CHRISSIE WALSH

THE GIRL FROM THE MILL

Complete and Unabridged

MAGNA
Leicester

First published in Great Britain in 2018 by
Aria
an imprint of Head of Zeus Ltd
London

First Ulverscroft Edition
published 2021
by arrangement with
Head of Zeus Ltd
London

This is a work of fiction. All characters,
organisations, and events portrayed in this novel
are either products of the author's imagination or
are used fictitiously.

A catalogue record for this book is available
from the British Library.

ISBN 978–0–7505–4869–4

Published by
Ulverscroft Limited
Anstey, Leicestershire

Printed and bound in Great Britain by
TJ Books Ltd., Padstow, Cornwall

This book is printed on acid-free paper

THE GIRL FROM THE MILL

In the drab Yorkshire town of Garsthwaite, Lacey Barraclough works hard in the textile mill, determined to fight for improvements to the dismal working conditions she and her fellow weavers face. But she hadn't reckoned on falling in love with the boss's son, Nathan. Nathan returns her love, but to succeed they must overcome the class divide.

Before Nathan and Lacey can make a life together, World War I breaks out and Nathan enlists to fight. When Nathan heads off to the Front, Lucy must find a new way to face the future. As hard times come to Garsthwaite, will there be a home for the returning heroes to come back to? And for those men who do make it back from France, can they ever outrun the horrors they have witnessed, and learn to love again?

This book is dedicated to my mother,
Dolly Manion, my inspiration in all things.

In memory of my husband, Billy, who
believed in me.

1

Long before Lacey Barraclough reached the out-
skirts of Garsthwaite, a dirty little mill town in
the Colne Valley, her armpits and the hand that
held her basket were already sticky with perspiration. It was shortly before six o'clock on a bright
June morning, and the sun's strengthening rays
signalled that today would be a scorcher.

With the moorland and hillside farms behind
her, Lacey entered the depths of the town. As
she hurried along Towngate she was plunged into
sudden gloom, the sun shut out by towering, soot
blackened mills and the air thick, every crevice
filled with the rank stink of raw wool, acrid smoke
and foul smelling dyes. Behind the mills ran a
tumbling river and the slick, still waters of a canal.
Today, the canal added its own stink, the pungent
reek wafting through the mill yards and into the
street. Lacey's nose wrinkled.

When she reached Turnpike Lane, a shabby little
terrace of two up and two down houses, she darted
up to number thirteen and rapped on the door.

It opened instantly.

'You're late,' Joan Chadwick exclaimed, slamming the door behind her.

'We'll have to dash if we're to get there before
the hooter blows.' Joan hoisted her basket into the
crook of her arm and set off at a run, Lacey keeping pace with her cousin.

At the end of Turnpike Lane they crossed the

1

main road, dodging the constant stream of horse drawn carts and the new, motorised lorries that plied their trade between Liverpool, Manchester, Huddersfield and Bradford.

Lacey leapt for the pavement. 'Phew, that were a bit close. You forget how fast them things can travel,' she panted, as a huge lorry rumbled past, its horn blaring. She adjusted her basket then ran the last few yards to Brearley's Mill, Joan hot on her heels. As they hurtled under the arched gateway a piercing shriek reverberated from the Mill's tower; the six o'clock hooter.

'If tha'd a bin a second later tha'd a bin locked out,' the wizened old gatekeeper shouted as they scooted past him. The ornate iron gates clanged shut, the gatekeeper deaf to the pleas of a woman left outside.

Lacey half turned. 'Let her in, you mean old sod, it's nowt to you,' she shouted.

Joan threw the woman a pitying glance. 'Thank God that wasn't us,' she said, both girls knowing had they been any later they too would have been locked out for the next two and a half hours. It was policy in all mills in the valley to punish tardy employees by keeping them out until breakfast time at eight thirty, thereby losing them a quarter of their day's wages. Making a final dash across the cobbled yard, Lacey and Joan entered the weaving shed, the smell of linseed oil, sized warp and greased leather assailing their senses.

'Whew! It's hot in here,' gasped Joan, flapping a hand under her nose as she followed Lacey into an alcove in the back wall of the shed.

'It'll get worse afore the day's done,' replied

2

Lacey, undoing the buttons on her blouse. Joan followed suit, the girls stripping down to their underwear and at the same time keeping a sharp eye out for Sydney Sugden, the lecherous overlooker. The women in the weaving shed called him Slimy Syd, his proclivity for sexual harassment earning him the nickname. It wouldn't do to let him catch them in a state of undress; he didn't need encouragement.

Lacey was just tying the strings on her sleeveless, cross-over pinny, the sort most weavers wore to keep the fluff off their clothing, and Joan was wrapping hers across her plump little belly when Syd slunk from behind a loom, the disappointment at being too late plain on his face.

Syd stomped off, and the girls, giggling at having thwarted him, covered their heads with cotton headscarves to protect their crowning glories from the savage thrash of their looms or the overhead, low hanging leather belts attached to the drums and pulleys that powered them. Together, they hurried down 'weaver's alley' — the wide space that separated row upon row of looms — and standing between the two looms she minded, Lacey called across the alley to Joan.

'Syd'll be as mardy as hell since he didn't get a chance to see you in your knickers.'

Joan's saucy reply was lost as the hooter blasted again, the shed echoing with a grinding roar as the weavers set their looms in motion. Shuttles trailing fine woollen yarns flew forwards then backwards, the strategy of advance and retreat interlacing wefts with warps, the beaters thrashing faster than the eye could see. Oblivious to the monotonous clatter, Lacey kept a constant lookout for broken threads, empty bobbins or flaws that might suddenly mar the fabric's parallel perfection.

Golden shafts of sun pierced the shed's glazed roof, descending through a haze of shimmering dust motes to glint on the oily machinery below, and as fine Yorkshire worsted smoothly lapped thickening cloth beams, the heat in the shed intensified.

A stream of sweat wormed its way under Lacey's chin and trickled between her breasts. She plunged her hand inside her overall to wipe away the discomfort, withdrawing it just as quickly to catch and secure a loose end.

When Joan glanced in Lacey's direction, Lacey raised two fingers to her lips indicating she was about to speak. Although the noise of machinery eliminated normal conversation, Lacey, like all weavers, was adept at mouthing and lip reading; in the cacophonous din of the weaving shed gossip flowed as easily as it would in the quiet of a churchyard.

'Them windows need opening; I'm sweating cobs,' mouthed Lacey, gesturing to the high transoms that ran the length of both sides of the shed.

'Me an' all; I'll faint if it gets any hotter,' Joan mouthed back.

Lacey watched out for Syd to ask him to open the windows, but the overlooker was nowhere to be seen. Typical, she thought; when you want him he's never there.

At half past eight the hooter blew again, the looms shut down and mill hands poured out into the yard, hungry for breakfast. In the shade of the

4

dye house wall, Lacey and Joan ate drip bread and drank cold tea. Half an hour later they were back in the hot, dusty confines of the weaving shed.

Sweat stained and weary, Lacey roved between her looms. Spotting an empty pirn she removed it, the thin metal rod slipping from her sweat soaked fingers. As she stooped to pick it up, she felt a hand grope her backside. She shot upright and swung round.

'You've a lovely arse on you, Lacey,' cackled Syd, standing too close for comfort, his knowing leer displaying stumps of rotten teeth.

Lacey stepped back, her nose wrinkling at his fetid smell. 'Any chance of opening them windows, Mr Sugden?' She gestured upwards. 'An' the doors an' all; let a bit of air in.'

Syd licked his teeth. 'Tha knows what tha has to do for a favour, Lacey.'

His grimy hand pawed her breast. Lacey slapped it away, her swingeing contempt making Syd curl his lip as he leaned into her face hissing, 'Watch what you're doin', Lacey. I wouldn't want to fine you for shoddy work.' He smirked and strode off.

Lacey watched him go, her blood boiling. Syd could easily dock her pay by a shilling or two, saying her piece was flawed even if it wasn't. In bad grace she carried on working, only to be distracted by a commotion further along 'weaver's alley'. Lizzie Isherwood, the 'Mrs Weaver' in charge of training the women hove into view shouting, 'Get 'er up an' out in t'fresh air.'

Flo Backhouse had fainted. A short while later it was Gertie Earnshaw's, then Maggie Collier's turn to be carried out.

The windows stayed closed and, as the temperature rose, so did Lacey's ire. By midday she was raging; injustice of any sort always raised her hackles. 'We're treated worse than animals,' she fumed to Joan. 'We have rights and I'm going to see we bloody well get 'em.'

At half past twelve the perspiring weavers stilled their looms and trudged out into the yard, scrabbling for shady places against the shed walls to eat their dinners. Flopped down on the cobbles, they dabbed their sweating faces and armpits.

'I asked Syd to open t'windows and t'doors but the dirty sod wanted payin' for it,' Lacey told the women sitting nearby. The women's faces registered their disgust; they all knew Syd's game.

Disconsolate, Lacey munched her cheese sandwiches and drank cold tea.

She felt cheated and abused. Thirsting for retribution, she moved from one group of women to another, exchanging whispered words. Some, their eyes flashing in anticipation, nodded their heads in agreement, the faint-hearted objecting for fear of dismissal or docked wages.

The one o'clock hooter wailed. The women got to their feet but remained standing on the spot. Syd appeared in the shed doorway. 'Oy, are you lot bloody deaf? Get in here an' get back to work.'

Lacey stepped forward. 'It's not right that we should have to work in that heat. We're not going back in until you've opened them windows.'

'Aye, get your long pole out, Syd,' a raucous voice yelled, and the women roared with laughter.

'Go on, Syd, you like getting your pole out.'

'Aye, an' shoving it where it's not wanted.'

6

'Aye, he does. The dirty bugger asked me to hold it for him yesterday morning.'

'From what I've heard, it's not long enough or stiff enough to open t'windows.' Screeching laughter rose to a crescendo.

Syd dithered.

Lacey struck again. 'Closed windows means idle looms, Syd,' she yelled above the hubbub. 'Open 'em and we'll come back in.'

The racket brought Jonas Brearley to his office door, the mill owner glancing at the timepiece he'd taken from his waistcoat pocket. 'What's going on here?' he barked. The women fell silent.

Lacey stepped forward. 'The shed's too hot work in, Mr Brearley, sir.

Some lasses fainted this morning because of it. We'd like t'windows opening to let a bit of air in.' She looked pointedly at Syd then back at Jonas.

Jonas Brearley stared quizzically at the tall, slender girl whose direct gaze met his.

He noted her fine features and vibrant green eyes; eyes full of passion.

Inwardly admiring her courage and forthright manner he raised his hand to his mouth to hide the smile forming on his lips. A firebrand if ever he saw one.

He stepped down into the yard. 'And am I to presume you asked for the windows to be opened?' Now it was his turn to look pointedly at Syd.

Syd quailed, visibly.

'That's right, sir. The dirty lummock wanted a favour for . . . ' Lacey changed tack. 'I asked Mr Sugden to open 'em.' Then raising her chin defiantly, she added, 'It wa' me who told the lasses

7

not to go back in until he'd done summat about it, 'cos you'll not get good work out of 'em if they're fainting an' their hands too sweaty to change a pirn or catch loose ends.'

Jonas eyed her closely; not only was she a beauty, she was shrewd too, and a damned good weaver so he'd been told. He turned his attention back to Syd and let out a roar. 'Well, what are you waiting for, man? Open the blasted windows. And you lot,' he addressed the women, 'no more complaints. Get back to work.'

Syd scuttled off, and before all the women were back at their looms the windows and doors were open, the escaping heat making conditions tolerable. Lacey was ecstatic. She'd fought for her rights — and won.

Jonas Brearley returned to his office, a thoughtful expression on his face.

He admired strong women, but he'd have to watch that one; it wouldn't do to let her get too cocky. He'd not sack her; he'd keep her in check — dock her wages or put her on short-time if need be.

Back at her looms, Lacey mentally replayed her altercation with Jonas.

She'd been surprised at the outcome. The more she thought about it, the more dumbfounded she was. He could have sacked her on the spot. After all, she couldn't expect Jonas Brearley to identify with the hardships his employees endured.

But she was wrong. Jonas was well aware of the hardships.

Hector Brearley, Jonas's late father, unlike many of his counterparts, had not sent his son

8

away from home to receive an expensive education, and return a gentleman. Instead, Jonas had worked in the mill as soon as he was old enough, learning every process at first hand. This hugely beneficial experience had led to his success. Now he was one of the most prestigious manufacturers in the West Riding, and if his unrefined manner of speech and his intricate knowledge of every warp and weft, thrum and bobbin in his mill made him a figure of fun amongst his more gentlemanly rivals, he cared not one jot. His mill outstripped most of the others in the valley.

Now, as he sat down at his desk, his waistcoat stretched tight over his ample paunch, Jonas was pleased with his recent decision, telling himself he wasn't a cruel taskmaster but a wise and generous employer.

★ ★ ★

'Did you see t'look on Slimy Syd's face when Mester Brearley shouted at him; it were priceless,' chortled Joan as, at half past six that evening she and Lacey walked arm in arm out through the Mill gate and along Towngate.

Lacey, still flushed with triumph at her small victory, grinned broadly before saying, 'Aye, happen next time it'll make him think twice, 'cos there will be a next time. We've got to stick up for us selves, Joanie, else we'll always be treated like muck. It's badly wrong when them that think they're our betters deny us our rights as human beings.'

Lacey warmed to her theme as they made their

9

way out of the town and along the road leading to Netherfold. Joan often went to Lacey's home after work to spend an hour or two with her cousin before going back home to Turnpike Lane. As they walked and talked, Joan somewhat in awe of her cousin, they exchanged the mean grey drabness of narrow streets of shabby houses and towering mills for hawthorn blossomed hedges and grassy banks golden with buttercups and dandelions. On either side of the road were steep hillsides dotted with clusters of weavers' cottages, some derelict, the sun glinting in the long rows of little windows in their upper storeys; a reminder of the days when the occupants of these dwellings had toiled over looms in their own homes. Now all the weaving in the Colne Valley took place in huge mills such as the one Lacey and Joan worked in.

'We've come a long way since then,' said Lacey, pointing to the cottages. 'Then we were our own bosses. Now we slave for greedy mill owners but it doesn't mean we don't have rights.'

Joan sighed. 'Folks like us will always be put down by t'bosses, Lacey. We're too poor to do owt about it.'

Lacey stopped in her tracks, and pulling her arm free of Joan's, turned to face her. 'We might be poor but we're not ignorant. I'm as good as anybody, an' so are you, Joanie. We deserve respect; fair treatment for a fair day's work. It's about time we did summat about it.' She walked on, her back straight, her head high.

In the near distance the evening sun shimmered on vast swathes of green bracken, purple heather and the rocky outcrops of black millstone grit on

Marsden Moor. In a sheltered cleft on the edge of the moor, Lacey could see the sun's rays glinting on the cobblestoned yard and warming the red doors of the outbuildings of the farmhouse that was home. She quickened her pace. For all its close proximity, Netherfold Farm seemed a world away from drab, dirty Garsthwaite.

Joan hurried after her.

'I'm fair looking forward to t'works outing next Saturday,' she said when she caught up.

The annual Mill outing, always a source of great excitement, was something the mill workers anticipated all year. On Saturdays throughout the year they were expected to work until midday but on the day of the outing Jonas Brearley not only released them from their duties, he also arranged a day of pleasure. To this end the workers contributed two pence a week, Jonas footing the rest of the bill. Sometimes they visited a grand house with parkland open to the public, or a place noted for its beautiful scenery. This year a barge trip down the John Ramsden canal would be a first for many.

When Lacey didn't immediately respond, Joan said, 'I've never been on t'canal before. Do you think we'll be safe?'

Lacey, her thoughts still on the altercation with Jonas Brearley, said, 'You know, when you come to think about it, Brearley's not a bad sort. He took our side this morning over t'windows, an' I bet he didn't half give Syd a wiggin' when he got him on his own. What we need to do is make old Brearley see our point of view more often.'

Joan raised her eyes to the heavens. When Lacey got a bee in her bonnet there was no talking to her.

11

2

Lacey glanced up at the clock on the high mantelshelf above the kitchen range. In one swift movement she drained her mug of tea, pushed her chair back from the large table and hurried out into the passage. At the foot of the stairs her cry would have wakened the Sphinx.

'Come on, our Jimmy, it's almost quarter past five; time to go.'

An answering grunt and a thud from above had her darting back to the kitchen. From the large teapot she filled four bottles, stoppering them tightly before placing two in a canvas knapsack and the others in a basket.

Jimmy Barraclough, hair tousled and half asleep, shuffled into the kitchen. 'Is me snap ready?' he enquired belligerently, lifting the milk jug and drinking from it.

Lacey glared with distaste at her youngest brother. 'Aye, an' I've given you an extra bottle of tea. Today looks like it's going to be another scorcher.'

Jimmy picked up the knapsack and plodded to the outside door.

'Don't bother to say thanks,' she called after him, her tone heavy with sarcasm.

Without another word Jimmy opened the door, letting in a cacophony of honking and squawking and the furious flapping of wings. He stepped outside and Lacey, basket in hand, followed him scrunching her face as her ears and eyes were assaulted by the rumpus. Jimmy, oblivious to the pandemonium, trudged across the yard to the gate that led into the lane.

Lacey, on the other hand, took a few tentative steps in the opposite direction, careful to avoid the beady eyed bobbing heads and vicious beaks of the gaggle of geese that gobbled and skraiked around her mother.

'I'm off now!' Lacey yelled, her words drowning in the din. Edith, her back turned and a bucket swinging from her hand, flung handfuls of corn into the frenzied melee of long white necks and flurried wings. Reaching her side unscathed, Lacey tapped Edith's shoulder. 'I'm off now. See you teatime.'

Edith swung round, a handful of corn dusting Lacey's boots. 'Right you are, love.' Edith squinted up at the sky. 'Another scorcher if I'm not mistaken.' She gave Lacey a meaningful look. 'Don't go getting into bother.'

Lacey grimaced. 'I'll do what's right, Mam.'

'Our Jimmy says you're causing trouble. You could get sacked.' Edith swivelled her eyes, searching for Jimmy.

'He's already left, Mam.' Lacey watched Edith's face crease with disappointment.

'He never used to go without saying, but,' Edith essayed a smile, 'I suppose he's getting too big to bother wi' such things.'

'Too big my arse,' said Lacey, irritated by Jimmy's thoughtlessness. She dropped a brief kiss on Edith's cheek before repeating her hazardous journey through snapping beaks and clawing feet

13

and hurried out of the yard into the lane, walking briskly along the rutted path leading to the main road.

At the end of the lane she lingered for a few precious minutes, letting her gaze drift over Netherfold and the wild expanse of moorland beyond it. Out there her Dad's sheep roamed the bracken and heather and she wished she could join them. But aware of time wasted she quickened her pace, her boots drumming the road that would take her to Garsthwaite.

★ ★ ★

In the week leading up to the outing, the weather holding good, Syd had the windows open wide every day. Even so, the women baited him, Syd taking his revenge by finding fault with Lacey's work. But she didn't care; she'd bested him on this occasion and would do so again if necessary.

All week the women talked of little else other than Lacey's small triumph, and when they weren't talking about that they talked about the outing. Come Friday evening, expectations were high.

'See you tomorrow, bright an' early,' they called to one another as they hurried through the mill gates.

'What'll you be wearin'?' Joan asked, as she and Lacey walked out of the town, and wondering why Lacey had been most insistent that she should go home with her that evening.

Lacey shrugged carelessly, but there was a gleam in her eye as she said,

'Wait an' see.'

14

'Hello, Auntie Edith,' Joan said, as the girls entered the kitchen at Netherfold Farm. Edith smiled a welcome and carried on chopping turnip into small cubes. Lacey went and plopped a kiss on her mother's cheek.

After a quick wash and a bite to eat, Lacey beckoned Joan to follow her upstairs. 'You can't come in just yet,' she said, closing her bedroom door in Joan's face.

Puzzled, yet willing to play along, Joan stayed out on the landing. Lacey was up to something, of that she was certain.

In her bedroom, Lacey stripped to her underwear. A rustle of silk followed by the fastening of plackets and she opened the door. 'You can come in now.'

Joan's eyes widened in amazement and an overawed 'oooh' floated from her lips as she entered the room. Sinuously, Lacey adopted an artful pose, one foot flat on the floor with the other on tiptoes, her left hand on her hip and her right hand drooping from her extended arm.

Joan simply stared.

Lacey tilted her head upwards and, lowering her eyes seductively, performed a slow twirl. 'La Parisienne model awaits madame's opinion,' she purred in a mock French accent.

Joan chuckled.

Lacey dropped the pose and reverting to her native Yorkshire asked, 'So Joanie, what do you think? Is it like that dress in the magazine?' She performed another twirl, the dark green silk catching the last

15

vestiges of a glorious sunset streaming through the window.

Joan's expression was a mixture of admiration and envy. 'It's beautiful — an' that green matches your eyes.'

'Does it?' Lacey sounded pleased and surprised. She walked a few paces then paused, flicking one ankle to show off the new, shorter length of the narrow skirt.

'You don't think it's too short do you, Joanie?'

'No, it's just right: very fashionable. It's the one we liked best, isn't it?' she said, confirming that the dress with its two tiered skirt, elbow length sleeves and square neckline was almost identical to one they had seen in a copy of *Weldon's Ladies Journal*. Whenever the ladies Joan's mother cleaned for threw out the magazines she brought them home for Joan and Lacey, the girls devouring them page by page.

Pleased by Joan's comments, Lacey performed another twirl. In the past she'd refashioned several items in her wardrobe and made skirts and blouses, but never before had she made a dress simply by copying it from a picture in a magazine. She grinned. 'Ta, Joanie; you say the nicest things.'

Joan stroked her fingers over the silky fabric. 'It's lovely material. Where did you get it?'

'Grandma Barraclough's trunk in the attic: after she died me Mam packed Grandma's stuff into it when she cleared out her bedroom so I could have it. I made this dress out of one of hers. There were umpteen to choose from.'

'Fancy that,' Joan murmured pensively, her

16

gaze straying from the dress to take in the spacious upper room in Netherfold Farm. Her thoughts found a voice. 'You're lucky to have a bedroom of your own.'

'I know,' said Lacey, understanding her cousin's dejection and feeling sorry for her. Joan shared a bedroom with two younger sisters in the poky little house in Turnpike Lane, the home of Edith's widowed sister, May Chadwick, and her three daughters.

'The only reason I have a bedroom of me own is because I'm the only girl in the house,' said Lacey, 'and that has its drawbacks, believe you me.

You don't see our Matt or our Jimmy washing up or ironing, do you?'

'That's 'cos your Mam spoils 'em, them being lads.'

'Never a truer word said, Joanie.'

At the mention of twenty-one year old Matt and Jimmy, sixteen, the girls' faces registered cynicism, both girls knowing full well that Edith pampered her sons.

Joan sighed. 'Aye, either being the only girl in the family or, in my case, the oldest means you're expected to do twice the work, an' I'm fed up of it.

Me Mam never makes our Maggie or our Elsie do as much as I do. I'm turned twenty-one; at my age I should be married with a house of me own.'

She looked close to tears.

Saddened to see Joan so despondent, Lacey struggled to keep secret the surprise she had for her: a surprise that would surely put a smile on Joan's face. She slipped off the green dress and put on the skirt and blouse she'd worn earlier.

Joan looked on, a doleful expression masking her plump, pretty features as fleetingly and unfavourably she compared her own dumpy shape and blonde curls with her cousin's attributes. Even with her finery removed Lacey still managed to look beautiful.

Tall and slender with an ample bust and small, neat waist, her striking features were topped with a mass of glossy brown hair. And what was it about Lacey tonight that made her glow with an inner light? Naturally, she'd been excited showing off the dress but even now, the dress put away, there was an air of anticipation filling the room.

'There, that's me sorted,' said Lacey, her smile fading when she saw Joan's woebegone expression. 'Oh, don't look so miserable.'

Joan shrugged. 'It's all right for you. You look lovely in whatever you have on, and you can sew. Me, I can't sew to save me life.'

'You'll never have to, Joanie, I'll do it for you.' Thinking it wise to mention one of Joan's best attributes Lacey added, 'you might not be much use on a sewing machine but there's nobody makes a better sponge cake.'

Joan grimaced. 'I can't wear a sponge cake. I'll have to make do with that blue gingham you made for me last Easter. Tomorrow you'll turn the heads of all the lads on the outing in that one.' With her thumb she gestured at the wardrobe.

'Ah, but remember, Joanie, the way to a man's heart is through his stomach. You'll catch a lad before I do. Anyway, you look lovely in blue. It sets off your blonde curls and,' Lacey grinned mischievously, 'it matches the colour of your

18

eyes.' She reached into the wardrobe. 'That's why I made this for you.'

'Ooh Lacey, it's gorgeous, just gorgeous!' Joan squealed, as Lacey flourished a kingfisher blue dress, its square necked bodice and slender skirt cut in the latest style. Joan leapt to her feet. 'Here, let me try it on. Will it fit me?' She began shedding her outer clothes, tears brimming her eyes, her cheeks flushed with pleasure.

'It should. I used the measurements I took when I altered that grey wool dress Mrs Hibberd gave you a couple of months ago.' Joan's mother also cleaned for Reverend Hibberd, the Methodist minister.

Joan slipped the dress over her head, jigging up and down impatiently whilst Lacey fastened the plackets. Then, almost afraid to look, she approached the mirror. 'Ooh Lacey, I never had anything so grand; an' it fits perfectly. We'll both turn heads tomorrow,' crowed Joan, dancing round the room, the cut of the dress making her appear slimmer and taller.

Lacey smiled, but try as she might she couldn't conjure up a face or a name of any lad whose head she wanted to turn. Not that she wouldn't get offers; she would and plenty of them. She'd had boyfriends in the past but none of them were what she was looking for.

The dress perfect, no alterations required, Lacey gathered up her tape measure, scissors and thread. Hands full, she walked over to the sewing machine in front of the window, carefully replacing the items in the narrow drawers either side of the wrought iron treadle. Then she covered the

19

machine's working parts with the top box to keep out the dust. The sewing machine was Lacey's most treasured possession.

'There,' Lacey said, dusting her palms, 'that's me tidied. And you, Joan Chadwick, take that dress off before you wear it out with all that jigging. There's a big paper bag in the bottom of the wardrobe. You can carry it home in that.'

'Can I show Auntie Edith first,' Joan begged.

'Aye, I'll give her a shout. She's already seen it but she'll get her eyes opened when she sees you wearing it.'

A shout down the stairs and Edith came up, wiping her wet hands on her apron. 'You've done titivating then,' she asked as she entered the room, her eyes widening when she saw Joan. 'My, you look a picture, our Joan. I've never seen you looking so lovely.' Joan giggled, her cheeks pinking at the heartfelt compliment.

Lacey groaned. 'Don't say any more, Mam. She's likely to swell up with that much pride it'll not fit her tomorrow and,' Lacey addressed Joan, 'if you don't get a chap on this outing I'll strip you down to your knickers an' chuck you in t'canal.'

Lacey's mocking threat had Joan laughing until tears ran down her cheeks. Lacey always did something kind or had something cheeky to say so in her company she rarely stayed miserable for long.

Edith went back downstairs to the scullery. She'd just slopped a shirt out of the washtub and wedged it between the wooden rollers of the mangle when Lacey and Joan joined her.

'Mam, it's Friday night,' Lacey expostulated,

20

'Why on earth are you washing?'

'It's only a shirt. It's our Jimmy's favourite. He wants to wear it for t'outing, bless him.' She turned the mangle, the shirt gradually disappearing between the rollers, then plopping into a wicker basket on the floor. 'He forgot to put it to wash. I'll dry it in front o' t'fire an' iron it afore I go to bed.'

Lacey raised her eyes to the ceiling, irritated by Jimmy's thoughtlessness and her mother's acquiescence. 'You should have told him to wear summat else. Just because he forgot, doesn't mean you have to dance to his tune.'

Edith looked pained. She didn't like to hear Jimmy criticised. She marched from the scullery into the kitchen. The girls followed. Seeing the hurt she had inflicted, Lacey took the shirt from Edith's grasp and draped it over the clothes horse. 'You put the kettle on for a cup of tea an' I'll iron the shirt after I've seen our Joan off.'

Lacey knew how hard Edith worked. She constantly chased her tail as she juggled the household chores around the demands of the smallholding.

However, Lacey rarely left her to struggle alone.

'You're a good lass, Lacey.' Edith plodded to the sink, kettle in hand.

The outer door opened and Matt came in. 'Are you ready for off, Joanie?'

He always walked Joan back into Garsthwaite on the evenings she came up to Netherfold, stopping off on the return journey for a pint or two in the Plough Inn.

'Goodnight, Auntie Edie,' said Joan, pulling on her coat then picking up the paper bag containing her dress.

Matt walked on ahead, Joan and Lacey walking behind him up the lane.

'Don't be late up tomorrow,' Lacey advised, as they reached the spot where they would part, 'Me an' our Jimmy'll call for you at nine. The charabancs leave at half past an' we don't want to miss 'em.' She raised her eyes skyward. 'I hope it stays fine. A day out on t'canal won't be much fun if it's raining.'

'It'll not rain.' Joan pointed in the direction of the moor. 'There's a red sky, an' you know what they say.' Together the girls chanted the old adage.

'Aye, but we're not shepherds, we're weavers. Does it count?'

'Course it does.'

Joan hugged Lacey. 'Thanks for the lovely dress. You're the best cousin in the whole world.'

'That makes two of us,' quipped Lacey. 'See you tomorrow then.'

'Come on, Joanie,' Matt shouted, 'don't stand nattering all night.'

Lacey walked back down the lane, the night time sweetness of yarrow and wild parsley stirring her senses. She loved living on the moor, away from the mills and the narrow, mean streets surrounding them. Barracloughs had farmed Netherfold for four generations, her ancestors tending sheep or planting swedes and beet in the unforgiving rock strewn fields behind the farmhouse as did her father, Joshua, and her brother, Matt. Lacey couldn't imagine living anywhere else.

At the end of the lane Lacey leaned on the yard gate, and as the night sky darkened to deepest

22

purple, her thoughts turned to tomorrow's outing — and romance. She considered her options. Maybe she'd give Sam Barton another chance: of the lads she'd courted he was the most likeable, and he was good looking. After all, she was nearly twenty and some of the girls she worked with of a similar age were now married with children. She didn't want to rush into marriage for the sake of it, but she would like a romance: one that made her blood tingle and her heart beat faster because she was with the right man.

Lacey gazed up at the darkening sky and sighed. Finding the right man was the problem. She wanted one who shared her interests: a well read man, interested in local politics and with enough get up and go to improve his station in life. She didn't want to be married to a mill hand like Sam, content to talk whippets and horse racing. Neither did she want to be a weaver all her life; for now it was a necessity, but Lacey had aspirations that led her to dream of much better things.

If I stay out here all night I'll not come up with any answers, she told herself. All I know is that I want to do something really worthwhile with my life and do it with someone I truly love.

By the time Lacey was back in Netherfold's kitchen, Joan and Matt had reached Turnpike Lane. 'Be seein' you, Joanie,' said Matt, leaving her at the end of the street.

'Night Matt, thanks.' Joan walked the last few yards to her door alone; Matt headed for The Plough and a pint.

Turnpike Lane was just one of several narrow streets of Victorian terraces Hector Brearley had

had built more than fifty years before to house the mill workers in his employ. Joan had always lived here, and as she walked between the rows of cramped and fetid houses she pondered on how miserable life would be without the solace of Netherfold Farm and Lacey's staunch friendship.

3

Saturday dawned dry and bright, the early morning sun promising another hot day. Lacey, still in her nightgown, packed a basket with sandwiches, buns and bottles of Ben Shaw's pop whilst her brother Jimmy washed in the kitchen sink.

'Your shirt's on the winter-edge, our Jimmy.' Lacey gestured to the wooden clothes horse on which the freshly washed and ironed garment now hung. 'An' next time give Mam a bit more notice. You should have thrown it to wash earlier in t'week.'

Jimmy glanced over at the shirt and shrugged. 'I never thought,' he said, 'I din't realise it wa' mucky 'til last night.'

'That's the trouble wi' you, Jimmy. You don't think. You wait for others to do it for you.' With this riposte Lacey left the kitchen and climbed the stairs.

In her bedroom she slipped into the green dress, the feel of silk against bare skin making her shiver with delight. It was too hot to wear stockings so she popped her bare feet into shiny brown sandals with T-bar straps and little heels. Pleased with the effect she sat in front of the cheval mirror, rolling and pinning her long chestnut hair into thick glossy coils then, careful not to disturb them, she pinned on a straw hat decorated with a bow made from a strip of left over green silk. A final glance in the full length mirror and she descended the stairs, ready for the day ahead.

In the kitchen, Jimmy hopped impatiently as Edith fluttered round him like a mother hen. Spruced up in his clean shirt and Sunday trousers, his unruly curls parted and flattened with a liberal application of sugar and water, he was a handsome young man.

'Come on,' he urged, 'we don't want to miss the charas.'

Edith gave Lacey a fond smile. 'You look lovely, our Lacey: now get off the pair of you and have a good time.'

Out they went into the sunshine, Jimmy marching on in front, heedless as to the last minute problems his clean shirt had caused, and utterly oblivious to Lacey lugging the heavy picnic basket.

At nine o' clock sharp, Lacey rapped the door of number thirteen, Turnpike Lane. Joan bounced out, a basket over her arm, her eyes alive with anticipation. She looked so fetching in the kingfisher blue dress, her blonde curls newly washed and fluffed out under a straw boater, that Jimmy whistled and gave her a sly wink.

'Eh, Mr Cleverclogs, none of your cheek,' Joan admonished, although Jimmy's open admiration had her flushing with pleasure.

'Let's be off,' Lacey said, 'we've to be at Townend for half past. The charas won't wait.'

Arms linked, Jimmy in the middle, they walked smartly down Towngate to Townend, meeting with fellow mill hands heading in the same direction.

As they approached the crowd of waiting workers Gertie Earnshaw ran to meet them, full of

26

excitement. 'Guess what! The boss's son's coming on t'canal wi' us.'

Jimmy guffawed. 'Yer daft clout; Nathan Brearley'll be doing nowt o' t'sort. Them lot don't bother wi' t'likes of us.'

Gertie pointed to a group of Mill office workers. 'Look! He's there; the tall fellow wi' fair hair.'

Lacey looked over at the group.

Nathan Brearley stood head and shoulders above his companions, his bright hair gleaming in the sunlight, a bemused expression on his handsome face. He doesn't look too comfortable with the situation, thought Lacey.

Had his father forced him to come? Was it part of his training? Getting to know the workforce before he took over the running of the Mill.

It was well known that Jonas was keen for Nathan to learn the business first hand. For more than a year now, on his return from school, twenty year old Nathan had been involved in the process of worsted manufacture; carding, spinning, winding, weaving and finishing.

Lacey had seen him at the Mill but, to her disappointment, his time in the weaving shed had been spent with the 'Mrs Weaver', Lizzie. Until today she hadn't seen him for several weeks. Unbeknown to her, Jonas had sent Nathan on a research tour. Whilst the Mill manufactured the finest worsted in the valley, Jonas was keen to meet the increasing demand for cheap woollen cloths that imitated Scotch tweeds so, with Brearley's always to the forefront, it had been Nathan's job to investigate the possibilities.

Now, seeing him again, Lacey's heart skipped a

27

beat. Not for the first time, she noted how handsome he was. Now there's a head I wouldn't mind turning, she thought, recalling Joan's words. No sooner had the thought crossed her mind than Nathan Brearley looked in her direction. Their eyes met and Lacey's heart skipped a few more beats.

★ ★ ★

The charabancs trundled down the valley into Huddersfield town. At Aspley Basin on the John Ramsden narrow canal they drew to a halt, the passengers tumbling out, some still singing the catchy tunes they'd sung on the journey. On the wharf they admired the newly painted barges waiting to take them down the canal to Hopton.

It was customary for the bargees to paint their crafts for such outings and the owners of these had spared no effort. Bright blues and yellows clashed with greens, reds and white. All gaily decorated with flowery symbols, they contrasted sharply with the dingy coal barges moored nearby.

The Mill manager, officious as usual, chivvied everyone onto the barges.

Jimmy chose the one painted blue and yellow, the girls following him aboard. Lacey glanced round to see which barge Nathan was on but sadly it wasn't theirs.

Ropes cast off, the horse straining in its harness, the barge glided away from the wharf, its passengers leaning over the side to watch the dark, oily ripples as it ploughed through the water.

'Do you remember 'The Titanic', Joan?' Jimmy

made his voice deliberately scary.

Forced to recall the disaster of the previous year, Joan shuddered. 'Ooh, don't be saying that, Jimmy.' She whirled round to address Lacey. 'Do you think we could sink?'

Lacey rolled her eyes. 'It's highly unlikely, an' I'm absolutely certain there's no icebergs on t'canal.'

Huge mills and engineering factories lined the canal banks, the barge sailing sedately between walls green with slime. The passengers crowded the deck, laughing, chatting, singing and calling out to their workmates on the red and white barge cruising behind. When the barge negotiated the first lock the noise suddenly subsided.

'Oh, I can't say I like this,' squeaked Joan, as the barge entered the gloomy lock chamber, its towering walls on either side festooned with slimy green clumps of waterweed and lichens. Lacey held her breath. The lock gates shut and the water rushed in, the barge's gradual ascent into the sunlight accompanied by Joan's screams.

Lacey chirped, 'Better get used to it, Joanie, there's nine more locks before we reach Hopton.'

The mills and factories behind them, the barges glided through open countryside, the towpaths lined with hawthorn, grasses and wild flowers, the passengers no longer afraid of the locks. A kingfisher skimmed the water. 'Look at that!' Jimmy pointed to where the bird, now perched on a branch of overhanging willow, preened itself.

Lacey looked to where he pointed. 'Ooh, look at the colour of its feathers, Joan. It matches your dress.'

'Aye, Joan's t'bonniest lass out today.' Jimmy's remark caused Joan to blush yet again.

'If I didn't think he was too young, I'd say our Jimmy fancies you, Joan,' said Lacey. This time it was Jimmy's turn to blush.

The barges eventually arrived at Hopton and the holiday makers disembarked to stroll along the towpath to a pretty public house close by an open field and a small wood. Lacey and Joan found a comfortable spot in the field and unpacked the picnic baskets. A rowdy game of football kicked off, and the men who hadn't sloped off to the pub joined in or ran races the length of the field. The girls and older women sat in groups, chatting or watching the antics of their male colleagues. The office workers kept to their own company, Nathan among them.

'It's lovely to be out in t'open air away from all the fluff,' Lacey commented, having just taken several deep breaths. Inhaling the loose, hairy fibres that floated from the fine woollen worsted they wove was one of the many daily hazards the weavers had to contend with; congestion of the lungs a common complaint. She gestured towards the footballers. 'Even the racket that lot's making is better than clattering looms.'

'Aye, it's fair grand,' said Joan, stretching out her legs and leaning back on her hands, her head tilted to feel the sun on her face. A sharp nudge from Lacey soon brought her upright.

Joan squinted, startled to see Stanley Micklethwaite looming over her. He coughed nervously. 'I wondered if you'd like to take a stroll, Joan. I fancy a walk on t'towpath an' I thought you might

30

like to join me.' Joan looked to Lacey for an answer.

Lacey rolled her eyes and pouted her lips, her comical expression hinting at pleasures to come. 'Aye, off you go, Joanie. I'll be grand.'

'Are you sure you don't mind?' Joan took Stanley's outstretched hand and he pulled her to her feet.

'Not at all; go off an' enjoy yourselves.' Lacey closed one eye in a naughty wink. She knew her cousin admired Stanley and that he had hankered after Joan for some time but was too shy to do anything about it until today. Lacey wondered if he'd been to the pub for a drop of Dutch courage. Lost in thought, she was surprised when someone spoke her name.

'It's Lacey, isn't it? Lacey Barraclough.'

Lacey gazed up into Nathan Brearley's enquiring grey-blue eyes, noting the long, fair lashes and the way his tawny blonde hair fell over his forehead and curled round his ears. Oh but he was a good looking man. He lowered himself down on the grass beside her. Lacey slid her eyes sideways to admire his tall physique and neatness of dress, thinking how clean and fine cut he looked.

'That's right,' she replied. 'Fancy you knowing my name.'

'Lacey's a rather intriguing name, not one you'd easily forget. How did you come by it?'

'I've me mother to thank for it. She's a great one for reading an' remembering old stories. Apparently there was an important family lived in these parts a long time ago called De Lacey. She liked the sound of it, and what with it being part of the history of Garsthwaite she thought I should carry

31

it on.'

'I like that,' Nathan said. 'I'm interested in both history and reading. Do you read much yourself?'

They chatted for some time about books and then Nathan's travels to mills as far north as Scotland. Intrigued, and eager to prolong the conversation, Lacey asked lots of questions about the places he had seen, at the same time thinking she had never before talked with a man who stirred her spirits as did Nathan Brearley. He didn't drone on about whippets and betting on horses or talk down to her as did other chaps she'd courted; he openly acknowledged she had a brain and knew how to use it. Even so,

Lacey couldn't help thinking he'd soon move on, that on days like this he probably considered it his duty to chat to the workers. But she was wrong.

Captivated, Nathan listened to her unpretentious opinions on literature and life in general, fascinated and impressed by her intelligence and easy charm. Furthermore, he liked the way she responded to him; no hint of servant to master as was usually the case when speaking with other mill workers. That, combined with her glossy brown hair, the richness of her full mouth and those eyes fringed with long sweeping lashes had Nathan wishing he could stay forever.

After a while Nathan stood and stretched his legs, Lacey saddened to think he was moving on to socialise elsewhere, but to her surprise he suggested they go for a walk in the woods, saying a stroll in the shade would be welcome.

Lacey jumped up and smoothed her skirts.

Nathan silently admired her trim figure. Just then Jimmy arrived back, having abandoned the football game. 'Where's Joan?' he asked.

'Gone for a walk with Stanley Micklethwaite.' Crestfallen, Jimmy helped himself to a ham sandwich from the picnic basket and ran back to the game.

Lacey smiled fondly after him. Poor Jimmy, he was smitten, but he was almost four years younger than Joan and his love was unrequited.

Nathan offered Lacey his arm and they crossed the field into the shade of the trees. Not once did they run out of conversation, Lacey silently blessing Stanley Micklethwaite for taking Joan for a walk.

When Lacey and Nathan returned to the field they met with sidelong glances and murmured innuendo. 'You taking a walk with me has caused quite a stir,' she remarked. 'The gossips are having a field day in more ways than one.'

Nathan flushed and shuffled his feet. Then, his tone formal and polite he said, 'Thank you for sharing your time with me, Miss Barraclough, it was most enjoyable. I hope we'll meet again soon.'

To Lacey's disappointment he didn't specify a time or place and, striding briskly across the field, he joined the managers and office workers.

4

On the Monday morning after the Canal Trip, Lacey met with a barrage of comments and questions as soon as she arrived at the Mill gates.

'Hey Lacey! What did you an' t'boss's son get up to yesterday when you wa' in t'woods?' bawled May Skinner.

'Aye, we all saw you,' Gertie Earnshaw cackled, 'an' we all know what his sort do wi' lasses like us.'

Lacey's face flamed. 'We weren't doin' owt we shouldn't. We were just talking,' she replied tartly, and head high she marched into the weaving shed. The women piled in after her, eager to have their say.

'Take no notice of 'em, they're just mucky minded.' urged Joan as they changed into their overalls; she made this last remark loud enough for the other women to hear but rather than deter them, it egged them on.

'Aye, what sort o' mucky stuff do toffs like him do when they get you on your own?'

Lacey clenched her teeth and concentrated on tying the strings of her pinny. One of the older women gave her some sympathetic advice. 'It's not right dallying wi' t'boss's son, love. His sort aren't really interested in the likes o' you. He'll be out for one thing, an' you know what that is.'

'Aye, he's leadin' you on, lass. He's seen a pretty face an' fancies he'll get what he wants.'

34

'That's if he hasn't already had it,' sneered May.

The women's ribald laughter ringing in her ears, Lacey fished a cotton head square from her overall pocket, and as she tied it over her hair she mused on the women's logic. She knew exactly how the hierarchy in the mills functioned. The owners, their sons, the managers and the overseers considered every girl fair game, assuming the right to foist their sexual perversions on them. It was a hazard of working life, and one Lacey had had to deal with on several occasions. So far she had been lucky, her quick wits and feisty nature protecting her. But Nathan wasn't like that she consoled herself; he respected her. Arguing with the women was useless, so, giving a withering glance to all concerned she walked away.

'You've some neck on you, Lacey Barraclough, I'll give you that,' said Flo Backhouse, shouldering past her as they walked to their looms.

'Aye, what makes you think you're good enough for the likes of Master Nathan?'

Lacey's temper flared, her determination to rise above the cat-calling and treat it with the contempt it deserved blown away by Maggie Clegg's taunting remark. She whirled round to face the women standing at her back.

'I'm as good as he is any day,' she cried. 'I might work in his Mill but it doesn't mean I'm any less a person. The trouble wi' you lot is you think you're worthless, an' if you carry on letting the upper classes treat you like serfs, that's all you'll ever be. It's 1913 for God's sake, not the dark ages. It's about time you lot bucked up your ideas; have some respect for yourselves, stop crawling round in the slime.' She stomped over to her loom calling back, 'An' any road, I happen to believe God made everybody equal.'

The women stared wide-eyed at Lacey's tirade then, at a blast from the hooter they shuffled off to their looms, muttering and casting curious glances over their shoulders.

Once her looms were in action Lacey kept her eyes on the job, her bad temper gradually dissipating. She was glad she hadn't retaliated to the slurs with a slap or a kick. It wouldn't do for her to be seen scrapping over the boss's son. Perhaps she'd been a bit harsh on the women, but why did they have to assume they were lesser beings than the likes of Nathan Brearley.

They're just as bad as the upper class, she thought angrily, catching a loose end. They have such low opinions of themselves and their place in society they perpetuate the idea that a person must be born with a silver spoon in their mouths to have any worth. Think like that, she told herself, and you'll always be treated as worthless. Everybody has something valuable to offer. If it weren't for us women this Mill wouldn't function.

Round and round inside her head she contemplated the events of the morning so far, and as shuttles flew and cloth-beams thickened, the women's taunts hurt less and less. More than likely they were just jealous, and anyway, nothing would come of her afternoon with Nathan Brearley; he was just being nice. Feeling in a better frame of mind she signalled to Joan, mouthing, 'When are you seeing Stanley again?'

'Tonight, after work; he's walking me home,'

Joan mouthed back.

Lacey winked saucily, mouthing, 'Must be true love.'

Lizzie Isherwood hove into view. Whilst Lizzie wasn't a hard taskmaster, she didn't tolerate shoddy work, her tongue razor edged when she spotted carelessness. Lacey paid full attention to her looms; she'd suffered enough slanging this morning. Two hours later the hooter signalled breakfast time.

'Stanley says he's fancied me for ages,' Joan confided, as they sat with their backs to the dye house wall. 'He says he was just too shy to do owt about.'

'I could have told you that. I've seen the way he looks at you; he goes all cow eyed an' soppy.'

'Ooh Lacey, you make him sound awful, an' he's not, he's really nice.'

'So, is this the real thing?'

'I'd like to think it is 'cos he's ever so kind an' gentle, but it's a bit too soon to tell.' Joan gazed pensively at the dye house door.

'If he's seeing you again after work today it sounds like Stanley's got his skates on. He's making up for lost time.'

Stanley emerged from the dye house.

'Ooh look, there he is.' Joan scrambled to her feet. 'Do you mind if I go an' have a word with him?' She scooted off without waiting for an answer.

Left alone, Lacey smiled fondly at her cousin's eagerness. She was pleased for Joan who, at twenty-one years of age, was afraid of being left on the shelf. It would be nice if Joan and Stanley made a go of it, she mused, unlike me who will probably never spend another afternoon in Nathan Brearley's company. It was most likely boredom drove him to talk to me yesterday.

Even so, it had been an extremely pleasant experience, one she wouldn't mind repeating. But there won't be much chance of that happening, she told herself. He's a mill owner's son, and whilst I might think I'm his equal, I can't see him thinking the same. Shrugging off her misgivings Lacey finished her sandwich, and when the hooter blew again she went back into the weaving shed.

* * *

At midday Lacey walked the length of the Mill yard to a quiet spot overlooking the river, leaving Joan to share her dinner with Stanley and she herself removed from further taunting.

Leaning back against the warmed stone of the wash house wall, undeterred by the rank odour of wet wool, she opened her copy of *Virginia*, a tale of an enterprising woman who supports her husband, a struggling playwright. Disappointed when the husband proved to be an adulterer, Lacey set the book aside and closed her eyes.

'Will you always be sitting in the sun day dreaming whenever I come to find you?'

Lacey's eyes flew open. Nathan smiled down at her. 'I hoped I might see you today. I so enjoyed your company I wondered if you'd consider sharing more of your time with me. What do you say to continuing our interesting discussions one day soon?'

A warm glow suffused Lacey's cheeks. 'I'd like that,' she said. Although she appeared outwardly calm her blood tingled and her heart drummed a tattoo. Nathan perched on the low wall separating the Mill yard from the riverbank and gazed into Lacey's face, his eyes tracing the arch of her brow, the high cheekbones and full lips. She's beautiful, he thought, and electrifyingly alive.

'What are you reading?'

'Virginia.' Lacey held up the book.

This simple enquiry and its answer led to another interesting interlude, Lacey disappointed when the Mill hooter called her back to work. 'Where and when will we meet?' Nathan asked urgently.

'At the cairn on Cuckoo Hill, Sunday, two o' clock.'

Lacey ran up the yard, leaving Nathan hidden behind the wash house wall. She understood that it wasn't wise for him to be seen with her at the Mill.

Although their meeting had been unobserved, Nathan's ears reddened as he scurried past two women on their way to the spinning shed. In truth he was nervous of the rough, outspoken women who toiled in his father's mill.

But they're not all like that, he mused, his thoughts and his eyes on the girl who now hurried up the Mill yard in front of him.

Lacey had almost reached the weaving shed when she spotted Jimmy by the warehouse, deep in conversation with Arty Bincliffe. Lacey didn't like Arty. He was a blagger. Tempted to interfere, she was forestalled by the second blast of the hooter. Her curiosity unsatisfied, she headed back to the weaving shed.

'What wa' you talking to Arty Bincliffe about?' Lacey asked Jimmy, as they walked back to Netherfold at the end of the working day.

'Summat an' nowt.' Jimmy's reply was intentionally casual. He knew Lacey didn't approve of Arty.

'You want to keep away from his sort, he's bad, an' you shouldn't be bothering with him. He'll get you into trouble.'

'He's not that bad,' Jimmy argued. 'He wants me to go out wi' him and some o' t'lads on Saturday night.'

'I hope you told him no.'

'Why? There's nowt wrong wi' him. I can go if I want.'

'His lot are too old for you to bother with, an' they're always up to no good, so stay away from 'em.'

Jimmy tossed his head. 'Anybody 'ud think I wa' still a bairn.' He marched on, leaving Lacey to make her own way home.

Lacey watched him go, a worried expression creasing her brow. Jimmy worked in the Mill warehouse, a job requiring no particular skills, which was just as well considering Jimmy's lack of aptitude. Whilst he managed to earn his keep, he was an immature and gullible lad inclined to believe the best in everybody.

In his first weeks in the Mill his workmates, quick to spot his naivety, had made a fool of him. One day they sent him to the spinning shed to ask for a long stand. Jimmy set off, expecting to return with a piece of equipment. After he had stood and waited for twenty minutes the spinning overseer said, 'There lad, you've had a long stand, now bugger off back to t'warehouse.'

On another occasion they sent him to the Mill office for 'nip-scrotes and mankers'. Jimmy, unaware this was old Yorkshire dialect for penny pinching idlers, couldn't understand why the chief clerk clipped his ear before turfing him out into the yard.

When Lacey heard about these pranks she shrugged them off as just that, but when a group of particularly rough women from the spinning shed grabbed Jimmy in the Mill yard and 'sunned him' Lacey intervened, sorting the matter with fists and fierce tugging of hair. Whilst she didn't object to the ritual, harmless teasing all new workers suffered, she drew the line at sexual humiliation.

The women had Jimmy down on the ground minus his trousers, pouring oil on his genitals then manhandling him when Lacey had rushed to his rescue. Jimmy hadn't wanted to go back to the Mill after that, but within a matter of days a newer boy became the butt of his tormentors, and Jimmy was left in peace.

Lacey knew she couldn't protect Jimmy from every situation, but she determined to be watchful. It wouldn't do for someone to take advantage of Jimmy's innocence.

★ ★ ★

For the rest of that week Lacey's thoughts focused on the Sunday ahead.

41

Whilst she caught fleeting glances of Nathan as they both went about their work, he didn't approach her again. By Friday her anticipation had faded, Lacey convinced his request to meet her again would come to nothing.

Midday Saturday, the working week ended, Lacey walked home in low spirits. Nathan had made no attempt to confirm the Sunday arrangements.

By the time she arrived at Netherfold, she had reached the conclusion that he had had time to consider the consequences of walking out with an employee, and now thought it unwise.

Even so, at one o' clock on Sunday afternoon Lacey stood in her bedroom puzzling over what to wear for her meeting with Nathan. Should she wear the green dress again, or the blouse with a white sailor collar edged with navy and a matching skirt. Not wanting to appear overdressed for a walk in the countryside, she settled on the blouse and skirt, another of her creations made from cheap cotton remnants she'd bought last Bank Holiday at the Monday market in Huddersfield.

The weather still warm, she wouldn't need a jacket, which was just as well because she didn't have one to go with her chosen outfit.

Complementing her ensemble with a straw boater and a pair of white gloves, Lacey ran downstairs to the kitchen where, Sunday dinner over and the washing up done, Edith sat reading.

'By, you look a picture,' Edith remarked. 'Are you going somewhere special?'

'Nathan Brearley's asked me to walk out with him. I met him on the canal trip.'

Edith's eyes widened. 'Nathan Brearley: Jonas's son? Eeh, lass, you can't go walking wi' the likes of him.'

'Why ever not? He's a nice lad, and I enjoy his company.'

Edith frowned. 'He might well be a nice lad but he's the boss's son. The Brearley's won't approve. Don't go getting mixed up in summat that might cause you trouble, Lacey.'

'Mother! It's a walk on the moor I'm taking, not a visit to chapel to arrange the banns. I hardly know him. An' anyway, he more than likely won't bother to turn up.'

'It might be better if he doesn't,' Edith retorted, 'He's not your sort.'

Lacey's brow puckered and her tone had a hard edge to it as she said, 'Are you saying that I'm not good enough to walk out with Nathan Brearley? Would you rather I stuck to the likes of Sam Barton?'

Edith sighed. 'No lass, I've always thought you deserve somebody better than a carder in t'mill who's a bit too fond of ale, but Brearley's are gentry, and y . . . ' Her argument petered out, her eyes taking on a dreamy expression.

'Still, wouldn't it be grand if summat came of it?'

Lacey laughed out loud. 'Sometimes Edith Barraclough, your imagination runs riot. It must be all that reading you do.' Although Lacey's tone was tart, her amused expression was full of love and understanding.

Edith's vivid imaginings were a family joke.

'I only want what's best for you, lass.'

'So do I. I'll be off an' see what I can do about it,' Lacey pertly replied.

★ ★ ★

Nathan Brearley was there at the cairn when, shortly after two o' clock, Lacey topped the brow of Cuckoo Hill. When she saw him, resplendent in a smart fawn jacket and brown trousers, a gentle breeze ruffling his tawny curls she breathed a sigh of relief.

Nathan too breathed a sigh of relief. He hadn't entirely believed that this outspoken, independent girl, popular with many of the tough, brawny mill hands would be interested in someone as pale and insipid as he thought himself to be.

'Sorry to keep you waiting,' Lacey called out as she drew nearer, 'me Mam kept me talking.' She wouldn't tell him she'd doubted he'd be there.

'No need to apologise,' Nathan said, the words denying his fears that she wouldn't come at all, and his admiring gaze letting her know she was forgiven.

'What's it to be then?' Pointing left then right, Lacey allowed Nathan to choose one of the two paths leading from the cairn to the moor.

'I'm not familiar with either. I don't often come this way. What made you choose Cuckoo Hill?'

'I love it up here,' she said, her sweeping gesture taking in the panorama of wild moorland and below it in the valley, Garsthwaite, its skyline dominated by tall chimneys. From their high vantage point Lacey and Nathan could see Towngate flanked by narrow streets of terrace houses, and behind them the huge mills and the canal and the river slinking darkly on its long journey to the sea. 'From here you can see for miles an' miles.'

Nathan slowly turned full circle, taking in the view. 'Masters of all we survey,' he jested.

'I don't think so,' Lacey said.

Hearing the bitterness in her voice Nathan said, 'You sound angry; why so?'

'Because of the unfairness of it all: It's all about profit as far as the mill owners are concerned, and not enough about people's rights. I think we're treated badly, paid too little an' expected to work too fast for safety.' She shrugged dismissively. 'Apart from that I can't complain.'

Nathan looked serious. 'I know exactly what you mean. There's much to be done to improve working conditions. I frequently question the demands imposed by the managers.'

Lacey blinked her surprise. 'You do? Good for you; keep it up. An' one day, when you're in charge you can do summat about it before one of us weavers ends up chewed to bits in one of her looms.'

For a long moment Lacey and Nathan silently surveyed their surroundings, weighing up the awfulness of such a consequence. They were both familiar with accidents that frequently happened in the weaving and spinning sheds, the thrashing machinery inflicting terrible harm to those unfortunate enough to fall victim to it. Yet again, Nathan admired Lacey's outspokenness and the reasoning behind it. He was about to compliment her on this when she intervened.

'Hey up!' she cried, 'we're not here to make one

45

another miserable, so forget about the Mill for today an' let's go walking, Mr Brearley.'

They took the right hand path, Lacey pointing out Netherfold Farm tucked in a cleft of the moor on the edge of the town. 'That's where I live. Me Dad runs sheep on the moor an' grows swedes an' beet in the fields behind the house. We've a couple of pigs an' all. Me mother sees to them an' the geese an' hens. It's only a small place, not big enough to support us all, so only our Matt works with me Dad.'

'And Matt is . . . ?' Nathan was pleased to be learning so much about her without having to ask.

'Me older brother,' Lacey said. 'An' me younger brother, our Jimmy, works in the warehouse at Brearley's. You might have seen him around. He's a skinny little lad with a mop of brown curls an' a cheeky grin.'

'I'll keep an eye out for him. See if I can recognise him from your description.'

In this manner they walked over the moor, talking easily, sharing likes and dislikes regarding books and music and anything else that came to mind. As they made their way back to the cairn neither of them wanted the afternoon to end.

The cairn in sight, Nathan asked. 'What does it represent?'

Lacey looked askance. 'To say you've lived round here all your life you don't know much about your own place, do you?'

Nathan laughed uneasily. 'I was away at school most of the time. I had a sheltered childhood.'

'Aye, you must have done, 'cos I never saw owt of you when you were younger.'

46

Nathan didn't want to dwell on his own upbringing. Compared to the men Lacey usually kept company with, he thought she might think he'd been mollycoddled; a namby-pamby as she might say. 'I thought you were going to tell me about the cairn,' he urged.

'I am,' Lacey replied, and adopting a school-marm-ish voice said, 'Well, young man, for the benefit of your edification the cairn was built about a hundred years ago to commemorate a small community of home weavers who lost their lives in a disastrous fire that swept through an entire row of weaver's cottages up on the moor. It happened at night, the grease from the raw wool turning the houses into a roaring inferno whilst they slept.'

Nathan drew a sharp intake of breath. 'That's a tragic tale.'

'Aye, it is, but them as makes cloth have never had it easy.'

They were now at the bottom of Cuckoo Hill, the place where they would part, Lacey down the country lanes to Netherfold and Nathan along the road to Towngate and Fenay Hall.

'We appear to have ended our walk on a sad note,' Nathan commented, 'what do you say to doing this next Sunday afternoon? Avoiding the sad tales, of course.' He gazed into Lacey's eyes, his expression pleading for a positive response.

He got one.

'I'd love to,' Lacey said, her green eyes flashing delightfully. 'Cuckoo Hill next Sunday then.'

Nathan smiled his relief, the smile fading as he said, 'I'll see you at the Mill, no doubt, but I'll not draw attention to our friendship.'

This time Lacey's eyes flashed annoyance. 'Why! Are you ashamed to be seen with me?'

Nathan looked shocked. 'Not at all, but there are some who will object and I don't want our friendship to end before it's barely started.' He flushed. 'You must know what I mean.'

Lacey gazed into Nathan's face, and seeing a genuine plea for understanding she smiled gently, softening her tone when next she spoke. 'I do, Nathan. I can't say as I appreciate the women's gossiping, and I'm sure you don't. We'll just keep it to ourselves for the time being. That way we won't spoil things.'

It was Nathan's turn to smile. 'Does that mean you'll be here next Sunday?'

Lacey stretched up and pecked his cheek. 'There's your answer, Mr Brearley.' She turned and skipped down the lane leading to Netherfold Farm. Never had she been so happy.

5

'Stanley's asked me to marry him,' Joan said, as she and Lacey kicked their way through the last of the autumn leaves scattered in the lane at Netherfold.

'Oh, Joanie!' Lacey was thrilled because she knew it was what Joan had been hoping for. 'When will you do it?'

'Next spring, Stanley says. It'll give us a bit of time to save up for a place of our own an' buy a bit of furniture. I don't want to end up living with Hettie Micklethwaite if I can help it.' At the mention of Stanley's mother, Joan's euphoria dissipated. Hettie Micklethwaite was a termagant, renowned for her moaning and whiplash tongue.

'Lord no!' To dispel Joan's anxiety Lacey added, 'It'll not come to that. Stanley'll get you a house.'

'The wedding won't be a big do. Me mam's got nowt to give us and we won't have any spare money. Goodness knows what I'll wear. I'm not frittering money on a dress I'll only wear once.'

'You won't have to,' Lacey said.

Joan frowned. 'How do you mean?'

'Wait an' see,' Lacey said, her smile anticipating the pleasure Joan would take from the blue, crepe suit she'd make from one of Grandma Barraclough's dresses.

'Our Joan's getting married,' Lacey announced as soon as they entered Netherfold's kitchen.

Edith shoved the battered copy of Galsworthy's

49

A Man of Property down the side of the chair and hurried over to the hen's carcass she'd been plucking before abandoning it for her book.

'Eeh, that's grand news, Joan. Is it Stanley Micklethwaite?'

Joan affirmed it was. 'It's not till next spring, mind.'

'Is your mother pleased?' Edith's tone suggested that May Chadwick might not be.

'No, she says she'll miss me wages, but I told her I can't stay at home forever.'

'No you can't, an' our May shouldn't expect it. She knows she'll never go without as long as she's got us.' Edith didn't much care for her widowed sister's pessimistic outlook on life. 'Tell her she should be happy for you.'

Edith gathered the pile of feathers and stuffed them into a paper bag.

'Maybe one of these days our Lacey might find herself a chap who's free to marry her.' They all knew this remark alluded to Lacey's friendship with Nathan Brearley. 'But you never know,' chirped Edith, rinsing the plucked chicken under the tap, 'something might come of it yet.'

'Mother! Will you stop letting your romantic notions run away with you.'

Lacey addressed Joan. 'She reads one book after another an' expects me to be like the heroines in every story; the poor little match girl marries the wealthy landowner.'

'I just think you're destined for better things, our Lacey, an' there's no harm in hoping.'

★ ★ ★

Winter began its approach, the weather turning bitingly cold and windy.

Lacey and Nathan's Sunday walks were necessarily brief, daylight hours quickly fading to black night so, in order to redress the shortened time they spent together on Sundays, they took to meeting on the riverbank after work. There they snatched a few precious moments, Lacey saddened that Nathan never suggested an evening or Saturday afternoon meeting.

On the first Sunday in December they braved the icy cold and met at Cuckoo Hill.

Huddled in the shelter of the cairn the talk turned to Christmas and the New Year.

'I love Christmas,' Lacey said. 'People always seem kinder to one another at this time of year. It must be something to do with the spirit of giving; it brings out the best in 'em.'

'How will you celebrate it, Lacey?' Nathan posed the question tentatively.

'Oh, you know, the usual way. Folks drop in for hot toddies, bringing a bit of Christmas cheer with 'em so it usually ends up with a singsong an' a few daft games. Mam makes everybody welcome. We trim the parlour with fresh spruce and holly and Mam makes delicious mince pies and Christmas cake.' Lacey wrinkled her nose. 'Christmas has a smell all of its own, don't you think.'

'I'm afraid Christmas Day in our house is a sombre affair. We go to church, eat an overly large dinner then sit around making desultory conversation with relatives we don't particularly like. It's not what you would call fun.'

'Eeh, you should come up to our place, you'd

51

enjoy it, what with the lads an' their mates an' the neighbours wassailing at all hours.' Lacey issued the invitation without thinking.

Nathan coughed nervously. 'Actually, I was going to suggest you might visit us. It would be an opportunity for me to introduce you to my family.

We have a rather informal gathering on the day after Boxing Day for the Mill managers and their wives. I'm to invite a guest; I thought it might be you.'

Lacey gave Nathan an enquiring look. 'Does this mean what I think it means? Are you saying you'd like me to meet your mother because . . .' she adopted an arch manner of speech, 'because you want us to be more than friends, Mr Brearley?'

Nathan looked perplexed. 'Of course I do, Lacey. Surely you know how much I love you.' He pulled her to his chest, mumbling 'I thought you loved me.'

Lacey gazed into his troubled grey eyes, her heart performing somersaults. 'I do, Nathan, from that first afternoon on the canal. I'm just taken aback to think you would choose a girl from the weaving shed when you could have an heiress. Not that I don't think I'm as good as one,' she blustered, 'but you come from a different background an' your sort usually stick to their own kind.'

Exasperated, Nathan threw his arms wide. 'Lacey, I don't care where you work or what your background is. You are the most beautiful, intelligent and interesting woman I have ever met. That's why I love you.'

52

Lacey stepped out from the shelter of the cairn, the chill breeze ruffling her hair about her cheeks. She gazed out over the moor, her mind in turmoil.

It was true she wanted more than just friendship — but did she want everything else it would entail; would Nathan expect her to eschew her family and friends, and give up the hopes and dreams she had for carving her own future? She knew she could not adapt her way of life to that of a lady of leisure, one who spent her days tea partying and ignoring issues that needed to be addressed in the real world; her world.

Nathan watched her struggle, his expression mirroring her own when she turned to face him. 'What makes you hesitate? Is it that you don't love me enough to overcome the problems we'll surely face.'

Lacey shook her head. 'If you're referring to the difference in our backgrounds, that's the least of my worries. I can hold my own with anyone, be they high or low; what I wouldn't want is for you to expect me to become a society lady,' she laughed derisively, 'that's even if I could. No, Nathan, if we were to marry I would still want freedom enough to follow my own ambitions and involve myself in matters that really concern me. I won't be a simpering, little woman whose days are filled with nothing but idle prattle and wondering what to wear.'

Nathan laughed out loud. 'I'm sure you won't, and I wouldn't want you any way but how you are. I won't change you, Lacey.' He drew her close. 'I don't think I could, even if I wanted to.'

Lacey grimaced. 'You're probably right about that. Maybe, given time, I might become a little more refined, but I wouldn't hold your breath.'

Nathan laughed again. 'I won't, but,' his humour evaporated, his expression one of undisguised irritation, 'you're right to say the difference in our backgrounds may cause problems, but it's up to us to convince the doubters that we have a future together.'

Lacey gave him a wry smile. 'We could have a fight on our hands — you more so than me. My family will assume I'll become too grand for them — and as for yours — they'll hate the idea.'

'I'll deal with them,' Nathan said, firmly. 'I won't let anyone stand in our way.'

'Brave words,' said Lacey, but she couldn't help thinking Nathan wouldn't find it that easy. In the deepening dusk they walked down Cuckoo Hill, each lost in their own thoughts. At the parting of the ways they halted, Lacey taking both of Nathan's hands in her own and saying, 'Words can't express how happy you've made me. I knew from when we first met that I wanted to spend my life with you. So, Mr Brearley, let's prepare for battle.'

Nathan bent his face to hers and they kissed for the first time, a long, warm kiss that made Lacey's spine tingle. The snow that had threatened to fall throughout the day found release, large white flakes settling on hats and shoulders, the soot stained world around them transformed to pearly white.

Another kiss and they parted, both glorying in wonderment at the shift in their relationship, and at the same time inwardly quaking at what the consequences might be.

★ ★ ★

'Our Jimmy's late again,' Edith remarked, as she banked the fire with slack to keep it burning overnight. Outside the ground was covered with layers of ice and fresh snow, it having fallen every day for the past week. 'He shouldn't be out on a night like this but just lately there's no keeping him in.'

'That's 'cos he's spoiled rotten,' Joshua Barraclough growled, 'you give in to him at every turn. He should be tending sheep wi' me an' our Matt, not working in t'mill. An' come spring when we're breakin' us backs ploughin' an' plantin' he'll still be there. What sort of a son is it won't work on his father's land?'

'Now Jos, you know as well as I do the land's not big enough to support us all,' Edith interjected. 'Without our Lacey's an' Jimmy's wages we'd be in a right pickle, I can tell you. There's weeks when this farm earns nowt.'

'Well it's not for t'want o' tryin'. I work me fingers to t'bone,' grumbled Joshua.

'We know you do, luv,' Edith said, patiently, 'but you shouldn't go taking your temper out on our Jimmy. You've been awful short with him lately.'

Lacey shut her ears to the argument; she'd heard it all before. Her Dad hated the mills and had been sorely disappointed when she had gone to be a weaver instead of staying at home to help Edith with the geese and hens.

Jimmy's defection three years later still caused

55

uproar, Joshua regularly voicing his objections. Yet, deep down, he knew the family couldn't manage without the money Lacey and Jimmy brought home; he was just too proud to admit it.

Lacey filled a saucepan with milk. 'I'm making a bedtime drink, Dad. Do you want one.' Prising the lid off a tin of Fry's Cocoa she measured spoonfuls into thick mugs.

'Aye, go on then,' Joshua said, mollified. 'I'll have that then I'll go to bed. I'm not waitin' up for him, the silly young bugger.'

Just then the door burst open and Matt came in, bringing with him a flurry of icy, white flakes. 'By, that's some bloody night out there,' he said, stamping his boots free of snow. He shrugged out of his coats.

'Did you check on them ewes an' lock up,' Joshua asked him.

'Aye, I did. They're well sheltered in yon fold.' Matt glanced round the kitchen. 'Our Jimmy not in yet?'

'No, he's not,' Lacey said. 'You wouldn't happen to know who he's running with lately, would you?' She had a nasty feeling it could be Arty Bincliffe and his mob.

Matt shrugged. 'Can't say as I do. You know me, I hardly go any further than t'Plough.'

The Plough Inn being the nearest public house to Netherfold, Matt rarely went into the heart of the town. He had no interest in women, or so it seemed, and his social life consisted of no more than a few pints of ale and a game of skittles. That he was Joshua's favourite went without saying.

Born to the land, Matt was happiest herding

56

sheep or planting turnips.

Matt took off his boots and went and sat by the fire. 'I checked on t'geese an' all, Mam. Fred Tinker told me somebody stole three of his turkeys.

Coming up to Christmas the thieving buggers'll be raiding coops all over t'place.'

Lacey handed out mugs of cocoa then joined her family at the fireside, Joshua and Matt toasting their feet on the fender, Lacey with her nose in a book and Edith darning Jimmy's socks. They listened for the sound of his footsteps.

Joshua drained his mug then slammed it down on the hearth. 'Well, I don't know about the rest o' you but I'm off to bed. I'll give that thoughtless bugger a right larrikin when I see him tomorrow.'

He stamped out of the room, Matt following shortly after. Every now and then Edith glanced anxiously at the outside door. 'You go on up, Mam,' Lacey said. 'I'll wait up for him. He'll not be long.'

'Right you are, love; but I'll not sleep.' Edith plodded from the kitchen.

Lacey read for a while then dozed for almost an hour, roused by the stamp of feet outside the kitchen door. It opened and Jimmy crept in, grinning sheepishly. 'I knocked snow off me boots afore I came in.'

Ignoring his childish placatory tactics, Lacey fixed him with an iron glare. 'Where were you?' Her accusatory tone made Jimmy flinch. 'And more to the point, who were you with?'

Jimmy's cheeks reddened. 'Some lads from t'Mill.' He shuffled his feet and hung his head, the picture of a naughty child.

'Arty Bincliffe,' Lacey spat. 'What did I tell you? Mam and Dad were worried to death an' if they knew who you were running with, they'd have a fit.' She shook her head in exasperation. 'Get over by t'fire; warm yourself. I'll make you some cocoa.'

Jimmy shuffled over to the hearth, the lamps on the mantel casting him in full light. A skinny lad, all elbows and ears, he stretched his scrawny wrists to warm his hands over the dying embers. Minutes later, Lacey handed him a mug of cocoa. 'What's that on your jacket?'

Jimmy shrank back as Lacey plucked a clump of down from the front of his coat. 'What have you been up to? You're covered in feathers.'

Jimmy put his mug on the hearth then brushed frantically at the front of his jacket, a red flush creeping up his neck into his cheeks.

Lacey's face registered her dismay. 'You've been thieving birds.'

Jimmy spluttered. 'We only did it for a laugh, Lacey. I didn't want to, but Arty said I wa' soft. I don't want 'em thinkin' I'm just a kid so I went along wi' it.'

'Along with what, Jimmy?'

'We pinched two o' Jem Baxter's turkeys.'

'An' you think that's funny, do you?' Lacey's voice rang with contempt and her eyes blazed as she brought her face to within an inch of Jimmy's.

'Would you think it funny if somebody pinched Mam's geese? Summat she's worked hard to rear all year to make a bit of money.'

Tears welled in the corners of Jimmy's eyes and

58

he seemed to shrink inside his jacket as Lacey berated him. 'Arty didn't steal the turkeys for a joke, you daft lummox; he'll sell 'em to the highest bidder come Christmas.' She prodded Jimmy's chest, hard. 'That's thieving, Jimmy.'

Chastened, Jimmy hurried to the foot of the stairs. 'I'm sorry, Lacey. It'll not happen again. I don't want me cocoa, I'm off to bed.'

Nursing the mug of cocoa, Lacey determined to have a word with Arty Bincliffe, warn him off, tell him to leave their Jimmy alone. She'd not mention this night's escapade to her Mam. It would only upset her. And she certainly wouldn't tell her Dad. His relationship with his youngest son caused enough problems. She'd deal with it herself.

6

The Sunday before Christmas was a bitterly cold
day when Nathan and Lacey met on the riverbank
behind the Mill. Underfoot the path was slippery
and overhead thick grey clouds threatened snow.

It was only just after two in the afternoon yet
already the sky was darkening, and Lacey shivered as they walked gingerly, hand in hand, over
the icy ruts. It was so dismal she couldn't help
thinking of the warm, jolly places they could be
were they not keeping their friendship secret.

Christmas Day being a Thursday, the Mill
would close until the following Monday and
Lacey, looking forward to the holiday, attempted
to lighten her spirits by talking of what she might
do. 'It'll give me chance to catch up with me sewing, an' there'll be folks coming and going at all
hours so I'll not be short of company,' she said, at
the same time hoping Nathan would suggest she
spent some of the time with him.

Nathan, sensing her forced jollity gazed down
at her, his heart heavy. She looked a picture in
her navy woollen coat with its nipped in waist, a
bright blue knitted scarf covering her glossy brown
hair and framing her lovely face. He desperately
wanted to say he would share every minute of the
holiday with her, yet he knew family duties would
claim him.

His spirits sinking even further, he reiterated
his request for her to meet his family. 'Do come.

There'll be other workers there so you won't feel out of place. We'll get it over with in one fell swoop.' To Lacey it sounded as though he dreaded the event so she said as much.

'Look, if you're not sure about this we can leave it for another time.'

'No, the sooner we get it over with, the better.'

For the rest of the afternoon Nathan was tense and distracted and they almost quarrelled when Lacey chose to discuss a topic close to her heart.

'They've arrested Emmeline Pankhurst again. I think it's disgraceful that women aren't allowed to vote. If I were in London I'd join the protest.'

Nathan stared at her, askance. 'She was involved in a bomb attack on Lloyd George's home. Surely you don't condone such actions.'

'They wouldn't have to resort to such actions if men were intelligent enough to acknowledge that women have an equal place in society,' said Lacey stoutly. 'I think Sylvia Pankhurst and her daughter, Emmeline, are extremely brave.'

'Foolish, more like; it all seems dreadfully unladylike to march in mobs, yelling and jeering at those chosen to run the country.'

'Aye — men — that's who runs the country an' women have no say — not even upper class women like the one's you're used to,' Lacey fired back, her cheeks pinking with the heat of her argument. 'Suffragettes fight for what they believe in. They're even prepared to starve to death for their rights. The way the government played 'Cat an' Mouse' with 'em was a dirty trick; releasing them from gaol when they went on hunger strike so's the women wouldn't get public sympathy. We've

61

as much right to the vote as any man.' Lacey paused for breath, her green eyes glittering and her expression steely.

Nathan watched the rapid rise and fall of her bosom. 'I don't entirely disagree with women having the vote,' he said reasonably, 'but I think they should let the law decide. These dramatic little displays of aggravation are getting them nowhere.'

'Dramatic displays!'

Lacey's shriek stopped Nathan in his tracks. She stared at him incredulously. 'You think Emily Davidson throwing herself under the hooves of the king's horse an' being trampled to death was just for show. Really Nathan, I thought better of you.' She turned, marching briskly away from him.

Nathan ran after her, catching her with both hands and swinging her round to face him. He kissed her passionately and when he released her, he laughed, 'Oh Lacey, my darling little firebrand. What am I to do with you? Of course I agree women should have the right to vote. I'm sorry I upset you; don't let's quarrel over things that don't concern us. We have little enough time together.'

And whose fault's that, thought Lacey, as he took her in his arms and kissed her again. She responded willingly but in the recesses of her mind she was thinking, the right to vote might not concern you, Nathan, but it concerns me. And why, when you're so intelligent and well read, are your opinions so skewed? It's as if someone was telling you what you should think, rather than what you believe. What's more, people of your social standing don't have to consider the needs of the lower classes. You have your rights, no matter what.

Before they parted, Nathan said, 'By the way, Lacey, I'd rather you didn't mention Mrs Pankhurst during your visit. Mother doesn't agree with suffrage. She considers it unladylike.'

Lacey sniggered. 'Oh, I can see me an' your mother will get along just fine.'

Nathan didn't look convinced.

★ ★ ★

On Christmas Eve morning the atmosphere in the weaving shed was more convivial than usual. Some of the women had decorated their looms with sprigs of holly and sparkling tinsel. At breakfast time Jonas Brearley supplied hot mince pies for everyone, this being the last working day before the Mill closed for the holiday.

Huddled in a corner of the shed, for it was bitingly cold and the ground outside still covered in snow, Lacey and Joan bit into their pies before settling down to gossip.

'Nathan's invited me to that party they give for the managers, though I'm not sure I'll go,' said Lacey, her tone deliberately casual.

Joan's blue eyes opened wide and her mouth turned down at the corners.

'Does Jonas know you've been asked?'

Lacey shrugged. 'Nathan thinks it will be a gentle way of introducing me to his mother.'

'Gentle be beggared. It'll more likely shock her into having a heart attack. You could lose your job over it, Lacey. Don't go.'

Lacey frowned. 'I know what you mean, Joanie, but if I don't go I'll never find out what way

63

the wind's blowing. If they go berserk and force Nathan to give me up then that'll be the end of it. He says he'll stand up to them, but I don't think he's thought how much he might lose if he does.'

Her glum expression tore at Joan's kind heart so to ease Lacey's pain she decided to commiserate by relating her own problems.

'I wanted Stanley to come to us for his Christmas dinner but his mother wouldn't hear of it. Caused a right stink, she did. She didn't invite me to their place so we'll not see one another until afterwards.' Joan's face brightened. 'We're both coming up to yours though, for a bit of a do later on.'

'Good,' said Lacey. 'I've asked Nathan to come but I don't know that he will. It's not the done thing for the boss's son to keep company with mill hands and farmers.' She grimaced. 'An' anyway, we'll more than likely shock the socks off him with our rowdy carry on.'

Joan grinned. 'If he's going to stay friends with you he'll have to get used to it.'

'Aye, maybe it'll loosen him up a bit — show him how the other half lives.'

They both laughed at Lacey's remark, but deep down Lacey was thinking that rather than make Nathan more carefree she ought to be encouraging him to show a bit more backbone.

Late that afternoon, as pick after pick increased her piece of woven worsted, Lacey thought of the larger than usual pay packet she would receive at the end of the day. The weavers were paid according to the number of pieces they had completed that week, each roll of cloth marked in black wax

64

crayon with a weaver's individual number. This enabled the wages clerk to calculate what was owed. This week Lacey's pieces had been good, and added to that she would receive her Christmas bonus.

Suddenly her elation turned to exasperation. The shuttle on one of her looms had come unthreaded. Swiftly gripping the stout handle that stopped and started the loom, she shifted the drive belt from a 'fast' pulley to a 'loose' pulley. The loom ground to a halt. Annoyed by wasting time, Lacey looked around anxiously for a tuner.

A loom tuner was the man who fixed breakdowns, and whilst Lacey knew she could rethread the shuttle herself she objected to the practice.

'Kissing the shuttle' as it was called, meant placing the thread in the shuttle's eye then sucking it through with a quick intake of breath. To do so she would be sucking fluff and dust into her lungs.

Better to let someone else do it.

The loom at a standstill, Lacey was startled when a pair of grimy hands encircled her waist and hot, fetid breath wafted over her shoulder. Half turning, she saw Syd's leering face, and through her overall and heavy woollen skirt she felt his manhood rising as he pressed against her buttocks.

Elbowing him aside she said, 'I need me shuttle rethreading. Will you do it for us, Mr Sugden?'

A sprig of mistletoe dangled from the peak of Syd's cloth cap. He had been drinking all morning, it being the custom at Christmas for the bosses to break open a bottle in the privacy of the office.

'Aye, I will, but I know what I'd rather be kissin'.
He leaned forward, lips puckered. Lacey stepped
back, wishing she hadn't asked for his help.

With one quick suck Syd rethreaded the shuttle
and returned it to the loom. 'Thanks,' said Lacey,
stepping forward to set the loom in motion.

Syd blocked her way. She gave an appeasing
smile and adopting a conciliatory tone said, 'Let
me get on, Mr Sugden, or I'll be all behind at
clocking off time.'

Syd bared his stained teeth in a grimace. 'I think
I deserve a bit more than thanks,' he cajoled. 'Go
out to t'lavvy an' I'll be right behind; you can give
us a Christmas present.'

Ignoring his request, Lacey turned her back on
him and, as though he were not there, she waved
to Joan then started up a silent conversation.

Joan, who had been keeping an eye on the situation, mouthed back.

Syd, realising they were making a fool of him,
yanked at Lacey's arm.

'Give us a kiss, yer miserable bugger.' He
pushed his face into Lacey's. She raised her knee,
ramming it into Syd's groin and he tottered away,
his face livid.

Lacey groaned. It had been unwise to anger Syd.
Now, too late to prevent it, Lacey contemplated
the misery of finding her wages minus the small
bonus Jonas Brearley gave each of his employees
at Christmas. For the rest of the day Lacey felt
miserable.

Shortly before clocking off time the head tuner,
Arthur Gibson, plodded through the 'weaver's
alleys' doling out the wages from a wooden tray

66

divided into numbered strips, each strip holding several small tins containing money. When he handed Lacey hers, she knew by its weight that her Christmas bonus wasn't in it. Damn Sydney Sugden, she silently cursed, counting the coins then shoving them into her overall pocket. It was no use complaining — she'd brought it on herself.

But complain she did, to Joan as they hurried out into the mill yard at the end of the day, the clatter of their clogs muffled by the thick snow underfoot.

'The dirty, rotten sod,' Joan commiserated.

Lacey chuckled. 'I just hope his balls are that tender he can't enjoy his Christmas dinner.'

'Do you think I should tell him to rub some goose fat on 'em,' scoffed Joan.

'I'd prefer to set me Mam's geese on him. They'd rip 'em off an' do us all a favour.'

At the bottom of Turnpike Lane, the girls parted. 'See you tomorrow then, Joanie; enjoy your Christmas dinner.'

'Aye, me an' Stanley'll come to yours about six.' Joan headed up Turnpike Lane and Lacey down Backhouse Lane to meet Nathan on the riverbank.

A chill wind blew up from the river, stinging her cheeks and making her eyes water, and as she trudged through the snow to the riverbank she couldn't help feeling peeved. Why did their meetings have to be so clandestine? When were she and Nathan going to spend time together like other courting couples?

In the shelter of the Mill wall Nathan held her close, Lacey warming to his kisses. 'Have you thought any more about coming up to our place tomorrow?' she asked, fearful she might not see him at all over the holiday.

There was a long silence before Nathan answered. A cold shiver fingered Lacey's spine. 'I don't think that will be possible,' Nathan said, 'I have family duties to attend to and, furthermore, don't you think it will seem rather odd, me celebrating Christmas with your people?'

A hot spurt of anger flared in Lacey's chest. 'What do you mean — my people? If we're ever to be together you'll have to learn to mix with my people just as I'll have to learn to mix with yours. If we mean anything at all to one another we'll rise above whatever other people might think.' She pulled away from him. 'Or maybe you don't love me enough, an' it's just a game you're playing, salving your do-gooding instincts by being nice to the poor little factory girl.'

Nathan blanched. 'No, Lacey! I love you truly. You mean the world to me. I just don't know how we are to overcome our different stations in life without there being ructions.' He hung his head, utterly dejected.

Lacey gave him a withering glare. 'If you truly loved me you'd put aside all this class nonsense and if, as you say, I mean the world to you then your world must be a very petty place indeed.'

Nathan clutched her to his chest. 'Please, Lacey; don't be like this. I'll come tomorrow evening, if I can get away.' He kissed her fleetingly on the cheek then turned and ran.

Lacey gazed at the fast flowing river. You know where you're going, she silently told it, whereas I don't know whether I'm coming or going. One minute I'm certain of Nathan's love, and the next I believe he doesn't mean a word of it.

Totally confused, she retraced her footsteps until she came to the bottom of Backhouse Lane. What a waste of time on a night like this, she thought, as she trudged up the snowy pavement, irked and disappointed by Nathan's feebleness.

At the top of Backhouse Lane she saw two men, both familiar, deep in conversation. She quickened her pace but failed to reach them before Jimmy ran off in the direction of Netherfold. Arty Bincliffe strolled towards her. Lacey blocked his way. Her eyes raked his pocked, weasel-like features. 'I want a word with you.'

Arty grinned lewdly. 'You can have owt you want wi' me, Lacey, luv.'

Ignoring the innuendo, Lacey glared. 'Leave our Jimmy alone,' she threatened, 'cos if you don't you'll have me to deal with. I know about them turkeys, so if you don't want me to report it was you as stole 'em, you'll tell our Jimmy to get lost next time you see him.'

Arty smirked, rocking back on his heels, unfazed. 'Ooh, you're scarin' me,' he mocked.

Lacey tried a different tack, despising the pleading tone of her voice as she said, 'Look Arty, our Jimmy thinks he's a big man running round wi' you, but he's only a daft little lad. Do us a favour an' leave him alone.'

'Can't say as I can, Lacey. Your Jimmy's my little lackey. There's nowt he wouldn't do for me.' Arty's cocky tone and smug expression confirmed Lacey's worst fears so she reverted to threats.

'I've not said owt yet to our Matt but if he hears

69

that you've been putting our Jimmy up to no good, he'll give you a bloody good hiding.'

This time she managed to dent Arty's arrogance. Matt Barraclough was a big, brawny man noted for being handy with his fists, whereas Arty Bincliffe was a weedy runt fit only for dominating the vulnerable. Astute enough to know Lacey had kept the incident of the turkeys from Matt to protect Jimmy, he shrugged carelessly. 'Rightio! Just for you, Lacey, I'll tell him to bugger off next time he comes lookin' for me. Mind, I'm only doin' it 'cos I fancy you. Do you want to go out wi' me?'

Lacey laughed in his face. 'You cheeky bugger; are you seriously expecting me to return the favour? I've said what I have to say, Arty, an' I mean it. Leave our Jimmy be.'

She left him standing like a dejected scarecrow and hurried home to Netherfold convinced she'd dealt with the problem successfully.

7

Nathan Brearley was bored and irritable. He'd spent the earlier part of Christmas Day attending to his filial duties, and now it was six in the evening and he needed to escape the drawing room at Fenay Hall. He'd partaken of a sumptuous turkey dinner and played numerous foolish party games, several of them resulting in his having to kiss his cousin, Violet.

That she had purposely arranged these forfeits did not escape Nathan's notice. But he didn't want Violet — he wanted Lacey.

'Oh, don't they make a charming couple,' Violet's mother gushed, waving her fan with one hand and clasping Jonas's arm with the other.

'Aye, they're a bonny enough pair,' Jonas agreed half heartedly, as he helped himself to another glass of port. Jonas was well aware that Alice Burrows, his wife's second cousin, had set her heart on making a match between Violet and Nathan. He concentrated his gaze on his son. Nathan was reluctantly standing under a crystal chandelier festooned with mistletoe, Violet on tip-toe clinging to his lapels and waiting to be kissed.

Unfortunately for Violet, her protruding upper teeth and pouted lips were not the prettiest sight. Hesitantly, Nathan brushed her lips with his, unhanded her and strode across the fine Turkish carpet to the drinks trolley.

He poured himself a hefty measure of whisky

71

and swigged it in one gulp.

Jonas smiled sardonically. Aye, he mused, they might look a charming couple to you, Alice, but my lad has no notion of your Violet. In his mind's eye he pictured Lacey Barraclough's vibrant face and commanding eyes and wondered if the rumours he had heard at The Mill were true. Maybe he should have a word with the lad. Excusing himself, he left Alice and went to the bathroom. When he returned to the drawing room Nathan was nowhere in sight.

★ ★ ★

At the end of the lane leading to Netherfold Farm, Nathan stopped to catch his breath. He'd run all the way, buoyed by the whisky and the half bottle of wine he'd downed before leaving Fenay Hall. Now, the cold sobering air made him think twice. What would the mill hands and Lacey's family think if he joined the party? Word that he had been there would be all over the Mill when they returned to work on Monday morning. Then there would be no hiding his relationship with Lacey.

Damn it, he ached to be with her, and to hell with the consequences. He'd socialised with the workers on the Mill outing at his father's request. What difference was there in sharing their company tonight? Before his nerve wavered, he set off again at a run.

★ ★ ★

72

The kitchen and parlour at Netherfold were crammed with the Barracloughs' friends and neighbours, all there to celebrate the festive season in high old fashion. It was something of a tradition for Edith to hold open house on Christmas Day evening. The sideboard was loaded with jugs of ale and bottled beer, the kitchen table swamped by a plentiful supply of cooked meats, mince pies and Christmas cake, much of it contributed by the revellers.

Lacey had decked the mantelshelf in the parlour with holly and ivy, the glossy green leaves and bright red berries glinting in the light from oil lamps and the blazing fire. A small spruce, aglow with baubles and tinsel stood in one corner. Spirits were high but Lacey felt detached from it all.

Nathan hadn't come; but what had she expected? He was lily-livered, his love for her not strong enough to defy his rearing.

'Give us a Christmas kiss for old time's sake, Lacey.' Sam Barton, his handsome features and warm brown eyes alight with mischief, and love, dangled a sprig of mistletoe above Lacey's head.

Lacey fleetingly pecked his lips. When he tried for more she pushed him aside. 'Go away, Sam. I don't feel like playing daft games.'

'Suit yourself.' Sam sauntered over to Mary Collier who obliged in an instant. Sam glanced over his shoulder to see if Lacey had noticed and, if so, was she envious.

Joan nudged Lacey. 'Don't take it out on poor Sam just because Nathan's not shown up. You didn't really expect him to, did you? I didn't. I said as much to Stanley.'

73

Lacey glared at her. 'Don't be discussing me and Nathan wi' Stanley,' she hissed. 'Nobody's supposed to know.'

'You can't keep owt secret in Garsthwaite, Lacey. You should know that,'

said Joan, a little peevishly. 'An' anyway, maybe you'd be better off wi'

Sam; he's really fond of you.' She turned on her heel, and linking her arm through Stanley's, left Lacey to her own devices.

Lacey stayed where she was. Perhaps Joan was right, she mused. With Sam there would be no problems regarding class; our backgrounds are the same. But I don't love Sam — I love Nathan — even if, at times, he seems spineless. Yet, the pure joy we find in each other, the lively wit and thoughtful conversation makes me happier than I ever could be with Sam.

A sudden lull in the noise level from the kitchen had her peering through the adjoining doorway. Joshua and Matt, along with a few farmers and mill hands were all gawping at the tall, fair, expensively dressed man standing at the open back door.

Joshua was the first to recover. 'Come in, lad, whoever you are, don't just stand there; make yourself at home. Here have a sup.' He thrust a bottle of beer into Nathan's hand.

Lacey stayed where she was, shock and overwhelming joy rooting her to the spot: he'd actually come.

'What about summat to go with it, sir?' Billy Northrop, from the dye house, shoved a plate of mince pies under Nathan's nose. On hearing Billy refer to Nathan as 'sir', Joshua's eyebrows shot up

74

and he looked questioningly at Billy.

'It's Master Nathan, from t'Mill, Jos; Jonas's son,' Billy explained.

Joshua's benevolent expression dissolved into a frown.

Quickly Lacey regained her composure. Thrusting her way through the crowd she held out her hand to Nathan and he took hold of it like a man clinging to a rock in a stormy sea.

'I'm so glad you came.' Lacey's voice was calm but her heartbeat raced and hot blood warmed her cheeks. 'Do come in and join us,' she said, leading Nathan past the puzzled faces that openly asked, what's he doing here?

In the parlour some of the male mill hands courteously touched their forelocks and the older women bobbed curtseys. The bluff farmers nodded greetings. Nathan took a deep breath. 'No need to stand on ceremony,' he said, his tone jovial, 'I just thought I'd join you for a while. I'm told this is where the fun is.' The tense atmosphere faded and Lacey could have kissed him.

Nathan observed the cheerful scene, his face alight with genuine admiration. 'It's jolly indeed, Lacey,' he said, glancing over his shoulder and apologising unnecessarily as a string of merrymakers jostled him from behind. Lacey steered him towards a vacant armchair in a corner, dodging in and out of the revellers circling the room and singing at the tops of their voices 'Here We Come A Wassailing.'

'They're inclined to get a bit rowdy,' she said as Nathan flopped down in the seat. Lacey perched on the arm. Safely tucked in the corner, Nathan

75

began to relax and enjoy the evening. Edith gave him a cautious welcome, as did Joan and Stanley.

When Sam Smethurst, a neighbouring farmer noted for his mellifluous tenor voice gave a beautiful rendition of 'If You Were the Only Girl in the World,' Nathan gazed up into Lacey's eyes and softly sang along.

Next, the girls from the weaving shed performed a lively version of 'Put Your Arms Around Me Honey, Hold Me Tight,' Lacey leading them in her clear, sweet voice. After that an old, retired weaver gave a bawdy version of 'The Foggy Dew', the company roaring with laughter at the lewd ditties.

Lacey sensed Nathan's discomfiture. 'It's only a bit o' fun, you've no need to feel embarrassed. We sing songs like that when we're in the weaving shed; it makes time fly. But just because they've got mucky words, it doesn't mean we behave like that.'

Nathan's smile begged for understanding. 'You must think I've had a sheltered upbringing, and I suppose I have. Maybe you'll open up a whole new world for me once we're married.'

Lacey thrilled at the words. He was such a gentle soul, and she loved him for it. 'I might just do that,' she whispered, her lips brushing against his ear.

Just then Arty Bincliffe loped into the parlour. Lacey jumped up. 'Who invited him?'

Jimmy's eyes flashed defiantly. 'I did. He's me mate.'

Arty, the worse for drink, swayed further into the room, a bottle in his hand. Some of the merrymakers eyed him with open distaste, surprised to see him there. His eyes lighting on Lacey, he staggered towards her.

'Ah, there you are Lacey, luv.' He lurched forward, a lascivious grin masking his spotty face as he slurred, 'Give us a kiss for Christmas.'

Lacey stepped back. 'You're not wanted here so take yourself off.'

'Don't be like that, luv.' Arty pretended to look hurt. 'If you want me to do you that favour you asked me about t'other night, you'll have to be nice to me.' He reached out to grab hold of her.

Before his hand could make contact, it was clasped firmly and twisted behind his back. Arty let out a yell and raised his free arm, the bottle flailing the air. Nathan dodged it neatly and spun Arty round.

'The lady told you to go away. Now do that.' He thrust Arty towards the door. Amazed, Lacey watched them go. Not so soft and gentle after all, she thought.

Matt hurried to assist Nathan, roaring, 'Who the bloody hell let him in?'

Between them they shunted Arty out of the parlour and through into the kitchen, ejecting him unceremoniously into the yard. 'Bugger off,' Matt yelled after him, 'an' don't come back.'

In the sudden lull the unpleasant incident provoked, Jimmy slunk into a corner, unnerved by the turn of events and afraid he would get the blame.

When Nathan and Matt returned to the parlour, loud cheering broke out.

A hand clapped Nathan's shoulder. 'Good for you, sir, you showed that bugger off rightly.' The mill hand's praise, echoed by several others, had

Nathan blushing to the roots of his scalp. Deeply self-conscious, he made his way back to Lacey's side.

Lacey bobbed a curtsey. 'Thank you, my gallant knight in shining armour.'

Nathan smiled modestly. 'I could hardly stand by and watch that lout pester you.' His brow creased. 'What was the favour you wanted from him?'

Lacey, disinclined to tell him of Jimmy's involvement with Arty, feigned ignorance. 'I've no idea. He's drunk, and drunks always talk rubbish.' She didn't want him thinking her family associated with scum such as Arty Bincliffe.

Nathan stayed far later than he intended. He chatted with Joshua and Matt about the farm, wished Joan and Stanley good luck for their forthcoming wedding and even spent time talking with Jimmy and some of the mill hands. Before he left he thanked Edith for her hospitality, his fulsome praise making her glow.

'Maybe he's not such a bad fellow after all. He seems fair set on our Lacey,' she remarked to Joshua as they watched him go.

Lacey walked him to the end of the lane. 'Thanks for coming. You've made it a very happy Christmas for me. I was proud to have you there with me tonight. You see; all manner of people can mix together if they have open minds. In the end nobody minded that you're the boss's son; they liked you for yourself, an' you got along with them rightly.'

'I thoroughly enjoyed myself,' said Nathan, 'for as you say, it's how we behave not who we are that makes the world a better place.' They kissed fondly, each reluctant to let the other go. 'I'll call for you at three on Saturday, the manager's tea party begins about four so we'll arrive in plenty of time for me to introduce you to my parents.' A final kiss and they parted, Lacey returning to the kitchen elated.

Walking back to Towngate and home, Nathan couldn't recall a pleasanter evening. He doubted Lacey would leave with the same euphoric feeling after her meeting with his family.

8

Lacey was apprehensive. She desperately wanted to make a good impression on her first visit to Nathan's home so she dressed with particular care. It wasn't a case of choosing what to wear; the green dress, her best and most fashionable one would have to do again. More than likely Nathan would recognise it as the one she'd worn the day of the canal trip, but so be it.

Seated in front of Grandma's cheval mirror she coiled her hair three times before she was satisfied with the result. Then she topped it with a ruched bandeau she'd fashioned from a piece of the green silk.

'There,' she said, releasing her breath gustily, 'you'll do, Lacey Barraclough. You'll not let yourself down.' Confidence restored she went downstairs to the kitchen to be met with Edith's abrupt, 'You're off then?'

Lacey gave an exasperated glare in return. 'I was invited.' she said tersely.

'I know you were but . . . ' Realising her doubts were unnerving Lacey, Edith hastily made reparation. 'You look ever so smart, luv. The Brearleys'll think their Nathan's bringing home a lady.'

Lacey's temper flared. 'He is. Just because I work in a weaving shed doesn't mean I'm not one.' To tell the truth Lacey was more nervous than she cared to admit and her response sharper than intended.

'Eeh luv, I didn't mean owt by it.' Once again Edith found herself making amends. 'Us Barraclough's are as good as anybody, and you are a lady. You've always kept yourself right an' there's nobody wi' a kinder heart.' She appraised her daughter and her eyes filled with love and admiration. To show she was forgiven, Lacey hugged her.

Joshua eased up out of his chair by the fire. 'Are you done chittering? Are you ready for off?' He too, doubted the wisdom of Lacey accepting the invitation but, with the ground covered in snow, he had offered to take her to the end of the lane in the cart.

Lacey draped a thick cape over her dress. She had made it out of a fent of worsted cloth. It was common practice for the Mill manager to sell off damaged pieces to the workers and Lacey had lined the worsted with flannel to make it more substantial. Dark green on the outside and pale grey on the inside, its fine seaming and frogged fastenings made it a garment befitting any lady.

'Thank goodness it's not snowin',' Lacey said, stepping outside. Joshua followed, Edith waving goodbye from the doorway. She did not look happy.

At the end of the lane Joshua and Lacey waited for Nathan to meet them, Joshua tutting impatiently as the minutes passed by and Lacey wondering if Nathan had had second thoughts. When eventually, he did arrive, driving a smart pony and trap, Lacey climbed up beside him and they set off for Fenay Hall, both tense and silent for much of the way. 'I'm later than I intended,' said Nathan, 'but I'll introduce you to my parents the first chance I

81

get.' He sounded positively lugubrious.

Lacey grimaced. 'You make it sound as though you're about to sign my death warrant.'

He might as well have been.

By the time they arrived at Fenay Hall, the drawing room was crowded with people. Perched on the edge of an ornate chair, Lacey admired the large, opulent room. Brocaded drapes adorned the windows and dark wood furniture gleamed against pale green walls. The body of the room was filled with small round tables covered with pristine white damask cloths, and at each table there were four chairs so the guests could sit to enjoy the lavish repast. Mill managers and their spouses sat or stood, many of them looking decidedly ill at ease.

Lacey scanned the dresses of the younger women in the room. Her green dress didn't look out of place although it was simple in comparison to those worn by the girls clustered about Constance Brearley, Nathan's mother.

Nathan was with them now; summoned by his mother.

Lacey had watched him go, striding nonchalantly across the parquet floor, a feeling of sadness creeping over her. Why hadn't he taken her with him and introduced her there and then? Feeling bereft she looked around for a familiar face. Catching the eye of Clara Johnson, the Mill manager's wife, sitting at the next table, she smiled and then said, 'Hello, Mrs Johnson; it's very impressive, isn't it?'

Clara Johnson gave her a sour look. 'I'd have put you down as having more sense than to come here,' she replied tartly.

'Why shouldn't I be here?'

'You know why.' Clara turned her back on Lacey. A few minutes later Nathan returned, but he'd barely spoken two words when a girl with a mop of blonde, frizzy hair and prominent teeth rushed over to them.

'Nathan, Nathan.' She grabbed his arm. 'Do come and say hello to Sylvia Oldroyd, she's simply dying to meet you.'

Muttering excuses, Nathan allowed himself to be dragged away.

Sylvia Oldroyd, mused Lacey. She must be the daughter of Edgar Oldroyd, a mill owner from further down the valley. She gazed over to where Nathan now stood, deep in conversation with the frizzy haired girl; a girl she presumed was Sylvia Oldroyd.

Lacey studied the tall, raven haired girl, noting her fine features and aristocratic bearing. She was smiling charmingly at Nathan, completely at ease in her surroundings. Now there's the sort of girl Nathan's mother would choose, thought Lacey, and by the looks of it Nathan himself might be tempted. A spurt of anger flashed through her. She stood up; she was going home.

However, her departure was delayed by one of the smartly uniformed girls hired to serve the repast. 'Is it just for one, miss?'

Lacey hid her chagrin behind a bright smile and was about to decline when Nathan arrived at her elbow. 'Oh, jolly good, tea and cakes.' He pulled out a chair, motioning for Lacey to sit, then sat across from her, apologising yet again for his neglect.

The delightful confectionary did little to lighten Lacey's spirits. Choking down a morsel of cake, she reflected miserably on the event so far. It wasn't at all what she had expected.

'Who's the frizzy blonde with the teeth?' Lacey knew she sounded ungracious but she couldn't help it.

Nathan groaned. 'That's cousin Violet. She's awfully difficult to refuse. She's so pushy it's easier to do as she asks, and it would have been churlish of me not to speak with Sylvia.' He pulled a face, indicating his displeasure at having to do so.

'You didn't look as though you weren't enjoying it,' Lacey riposted, aware that she sounded jealous, and gauche.

Nathan laid his hand on top of hers. 'Oh Lacey! It's what we do on occasions like this. I'm meant to socialise and be pleasant; I'm the son of the house.'

This remark made Lacey feel even more out of place, the 'what we do' inferring that she didn't understand upper class etiquette.

'Am I forgiven?' Nathan gave her beseeching look.

Although she was inwardly seething, Lacey merely nodded; this was hardly the time or place to quarrel. They made desultory conversation, Lacey admiring the paintings on the wall nearby and Nathan explaining them. By now several pairs of eyes were watching them acutely: none more so than Jonas Brearley's. He strolled over to their table.

Nathan stood. 'Father, allow me to introduce

Miss Lacey Barraclough.'

Jonas ignored Lacey's outstretched hand. 'We've already met,' he said bluntly. 'What's she doing here?'

Nathan flushed. 'I invited her. We've become friends, and Mother gave me permission to invite a guest.'

'I doubt she meant a lass from our weaving shed. I'll talk to you later.'

Jonas strutted across the room to join his wife.

During this exchange Lacey had kept her head down. She wouldn't make a scene. 'That went well,' she remarked, her tone laced with sarcasm. She got to her feet. 'It was a mistake to come. If you'll excuse me, I'll be on my way.'

She hurried out to the hallway, Nathan close behind. 'Please Lacey, don't be cross.'

Lacey glared. 'Cross? I'm not cross, I'm bloody raging.' A discreet cough from a footman standing in the hall stilled her tongue, lest she shame herself further.

'Nathan, come with me. I want to introduce you to Sir Humphrey.' Jonas Brearley grasped his son's elbow.

Nathan gave Lacey a panicked glance. 'I'll be back shortly to drive you home,' he gabbled before following his father into the drawing room. Lacey asked the butler to fetch her cape. She had no intention of waiting for Nathan even though it was a long walk home. Whilst she waited, she studied her reflection in a large gilt mirror. Two bright pink spots stained her cheeks and her eyes flashed green. Damn them all, she thought, then suddenly aware of another reflection in the mirror she turned to face Constance Brearley.

Constance gave a wintry smile. 'And who might you be, my dear? I don't think we've been introduced.'

Lacey took a deep breath. 'I'm Lacey Barraclough, Nathan's guest.' And you know damned well who I am, she thought.

A spiteful glimmer lit Constance's eyes. 'Nathan who, dear?'

'Nathan Brearley; your son.'

Constance frowned: 'My son, Nathan?' Mustering a withering look and a tone filled with contempt, she said, 'Why ever would he invite a girl like you as his guest.'

'A girl like me, Mrs Brearley?' said Lacey, throwing caution to the wind. 'You don't know what I'm like. Nathan, on the other hand, does. We've been walking out for months now, and whilst you might consider me unsuitable, Nathan doesn't. So that's why I'm here. But you needn't worry; I'm not staying. I'm particular as to the company I keep.'

The butler, his face a mask, helped Lacey don her cape. Nathan hurried towards her, Lacey almost knocking him off his feet as she swept to the front door, his offer to take her home ignored. Constance, her cheeks blazing, placed a restraining arm on Nathan's.

Outside, Lacey slowed her pace, half hoping Nathan might follow. He didn't, and as she plodded onwards in shoes totally unsuited to the snow and ice underfoot, she cursed herself for being so foolish. She should have listened to her Mam: it wasn't enough to think you were equal to all men, and women for that matter, because upper class snobs such as Constance Brearley would never allow it. Furthermore, she thought, as she squelched through Garsthwaite in sodden shoes, Nathan Brearley might try to deny the class barrier, but he's too spineless to surmount it. Better to forget all about him.

★ ★ ★

Later that same evening, Constance and Jonas Brearley sat side by side on a couch in Fenay Hall's drawing room. Nathan, subdued and nervous, sat facing them.

'Whatever were you thinking, lad?' Jonas's tone was thick with consternation.

Nathan squirmed. 'I wanted you to meet her; for you to realise what a beautiful, intelligent girl she is.'

Constance sneered, her words barbed. 'She's a common mill hand, one of your father's employees: a girl from the gutter. Hardly the sort for you.'

No longer contrite, Nathan retaliated. 'She's not from the gutter. Her father's a respectable farmer. Yes! She works for a living, but it doesn't make her inferior. She's far more interesting and intelligent than either Violet Burrows or Sylvia Oldroyd — and prettier too.'

'And you're a fool,' screeched Constance. 'You have your position to uphold. One day the Mill will be yours. What use will a common slut of a wife be to you then?'

Nathan leapt to his feet. 'I'll not stay to listen to you deride her in such a fashion.' He made to

87

leave but Jonas placed a restraining hand on his shoulder.

'Your mother has a point, lad. It's only natural you should be attracted to a pretty face' — and recalling the incident in the Mill yard, Jonas added — 'and a lively tongue. But you don't parade your feelings in public. You keep such pleasures away from prying eyes. That way, there'll be no stones cast when you choose a respectable woman.'

Constance sniffed. 'Are we to understand that is what you did?'

Jonas reddened.

Nathan shrugged Jonas's hand away. 'I have chosen a respectable woman; the one you insulted. She's not some passing fancy I'm using to satisfy my needs. I love Lacey, and I'll not be forced into a miserable marriage simply to uphold your stupid snobbery.' He barged from the room.

Constance burst into tears, Jonas patting her shoulder distractedly. 'Don't take on so. He's young; he'll grow out of it. It's only right for him to sow a few wild oats before he settles down. It'll not be long before he's had his fill and realises she's not for him. He's smart enough.'

Jonas truly believed this. In his younger days he'd dallied with a number of girls from the sheds. They were fun — and willing — but not the type a mill owner should take for a wife. When his father, Hector, had suggested he marry Constance, a mining heiress, Jonas had appreciated the logic: Constance had breeding and money.

Outside the drawing room, leant against the closed door to gather his senses, Nathan clearly heard Jonas voicing his opinion. He was shocked.

His father thought he was bedding Lacey, but he'd never laid a hand on her.

He was even more shocked when he heard his mother say, 'If he persists with this nonsense you will have to disown him.'

Nathan heard Jonas harrumph. Afraid to hear more, he fled.

Up in his bedroom he threw himself on the bed and stared up at the ceiling. Disinherited? He couldn't bear that. He took it for granted that, one day, the Mill would be his — and he dreamed of the changes he would make.

Inspired by the works of Engels, Shaftsbury and Cadbury, Nathan firmly believed that a workforce provided with safe, healthy working conditions and respect would result in improved production. Now, if he chose Lacey over the Mill, what would he do?

Perhaps his mother was right. If he chose a girl of his own standing the problem would be solved. But I love Lacey, he told himself, thumping his fist into a pillow. Question is: do I have the courage to relinquish my inheritance for her? Failing to reach a conclusion, he fell into an uneasy sleep.

★ ★ ★

A dank mist rolled in from the moor, shrouding the cairn on Cuckoo Hill.

The late February afternoon was drawing to a close. Lacey shivered and stamped her numbed feet. She'd waited for almost an hour, but Nathan hadn't come. Neither had he come on any of the previous Sundays when she had visited the cairn.

In fact she hadn't clapped eyes on him since the disastrous party in late December. He hadn't appeared at the Mill nor had he sent her a message explaining his absence.

So much for true love, she mused. It had been too good to be true. But what else should she have expected. He'd had her believing he was made of sterner stuff but obviously this was not the case. How could she have been foolish enough to believe him when he told her he cared nothing for status?

How many times had they discussed transcending class barriers, that they were outmoded in the modern world?

Hadn't they agreed that all men, and women, ought to be measured not by their wealth but by their contribution to society? All pie in the sky, Lacey concluded, as she made her way home. But such thoughts didn't prevent her from yearning to be with him.

Had she been aware of the reason for Nathan's absence, Lacey might not have felt so miserable. At his parents' insistence he was in Northumberland, negotiating the purchase of new yarns and visiting friends of his mother. At the same time as Lacey waited for him on Cuckoo Hill, Nathan was despondently trudging across a grouse moor taking part in a shoot organised by his host, Arthur Fearnley, a coal baron. At his side was Imogen, his host's daughter. Of a similar age to Nathan, he had come to the conclusion she was also part of Constance's plan to distract him from Lacey. Yet he cared not one jot for killing birds and even less for Imogen. He was determined to make up with Lacey as soon as he returned to Yorkshire.

9

It was a Saturday afternoon, and Lacey was not long home from work. Up in her bedroom, she sat at her sewing machine treadling furiously. Easter was less than two weeks away and she still had to complete three bridesmaid's dresses and a dress for Edith. Joan was marrying Stanley on Easter Saturday, and Lacey was to be a bridesmaid along with Joan's sisters, Maggie and Elsie.

Lacey was glad she'd had plenty to do in the past three months; it took her mind off Nathan. As she set a sleeve into the dress she was making for Edith she pondered on the unfairness of her own situation, Joan's forthcoming wedding making her own hapless romance seem all the more poignant.

Why did I have to fall for someone I can't have, she asked herself? It had all seemed so right at the start, Nathan swearing he loved me enough to cast aside any opposition to us being together. Then, at the first hurdle, he abandoned me.

The sleeve in place, Lacey stilled the treadle. Stop moping she chastised herself. Nathan doesn't want you so forget about him. Joan will be here any minute to try on her wedding outfit. Don't let your disappointment spoil her pleasure. Hearing the rattle of the outside door and voices in the kitchen, Lacey put on her bravest face and ran downstairs to greet Joan. She led her straight up to the bedroom.

Several minutes later, Joan gazed in awe at her image in the cheval mirror. 'It's beautiful, Lacey. It's like something you'd see in The *Women's Journal*.' The blue crepe suit, its hobble skirt fashionably short, draped gently over Joan's ample hips. The jacket, its lapels trimmed with white pique, sat wide on the shoulders and nipped in at the waist.

A satisfied smile curved Lacey's lips, the success of the outfit bringing with it a rush of adrenaline.

'What you need is a picture hat and a pair of shoes with heels to finish it off. Let's go into Huddersfield and buy them this afternoon. I've done enough sewing for one day.'

★ ★ ★

In Rushworth's, Huddersfield's finest emporium, Joan tried on hats, her enthusiasm waning as a patronising assistant quoted prices. A hat trimmed with white braid particularly took Joan's fancy.

'This is lovely but I can't afford it,' she whispered to Lacey, as she set it back on its stand. Lacey lifted the hat, and turning to one side craftily tweaked at the silk braid decorating the wide brim.

'It is, Joanie. It's just a pity the braid's loose.' Lacey pointed out the flaw to the arrogant assistant. 'You can't ask full price for it in this condition.'

The assistant peered at the hat, her hauteur diminishing. 'Mind you,' Lacey continued, 'if you were to knock a bit off she might still take it.'

'I'll see what the manageress says.' The assistant scurried away, her hopes of earning commission on the sale revived.

Joan dithered. 'It costs twelve and six, Lacey: nearly a week's wages.

Even if they knock a couple of bob off I still can't afford it.'

'Wait an' see,' Lacey ordered.

A few minutes later, back out on John William Street, Lacey and Joan performed a gleeful jig to celebrate their triumph.

'I never noticed it wa' damaged,' said Joan, sure in the knowledge that Lacey could fix it.

Lacey grinned. 'The braid wa' definitely missing a stitch or two so I thought I'd just help things along.' She picked at the air with her thumb and forefinger.

Joan stopped in her tracks. 'Ooh, Lacey Barraclough, you never did.'

'What's a fingernail between friends?' said Lacey, jiggling her fingers again. 'Now, out of the thirty bob you started with you've got plenty left over for a pair of shoes and some new underwear.'

Inside the Market Hall with its huge glazed roof and architectural ironwork they purchased two pairs of cotton drawers, a vest and a petticoat and a pair of Moroccan leather shoes with high, curved heels. Moroccan leather being the cheapest, the shoes were stiff and uncomfortable but, as

Lacey pointed out, Joan wouldn't be wearing them too often. Flushed with success they boarded the bus back home, Joan ready for her big day.

★ ★ ★

Easter Saturday dawned bright and clear. In the churchyard, clumps of daffodils circled the boles of blossoming lilac and cherry trees. Inside the church Joan and Stanley solemnly exchanged vows, Joan looking gorgeous in her blue crepe suit and picture hat, Stanley nervous and ungainly in an ill-fitting brown suit. As Joan and Stanley became man and wife, Lacey's thoughts were on Nathan.

After the ceremony the wedding guests gathered in front of the church to congratulate the happy couple. As they did so, a large shiny car drew up at the gates, its two female passengers alighting to watch the festivities. Joan deliberately tossed her bouquet in Lacey's direction but, whilst she instinctively reached out and caught it, Lacey doubted the validity of the time honoured custom. The car and its passengers drove away, the wedding guests filing into the Church Hall.

'Well, Mrs Micklethwaite, what does it feel like to be a married woman?' Lacey asked, as they enjoyed tea and ham sandwiches and cakes and buns Edith had helped May Chadwick lay on for the wedding guests.

'Can't really say as yet,' Joan replied, 'I don't feel any different. I'll tell you better after me honeymoon.' She tittered suggestively.

She and Stanley were going to Blackpool and had booked to stay overnight in a boarding house.

Lacey grinned wickedly. 'You'll find out afore that. You don't go to Blackpool till tomorrow.'

Joan blushed. 'Oh, I don't think there'll be much o' that sort of thing happening tonight. I don't think I could do it under Hettie Micklethwaite's roof. She'll be listening to every move we make.'

Knowing Joan dreaded the idea of living with her mother-in-law, Lacey lightened the mood. 'Listening did you say? If I know Hettie Micklethwaite, she'll be standing at the end of the bed telling you not to get up to any mucky tricks wi' her Stanley.'

Joan burst out laughing.

Determined to bolster Joan's spirits further, Lacey added, 'You'll find somewhere of your own soon enough, an' whilst you are living with her, stand up to her. You're a married woman now.'

★ ★ ★

The large, shiny car that had paused outside the church had now come to a halt on the gravel sweep outside Fenay Hall. The passengers tumbled out, the taller and prettier of the two girls stretching her arms wide and declaring, 'Oh, it's good to be home. I simply adored Switzerland but there's no place like Garsthwaite.'

The huge oak front door swung open, the butler and the chauffeur attending to the baggage as Felicity Brearley flew into the arms of her parents.

Freed from Jonas's grasp, Felicity turned to her companion. 'Pardon my manners, Amelia. I'm so excited I forgot to introduce you. Mama, Papa, this is my friend Amelia McKenzie. She's breaking her journey to stay with us for four days before she returns home to Scotland.' Amelia made welcome, they trooped inside to the drawing room.

'Come sit by me, darling,' Constance urged Felicity, 'tell us about Switzerland. You've hardly

95

written a word to us in the past six months. I want to find out if that finishing school has made a lady of you.'

Felicity burst out laughing. 'Mama, how dreadfully old fashioned you are.' She rolled her eyes. 'It was a dreary, dull place full of rules — but we made the best of it, didn't we, Amelia.' She winked broadly and Amelia winked back.

'I'll bet you did, you wicked girl.' At the sound of Nathan's voice, Felicity jumped up and ran into his open arms. He'd deliberately waited for the initial welcomes to be made before putting in an appearance.

He had arrived back from Northumberland late the previous night to Constance immediately quizzing him about Imogen. Nathan had answered rudely; her scheming had failed. If he couldn't marry Lacey Barraclough then he'd stay single. He wouldn't relinquish the Mill but neither would he provide them with future heirs. Constance had vented her disapproval; the homecoming had been ruined and now Nathan was uncomfortable in her presence.

Now, putting the horrors of the previous evening behind him, he danced his beloved sister across the drawing room; maybe Fliss would help ease the situation.

Over tea, Constance strove to divert Nathan's attention to Amelia, pointing out that she was the daughter of a Laird with a castle in Argyll.

Nathan was charming to Amelia but, whenever his mother's eyes met his, he could barely hide his contempt. Felicity, quick to sense Nathan's unhappiness, dominated the conversation.

'We saw the most charming little wedding as we drove through Garsthwaite. I insisted Cheevers stop the car so we could get out and watch.

The bride wore a gorgeous blue crepe suit and the bridesmaids were delightful in darker blue.' She paused for breath before adding, 'It was an unusually fashionable wedding for Garsthwaite; I wonder where on earth they purchased their outfits.' She sounded both surprised and curious. She swivelled round in her chair to address Jonas. 'I think the girls were from our Mill.'

'Aye, a chap out of the dye house and a lass from the weaving, so I heard; Micklethwaite's his name and she was Joan Chadwick.' Jonas prided himself on knowing the names of all his employees and the major events affecting their lives.

Nathan leapt up. Now he knew exactly where to find Lacey. Gabbling excuses, he dashed from the room. All morning he'd contemplated where Lacey might be, it being Saturday. He didn't dare call at Netherfold Farm for fear Joshua might object to the shabby way he'd treated his daughter.

In no time at all he arrived at the Church Hall, uncertain of his next move. He didn't have long to wait before his mind was made up for him.

The wedding reception over, the bride and groom stepped out of the Hall arm in arm, their guests crowding after them, cheering and yelling ribald remarks.

Lacey spotted Nathan before he saw her. For a moment she was rooted to the ground. Should she pretend she hadn't seen him, and walk on by with the rest of the guests, she wondered? Then, before she reached a decision he was pushing his way through the crowd towards her, and even from a distance she could see the pleading in his eyes. Shoving the bouquet she had caught earlier and her own posy into a startled Maggie's hands, Lacey ran towards him. Nathan met her halfway, his face alight with love and hope. Careless of the onlookers' curiosity, he caught Lacey in his arms and held her close.

★ ★ ★

Up on Cuckoo Hill, seated on heather warmed by the sun's strong rays, Nathan poured out his heart. In between kisses he explained the reason for his lengthy absence and about his confusion after Constance had suggested Jonas should disown him.

'It isn't that I want the Mill purely for financial gain or position. All my life I've dreamed of the day it would be mine to develop as I please. The process of making cloth intrigues me, and I've so many ideas both for the making of it and improving the way the Mill works, it just seemed so heartless to have it snatched away because of my love for you.' He buried his head in his hands and when he raised it he gazed into Lacey's face, beseeching her to understand.

'And what did your father say to that?' Lacey asked, her heart aching for him. She understood the quandary facing him.

Nathan's brow puckered. 'I didn't stay to hear, but if he agreed with Mother then so be it. I would give it up for you, Lacey, of that there's no doubt,

98

but I'd rather have both you and the Mill, and I'll do everything I can to make it so.' He squeezed her hand tightly and gave her a wan smile before adding, 'We're not beaten yet.'

Lacey gazed thoughtfully into the distance. 'Perhaps not,' she said, 'but if you gave up everything you've hoped and dreamed of to marry me, can we be sure it wouldn't poison our love for one another — you regretting the choice you made and me feeling responsible for your loss?'

'I would hope our love is strong enough to combat all that life might throw at us, no matter what path we choose, but for now we must concentrate on getting what is only right and fair.' He flopped back on the heather, his face masked with anxiety.

'Do you really think your father would disinherit you?' Lacey asked dolefully, the weight of responsibility lying heavily in her heart.

Nathan sat upright, chuckling wryly. 'Strangely enough he's said very little throughout all the rows. He's under the impression I'm sowing a few wild oats before I settle down. Apparently that's what he did in his youth.'

Lacey drew a sharp breath. 'The cheeky sod; what sort of a girl does he think I am?'

'That's just it. He doesn't know you — and neither does my mother. But they soon will. I've thought things through properly this time. I'll move heaven and earth to persuade them to meet you. It might take a while but I won't be doing it alone. I've told my sister, Felicity, all about us. She's offered to lend her support.'

Lacey was intrigued. 'Is that the sister who was in Switzerland, finishing off her education? You mentioned her when we first met.'

Nathan smiled fondly. 'That's the one — my only sibling. Fliss has no patience with stuffy proprieties. She's a very modern girl and does as she pleases.'

As they talked, the sun dipped over the edge of the moor, burnt orange rays streaking a purple sky, a sight so beautiful Lacey wanted to hold onto it. Taking it to be a good omen, she thought, maybe we can change the hearts and minds of those who are so hidebound by tradition they measure a person by wealth or social standing. Rich or poor, boss or employee, they actually encourage division of the classes. Out loud she said. 'My lot are just as bad as yours, you know. My Dad has you cast in the role of wicked squire and my Mam believes you're just leading me on, that you'll get me pregnant then dump me.'

'Surely they don't think that of me.' Nathan's shock apparent, he rubbed his chin thoughtfully. 'In that case it's up to me to alter their opinion.' He took Lacey's hand and pulled her upright and as they walked on, he said,

'We'll both have our work cut out convincing our parents we're right for each other, and the only way to do that is for them to get to know us as we really are; yours to understand I'm not an aristocratic bounder, and mine to see that your breeding is equal to my own.'

'Does this mean no more sly meetings?' Lacey asked coquettishly. 'Let everyone in Garsthwaite know about us. I think that lot at Joan's wedding have already got the message.'

'Indeed,' said Nathan firmly. 'From now on I'll

make regular visits to your home and you to mine. That way we'll make them understand how much we love one another and that they can't keep us apart.'

They sauntered hand in hand down Cuckoo Hill and before they parted Nathan begged her to be patient. 'It might take some time but believe me, we'll win.'

Feeling happier than she had felt for a long time, Lacey placed her trust in Nathan.

10

Lacey patiently waited for her loom to be gated. She'd finished a piece and now the tackler was busy setting the new warp between healds and reeds, ready for her to continue weaving. The process painstakingly slow, she waved one hand to attract Joan's attention then placed the fingers of the other to her lips. Catching sight of the gesture, Joan nodded.

'Well, what was it like?' Lacey mouthed, her eyes dancing wickedly, her grin wide.

Joan's cheeks turned pink at the mention of her honeymoon. 'It wa' lovely,' she mouthed back, 'just grand.'

'What wa', you know, like?' mouthed Lacey, a roguish glint in her eye.

Her cheeky enquiry regarding Joan and Stanley's nuptials went unanswered, the tackler fixing a card to an upright strut on her loom and pronouncing it ready for action. As she read the instructions for how to weave the new piece, Sydney Sugden leaned over her shoulder. 'Don't take all day about it,' he snarled, 'you've wasted enough time already.' He stomped off.

Suddenly, it occurred to Lacey that Slimy Syd hadn't pestered her for some time now. She'd been so wrapped up in her doubts about Nathan she hadn't given Syd a thought. At breakfast time she voiced this to her colleagues.

'What's wi' Slimy Syd these days? He wouldn't

leave me alone a short while back, now he hardly looks at me.'

'He's onto somebody else,' Maggie Clegg said.

'Aye, that new woman what he put on t'new looms. Her wi' red hair,' volunteered May Skinner. 'It's not right she should have got 'em. You can weave twice as fast on them as you can on them old rattletraps I'm stuck with.'

Flo Backhouse joined in. 'The rotten bugger said he'd let me have 'em but he gave 'em to her. An' to think I let him have his way wi' me on t'chance I'd earn a few extra bob each week. I'll bloody swing for him one day, an' that red headed tart.'

'As long as she keeps him off my back she can have all the new looms she likes,' Lacey said, 'although it's not right that we have to go along wi' Syd's mucky tricks so's we can earn us wages. Trouble is, the bosses treat us like chattels an' we've only ourselves to blame. As long as we let 'em walk all over us we'll never amount to anything. What we should do is join t'Union. Fight for us rights.'

Lizzie Isherwood scowled. 'Men don't want women in t'Union. The buggers don't think we have any rights.'

'If enough of us joined we'd make us selves heard,' Lacey insisted. 'We've as much rights as any man in this shed, but we don't do nowt about it.'

'I couldn't afford t'subscription even if I wanted to join,' Maggie grumbled.

'Aye, an' you never will as long as we let 'em pay us less money for doing t'same job as a man,'

103

Lacey pointed out. 'I think it's about time I gave a bit more thought to t'Unions. They can't keep us down forever.'

Mary Collier gave Lacey a sour look. 'Why would you join t'Union?

You'll not be workin' in t'weavin' shed much longer. Everybody knows you're walkin' out wi' t'boss's son. Afore long he'll move you into t'office to make you more respectable — that's if you open your legs wide enough.'

Some of the women cackled at this remark.

Lacey flew at her, catching her by the shoulders. 'You filthy minded bitch; it's not like that. I'll have you know . . . ' Mary retaliated by spitting in Lacey's face. Realising a full blown fight was developing, Lizzie Isherwood waded in and broke it up. The hooter blew and the women went back to their looms, Lacey wiping her face and seething with indignation.

* * *

'I'm beginning to think you were right after all when you said we should keep things under wraps,' Lacey told Nathan as they walked along Towngate after work.

'What changed your mind?'

Lacey scowled. 'Bitter minded folks an' their nasty tongues.'

Nathan looked concerned. 'I thought we weren't going to allow ourselves to be intimidated by other people's opinions. That we should let them get used to seeing us together.'

Lacey's temper flared. 'It's all right for you.

104

They don't dare blacken your character, but they have me marked for a whore.' Tears sprang to her eyes.

Nathan squeezed her hand. 'That's downright wickedness,' he cried, 'yet I understand the logic of it.' His expression changed from angry to remorseful. 'For centuries it's been common practice for bosses in the mills to abuse women workers.'

Lacey nodded miserably. 'Aye, I suppose it's only natural they think you're just using me.'

'I'd never do that, Lacey. Believe me, I've every intention of making things right. Father appears to be warming to our friendship already. He knows I meet you after work each day and on Sundays. As yet he's voiced no objections.'

'No, he won't, because he thinks I'm just a passing fancy, an' once you've had your way with me often enough you'll drop me an' move on to somebody more respectable.'

Nathan looked thoughtful. 'I'm not sure about that; I think he quite admires you in his own way.' He groaned comically. 'It's Mother who's the bugbear, but Fliss's working on her. She asks after you whenever we're together in Ma's company and I always answer favourably.' He managed a grim laugh. 'Just be patient. It won't be long now before she discovers for herself what a splendid creature you really are.'

★ ★ ★

However, patience was not one of Lacey's virtues, and whilst she waited, irritably, for the opportunity to show Constance Brearley what 'a splendid creature' she truly was, she found herself beset by problems of a completely different nature.

Although Jimmy swore he no longer hung around with Arty Bincliffe, Lacey suspected this wasn't entirely true. Of late, he had adopted a surly, devious manner. No longer the open faced, friendly lad who had a smile for everyone, he came and went at all hours, reluctant to say where and with whom he had been.

'He's a right temperamental teenager is our Jimmy. I never had that trouble wi' you an' our Matt,' Edith complained. She said this in Jimmy's hearing one night as he prepared to dash off without his dinner, having refused to give a reason why.

'That's 'cos our Matt never wa' a teenager. He were born an old man,' quipped Jimmy. 'That's why he's me Dad's favourite.' He slammed out of the house.

Lacey debated whether to have a word with Matt about her suspicions but reasoned Edith might be right. Perhaps Jimmy was finding the transition from boyhood to manhood hard to handle.

After all, she had no proof Jimmy was involved in any wrongdoing.

She'd not seen him with Arty since the day she warned Arty off, and whenever their paths crossed Arty grinned and winked lasciviously, giving no indication that he had outwitted her but rather that he still fancied her.

Her other problems, however, were of a more personal nature. Every day she ran the gamut of foul jibes and filthy innuendo delivered by a few of her workmates. 'Take no notice of 'em,' Joan

106

advised, 'they're only jealous.'

But it was easier said than done.

Lacey fleetingly considered pretending Nathan was no longer interested in her: thus proving them right. But cowardice didn't come naturally. It went against everything she believed in: equality, fairness and honesty.

Whilst the taunts hurt, they didn't annoy Lacey as much as Syd's renewed attentions and the spiteful tricks he played whenever she spurned him.

For the second time in a week, Lacey arrived at work to find one of her looms waiting for the tackler to fix the warp. 'What's going on?' she cried, throwing up her hands in consternation. 'How am I to make a decent wage if me looms aren't ready?'

'Syd's doing it on purpose,' said Joan, her plump face pink with irritation, for weavers were paid by the piece; idle looms meant loss of earnings. 'He'll not rest until he's had you.'

Lacey marched down 'weavers alley' in search of Syd, recalling the vengeful tricks he had employed in the past few months: no Christmas bonus, shuttles filled with shoddy yarn, and unnecessarily long waits for a tuner to adjust faults on her looms. She saw him hovering over one of the training looms, his grubby, wandering hands finding any excuse to grope the young girl learning the trade.

'Mr Sugden, why is my loom not warped?'

Syd ignored Lacey's cry. It wasn't until she was standing next to him that he bothered to give her his attention. He gave a mock sigh. 'Eeh, Lacey luv, you look fair pothered. What's wrong.' His leering eyes came to rest on her heaving bosom.

'You know what,' Lacey snapped, 'and I'm not

standin' for it.' Too late she regretted her choice of words.

'You could try lying down,' he said smirking at his own wit. 'You know what I want, Lacey. I've told you often enough. As long as you make me wait for it, I'll make you wait twice as long.'

Lacey contemplated confiding in Nathan but then dismissed the idea. If word got out that she was receiving special privileges, her workmates hackles would be raised even further. Besides, making him aware of Slimy Syd's obscene behaviour towards her might cause him to doubt her innocence.

If he truly loved her, he couldn't possibly think her so low, but that was another problem: was he just stringing her along? Whilst he swore his love for her at every meeting, there had been no further mention of him taking her to formally meet his parents.

* * *

On a bright Saturday afternoon in May, Lacey was shopping in Towngate when she came face to face with Jonas Brearley and Felicity. Prepared to bid them no more than good day, Lacey was surprised when Felicity brought Jonas to a sudden halt and greeted her enthusiastically. 'Hello, Lacey; isn't it a glorious afternoon, and might I say how much I admire your dress.'

Lacey blushed. The navy and white cotton dress she was wearing was one of her latest creations. 'Thank you,' she replied, 'I made it meself. I do a lot of sewing for meself and me cousin, Joan

Micklethwaite.'

Felicity looked thoughtful; she recognised the name. 'Is that the girl who was recently married in the Methodist Church. The one wearing a blue crepe suit?'

'Yes, that's her.'

'And did you make that delightful outfit as well?' Felicity turned to address Jonas. 'I'm sure you didn't know you had someone so talented in your employ, Papa.'

'I know she has a ready tongue on her,' Jonas said, indicating they should move on. Felicity delayed him.

'Would you consider making me something, Lacey? I'll be awfully pleased if you say yes.'

'I'd be delighted. Buy some material and I'll make it up for you.'

'No sooner said than done,' Felicity chirped, 'I'll be in touch. It was lovely to see you, Lacey.' She threaded her arm through Jonas's and led him away.

Lacey almost danced down the street.

★ ★ ★

'I'm to take you back for tea next Sunday,' Nathan told her as they climbed Cuckoo Hill. 'Mother has at last realised I've no intention of giving you up.'

Somewhat taken aback by such short notice, Lacey was both thrilled and apprehensive. As they sauntered over the moor she was so distracted by thoughts of how she should acquit herself, she paid little heed to Nathan.

'You haven't heard a word I was saying,' he

accused.

Lacey giggled. 'I was practicing my lines for when I meet your mother.'

Nathan groaned.

They found a cosy hollow sheltered by a rocky outcrop and cushioned with heather. At first they sat, Nathan's kisses soft on Lacey's lips. Passion flaring she found herself on her back, Nathan pressed against her. She felt his manhood rise and although her body said yes, her mind said no. She pushed him away and sat up, patting her hair to hide her desire.

Nathan rolled onto his back, staring up into the cloudless sky. 'Oh, Lacey, how much longer do I have to wait?'

'The answer to that is in your hands, Nathan.' Lacey spoke softly but firmly. She ached for him, yet she would not give in. 'If I let you have me now, an' believe me I'm tempted, I'll be the whore the Mill lasses already think I am. And I wouldn't want to face your mother knowing what we'd done here today.'

Nathan groaned again. 'I'm sorry, Lacey. You're right, as always.' He slumped forward, his arms wrapped around his bent knees, and in an attempt to quell his lustful hunger he turned his thoughts to dull matters.

'Father's seriously concerned about the slump in trade. We can't compete with foreign competition. He's thinking of putting the workers on short time.'

Having watched Nathan struggle to gain composure, Lacey understood the sudden change of topic was his way of cooling the situation. Suddenly she wanted to laugh out loud. What a fine pair we are, she thought, suppressing her laughter. One minute we're about to make passionate love and the next we're discussing Mill business.

Instead of voicing her thoughts, she echoed Nathan's words. 'Short time; isn't the Mill making a profit? We've plenty of work on.'

Nathan gazed at her, longing still burning in his eyes. Lacey's heart skipped a beat and the same warm feeling that had flooded her loins a short while ago surged through them again.

Nathan struggled to answer her question and Lacey forced herself to pay attention.

'Too many of our machines are out of date; we need more automatic looms and trouble in Europe is disrupting our trade networks.'

'Aye, I've read about that trouble in the Balkans, but surely with the price of raw wool staying steady for the last two years, your father must have made enough profit to buy new looms,' Lacey said.

Nathan was impressed. He hadn't reckoned on such an informed response. 'Yes, the Balkans and Russia are definitely stirring things up, and we are considering purchasing new machines, but for now things are looking pretty bleak for Brearley's.'

'They'll be a lot bleaker for them on short time than they will for your family,' Lacey said stoutly, ardour fading as they exchanged opinions on the issue. On this miserable note they left the sanctuary of their trysting place and walked back across the moor.

'Don't mention any of this over tea,' Nathan

111

advised, 'Mother doesn't like what she calls Mill talk.'

'I won't,' Lacey promised, 'although I can't say I'm not saddened to think I'll be earning less money if things don't improve.'

'You won't have to worry about money once we're married. I'll take care of you. In the meantime, concentrate on making a good impression with Mother.'

Lacey bristled. 'I'll not be a kept woman, Nathan; I thought I'd already made that clear. I have every intention of making my own way in the world — I might even impress your mother.'

Nathan rolled his eyes. 'I'm sure you will, Lacey.'

⋆ ⋆ ⋆

Yet again, Lacey dressed with care to visit Fenay Hall. This time she chose a cream linen dress, its dropped waistline and broad, flat pleats enhancing her slender hips. It wasn't new but Lacey thought its rather demure style fitted the occasion. She completed the outfit with a straw boater and cotton gloves.

'He's here again,' Edith hissed, as Lacey went to answer Nathan's knock.

'I hope you know what you're doing.'

'You look positively ravishing,' Nathan declared, when she opened the door. He'd called at Lacey's home three times during the past months, Joshua, Edith and Matt giving him a cautious welcome. They liked Nathan but they still doubted the veracity of his friendship with Lacey and didn't want to see her hurt. Joshua and Matt, in from

112

the fields for a cup of tea, exchanged quizzical glances, Joshua puckering his lips and Matt narrowing his eyes.

'How do, lad?' Joshua said by way of welcome as Lacey ushered Nathan inside. Matt just nodded his head.

'Good afternoon, gentlemen; and you too, Mrs Barraclough, I hope you're finding this fine weather to your liking.'

'Aye,' replied Joshua, 'I just hope it holds until we get last o' t'shearin' done.'

Edith fluttered between the sink and the stove, filling the kettle and rattling teacups. 'Will you take a cup of tea, Nathan?' She sounded almost breathless with anticipation.

'Mam, there's no need to fuss,' said Lacey.

Edith looked offended until Nathan, charming her with a smile said, 'Thank you, but no; we're having tea at Fenay Hall. I'm taking Lacey to meet my parents.'

Edith already knew this, and had objected strongly. Now, with Nathan standing there before her, she appeared to be absolutely delighted. 'How nice. How kind of you. Well, off you go and have a good time.'

Suppressing a groan of irritation, Lacey took Nathan by the arm and they made their farewells. Out in the yard, Lacey laughed out loud. 'Never mind 'em,' she said, 'they'll get used to you eventually.'

Lacey climbed into Nathan's newest purchase, an Austin A7. It being her first car ride she would have liked to sit upright and admire the view for

113

the entire journey, but when the little car chugged into Towngate she slid down in her seat, her head ducked. It wouldn't do to be seen by any of her workmates; come Monday morning, they'd mock her for 'showing off' and she had no desire to provoke them. During the drive, Lacey and Nathan had barely exchanged two words, Lacey feeling awkwardly conspicuous and Nathan staring stonily straight ahead, each lost in their own thoughts.

The afternoon was unusually warm even for July, and Lacey prayed she wouldn't perspire too much and make her dress limp. The nearer they got to Fenay Hall, the more apprehensive she felt. When Nathan brought the car to a halt, although Lacey had been here once before and admired its grandeur, the mansion now loomed ominously in front of her. Don't say too much, don't say the wrong thing and don't be intimidated, she silently admonished herself as they walked across the gravel sweep.

In the hallway, Lacey straightened her hat and flicked the pleats of her dress. 'You look beautiful,' Nathan said, squeezing her hand encouragingly.

When the butler turned his back on them to open the drawing room door, Nathan gave Lacey a swift kiss before whispering, 'Let battle commence.'

Constance and Felicity were seated on a couch and Jonas in a chair by the hearth. Nathan led Lacey forward, a brave smile on his face. 'I know you've already met but allow me to present Miss Lacey Barraclough of Netherfold Farm.' Lacey blushed at this grandiose introduction.

'Good afternoon, Mrs Brearley.' Lacey proffered her hand. Constance responded, her fingers

114

unwilling.

'Hello, Lacey,' Felicity chirped, a warm smile on her face. 'So glad you could come.' At Felicity's welcome, the tension stiffening Lacey's body eased. She adjusted her posture. Pushing back her shoulders and standing tall and straight, she assembled every whit of her naturally feisty spirit; today no-one would make her feel less than equal, try as they may.

Jonas got to his feet. 'How do, lass. Sit down, make yourself comfortable.' He indicated a couch sitting at right angles to the one Constance and Felicity occupied. Lacey sat down carefully, her knees together, her feet to one side and her hands resting in her lap — exactly as the Women's Journal dictated. Nathan sat beside her.

Constance gave her an icy smile. 'So — Miss Barraclough — do tell us something of yourself. Nathan has been rather remiss in giving us the details.' Rattled by the imperious tone, Lacey fought to control her feelings.

Nathan interjected. 'Mama, for goodness sake, it's not an inquisition.'

Lacey placed a restraining hand on his knee. 'It's not a problem, Nathan. If we're to get to know one another it's only right I answer your mother's questions.' She smiled at Constance but didn't receive one in return. 'As you already know, I work in the weaving shed at the Mill. I've been there seven years come next spring. My father and mother own Netherfold Farm, up on the moor. Matt, my elder brother, helps farm it and Jimmy, my younger brother, works in the Mill warehouse.' Lacey sat back, wondering if she had satisfactorily

115

acquitted herself.

'Barracloughs of Netherfold, you say?' Jonas turned in his chair to face them, smiling warmly at Lacey. 'An old, respected family, and damned good sheep farmers so I've heard.'

Lacey beamed her gratitude. Constance sniffed. 'I can't say I'm acquainted with your family, Miss Barraclough, but then — she paused, artfully — 'I don't associate with farmers or mill hands.' Her supercilious deprecating smile cut Lacey to the bone. Sensing her discomfort, Nathan enlarged on the attributes of Netherfold Farm, Felicity coming to his aid.

'You haven't told Mother about the marvellous sewing you do.' She turned to address Constance. 'Lacey makes the most wonderful outfits. They're as fine as anything you'd see in Rushworth's or Brown Muff's. I suppose you made the dress you're wearing now.'

Lacey said she had, flattered that Felicity likened her creations to those sold by two of the best fashion houses in the West Riding.

Ignoring Felicity's remarks, Constance returned to the subject of Joshua's occupation.

'So, your father's in agriculture,' she said, her tone casual. 'Mine was in coal on the borders of Scotland.'

Duped into believing Constance was putting her at ease by telling her that her own father had been a working man, and thinking they were at last conversing on an equal footing, Lacey readily responded. 'That's a hard life, and dangerous, too. It takes a brave man to work underground, hacking coal from . . . '

Jonas's barking laugh and Constance's sharp intake of breath stopped Lacey in full flow. Constance glared haughtily. 'My father didn't work down the mines, Miss Barraclough; he owned them.'

Jonas smothered his laughter with a coughing attack and Nathan and Felicity looked at one another, lips quirking and eyebrows raised in amusement. Lacey clapped her hand to her mouth.

Then, unabashed, she said, 'Well, if he did I hope he respected his workers enough to provide them with safe working conditions and decent wages. From what I've read, some of the pits are appalling, and what with the Unions withdrawing their support and the Government reneging on deals, the poor miners' demands are never met. That's why they keep striking.'

Jonas chortled merrily. 'She has you there, dear.'

His wife threw him a dirty look, then smiled ingratiatingly at Lacey. 'You have an interest in politics then, Miss Barraclough?' She sniffed derisively. 'Personally I consider it unfeminine; and as for those dreadful suffragettes . . . ' Constance threw her hands into the air dismissively.

Before Lacey could respond she felt Nathan's thigh press hard against her own, and when she turned to look at him his eyes begged her not to respond. For his sake she swallowed the retort she had been about to make.

Tea was served, Felicity and Nathan driving the conversation towards literature and the arts. At ease with both subjects, Lacey joined in willingly,

117

voicing her knowledge and opinions clearly and cleverly.

Jonas watched and listened, his admiration growing by the minute. Not only was the girl well read, she was well informed with regards to the world outside Garsthwaite. It took him by surprise.

Up to this moment Jonas had convinced himself that Nathan was merely attracted by the pretty face and the pert figure and would soon tire of her.

He'd said as much to Constance shortly before Nathan and Lacey arrived.

'He'll come to his senses. Let him find out for himself that she's unsuitable.

The more you object the more determined he'll be to have his way.'

Now, Jonas was finding it difficult to support his own argument. He understood what Nathan saw in her. She was intelligent, interesting, a girl with fire in her blood. If Nathan truly loved her, as he swore he did, he'd have a marriage filled with passion and shared interests: unlike his own loveless union.

He gazed sadly at Constance. She had refused to partake in what she considered the distasteful side of married life once she had produced a son and heir, and a daughter. She even denied Jonas licence to share the Mill's problems or triumphs, whereas Lacey would understand whenever Nathan talked Mill talk, as Constance called it. The more Jonas thought about it, the more inclined he was to brook no opposition to Nathan and Lacey's relationship.

★ ★ ★

'Whew, that was a nightmare,' said Lacey, releasing a deep breath as the butler closed Fenay Hall's front door behind them.

Nathan chuckled. 'I'll admit there were one or two sticky moments but we've broken the ice. I thought Father was about to choke when you misunderstood Mother's remark about her father. She's such a snob, yet I think she was surprised by how well read you are, and Father was definitely impressed by your wealth of knowledge.'

Lacey gave a mock curtsey and sarcastically said, 'So can I come again, kind sir?'

'You most certainly can.' Out of sight of the house now, Nathan pulled Lacey behind a large rhododendron and kissed her. Lacey kissed him back, pleased by the relative success of the visit.

⋆ ⋆ ⋆

The following Wednesday evening Nathan brought Felicity to Netherfold Farm along with a length of dress material she'd purchased in Bradford the day before. The girls went up to Lacey's bedroom, leaving Nathan in the kitchen with Joshua and Edith.

Felicity opened her parcel, showing Lacey what she had bought. 'I want you to make me a dress, but only on one condition: you allow me to pay you the same rate as I pay my dressmaker in Huddersfield.'

'I'd make it for free, just for the pleasure of working with such lovely material,' said Lacey, fingering the luxurious hyacinth blue voile. Felicity was adamant she must pay her and Lacey

119

acquiesced.

They sat on the bed, Lacey showing Felicity her compilation of paper patterns, magazines and some of her own sketches. 'I copy the magazine illustrations as best I can and then work out a pattern,' Lacey told Felicity.

For the next hour or so they perused the fashion magazines, commenting on likes and dislikes. To an uninformed observer these two young women, similar in age, might have appeared to be the best of friends. So easy was their rapport that at one point, Lacey quite forgot herself.

She pointed to a modish, tiered dress in the latest fashion, exclaiming,

'Ooh, this 'ud suit you. Your figure's quite boyish and frills don't suit you, whereas the simple cut of this one will bring out your best features. You've got lovely narrow hips and you're quite flat chest . . . '

Lacey clamped her hand to her mouth. 'Oh! me and my big gob,' she groaned, apologising for fear she had overstepped the mark by being too familiar.

'Stuff and nonsense,' Felicity hooted. 'I've little patience with people who don't say what they think.' She softened her tone. 'We're friends, Lacey, not mistress and servant,' and taking the magazine looked closely at the illustration and then exclaimed, 'and if you can make me look like this we'll be jolly good friends.'

'I'd like that,' said Lacey, 'and as for the dress, I'll do me best.'

Heads close together, Felicity watched whilst Lacey made a few quick sketches, explaining what she intended as she drew. Then she took Felicity's measurements, recording them neatly in a book she kept for that purpose. Felicity admired her professional approach.

'Will it be ready by the seventh of July? I'd love to show it off at my birthday party; you'll be invited, of course.'

Lacey's heart swelled. 'I'll make sure it's ready.'

They went back down to the kitchen to find Nathan and Matt laughing and joking over a game of cards, Joshua and Edith looking on, amused.

Edith made supper, Nathan and Felicity complimenting her drop scones.

Nathan gazed adoringly at Lacey, overjoyed by the successful evening.

When it was time for them to go, Felicity said, 'We've had a simply lovely time, haven't we, Nathan? We must do it again.' Thanks and farewells delivered, Lacey walked with them to the car. Felicity pecked Lacey's cheek before climbing in. Nathan gave her a lingering kiss and then whispered into her hair, 'I love you, Lacey Barraclough. You have a knack for making people happy: most of all me. I have a feeling that from now on our future will be filled with happiness.'

Lacey watched the car trundle slowly down the rutted lane and out of sight. Too elated to go straight indoors she gazed out over the moor. The darkening sky was streaked with pink and red: shepherds' delight. Resting her elbows on the wall's ancient stone, she breathed in the sweet smell of night-scented stock and the wallflowers Edith had planted. Everything's perfect, she mused, Nathan loves me and I love him. My family accept him and his accept me — almost. Constance's haughty face crept into her mind's eye. I'll win her round, she told the rising moon; see if I don't. Then, like Nathan says, we'll have a lifetime of happiness.

11

Joan caught Lacey's hand and squeezed it as they strolled towards Brearley's Mill. 'I'm ever so pleased everything's going right for you and Nathan,' she said. They were early and enjoying the walk on this bright, warm morning.

Lacey returned the squeeze. 'Thanks, Joanie; it's a weight off me mind, I can tell you. Mind you, his mother's still a bit frosty, although the more she sees of me the less obvious it is. She's either given up in disgust or she's beginning to realise I'm not something nasty she trod in.'

Joan sniggered. 'She'd be daft not to see how grand you are. I'll bet before long she'll genuinely like you. Stanley's Mam hates me.' Her shoulders drooped and her face wore an expression of defeat. 'I can't do anything to please her. She finds fault with everything I do an' she interferes in every conversation me an' Stanley have. We've no privacy except when we're in bed, an' even then she's laid on t'other side o' t'wall listening.'

Lacey's heart went out to Joan: Hettie Micklethwaite was the kind of mother-in-law every girl dreaded. 'Poor Joanie,' she said, giving her a sympathetic hug as they paused on the kerb to let the traffic go by, 'does Stanley know how miserable you are? Is there no chance of you finding your own place?'

Joan shook her head. 'What with Hettie taking most of Stanley's wages for letting us live with her we can't save enough to rent anywhere else. Most landlords want four weeks rent up front.'

There being no solution to Joan's problem, Lacey voiced her own as they reached the Mill gates. 'I'm worried about our Jimmy. He's ever so sly these days. He riles Mam and Dad something shocking. He's out till all hours and gives cheek whenever he's in the house. You haven't seen him up to owt, have you?' Joan living in the town, she was more likely to know what he had been up to there.

'I've seen him hanging around wi' Arty Bincliffe once or twice. I would have mentioned it 'cos I know you don't like Arty, but what wi' you having problems at work an' wi' your love life I didn't like to say owt.'

Lacey shook her head in exasperation. 'Let me know next time, Joanie. I'll have to sort something out.'

★ ★ ★

Lacey glanced at the clock on the mantelshelf. It was almost ten thirty and Jimmy was not yet home; again. Joshua and Matt had retired at nine and Edith not long after, all three grumbling at the late hours Jimmy kept. 'It's a wonder he can get up for his work of a morning,' Edith moaned. 'Who he's with an' what he's up to at this time o' night 'as me fair pothered.'

Saddened to see her mother so worried, and plagued by her own suspicions, Lacey decided to have a word with Matt in the morning and to tell him about Jimmy's friendship with Arty Bincliffe.

Maybe then Matt would make Jimmy see sense, and failing that he'd deal with Arty in his own way. By, but she'd give Jimmy a piece of her mind when he came home.

She picked up the book Nathan had given her earlier in the week. 'Read this,' he had said, 'it's considered quite intriguing.' It was a copy of *Sons and Lovers* by a new author called D.H. Lawrence.

Lacey was soon lost in the story, but rather than enjoying it she found herself assailed by niggling doubts about her own relationship with Nathan.

Had he given her the book simply for her to draw comparisons between their association and that of the characters in the novel? Did he see himself in the woman who marries out of her class and is bitterly disappointed? Or did he cast himself in the role of the son who denies his own happiness for the love of his domineering mother? Had Nathan bought the book for himself and, after reading it, thought it an easy way to point out the pitfalls awaiting them should they marry; was this his way of letting her down gently? Lacey closed her eyes, deep in thought.

Cinders rattled in the grate. Startled, Lacey opened her eyes, surprised to find herself in the chair by the fire and not in bed. She glanced up at the clock on the mantel; half past four, she'd slept for almost six hours.

Suddenly remembering why she was in the chair, she leapt up and climbed

the stairs to the bedroom Jimmy shared with Matt. Matt lay flat on his back with his mouth open, his snores reverberating in the sparsely furnished room. Jimmy's bed was empty. She woke Matt.

★ ★ ★

The Black Maria trundled down Manchester Road on its way to the Police Station in Huddersfield. Jimmy sat in the back, his head in his hands, Arty and two of his mates alongside. Jimmy pressed his fingertips into his eyes to stem tears he was desperate to suppress. Arty and the other lads sat back nonchalantly, legs outstretched, cocky expressions on their faces. A ride in a Black Maria was not a new experience for them.

Inside the Police Station the desk sergeant recorded details in a thick ledger: names, addresses, the part each man had played in the robbery.

When Jimmy gave his name the desk sergeant said, 'Joshua Barraclough's lad?' He sounded shocked. Jimmy hung his head, ashamed.

'You silly young bugger; how did you get mixed up wi' that lot?' the arresting officer said, as he pushed Jimmy into a cell and slammed the door.

★ ★ ★

At first light Matt went in search of Jimmy. He came back with the news that the warehouse at Brearley's Mill had been broken into, the thieves attempting to steal bales of finished worsted and four men had been arrested.

Later that morning a police car drew up outside Netherfold's yard gate.

126

Through the kitchen window, Lacey watched two policemen climb out, her heart heavy. She had taken the day off work; she had a terrible feeling Edith would need her. Joshua and Matt sat by the fire, sheep temporarily forgotten. Edith stood aimlessly at the sink.

Lacey opened the door, the policemen shuffling in and removing their helmets. Four pairs of eyes fixed on them but no-one spoke. The policemen, faced with the abject misery of those they counted as friends, looked uncomfortable.

At last, Joshua broke the silence. 'Go on then. How bad is it?'

'Bad enough, Jos,' said Bert Pickles, the older of the two policemen,

'that's if I'm right in saying your lad's James Barraclough, seventeen years of age, and currently employed in the warehouse at Brearley's.'

Joshua's face crumpled. He rose unsteadily to face Bert. 'What's he done?'

'He says he were asked to leave one o' t'warehouse doors unlocked at finishin' time so's Arty Bincliffe an' his lot could get in later. Trouble is, the daft young bugger hung about an' helped 'em rob the place.'

Lacey's heart sank. Typical Jimmy, trying to prove he was a big man. 'Is our Jimmy being charged with robbery,' she asked.

Bert sucked on his teeth. 'It's worse than that. T'nightwatchman, Fred Sykes, spotted 'em an' raised t'alarm. It appears Jonas Brearley's not as soft as you might think. What with there havin' been a few robberies in t'valley in t'past months he'd taken precautions by employing an extra fellow, armed wi' a shotgun. They —'

Edith's cry split the air. 'Has our Jimmy been shot?' She clutched Joshua's arm, her eyes riveted on Bert.

'Nay lass, don't take on,' Bert said kindly. 'Nobody wa' shot, but in t'altercation Fred Sykes were clobbered over t'ead. He's in a bad way; very bad.' He paused to let the importance of his words register. 'What wi' a badly injured man to take into consideration, they could all be sent down for a long spell.'

'Gaol!' An image of her feckless younger brother incarcerated with rough, tough criminals flashed before Lacey's eyes. 'Was it our Jimmy injured Fred?'

Bert raised his brows and clamped his lips, his expression bemused.

'That's just it, lass, nobody's saying, an' unless one of 'em owns up they'll all be to blame.' He shook his head despairingly. 'What wa' your Jimmy doin' mixed up wi' that lot any road?'

No-one answered, not even Lacey.

Bert replaced his helmet, adopting a more formal attitude. 'We'll keep you informed. He's been charged an' will plead his case in court afore t'end o' t'week.' Then, reverting to being a family friend, he added, 'You might like to go down to t'station an' see if there's owt you can do.'

Bert and his colleague departed, the Barracloughs stunned into silence until Lacey cut through the shrouds of misery cloaking them. 'I'm to blame for this,' she said. Uncomprehending, Joshua, Matt and Edith stared at her.

'I knew our Jimmy was hanging about with Arty

Bincliffe; I told him to put a stop to it. He promised me he would and I wanted to believe him. I even warned Arty off. I threatened I'd get our Matt to sort him out.'

'Why the bloody hell didn't you then?' Matt roared. 'Why didn't you say summat afore now?'

Lacey shook her head, tears springing to her eyes. 'I didn't want our Jimmy to think we were picking on him, us making out he wasn't to be trusted. He wants to be thought of as a grown-up, as smart and tough as the rest of 'em. Trouble is, he's just a silly young lad trying to be a man. We've got to help him.'

'Trusted! A man!' Joshua thrashed the air with clenched fists, his cheeks puce. 'He's no son o' mine after what he's done. Bringin' shame on our family, us as have had a good name in this valley for generations. He'll not be back in this house, let me tell you. He can go to prison for all I care.'

'Oh, don't say that, Jos,' wailed Edith. 'Our Jimmy won't last a crack in gaol. He's only a bairn. We've got to help him. We can't just pretend it never happened.'

Joshua threw himself into a chair by the fire. 'Aye, well, you lot can go an' make fools o' yourselves but I'm done wi' him.'

'We don't even know if he's guilty,' Lacey cried. Even to her ears, the words sounded pathetic.

'Course we do,' Matt shouted. 'Bert Pickles wouldn't get summat' like that wrong. An' if Arty Bincliffe did threaten him, our Jimmy had only to come to me an' I'd have sorted it.'

'I thought I already had,' Lacey said, inwardly cursing her own stupid arrogance for believing she'd frightened off a man as devious as Arty. She grabbed her coat from the hook behind the door. 'I'm going to the Police Station. If anyone cares to join me, you're welcome.'

★ ★ ★

In the Police Station Lacey, Matt and Edith listened patiently as the desk sergeant repeated what Bert Pickles had already told them: the only fresh information being that Jimmy hadn't denied the charges, neither had he implicated the person who had struck Fred Sykes.

'Can we see him?' Lacey begged.

The desk sergeant frowned; then unable to resist the pleading green eyes and the pretty face he asked them to follow him. He left them in a small room furnished with a table and three chairs. A short while later a different officer entered, leading Jimmy by the arm. Indicating for Jimmy to sit in one chair and Lacey and Edith the others, the officer leaned against the wall by the door and Matt stood behind Edith's chair, a comforting hand on her shoulder.

Pale and clearly terrified, Jimmy perched on the chair, his head down.

'I'm sorry,' he mumbled over and again.

'Sorry you got caught, or sorry that you've shamed this family? Look what it's done to your mother,' snarled Matt.

Edith, her face leached of colour and tears brimming her eyes, gazed at her precious younger son. 'Wa' you thievin', Jimmy, or did somebody force you to do it?' she asked, her voice no more

130

than a whisper.

Jimmy stared at the floor.

'Answer your mother,' Lacey snapped, then more kindly added, 'tell us your side of it, Jimmy.'

'There's nowt to tell. We wa' doin' a job an' we got caught.'

'Was it Arty who forced you to do it?' Lacey didn't want to believe Jimmy had carried out a robbery of his own free will. 'You must tell 'em if it was.'

'You don't split on your mates.'

At that Lacey lost patience. 'Mates! Mates don't involve you in robberies, Jimmy. They used you and you were willing to let 'em because it made you feel like a big man.'

Jimmy flushed and glancing across at the policeman asked, 'Can I go now?'

Shocked to think he was dismissing them, Lacey jumped up. 'You can't leave it like this, you little fool. You're admitting you're guilty.'

'I am.' Jimmy stood up and walked towards the door. 'I wa' doin' it for you, Lacey.' He slouched out of the room.

* * *

In the weaving shed the next morning, Lacey ignored the pointing fingers and the gossiping mouths as news of her brother's involvement in the robbery flitted from loom to loom. She had been in two minds about whether to stay at home, but knowing she would have to face up to the scandal sooner or later she decided otherwise. What would Nathan — and Jonas — think of her

131

now? And what had Jimmy meant when he'd told her he did it for her sake?

'Not so high an' mighty now are you, you jumped up little tart,' Mary Collier mouthed. 'The boss's son'll not be so fond of you after this mullarky.'

'Don't mind her, Lacey,' Joan mouthed, her plump face wreathed in sympathy. 'If it wa' one of hers had done it she'd keep her gob shut. It's not your fault.'

Lacey didn't bother to mouth back that she thought it was exactly that.

She could have stopped Jimmy going off the rails had she not kept the knowledge to herself. Her head throbbing in tandem with her loom, Lacey puzzled over how she might help Jimmy.

By the time the hooter signalled breakfast time, Lacey felt ill. She didn't want to go out to the yard but her frazzled nerves and the heat in the shed made her nauseous; she needed fresh air. Yet she dreaded coming into contact with Nathan or Jonas.

Halfway down the yard, on her way to the riverbank, Nathan appeared at Lacey's side. He usually avoided drawing attention to their relationship but, given the circumstances, Lacey was hardly surprised to see him. He hurried her into a secluded corner behind the spinning shed.

'Is it true your brother was involved in last night's robbery?'

Lacey nodded dumbly.

Nathan's face darkened. 'That's terrible. What on earth was he thinking?'

Lacey sighed. 'Our Jimmy doesn't think; he's young an' feckless. I'm not defending what he

132

did, it was wrong, but I believe he had a reason for doing it.'

'For the money, I imagine?' Nathan said, harshly.

'No,' Lacey replied, despairingly. 'There's more to it than that, but I don't know what. At first I thought he'd gone along with it to impress his so-called friends; that he thought he was being manly. Now I'm not so sure.' Her eyes filled with tears. 'The last thing he said before we left him at the Police Station was that he'd done it for me.'

Nathan looked askance. 'For you: whatever did he mean by that?'

'I've no idea,' cried Lacey. Utterly distraught, she dashed her knuckles against the rough stone of the spinning shed's wall, wincing at the self-inflicted pain. 'There must be something we can do; find a solicitor, someone to plead his case. Let the judge know Jimmy's not a hardened criminal, just a foolish boy, easily led.' She gazed hopefully into Nathan's face.

Nathan leaned back against the wall. 'You're clutching at straws, Lacey. Your brother was caught red-handed. He'll more than likely receive a custodial sentence, maybe two or three years in gaol.'

Lacey sagged visibly. She had thought Nathan would support her; tell her what to do to help Jimmy. She clutched at his chest, sobbing uncontrollably.

Instead of comforting her, Nathan said, 'It'll do your reputation harm; mine too.' He pulled away from her, adding reflectively, 'Just when everything was going so well for you with my family.'

133

A spurt of anger flared in Lacey's chest. She looked into Nathan's eyes, her own flashing dangerously. 'It'll not do much for our Jimmy's either.

An' if it bothers you being involved with somebody whose reputation's tarnished then I suggest you leave me alone; forget all about me.'

Nathan gazed at her sadly. 'I don't think I could do that, Lacey, but your brother's actions have forced me into this situation. It makes our relationship look ridiculous. Don't forget, it's my Mill he robbed.'

This last remark, accompanied as it was by a look of utter revulsion, stabbed Lacey to the core. Did Nathan have to condemn him and be so pompous when all she needed was his love and support?

Nathan walked a few steps away from her. 'I just hope Mother doesn't hear of his involvement and connect it to you. I didn't realise your brother was a thieving, no-good tearaway.'

Lacey jumped to Jimmy's defence. 'He isn't. He's just a foolish lad who's been led astray.'

Nathan's expression was a mixture of disappointment and frustration masked with contempt 'He's a thief, Lacey.'

Lacey's laugh was harsh and bitter. 'I can't fathom you, Nathan Brearley. One minute you're eulogising in defence of the working classes and the next you're kicking a poor, misguided lad when he's down. You're more concerned with your mother's disapproval than you are for me. I didn't rob your bloody mill!' She sagged against the wall, the fight knocked out of her. In a low voice she said, 'If you truly loved me, you'd understand.'

Exasperated, Nathan said, 'He robbed our Mill, Lacey.' He looked away from her, his gaze fixed on the flowing waters of the river. In the distance, thunder rumbled. Lacey looked towards the sound. The sky was darkening, huge rainclouds banked up one on the other. Suddenly, a jagged flash of lightning swiped the sky. The Sword of Damocles, Lacey thought.

When Nathan next spoke the anguish in his voice broke her heart. 'He ruined our chances: yours and mine. I'll always love you, but,' he paused, searching for words, 'whatever we had has been damaged beyond repair by your brother's behaviour. My father's bound to withdraw his approval of us given the circumstances, and I'm not prepared to give up the Mill for the sake of a thief. And I only mentioned Mother because if we were to marry she'd object to having a convict in the family.'

Lacey tossed her head and glared at him. 'Did it ever occur to you that I might object to marrying into a bunch of self-righteous, unforgiving snobs?' Too late she added, 'I think we'd better leave it at that, Nathan, before we both say something we regret.' She stepped away from him and, shrouded in misery, she ran back to the weaving shed.

12

Up in her bedroom, Lacey set the lamp on the deep windowsill. Its newly trimmed wick burned brightly inside the freshly washed glass chimney; a good light to sew by. She'd promised to have Felicity's dress ready for collection the following day, Friday.

Lacey had not seen Nathan since the robbery, and although it pained her to look at anything reminding her of him, she dutifully pulled a chair into the pool of lamplight and sat down, Felicity's dress draped across her lap.

Three times without success, she attempted to thread her needle. Holding it up to the light and cursing under her breath, she tried again. Finally, the length of purple embroidery silk penetrated the needle's eye and Lacey began to sew, her vision blurred by unshed tears. Would Felicity even wear the dress after all that had happened, she wondered, taking a deep breath and firmly telling herself to keep a clear head and a steady hand.

An hour later she placed the finished garment on a hanger, scrutinising it with a practised eye. Although she felt utterly joyless, she released a deep sigh of satisfaction. The dress looked beautiful. Around the hems of the voile tunic and skirt she had embroidered deep purple and mauve cornflowers; cornflowers signified friendship. But Felicity was no longer her friend. How could she be after what Jimmy had done?

Saddened to think she wouldn't be at the party to see Felicity wearing the dress, Lacey prepared for bed thinking, I could swing for you, Jimmy Barraclough. If you were here now I'd beat the living daylights out of you.

She climbed into bed, but the thought of Jimmy in gaol awaiting trial made sleep impossible.

★ ★ ★

The following evening Lacey stood by the yard gate, her eyes scanning the lane and her heart hoping against hope. Sunlight flashed on metal, Lacey's

spirits soaring then rapidly sinking as she realised the car trundling down the rutted lane was not Nathan's little Austin but the large, black chauffeur driven car that ferried Jonas Brearley to and from the Mill.

However, she prayed that Nathan was in it, bringing Felicity to collect the dress. Perhaps today they could retract the terrible words they had exchanged on the riverbank and be friends, at least.

The car drew to a halt outside the gate. Cheevers climbed out. 'Parcel to collect for Miss Brearley.'

Lacey walked dejectedly into the kitchen, returning with the carefully wrapped brown paper parcel. 'I thought Mr Nathan and Miss Felicity might have called for it,' she said with forced cheerfulness.

Cheevers took the parcel. 'Miss Felicity's busy with arrangements for tomorrow's party and Mr Nathan's getting ready to go to Northumberland.

He's leaving the day after.'

Cheevers marched smartly to the car.

'Wish him a safe journey for me,' Lacey called after him, her words wasted as Cheevers revved the engine and drove off.

★ ★ ★

Lacey walked to work on Monday morning, her heart heavy with the knowledge that Nathan would not be there so she'd have no chance to make amends. She asked herself did she even want to heal the rift, considering the cruel words they had exchanged behind the spinning shed? Maybe Nathan was going to Northumberland to purposely avoid her? Or was it to further his friendship with Imogen, the coal baron's daughter?

Lacey had laughed when Nathan described Constance's clumsy plot to involve him with Imogen, but perhaps now he'd decided to heed his mother's advice after all and marry a girl of his own class. I'm not laughing now, she mused, and what with losing Nathan and the possibility of Jimmy being sent to gaol, I'll probably never laugh again.

★ ★ ★

Nathan's absence left Lacey feeling utterly confused. Time and again, as she tended her looms or walked the moor, she asked herself could she truly love a man whose beliefs were at odds with her own. Had his natural charm and protestations of love lulled her into thinking it was possible for him to ignore the rules that governed the upper classes? Was he too weak willed to relinquish the prejudices that had been drummed into him from birth?

The more Lacey thought about it, the more convinced she became. It was true, Nathan harboured idealistic notions about society and change, but each time he had been faced with an incident emphasising the difference in their backgrounds he had been thrown into turmoil. For all his fine words it seemed he lacked the moral fibre to begin changing a system that, throughout history, had by dint of birth divided people, placing some on pedestals and others in chains. Like her Mam said, there was one law for the rich and one for the poor.

* * *

'I've given up on Nathan,' she told Joan one morning as they walked to work a week after Nathan had left for Northumberland. 'I was fooling myself thinking we could make a go of it. We come from two different worlds and Nathan doesn't seem capable of accepting mine, even though I'd have tried my bloody hardest to accept his.'

'I know you would, Lacey, 'cos I know how much you love him,' said Joan as they crossed the road to the Mill gates. 'Mebbe it'll come right in the end.'

Lacey wasn't convinced, and although she steeled herself to admit their love affair was over it took every ounce of strength for her not to dwell on all that they had shared. She missed catching

139

a glimpse of him through the office window or walking across the yard, and most of all she missed their trysts down by the river or up on Cuckoo Hill. Gone were the hours of lively conversation and the accompanying hugs and kisses.

A brief thank you note from Felicity did little to lighten her spirits. Even the words 'complemented the stylish cut and exquisite needlework' failed to impress, as did the enclosed crisp ten shilling note.

* * *

On a dismal Friday morning in late July, Lacey, Edith and Matt sat in Huddersfield County Court, numb with dread. Jimmy and his co-accused sat in the dock, Jimmy shrunken and fearful. He fidgeted with his shirt collar, a clean one sent in by Edith, and chewed on his fingernails. Every now and then he raised his eyes and stared across the courtroom at Lacey.

Lacey smiled back whenever their eyes met: a warm, encouraging smile.

Outwardly she appeared perfectly calm but inside she felt as though her stomach might turn in on itself.

Formalities dealt with, the magistrate addressed each of the accused in turn asking what they had to say in their defence. Both Tom Jagger and Bill Johnson shook their head mutely. Arty gave the magistrate a malevolent glare and replied 'Nowt.'

The magistrate addressed Jimmy, Lacey moving to the edge of her seat, her fingernails digging into the palms of her hands, her eyes riveted on

Jimmy's ashen face. Edith gave a shuddering sob and Matt bowed his head.

Jimmy fixed his gaze on Lacey.

The magistrate repeated the question. Jimmy glanced wildly at his partners in crime. The magistrate gave an exasperated sniff. 'Speak up, man, we haven't all day.'

Jimmy swallowed noisily, his Adam's apple jerking visibly. He looked intently at Lacey.

'Louder; speak louder.'

Jimmy's eyes flicked from the magistrate to Arty, then back to Lacey. He essayed a tremulous little grin, took a deep breath and then faced the magistrate directly. When he spoke his voice was clear and shrill.

'I only did it because he said he'd hurt my sister if I didn't do what he told me.' He pointed his finger at Arty. 'He said he'd rape her if I split on 'em.'

Lacey's sharp intake of breath whistled in her throat. Jimmy had been protecting her.

'You bloody liar.' Arty's roar ricocheted round the courtroom.

'Silence,' barked the magistrate, 'address the court in such manner again and I'll charge you with contempt.'

'An' it were Arty what hit Fred Sykes over t'head,' blurted out Jimmy,

'Bill tried to stop him.'

The magistrate pursed his lips and stared hard at Jimmy. 'We only have your word for it that Bincliffe threatened such actions.'

There then followed a series of questions and answers, Jimmy defending his statement, Arty

141

denying it with vitriolic glares.

'Can I say somethin', your worship,' interrupted Bill Johnson, the fourth and oldest member of the gang.

The magistrate glared at him. 'Well, speak up.'

Bill gave Jimmy a pitying glance. 'What young Jimmy says is true. Arty wa' always threatenin' to hurt Lacey Barraclough. Jimmy din't want to go robbin' but he wa' scared o' what Arty might do. I'm only sayin' this 'cos I don't like violence against women, an' what he did to Fred Sykes wasn't right either. I've nowt to say in me own defence but I'll not stand by an' see a young 'un like Jimmy go down for summat as wasn't his fault.'

Lacey's heart pounded and she held her breath as she waited for the magistrate's response.

'Is this true; remember you are under oath.'

'Aye, it is,' Tom Jagger growled. Jimmy threw Bill and Tom grateful glances. Then he looked over at Lacey, his eyes full of love.

After some private discussion with police and court officials the magistrate announced his verdict, sentencing Jagger and Johnson to two years in gaol. Arty, guilty of committing robbery with grievous bodily harm, was given five years with a further two for coercion, confinement to run consecutively. As the magistrate outlined the terms and conditions, Arty's shoulders slumped and his cocky expression faded. However, he did manage a final glare in Lacey's direction before he was taken down.

Then Jimmy, Lacey, Edith and Matt anxiously awaited Jimmy's fate. The magistrate adjusted his cuffs, a stern expression on his face. Lacey held her breath.

'James Barraclough, in view of your tender years and previous good conduct I am prepared to be lenient with you. It is obvious to me that you were subject to undue coercion by Arthur Bincliffe, therefore, provided you are of good behaviour for the next three years, I will release you into the care of your parents. You are free to go.'

Matt waved a triumphant fist; Edith's tears wetting Lacey's shoulder as they clung to each other.

Outside the court, hugging Jimmy tight, Lacey praised him for his courage. 'You really were doing it for me,' she marvelled.

'I'd do owt for you, Lacey, even though I didn't take any notice when you told me to keep away from Arty.' Jimmy flushed to the roots of his hair.

'At first it wa' a bit of fun. I wa' tryin' to be a big fellow, then Arty started fillin' me head wi' the awful things he wa' gonna do to you. I wa' scared he'd get you one night an' really hurt you.'

'Why din't you tell me?' Matt demanded. 'I'd a soon sorted the bugger.'

Jimmy looked shamefaced. 'I daren't. He said if I said owt to you he'd make sure Lacey 'ud get it 'cos if he didn't do it himself he'd get somebody to do it for him.'

Edith gasped. 'The evil swine!' She pulled Jimmy round to face her, gazing intently at him. 'And whatever made you take up with him in the first place, our Jimmy, I'll never understand.' She started to cry.

Jimmy's eyes brimmed. 'I'm sorry, Mam.' He threw his arms round Edith, pressing his face into her chest, their mutual tears absolving any blame.

When they broke apart, Matt took Edith on one arm and Jimmy on the other. 'Let's go home,' he said gruffly, 'put this behind us.'

But Matt wasn't finished. As the Barracloughs waited for the bus that would take them back to Garsthwaite, he addressed Jimmy angrily. 'You still haven't told us why you didn't say owt afore it got to this?'

Jimmy looked to Lacey for understanding. 'I daren't say owt at first in case they let him off an' he came after you. It wasn't until I realised we'd all get gaol that I knew Lacey 'ud be safe.' He turned to her. 'I'd a gone down for you, Lacey; honest.'

'It's a bloody good job Arty didn't try owt wi' our Lacey. He'd a got his come-uppance if he had. She's like a hell-cat if you cross her. I'd say Arty had a lucky escape,' joked Matt, not wishing to dwell on the awfulness of the past few hours.

Later that night in bed, Lacey hugged herself for joy. Jimmy, her protector, was free and innocent. She wondered what Nathan would say when he heard the facts. She wanted to run and blurt out the truth in his face but Nathan was still in Northumberland and she didn't know when she would see him again.

* * *

In the days following Jimmy's release, Lacey's emotions fluctuated from joy to despair. In daylight hours she managed to focus her thoughts on things that made her happy; Jimmy saved from gaol, and Joan's recently revealed pregnancy.

144

She also gloried in the marvellous weather they were experiencing, taking long walks over the moor lost in her thoughts; Joshua's prediction that this was going to be one of the longest, hottest summers in living memory holding true.

Nights however were a different matter. Sitting at her machine or lying in bed, the futility of her love for Nathan invaded every thought. She, who had once been so carefree, had never imagined love could be so painful. Neither could she have envisioned the events that were about to unfold; events so dynamically catastrophic they would change the lives of every man, woman and child in the British Isles.

13

'Stanley says there's going to be a war,' said Joan, when she met Lacey at the Mill gate one morning in early August. 'Do you think there is, Lacey?' she asked.

'He could very well be right. There's a lot of trouble in Germany; the newspapers are full of it.' Lacey's response sounded distinctly lacklustre.

Compared to her own misery the death of some Archduke and his wife in Sarajevo had made little impact; awake or asleep she was consumed by her own loss.

'What's it got to do with us?' Joan persisted, as they crossed the Mill yard.

'It's to do with a treaty we have with Russia and France. The Germans are rampaging through Europe and we'll have to help defend the countries that are our friends.'

'Will our soldiers have to fight the Germans?'

'Something like that, Joanie.'

Lacey's simplification of the machinations of war satisfying Joan, she followed Lacey into the shed, the heat of a glorious summer's morning already thickening the air. Joan wiped perspiration from her face and then put on her overall, the cross-over cotton flaps stretched over her burgeoning bump. 'This baby doesn't like it when I start to sweat. It gets too hot for it in there.' She patted her abdomen. 'I hope it's a boy. Stanley wants a son.'

146

'So you keep saying, Joanie.'

The hooter's blast had them scurrying to their looms, and throughout the day the women talked of little else other than how they might be affected should the country go to war.

'I can't see it happenin' meself,' asserted May Skinner, 'it's got nowt to do wi' us.'

'It will 'ave if them bloody Germans come here.' Gertie Earnshaw sounded as though she wished they would.

'Do you think t'Mill'll close down?' Maggie Clegg sounded horrified.

'Will it hell, you daft clout-head,' scoffed Flo Backhouse, 'folk's still need cloth no matter what.'

'They do,' agreed Lacey, 'but if the Germans block trade routes we'll soon run out of raw wool, an' then there'll be no business between us an' Europe.'

'There'll be no men either,' said Mary Collier, 'they'll all be off fightin'.'

At clocking off time Slimy Syd, full of his own importance, strutted in between the looms waving the evening edition of the Huddersfield Examiner.

'Herbert Asquith's given t'Germans till midnight to pull their troops back. If they don't, we'll be going to war, lasses.'

'Hey, Syd, if you go I hope them bloody Germans shoot you,' shouted Maggie Collier. Laughing uproariously, the women trooped out of the shed.

They returned the following morning in a sombre mood for they now knew England was at war.

By mid-afternoon, the temperature in the weaving shed was unbearable, Lacey's breath catching in her parched throat as dust and fluff from the thrashing looms clouded the fetid air. Earlier that day she had stripped down to her petticoat, the neckline of her loose overall exposing her cleavage. As perspiration wormed its way down her face and neck to settle in the hollow between her breasts, the thrum of the beaters, the flashing shuttles and the dancing dust motes began to make her feel nauseous. She stopped her looms and, mouthing her intentions to Lizzie, she tottered out of the shed and across the yard to the lavatory.

Inside the filthy closet, the stench exacerbated her nausea. Lacey vomited. Clammy with sweat, her head throbbing, she staggered outside and leaned against the wall, gulping deep breaths of soot laden air into her lungs and waiting for the churning in her stomach to calm itself.

A door across the yard slammed shut. Sydney Sugden came into view.

Instantly, Lacey prised herself from the wall, but Syd had seen her. Dashing over the cobbles he closed in on her, pushing her towards the closet's open door. Lacey lashed out but Syd persisted. 'Come on, Lacey,' he panted, ogling her bare cleavage, 'I've waited long enough.'

As Lacey struggled to escape Syd's clutches, Nathan walked out of the office, a sheaf of Jacquard patterns in his hand. As he crossed the yard to

the weaving shed he heard a woman's high pitched cry and, recognising the voice, he dropped the patterns and ran towards it.

Lacey swiped Syd's face, a slap so forceful she lost her balance. Syd's grip loosened. Lacey fell flat on her back on the flagstones. Stunned by the fall, she was vaguely aware of scuffling feet and shouting.

Slowly, she rolled over onto her side, regained her feet and then stared in amazement. Syd and Nathan were locked in combat, fists and feet flying.

Like a man possessed, Nathan punched Syd's jaw, Syd sprawled on the cobbles, defeated. Ignoring his pleas, Nathan dragged him upright, shaking him and shouting, 'If you ever go near her again I'll kill you, you filthy scum.'

Nathan tossed Syd aside then clasped Lacey to his chest, oblivious to the mill hands spilling from the sheds at word of the rumpus.

'Thanks,' Lacey said, her voice initially unsteady, then breaking into a relieved chuckle. 'By, Nathan Brearley; when you decide to make a stand you don't do it by halves.' She glanced at Syd, prostrate on the cobbles.

Nathan gazed into her eyes, his own so full of love that Lacey's breath caught in her throat. She knew people were watching, their voices drifting in and out of her hearing, but she seemed to be caught in a bubble where only she and Nathan existed. She rested her head against his chest and he wrapped his arms around her.

Cheers from the crowd brought them back to reality and they broke apart.

Nathan nudged Syd with the toe of his boot. 'Get your cards, you filthy swine; you're fired.'

'We'll all be grateful for that, Master Nathan. He's been a bloody nuisance for far too long.' As Lizzie Isherwood championed Nathan, the women looking on roared their approval.

'I'd best get back to me looms,' Lacey said quietly. 'Will I see you at Cuckoo Hill after clocking off time?'

★ ★ ★

He was there at the cairn as Lacey topped the brow of the hill, watching anxiously for her approach. She ran to him, Nathan enveloping her in his arms as though he would never let her go again. Returning kiss for kiss, Lacey felt all the pain and disillusion of the past few weeks easing away, leaving her rapturously lightheaded.

'You can't imagine how much I've missed you,' Nathan said, his voice shaking with emotion.

'I can,' Lacey replied solemnly, 'for I've missed you twice as much. We were foolish to quarrel when we should have stayed strong for one another. Our Jimmy — '

Nathan gently placed his finger on Lacey's lips. 'I heard all the details in the Mill office the moment I arrived back this morning. Let's not talk about it. We've more important things to discuss; like how much I love you and how I never want to be parted from you again.'

14

Constance sat facing Nathan over the breakfast table at Fenay Hall, her expression a mixture of disgust and dismay. It was a week or so after the fight at the Mill, Jonas was still in bed and Felicity was in London for a few days.

'Is it true you have resumed your relationship with that mill girl?'

Nathan's spirits drooped. As he lifted the cover on a serving dish containing rashers of grilled bacon, he wondered who his mother's informants were. Although she would deny it, Constance was always conversant with village gossip.

'It will ruin your reputation. We'll be the talk of the valley,' she persisted.

She would have said more had Nathan not slammed down the cover with a resounding clash. Constance's cutlery clattered on her plate, her shocked expression egging Nathan on.

'Yes, I have, and furthermore I intend to marry her. I don't care a jot for what you and your high minded friends in the valley think.'

Constance blinked fat tears down her cheeks and clutched at her chest.

'See what this is doing to me, Nathan, and to you,' she sobbed, 'you never used to take that tone with me.'

Nathan stood, determination making him appear taller and stronger. 'I do so because you have no regard for my feelings, Mother. I love

151

Lacey Barraclough regardless of her status in society and you had best get used to the idea.' He made to walk away, saying, 'I'll bring her to meet you again. You will, I hope, make her welcome and treat her with respect.'

Constance pushed back her chair, tears forgotten. 'Indeed I will not. I forbid you to marry that trollop. Do you hear me, Nathan?'

'Yes, Mother, I hear you; I'll invite her to call on you on Saturday afternoon, and if you have any love for me at all you will welcome her with the respect she deserves.' And with that he stalked out of the room.

★ ★ ★

For the third time Lacey sat in the opulent drawing room at Fenay Hall, this time with only Constance for company. Before leaving her there, Nathan told Lacey that Constance had met his announcement that he intended to marry her with reservations and that it was now up to Lacey to persuade her to give them her approval. Speak with Mother, woman to woman, he had said, so with these words in mind, Lacey now faced Constance with outward calm and inner foreboding.

Constance sat ramrod straight, her mouth a grim line of dissatisfaction, her statuesque bulk filling the leather armchair directly opposite the one in which Lacey sat. For several minutes she didn't speak, her eyes flicking from Lacey's face to her shoes and back again as though she was measuring her for the oven. Lacey didn't flinch.

Constance broke the silence, her tone harshly

152

imperious. 'It appears Nathan has some foolish notion regarding you. He says he intends to marry you.'

'That's correct, Mrs Brearley. Nathan and I have been friends for more than a year. We enjoyed one another's company from the start, and now we've fallen in love. It's only natural we should want to marry. I think we're well matched; we have a lot in common.'

Constance glowered. 'Don't be ridiculous. The only thing common is you, girl: a common mill hand. What on earth can you offer Nathan, a boy privately educated; the son of an esteemed factory owner?'

Lacey ignored the insult. 'I would love and respect him, share his interests and make him happy,' she said firmly. 'He loves me, Mrs Brearley.'

'Pshaw! Nathan has no experience of love. He's simply bewitched by a pretty face and the pleasure he takes in raising you above your station. Poor Nathan is given to flights of fancy. He has a romantic view of the world.' Constance gave Lacey a withering glare. 'You can't expect him to present you to our circle of acquaintances. He'd be a laughing stock, the heir to a mill married to a weaver.'

Determined not to be drawn into an inflammatory exchange no matter how rude Constance was, Lacey suppressed an angry retort and said, 'Weaving's a worthwhile and necessary occupation, Mrs Brearley. I might not have had the benefit of a private education but I'm as well read and equally as intelligent as many another young woman of your acquaintance.'

153

Constance sneered. 'Those women you refer to are ladies, something you will never be, regardless of your reading.' She waved her hand dismissively and then sighed heavily. 'If you're as intelligent as you would have me believe, you'll appreciate how preposterous his suggestion of marriage is.

You no doubt impress him with your hoity-toity, outspoken manner, but he's simply playing with you, the foolish boy.'

Lacey's eyes blazed. 'He's not a boy; he's a man. A man who knows what he wants from life. Your opinion of him is demeaning, to say the least.' She leaned forward and looked directly at Constance, her tone softer but no less intense. 'I might not be the right class of girl in your opinion, but I'm as well reared as anybody. My father's a respected farmer and yes, he isn't prosperous, but he earns his living honestly.'

Constance's eyes glittered. 'Talking of honesty, wasn't your brother involved in the robbery at the Mill.'

Lacey's heart plummeted and some of the fire went out of her. 'He was, but only out of loyalty to me. He's not a bad person.'

'Bad enough to associate with criminals.' Constance smirked. 'Now, if you take my advice you'll stop playing on Nathan's sensitivities and allow this stupid romance to fizzle out, as I'm sure it will if you would desist from pestering him.'

Her patience tried too far, Lacey readily abandoned her resolution to stay calm at all costs. 'Mrs Brearley, just because you're the daughter of a mine owner and wife of a mill owner doesn't give you the right to dictate what I do. I'm a woman

154

with a mind of her own. I won't always be in servitude to you and your kind.'

'And you think to better yourself by inveigling my son into marrying you,' Constance spat back, 'is that your plan?'

Lacey jumped up, standing tall and proud. 'Nothing could be further from my mind,' she said vehemently, 'I'm not marrying Nathan to climb the social ladder; I'd marry him even if he were a pauper. As for bettering myself, I can do that without him. It might surprise you to know that women can improve their standing in society without doing it on the coat tails of a man.'

Constance opened her mouth to intervene but Lacey, now in full flow was determined to have her say.

'Just because you come from a privileged background and made a fortuitous marriage shouldn't blind you to the fact that there are many different ways in which a woman can prove her worth — even though some choose to live in the shadow of their husbands.'

Constance had the grace to look abashed, but Lacey wasn't finished.

'Look around you, Mrs Brearley. It's women who'll make the world a better place once we cast aside our subservience to men. I consider myself equal to your son in every way.'

Constance's lip curled. 'I might have known it. I suppose you are one of those tiresome women involved in suffrage and the right to vote. How unladylike.'

Lacey chuckled. 'Yes, I am, and it's not unladylike. It's our right to be recognised as worthy

155

contributors to society. It's wrong for men to treat us as second-class citizens.' She paused for breath, an impish smile curving her lips. 'Have you seen the state of the one lavatory a hundred and more women have to use at Brearley's Mill?'

Constance's eyes popped, a look of utter confusion on her face.

'No, I thought not,' Lacey continued, 'because if you had you'd understand why I'm going to join the Trade Union. I'll fight for better conditions for working women like me and at the same time, if Nathan wants to marry me, I'll do that as well.'

'Lavatories! Trade Unions! I've heard enough of your nonsense.'

Constance's cheeks flaming and her breathing uneven, she charged to the door and flung it wide open.

'I bid you good-day,' she shrieked.

Lacey strode towards the door and then paused. 'Thank you for giving me your time, Mrs Brearley,' she said courteously, the hand she proffered left unshaken.

'I don't ever want to see you again,' Constance hissed, as Lacey stepped into the hallway. 'And should Nathan persist in this foolishness, I will do all in my power to put a stop to it.'

Lacey turned. 'Do as you please, Mrs Brearley, for I certainly will.'

Without waiting for Nathan to appear she marched out of Fenay Hall for what she was sure would be the last time.

★ ★ ★

Later that afternoon, Lacey walked up Cuckoo Hill to the cairn, sure of finding Nathan there. It was a warm, balmy evening, the last rays of sun turning the heather to deepest purple and the dips and folds in the valley to gold: pauper's gold her Dad called it, theirs for free to alleviate the misery of reality.

Nathan leaned dejectedly against the cairn, his hands stuffed deep in his trouser pockets. She could tell he was out of sorts — but then so was she.

There were no welcoming smiles or kisses, both of them barely able to conceal their frustration. She waited for him to speak.

'You certainly infuriated Mother this afternoon. What on earth did you say to her?' He sounded like a pompous schoolmaster rebuking a naughty pupil.

'I told her a few home truths,' Lacey said jauntily, an unpleasant edge to her voice. 'She didn't want to hear them. She thinks I'm a low-class girl using you to climb the social ladder, and that once I stop pestering you, you'll soon forget me.'

She paused, judging Nathan's reaction, not liking what she saw. His expression conveyed neither sympathy nor outrage on Lacey's behalf, nor did he make the quick rebuttal she had been expecting about him soon forgetting her. Shrugging off his silence, Lacey continued. 'She thinks you only imagine you're in love with me.'

Nathan emitted a deep sigh. 'What exactly were the home truths, as you call them?' He sounded wary, as though he dreaded hearing them, and paled as Lacey bluntly related the facts. She watched his

157

frown deepen and his grey-blue eyes darken.

Nathan drew breath, sharply. 'You were meant to endear yourself to her, not insult her. No wonder she dismissed you.'

Lacey's shoulders slumped. It was useless to argue that it was she who had been insulted. She gave him a pitying look and shrugged her resignation. 'There you go again, Nathan. Twisting the facts in favour of the upper class. The day you truly believe in equality is the day I'll want you. Until then I think it best we stay apart.' She turned and sped down the hill, Nathan's pleas for her to come back ringing in her ears.

15

The group of women in the Mill yard listened with mixed reactions to what Lacey was telling them. Some sniggered out loud whilst others muttered under their breath, refuting her suggestions. A few leaned forward, ears cocked, nodding in agreement.

Lacey challenged them further, for whilst she waited for Nathan to decide what his aspirations truly were, she had decided to further her own.

'So you see, lasses, the more of us joins the Weaver's Union the louder we'll be heard. We've as much right to have our say as the men we work with. If we sit back and let 'em walk all over us we'll get nowhere.' Hands on hips, she glanced from one face to another, awaiting their response.

'Men don't want women in t'Union. They've made that clear.'

'If it 'ud mean a raise in wages, I'd join.'

'Aye, why should we be paid less than a man for doin' t'same work?'

'We'll get the bloody sack if old Brearley hears about this.'

Lacey raised her voice above theirs. 'If the Union demands summat, Brearley has to listen to 'em, an' if they make a strong enough claim he has to do summat about it. That's how Unions work. That's why we need to join and make our voices heard. An' remember, Brearley can't do without us.

It's us that makes him his brass.'

A chorus of 'I'll join,' was in danger of being drowned out by the jeering

'Go an' waste your bloody time if you've nowt better to do.'

The hooter blew, Lacey hurried to her looms, elated. At least half the women had been supportive, and if they held their nerve the Union men were in for a surprise next Monday evening.

* * *

On Saturday afternoon Lacey knocked at the door of a neat terrace house in Wormald Street. When it opened, Lacey found herself gazing into the sharpest blue eyes she had ever seen. The elderly woman, head tilted enquiringly, waited for Lacey to speak.

'Miss Amelia Broadhead?'

'I am she. What can I do for you?'

The brisk tones and perceptive gaze were somewhat at odds with the wrinkled cheeks and untidy mop of silver hair. Surprised, Lacey smiled.

Amelia smiled back.

Lacey took a deep breath. 'I need to learn about women's suffrage and the Trade Unions. I thought you might give me some advice. I've heard you are actively involved in the women's movement and know a lot about such matters.'

Amelia's smile widened. 'You heard correctly, although these days I'm far less active than I'd like to be.' She shook her head ruefully. 'Old age has nothing to recommend it, my dear, however . . . ' she stepped back perkily, 'my heart still beats to

160

the same drum. Perhaps you'd better come inside.'

Two hours later, Lacey was back on the street, her head buzzing with the exploits of Annie Besant, the Pankhursts and Isabella Ormston Ford: Annie, who had fought for the rights of women employed in the Bryant and May match factory, had forced their employers to stop using the white phosphorous that formed the match heads, a highly toxic substance that gave the women something they called phossy jaw; a terribly painful condition that disfigured and rotted the jawbone. Isabella had rallied the overworked, underpaid women who worked in the sewing sweatshops in Leeds and Bradford to march through the streets of those cities, demanding better working conditions and improved wages, and the Pankhursts had campaigned for women's right to vote.

Amelia had described these women as having fire in their bellies. That's what I have, Lacey told herself as she walked back home. If they can do it, so can I.

★ ★ ★

On Sunday afternoon Lacey walked to Cuckoo Hill, her thoughts flitting from one issue to another; the Union meeting she would attend tomorrow night, the depressing newspaper reports on the war in France, and Nathan.

She sauntered over the moor, settling down in a sheltered spot overlooking the valley. From this vantage point she could see Garsthwaite.

It looked innocuously peaceful.

But England was no longer at peace. Every day

161

the worsening effects of war were felt throughout the land: husbands, fathers, sons and uncles leaving home to enlist and fight in a war not of their making; a slump in trade and the threat of short-time in the mills; the risk of food shortages and the ever present menace of invasion. Would German soldiers be marching over these moors before long, Lacey wondered? Would everything she held dear be changed forever?

Her gaze roved the rolling heather until the grey slate roof of Netherfold came into view, just visible in its cosy cleft on the edge of the moor. Please, God, protect us from all harm, she silently intoned, her gaze drifting to include the drab conglomeration that was Garsthwaite.

She fixed her eyes on the larger houses in Towngate; the better end of the town as Edith called it. Mill managers, businessmen and shopkeepers lived here, their substantial three storey dwellings in sharp contrast to the rows of terraced houses huddled in narrow, cobbled streets under the shadow of the mills. Eventually her eyes settled on the largest and most impressive of all the houses; Fenay Hall.

She wouldn't visit there again, she told herself forcefully. She was done with Nathan Brearley playing fast and loose with her affections, adoring her one day, castigating her the next.

Her mind made up, Lacey bounced up and skipped across the heather, an exhilarating sense of freedom spurring her on. In time she'd find someone else, she thought, someone who would go through hell and high water to marry her. The cairn in sight she quickened her pace, eager to reach home and those who truly appreciated her.

Nathan stepped into view. Shocked, Lacey faltered to a halt in front of him. 'I thought I'd find you here,' he said.

The very sight of him shaking her recent conviction to let him go, she steeled herself and snapped, 'Why would the likes of you come looking for the likes of me?'

'You know why. I love you.'

Lacey smiled sadly. 'Aye, but is it enough: enough for you to want to share your life with me?'

Hurt by her words, Nathan grasped her by the shoulders, pushing his face close to hers. 'Of course it is. I'm shocked you doubt me. I'll marry you as soon as I can.'

'Does that mean we have to wait until your mother's no longer with us?'

Nathan's face darkened and he stepped back. 'What sort of a question is that?'

'It's simply this, Nathan. If you were to marry me could you bear your mother's disapproval?'

Nathan flinched. Lacey knew she had touched a nerve.

'It won't come to that. She'll learn to accept you.'

Lacey laughed bitterly. 'No, she won't. You're fooling yourself again, Nathan. I'm a mill girl, the daughter of a penurious smallholder. She and the people you associate with will think you're marrying out of your class; and they'd be right. I've had no education to speak of, I consort with weavers and spinners, folk who toil in muck and dust twelve hours a day. I don't keep company with bank managers an' the like, neither am I the simpering, well bred young lady your mother expects

163

you to marry. So you see, Nathan, you have to be strong enough to contend with all our differences. If you marry me it might make me happy but it'll be a hard road for you.'

'So be it,' Nathan said, a glimmer of a smile lighting his face. 'I'd already reached that conclusion without you bullying me into it. No matter the problems, I'll move heaven and earth to make you my wife.'

Lacey's blood sang in her veins and she knew her face expressed the joy she felt, yet Nathan's didn't mirror it. 'Sadly though, Lacey, marriage will have to wait, and not because of Mother. I came to tell you I've signed up. I join my regiment in five days' time.'

Astounded, Lacey digested Nathan's words. When he pulled her into his arms and kissed her, Lacey responded with equal passion, at the same time dreading the thought of losing him.

'I can't imagine you as a soldier,' Lacey murmured.

Nathan smiled wanly. 'Neither can I, but I'd be a coward if I didn't do my duty. My old School, Sedbergh, had an Officer Training Corps and although I was a member I didn't exactly enjoy it. It's seems somewhat immoral, training to kill your fellow man. If I have to fight I will, although it'll hardly come to that. The War Office says it will be over by Christmas.'

'Then Christmas can't come soon enough,' Lacey replied fervently.

★ ★ ★

Jonas sat facing Constance in the library at Fenay Hall, an exasperated expression reddening his features. 'For God's sake, woman, the lad's going to war. Let him leave on a happy note. I don't understand why you're making such an infernal fuss over the girl. She's his choice and not a bad one at that.'

Constance retaliated. 'How like you to hold such an opinion; you've mixed with mill hands for so long you even think like them.'

Felicity entered the room, glancing disdainfully from one parent to the other. 'You're not still arguing over Nathan and Lacey, are you?' She went and stood in front of Constance, towering over her like a strict governess would a naughty child. 'Mother, he loves her, and Father and I are fond of her. She makes Nathan happy; be happy for him. Particularly now when he's going away to fight in this awful war.'

Constance fiddled with the string of pearls round her neck. She heaved a sigh. 'Very well, if and when he brings her here again I will be on my very best behaviour — but only for Nathan's sake.'

Jonas chuckled. 'I'll hold you to that.'

'Hold who to what?' Nathan asked as he entered the library.

Instantly, Jonas fabricated a lie. 'Your mother, she's promised to attend the next Woollen Manufacturer's Conference with me.' In the circumstances he did not want Nathan to know Constance had been badgered into accepting Lacey.

Nathan raised his eyebrows at Constance. 'You surprise me. You've never gone before. What changed your mind?'

Constance smiled sweetly. 'There are times, Nathan, when I think perhaps I am too staid. I'm trying to be a little more adventurous in my outlook.'

Jonas glanced at Felicity, his eyes twinkling triumphantly. 'Will we be seeing owt of Lacey before you leave us, lad?'

Nathan frowned in Constance's direction. 'That all depends on Mother. I intend to spend most of my time with Lacey in the next few days but I won't bring her here to be humiliated.'

Constance flushed. 'Oh, darling, that was a misunderstanding on my part. I've regretted it ever since. Bring Lacey to see me again and I promise I'll make her more than welcome.'

* * *

'So, he's joined up, has he?' Joshua met Lacey's news with his usual equanimity.

'I suppose he'll go in as an officer; his sort usually do,' commented Matt, a hint of derision in his voice.

'Exactly what do you mean by that?' asked Lacey.

Matt shrugged carelessly. 'Nowt, except he more than likely won't be in as much danger as them poor buggers who are just cannon fodder for t'Germans.'

'But he'll be there, fighting for king and country, which is more than you'll be doing,' Lacey retorted.

'Farmers are exempt,' growled Matt, 'an' I wa' only sayin' what's obvious. I'm not makin' out

166

he's a coward.'

Lacey's eyes moistened. Secretly, she had accused Nathan of being just that whenever she felt he had let her down, but she wouldn't allow Matt to do the same.

'Now, now,' Edith intervened, 'it's a bad do all round and we don't want to be falling out over it. There's enough trouble in t'world without making more.' She poured water from the kettle into the teapot. 'I just hope it's all over afore our Jimmy's old enough to be called up.' She lifted the teapot and poured. 'There, drink your tea, and no more sad talk. We should be proud our Lacey has such a courageous young man.'

Edith picked up her mug and sipped thoughtfully. Perhaps when Nathan was away, Lacey would give up this notion she had of him — and he of her.

It would save an awful lot of bother.

* * *

On Monday evening Lacey didn't attend the Union meeting; there would be plenty of time for that when Nathan was away. Instead, although she had vowed never to return, Nathan opened the door at Fenay Hall and Lacey stepped inside, a determined smile hiding her inner misgivings.

'Are you ready for this?' he asked, his own smile wavering at the thought of what he was about to do.

'You don't need me to bolster your confidence. You proved what a man you are when you battered Syd Sugden in the mill yard. This'll be easy

167

by comparison. At least you won't have to use your fists.'

Nathan laughed shakily. 'I would hope not.' He ushered Lacey into the drawing room. Constance looked up from the magazine she was reading, a warm smile lighting her face when she saw them.

'Ah, there you are, darling, and you brought Lacey with you; how delightful.' Lacey was dumbstruck. Although Nathan had assured her his mother no longer objected to their relationship, the effusive welcome surprised her.

Constance patted the chair next to hers. 'Come Lacey, sit here and give me your opinion on this.' She flourished the magazine in her hand. Lacey sat, focussing her attention on a fashion photograph of a suit with a three-quarter length coat.

'It's very elegant,' Lacey said and, casting aside any apprehension, added, 'it would become you perfectly, Mrs Brearley.' Lacey ran her index finger round the outline of the coat. 'See how it flares out at the bottom. With your height you'd carry off that style very well.'

Constance pouted prettily.

Lacey's thoughtful expression broke into an enthusiastic smile. 'It would hang beautifully if you had it made up in a length of fine worsted like the sort I was working on last week. If I was you I'd go for the blue, it would bring out your colouring . . . ' Realising she had been overly familiar, Lacey mumbled. 'We wove it in lovat and tan as well.' She cast a sidelong glance at Constance, nervous of her reaction.

Constance was beaming. 'How clever you are, Lacey; I should have known I could rely on your advice. After all, the dress you made for Felicity was splendid; everyone admired it. By the way, Felicity's longing to see you again; she'll be down shortly.' She glanced at the ornate grandfather clock and sniffed. 'She's never late for dinner.'

Nathan chuckled, his relieved expression patently obvious. He spoke for the first time since he and Lacey had entered the drawing room. 'Lacey is taking a few days off work and she and I are going to Fountain's Abbey tomorrow, Mother. Lacey has yet to see it and I'm sure she'll be impressed.'

Constance smiled endearingly at him. 'What a splendid idea, and afterwards you must take her to one of those splendid little teashops in Harrogate.' This being news to Lacey she glanced from one smiling face to the other, pleasantly surprised but somewhat bemused by such a change in Constance's attitude. The last time they had met, Constance had called her 'common' and 'unladylike'. She had even accused her of being a fortune-hunter. Now she was urging Nathan to take her on a splendid day out.

Felicity bounced into the room. 'Lacey! How lovely to see you. I hear Nathan has plans for you,' she cried, holding her arms wide.

'A full itinerary for the next few days.' he said.

'Super,' chortled Felicity.

* * *

'I did as you asked,' said Constance, dinner over and Nathan taking Lacey back to Netherfold. 'I made the girl welcome and to my surprise I found

169

her quite charming. Of course, once Nathan's in the army he'll forget all about her.'

'Mother!' Felicity threw up her hands in exasperation.

★ ★ ★

A further three visits to Fenay Hall met with a similar welcome from Constance, Lacey was pleased for Nathan's sake. However, she sensed an undercurrent of subterfuge in his mother's unctuous manner, as though Constance was playing a part; and Lacey knew exactly what that role was.

She's still living in hope that once Nathan and I are apart he'll forget all about me, she told herself, as Constance fussily conjectured how different things would be after Nathan's departure.

'They say absence makes the heart grow fonder, but I find it usually means one forgets quite easily,' she commented airily, as they sat down to tea.

This, and several other pointed remarks were not lost on Lacey. However, Nathan, Felicity and Jonas appeared oblivious to Constance's subtle jibes.

You might have them fooled, thought Lacey, but I know your game; you might admire my dressmaking skills but you still don't want me for a daughter-in-law.

'Don't be afraid to visit mother as often as you like,' Nathan urged after the final visit, 'keep up the ties you've formed.'

Lacey set aside her misgivings and promised she would.

The chauffeur driven car purred through the valley on its way to Huddersfield, Nathan pensively gazing out at the familiar landscape, Lacey sitting silently between him and Constance. Felicity sat opposite on the rumble seat and Jonas was up front with the chauffeur.

When he brought the car to a halt in St George's Square his passengers alighted, Lacey gazing up at the tall Georgian columns and Classic pediment that fronted Huddersfield Railway Station. One of the finest pieces of architecture in the north of England, it loomed ominously in front of her. This was where Nathan would say his goodbyes.

Inside, the station platform bustled with troops arriving and departing.

Mothers and fathers, wives and children and sweethearts clustered round their men, smiles of welcome and relief on some faces, others stoically but sadly preparing to say farewell.

Lacey silently observed the soldiers crowding the platform, categorising them by the expressions on their faces: bright eyed young men who had yet to do their training waited noisily, eager for the opportunity to serve king and country. The empty eyed, weary men home on leave, their faces lined and grey, had already witnessed death and destruction.

The train pulled into the station, steam and smoke billowing onto the platform. Through the windows of the carriages already filled with troops from towns and cities further down the line, Lacey could see the faces of men who had already said

171

their goodbyes. Doors flew open, the bright eyed young men on the platform surging forward, keen to be on their way.

Lacey felt the tension in Nathan's lean frame; he too was experiencing the excitement of the call to arms. But when he lowered his gaze to meet hers, his zeal faded. He held her close, his eyes memorising every detail.

Lacey held his gaze, seeing in his eyes a love so deep she felt as though she was drowning. 'I love you, Nathan Brearley. I always will. Come back soon.'

Nathan shook Jonas's hand then hugged his mother and Felicity.

Constance dabbed her eyes with a lace handkerchief. 'Take great care, darling,' she urged. Jonas echoing the sentiment, Constance was shocked when Felicity slapped Nathan's shoulder, saying. 'Give 'em hell, brother.'

A whistle blew, Nathan leaping aboard the train as it pulled slowly away from the platform. Lacey watched until it disappeared from view.

16

Lacey waited on the corner of Towngate for the women who had promised to meet her there, her moral fibre wilting as the hands on the church clock ticked relentlessly towards seven thirty. She glanced up and down the street but none of those who had shown interest in attending the Union meeting were in sight. Even Joan had let her down.

Disappointed, Lacey entered the room at the rear of the Bull's Head public house where the members of the Weavers' Association held their Union meetings. Heads turned as she stepped inside.

Twenty or so men sat on benches facing a long trestle table behind which sat four others, papers set out in front of them. Ascertaining these were the Union officials, Lacey walked towards them, ignoring the banter aimed at her from the body of the room.

'Atta lookin' for your old man, luv?'

'Oy, if you're lookin' for custom you need to go round to t'public bar.'

Whilst his allusion to her being a prostitute irked Lacey, she was even more annoyed to find herself flushing at the remark. 'I've come to join the Union,' she said to the men behind the long table. Much to her satisfaction her voice rang out clear and unwavering.

A sudden hush in the room was just as abruptly broken. 'This is no place for a woman. Bugger off home an' mind your bairns.'

Lacey turned to address the heckler. 'I don't have any, but if I did I wouldn't want you to be the father of 'em.'

The men laughed at the sharp response, one shouting, 'Hey up, we've got a right one here.'

Lacey's eyes roved her audience. 'You have, and talking of rights, mine are just as important as yours. Like all of you I'm a weaver who wants the same improvements in wages and conditions. The more members you have the stronger you become, even if some of those members are women.'

'Order, order,' called one of the men behind the table, a man whom Lacey knew to be Harry Clegg. The noise abated. 'Now lass, what can we do for you?' His tone kindly, Lacey suspected he was merely appeasing her before refusing her request.

'Like I said, I want to join the Union. You all know me, or at least you've seen me at work in Brearley's Mill. Some of you I work alongside, so you know what I do. I'm willing to pay me subscription an' abide by Union rules, so I don't see how you can refuse.'

Somewhat surprised by the directness of her answer, Harry Clegg looked from one to another of his colleagues, scratching his head as he awaited their intervention. None forthcoming he proceeded to deal with Lacey's request unaided.

'You're right in what you say, lass. If you pay your dues and abide by the rules we've no reason to refuse you membership but . . . ' He scratched his head again, searching for words before adding, 'we're not used to women at meetings. T'language

174

can be a bit rough sometimes, lass.'

Lacey widened her eyes. 'Mr Clegg, I've worked in t'mill for years. Don't you think I'm used to a bit o' cursing and swearing by now.' Her reply raised a ripple of laughter. Lacey relaxed.

Harry hid a smile. The girl's forthright manner was refreshing and he was enjoying the unsettling effect it was having on the other members. 'Give us your details, lass, an' sign there.' He pushed a sheet of paper across the table. Lacey signed with a flourish.

★ ★ ★

The hot summer days faded into glowing autumn, the moors around Garsthwaite burnished with browning bracken and the ugliness of the town itself muted by early morning or evening mists. However, the townspeople's attentions were elsewhere. As the war in Europe escalated it seemed to Lacey that everywhere she went people were discussing the implications of Britain being dragged into a war not of their making.

'What's it got to do with us?' Joan wanted to know.

'A hell of a lot,' replied Lacey. 'Rumour has it we'll be on short-time afore long.'

'But why?' groaned Flo Backhouse.

Lacey had the answer. 'Because there's a slump in the demand for worsted cloth; trade all over Europe's being affected because countries are concentrating on killing each other rather than buying the stuff we make for export.'

'How come you know so much?' Flo asked.

175

'Union meetings,' replied Lacey, 'you should come along.'

★ ★ ★

Within days rumour became reality when mill workers throughout the valley were reduced to working a three day week. The sudden drop in income caused hardship to many, particularly Joan who still lived with her mother-in-law, the dreadful Hettie Micklethwaite.

'Now we'll never save enough money to get a place of our own,' Joan grumbled. 'What with this baby coming we'll be stuck forever, but there's nowt we can do about it.'

They were sitting in Lacey's bedroom, Lacey at her sewing machine and Joan sewing buttons on a dress for Lily Hopkinson, landlady at The Bull's Head pub.

'Listen Joanie, I've been thinking,' said Lacey, easing her foot off the treadle. 'I'm still earning because I've a suit to finish for Mrs Brearley. Then Felicity an' her friends, Miss Murgatroyd and Miss Earnshaw, all want dresses an' I've more orders for alterations than I can cope with. If you help me run a little business on the side when we're not at the Mill we can both make money.'

'But how can I help?' wailed Joan. 'I can't treadle or cut out.'

'No, but you're good at hand sewing,' Lacey told her. 'I'll do all the cutting out and making up, you'll do the finishing touches; the fiddly, time consuming jobs.'

Joan's face lit up. 'I could, Lacey; oh yes, I

could.'

Cheered by the prospect of increasing her earnings, Joan sewed the last button on Lily Hopkinson's dress, the awfulness of living with Hettie Micklethwaite diminished. In return for Lacey's ingenuity, Joan volunteered to attend Union meetings.

★ ★ ★

'There, that's finished. What shall I do now?' Joan snipped at the thread she had used to sew buttons on a coat Lacey had altered for the Baptist Minister's wife, Mrs Pendlebury.

Lacey looked up from the fabric she was cutting, using one of the new paper patterns now on sale in the haberdashers in Huddersfield. 'Start on those,' she said.

It was the sixth week of working short-time in the Mill. Joan began to tack pieces of flimsy white muslin; two First Communion dresses for Lizzie Isherwood's granddaughters.

Lacey set aside her scissors. 'We could end up with more money in our purses than we earn in the Mill once we've finished this lot,' she said, gesturing at the garments cluttering the bedroom. She pointed to the now altered, outmoded heavy brown coat belonging to the Baptist Minister's wife. 'If I've managed to make that fashionable enough to satisfy Mrs Pendlebury, we might get more orders from the upper crust in Garsthwaite.

We can charge them a bit more than we do the lasses from the mill.'

Lacey picked up the scissors and resumed work.

177

Alleviating her cousin's financial distress pleased Lacey, but more importantly her little business had planted the seed of ambition.

★ ★ ★

On Monday evening Lacey and Joan hurried along Towngate, Lacey clutching a parcel containing Lily Hopkinson's dress. They were going to the Union meeting in The Bull's Head. 'Will you raise the matter of the lavatories, Lacey?' Joan's eager tone had Lacey smiling at her new recruit.

'I will if I can get them to stop talking about substitution and dilution for two minutes.' Noting Joan's blank expression Lacey elaborated.

'Substitution means a man is being replaced by a woman who can do the job just as well as him, therefore she should be paid the same rate. Dilution means replacing men with women who don't have experience, so they'll be paid at a lower rate. Seeing as how we've always been paid less for doing the same jobs as men, I can't rightly understand the argument. I know I work as hard as any o' them fellows in our shed, an' so do you, Joan, yet we're paid nearly four bob less for every piece.'

'We should bring that up at the meeting as well,' Joan said, 'equal pay for equal work.'

Lacey laughed outright. 'Listen to you. You haven't attended a meeting yet and you're talking like a lifelong member. We might mention it, but we've to go easy; we don't want to get their backs up.'

In the room at the rear of The Bull's Head, Lacey and Joan sat with Lizzie, Maggie and

Sarah, Lacey gratified by the increased female contingency. She'd delivered the finished dress to a delighted Lily Hopkinson and, receiving a shilling more than she'd asked for, Lacey felt ready for action.

The meeting was called to order and the new recruits sworn in. Then there followed a heated discussion on substitution and dilution, the men arguing that if they enlisted in the army and were replaced by women in their absence, was there any guarantee they would get their jobs back once the war ended.

'It'll all be over by Christmas, so they say,' argued one man, 'an'

Christmas is only weeks away so I don't know why we're bothering talking about it.'

'I know where you're coming from,' said Lacey, sympathetic to their argument, 'but women should be paid at the proper rate while they're doing the job. I'm sure they'll be only too glad to return to being housewives once their men return.'

The debate fizzled out, Lacey taking the opportunity to speak again.

'It might seem trivial at times like this, but there is only one closet for all the women at Brearley's, an' that not fit for use.'

'That's right,' Joan interjected, 'sometimes at breakfast an' dinnertime t'queues that long we don't get chance to go before t'hooter blows us back to work.' Thrilled at contributing to an issue she understood, Joan added,

'An' it doesn't even have a lock on the door.' She sat back, eagerly awaiting a response.

'Did you come here to waste our time talkin'

about women's shit holes,' one of the men scoffed, 'cos if you did you can bugger off.'

Joan flushed; squirming in her seat she turned beseeching eyes on Lacey. Lacey stood up, requesting permission to speak. Permission granted she turned to face the aggressor.

'I know it might not seem important to you but it is to us women. If the Unions can persuade employers to improve working conditions in any way, no matter how small, then they're doing their job. Every improvement is an achievement — even lavatories. If we can force Jonas Brearley to install decent facilities it shows the workforce we have their interests at heart.

Therefore I propose the Union should approach Mr Brearley an' ask him to deal with the matter.' She glanced down at Joan. 'An' I thank Sister Micklethwaite for her contribution.' Joan flushed again, this time with pride.

'She's right tha knows,' said an old codger at the back of the room.

'Make bosses give us a bit o' respect, no matter that we're on'y asking for shit holes.'

The motion was carried and the meeting ended. The girls departed, their steps buoyed with the sense of having made small but worthwhile progress.

The following day news of their minor triumph flew round the sheds, women weavers and spinners congratulating Lacey and Joan for raising the issue of the lavatories. The next meeting of the Weavers' Association boasted six more new female recruits and Lacey was triumphant.

'This war's getting worse,' complained Edith, setting aside the Huddersfield Examiner. She read it from end to end every evening, commenting on the news as she went. 'Here's me thinking it 'ud all be over in no time, an' now they're saying,' she picked up the paper and quoted.

'Conflict in Europe intensified.'

Lacey snipped at the thread she was using to sew buttons on a coat she was altering for the coalman's wife, then pinned the needle to the front of her cardigan. 'There's no sign of it coming to an end. You can see that everywhere you look. Nearly all the young lads in the Mill have answered Kitchener's call, an' most of 'em have no idea what they're letting themselves in for, poor sods.' She shook her head despondently. 'An' now they've ordered women to take over their jobs there's hardly a fellow under fifty in the spinning and weaving sheds. She gave a wry laugh. 'It's the same in all the mills in the valley; it must be the first time in history that women have been recognised for their true worth.'

'Not that there's that much for 'em to do, what wi' you being on short-time,' said Edith, going to the sink to fill the kettle.

Lacey grimaced. 'Aye, I'm lucky I've got me sewing; even though most of it's just alterations. It's only the nobs can afford to buy new material these days.'

'Well,' said Edith slowly, as she placed the kettle on the stove, 'if you keep in with the Brearleys maybe they'll send more custom your way.'

Lacey chuckled. 'You make it sound as though I'm only marrying Nathan to make a few extra bob out of his wealthy friends.'

Edith measured tealeaves into the pot and poured in boiling water, a thoughtful expression creasing her face and her tone speculative as she said.

'You'll not need to work at all once you're wed.'

'That's where you're wrong, Mam,' Lacey retaliated, 'I won't be a kept woman. I've made it clear to Nathan that I'll make my own way in the world. There are things I want to do, and if I don't I'll not be the person I aim to be.'

Edith shrugged. 'Suit yourself, you usually do. Most women would give their eyeteeth not to have to work.' She filled two mugs, setting one down in front of Lacey.

Lifting it in celebratory fashion, Lacey retorted, 'Ah, but I'm not most women, am I?'

* * *

The following week, having made a visit to Fenay Hall, Lacey arrived home in a jubilant mood. 'Guess what Jonas told me,' she chortled, as soon as she entered the kitchen. 'Brearley's have won a contract to make cloth for uniforms for t'British Army. We'll be back working full time, weaving khaki and serge by the mile.'

She took off her coat and flopped into a chair by the fire. 'Thank God for that! Short-time's a curse. Some of the lasses have been really hard up this last while back, but this'll give 'em a chance to earn some decent brass.'

Edith placed a plate of bread and butter on the table to eat along with coddled eggs. 'I don't know how you'll manage when you do go back, you've been that busy dressmaking.' She tutted irritably, then said, 'You take too much on, Lacey.'

Lacey sniggered. 'You weren't saying that the other day when Constance Brearley called to collect her suit.' It had amused Lacey to see how thrilled Edith was by Constance's visit, and how she had been even more flattered when Constance, accepting a cup of tea, had complemented her on her boiled cake.

Edith allowed herself a sheepish smile. 'Aye, I'll admit I was pleased to see her, for it settled my mind.' She did not openly acknowledge that up until then she had doubted the veracity of Nathan's feelings for Lacey, and with him in mind she asked, 'How did Nathan seem in that letter you got this morning?'

'He sounds cheerful enough. The training camp's not as grim as he thought it might be and he says he gets on with the men. He's asked me to knit him some thick socks but I think I'll leave that to you.'

Edith grinned. 'Aye, you might well. You never were a good hand at turning a heel. He'd be marching cockeyed if it depended on you.'

★   ★   ★

The following evening, Felicity called at Netherfold, her voice rising above the monotonous clack of the treadle as she and Lacey chatted. These visits, along with the occasional ones Lacey made

183

to Fenay Hall brought Nathan closer, and in her letters to him she wrote of 'building bridges' for their future happiness. She made no mention of her suspicions regarding Constance's duplicity, for whilst Constance accepted Lacey as a worthy dressmaker, Lacey sensed her reluctance to accept her as a prospective daughter-in-law.

17

After his brush with the law, Jimmy Barraclough hadn't returned to work in the Mill. He'd stayed at home, helping Joshua and Matt with the sheep on the moor or planting root crops in the fields. Joshua, presuming his younger son had come to his senses, was overjoyed to see him showing an interest in farming. Matt, being more wary, kept a close eye on his little brother whereas Edith and Lacey, saddened that Jimmy had learned his lesson the hard way, cosseted him with that special affection reserved only for the baby of the family.

The surly exterior he had adopted while under Arty Bincliffe's influence reverted to its former cheery cheekiness, Jimmy seemingly content to spend his days at Netherfold and his evenings in the company of his mates; nowadays nice lads he'd gone to school with. Therefore every member of his family was shocked to the core when, on his one day off in the week, he arrived back from Huddersfield an enlisted man.

'Oh, Jimmy, you haven't,' cried Edith, images of trench warfare springing to mind.

Edith, the avid newspaper reader, knew all about the horrors facing the soldiers in France and Belgium: Mons, Liege and Ardennes, place names she had never before heard of, were now as familiar as Huddersfield, Leeds and Bradford, as were tales of poison gas and zeppelins.

'Stay here, lad,' she begged, clutching him to

her breast. 'I couldn't bear it if owt happened to you.'

Jimmy pulled away, embarrassed. 'I'll be all right, Mam. It's me duty; a chance to put right the things I've done wrong.' He flushed at the memory of the robbery, then added jauntily, 'I'll be off as soon as me papers come through.'

When Lacey heard the news, she smiled sadly at his boyish eagerness. Still the same old Jimmy, willing to dive into whatever was on offer with no thought for the consequences. She thought of the young lads from Garsthwaite, some she had worked with, who had already lost their lives.

She hugged him tightly. 'You've nothing to prove, Jimmy. You didn't do anything wrong; you did it for me.'

Joshua was devastated and Matt incredulous so they blustered at the foolhardiness of his decision. 'You don't have to go; farmers are exempt.'

Jimmy smiled kindly at his father. 'I'm not a farmer, Dad, never was, never will be. I want to fight for what's right. Tommy Smith an' Jimmy Ollerenshaw are going an' all, so I'll not be on me own.'

After a subdued evening meal Jimmy went out to see his mates, leaving his family to mull over the shocking news. Joshua, Edith and Lacey feared for him, Matt however, was impressed and bemused. 'Our Jimmy a soldier.'

He grinned. 'He'll be like a terrier pup wi' a rabbit. He'll worry t'Germans to death. For two pins I'd go meself but somebody as to feed the nation. You can't fight on an empty belly.'

A chill wind nipped Lacey's cheeks as, deep in thought she walked down the lane from Nether-fold, her warm breath clouding with every step. It was two weeks to Christmas, the rutted mud under her feet hardened to an icy crisp, the last red berries on frost rimed hawthorns cheerful against the ghostly white.

Christmas wouldn't be the same this year with neither Nathan nor Jimmy to celebrate the fes-tive season with her. It was more than two months since she'd last seen Nathan, and whilst his let-ters were full of loving thoughts for her and his humorous accounts of life in Catterick Camp kept her amused, she didn't envisage a happy Christ-mas. Furthermore, although she had raised the matter at the last three Union meetings, nothing had been done about the women's lavatories at the Mill.

By the time she reached the Mill gates Lacey had somewhat consoled herself with the thought that at least Nathan was still in England and not in France, and Catterick was less than a hundred miles away. Feeling thankful for small mercies Lacey trotted into the Mill yard, curiosity aroused when she saw a team of builders unloading their tools. 'What's to do?' she asked a young lad hump-ing a bag of cement.

'We're building three new water closets over there,' he said, pointing to a gap between the weaving and spinning sheds. He heaved the bag back to his shoulder and strolled away.

At that moment, Jonas Brearley stepped out of

the Mill office and strutted over to where Lacey, barely able to contain her excitement, stood.

'I gather you're behind this,' Jonas barked, gesturing towards the builders.

Although he admired Lacey's forthrightness and had no strong objections to his son's relationship with her, he still had certain reservations. She was an employee and even though she had been made welcome in his home, Jonas was at a loss dealing with her at the Mill. Furthermore, the heavy dinner he had consumed at the Rotary Club the night before had left him with heartburn.

'That's right, sir. It was me suggested the Union approach you with the idea of getting better lavatories for the women.'

Jonas's eyes bulged in their sockets as he swallowed the acid bile burning his gullet. 'Are you taking advantage of me because of my son?'

Undeterred, Lacey met his grim expression directly. 'No, sir; it has nothing to do with that. I promised the women I'd see they got better facilities an' I don't like going back on me word.'

'Your word! Who the bloody hell do you think you are?' Jonas looked fit to burst.

'You know who I am, Mr Brearley.'

Jonas, his bluster evaporated, gestured again at the builders, 'Well, as you can see, you've got your way. Now get to work.'

Lacey bobbed her head deferentially and said, 'Thank you, Mr Brearley, sir. I'm most grateful.'

Heart singing like a bird, Lacey dashed into the weaving shed. She had taken the bull by the horns and had won a small victory. For the rest of the day the women who had joined the Union

188

congratulated Lacey and themselves on the new lavatories under construction.

The clocking off hooter had barely ceased its long, mournful blast when Lacey, muffled in her coat and scarf, stepped out into the Mill yard ready for the long walk home. The sky was dark, a few stars gleaming brightly in the blackness. Leaving Joan to wait for Stanley at the dye house door she walked through the Mill gate. A tall figure caught her by the arm. 'Good evening, madam: first lieutenant Nathan Brearley at your service, desiring to walk you home.'

Lacey flung herself into Nathan's arms.

'When did you get back?'

'About an hour ago; I've wangled four day's leave before they send me elsewhere.'

Lacey shuddered at the thought of elsewhere but, unwilling to spoil the sheer bliss of having Nathan home for a few days, she put it to the back of her mind.

* * *

On the day before Nathan was due to return to barracks, Constance hosted a small party. Overjoyed to have her son at home, she wanted to celebrate.

Against her will she had invited Lacey, a girl she still merely tolerated. For whilst she admired her talents with a needle and thread and found her interesting and amusing, she was as opposed to her becoming Nathan's wife as ever.

Nathan was overjoyed to learn Constance had included Lacey in her guest list without him having to request it. Constance was curious to see if, in his absence, Nathan's desire for Lacey had waned and, in the company of girls like Violet Burrows and Sylvia Oldroyd — girls of his own class — he would find her wanting. Secretly she hoped he would.

* * *

The party was in full swing, Nathan waltzing with his mother when Alice Burrows and her daughter, Violet, cornered Lacey.

'Is the poor little mill girl enjoying herself?' tweeted Violet. Her eyes gleamed malevolently and spittle flecked her prominent teeth. 'It must be quite exciting for you to be in such elevated company. No doubt it's a change from the dirty, greasy mill hands you're used to dallying with.'

Lacey's clenched fist was itching to deliver a sharp punch to those offensive teeth, and she clenched it even tighter when Alice said, 'Your audacity shocks me. You're nothing but a jumped up, money grabbing little whore.'

Desperate to prevent a scene, Lacey swallowed the crude retort that threatened to burst forth and through gritted teeth said, 'It's your ignorance that shocks me. How dare you approach me in this manner? I don't want to ruin Nathan's party so I'll excuse your petty opinions and leave you to stew in your own malicious juices.'

Lacey began to walk away but Alice caught her arm. 'You think you've finally snared him, don't you? Well, you're sadly mistaken. I'll do anything to prevent you getting Nathan.'

'Getting Nathan what?' Nathan appeared unexpectedly at Lacey's side, placing his arm around her waist.

Alice blanched and, letting go of Lacey's arm, smoothly replied, 'A suitable Christmas gift for you, darling.' She smiled sweetly. 'Lacey was seeking our advice, seeing as how we are better acquainted with your likes and dislikes. After all, Violet has known you since you were both children and has always had your best interests at heart.'

Nathan grinned. 'Lacey's the only gift I want.' He caught hold of her hand. 'Come on, let's dance.'

Lacey twirled and swayed, a fixed smile on her face; another time and place and she'd have dealt with Alice and Violet with her tongue and fists.

Being a lady didn't come easy.

★ ★ ★

Two days after Nathan had returned to his unit, Lacey chanced to be in the mill yard when Jonas stepped out of his office. Seeing her, he crooked a beckoning finger.

Her thoughts whirling, Lacey tidied her hair and straightened her overall as she walked towards him. Had he heard about her altercation with Alice and Violet Burrows? Had they complained to Constance? Was he about to remind her of her lowly position? Well, so what! Defiantly, she threw back her shoulders and faced him.

Jonas rested his hands on the rail of the office steps, his corpulent belly butting the edge of it and his waistcoat, fashioned from his own finest worsted, almost bursting at the buttons as he glowered down at her. 'Well, lass, you got your way with the women's closets, now let that be an end to it.'

All thought of her earlier misgivings fleeing her mind, Lacey took a deep breath and said, 'It doesn't have to be. There's more to be done, so begging your pardon, I'll put it to you now.'

Jonas's eyes bulged, but curious to hear what she had to say, he barked, 'Well, make it quick; time's money.'

'Aye, it is,' agreed Lacey, 'and now we've got more than one closet, you'll feel the benefit. When we had only one there wasn't enough time for us all to use it at break times. That meant we had to stop our looms and go during working hours; everybody was losing out. Us because we're neglecting our pieces and you because the more pieces we finish, the quicker you can sell 'em to the British Army.'

Jonas, impressed by the flurry of words and their reasoning, acknowledged them begrudgingly. 'You make sense lass — but then you usually do — so I've noticed.'

Heartened by his response, Lacey decided to elaborate. 'It's like this, sir.

The more you do for your workers the more they'll do for you. Better facilities make working hours pleasanter and we work twice as quick and twice as hard. You see, weaving wi' a full bladder makes the lasses distracted and then they get careless, just like not having warm drinks on cold days leaves their bellies feeling cheated.'

Lacey paused for breath, Jonas opened his mouth to speak, but Lacey charged on. 'If we had a ready supply of hot water to make warm drinks to go with our sandwiches we'd feel better for it, particularly in this cold weather. Like the army, Mr Brearley, we fight better on a full stomach,' she concluded, rephrasing what she had read in the newspaper to suit her own ends.

Jonas chuckled. 'By, but you've a brass neck on you, lass, I'll give you that.'

'I'll take that as a compliment, sir,' Lacey said, hoping she hadn't overplayed her hand.

Jonas slapped his hand on the rail. 'Leave it with me, lass. Now bugger off back to t'weaving shed.'

Jonas watched Lacey go, his eyes alight with admiration. She was, he thought, a rougher version of his daughter, Felicity: feisty and full of ideals.

He strolled towards his waiting car, replaying the exchange. Lacey Barraclough might not be a lady, but by gum she knew the way a mill worked; a lass like that would make Nathan a splendid wife. Once they were wed she'd be happy to work alongside him, not as a weaver, of course, more in an advisory capacity.

On his homeward journey to Fenay Hall, Jonas was in reflective mood.

Perhaps too much soft living had made him neglectful of his duties to his fellow man — or woman. He chuckled heartily as he recalled Lacey's description of women's needs, his chauffeur wondering what had him so amused.

18

Standing on the platform of Huddersfield Railway Station saying goodbye to someone I love now seems to be part of my life, thought Lacey, as she waited for Edith to release her hold on her youngest son. Last week it was Nathan and today it's our Jimmy.

'Be careful and come back unharmed,' said Lacey, hugging him close. 'Write when you can. You know you'll always be in our thoughts.'

Joshua shook Jimmy by the hand. 'I'm proud of you, lad. Think on now, take care.' Matt slapped him on the back then grabbed him in a brotherly hug. The train snaked its way into the station, Jimmy lifting his bag with one hand and wiping his eyes with the other. Smiling bravely, he dived into a carriage and was lost in the melee of bodies already aboard. Slamming doors, clouds of steam and a whistle's blast and the train pulled away, the families of the departed soldiers shuffling miserably towards the station's exit, Joshua, Edith and Matt amongst them. Lacey hung back, her eyes riveted on a poster of Lord Kitchener urging men to do their duty. Staring into the Secretary of War's piercing blue eyes she prayed he would take care of Nathan and little Jimmy.

★ ★ ★

Christmas came and went without Lacey sharing any of the joys of the previous year, but she was not downhearted. Her persistence in the Union was paying off. She had achieved something worthwhile, her faith in human nature restored, her only sadness Nathan and Jimmy's absence.

On the first working day of the New Year, 1915, Lacey knocked on Jonas Brearley's office door. 'I came to say a proper thank you for listening to me and for providing the new lavatories and the hot water, sir. All the women are grateful.'

Jonas accepted the thanks with a flicker of a smile and a curt nod. As Lacey turned to go, he said, 'By the way lass, I hope you're taking time to write to that lad o' mine. You'll not forget him while he's away, will you?'

'There's no danger of that, sir. Wherever he is, he's in my thoughts and prayers, and always will be.'

★ ★ ★

Nathan's transfer to a camp in Staffordshire and Jimmy's to Newcastle seemed to Lacey as though the war was taking them further away from home bit by bit. To make matters worse sleet lashed the Colne Valley for days on end followed by blizzards of snow and the landscape was shrouded in a blanket of icy white. Slithering and sliding along the road morning and evening, Lacey journeyed to and from the Mill, cursing the weather, the war and her humdrum existence.

On a bitterly cold Monday morning in February she hurried towards the Mill gate, her thoughts on

195

the Union meeting she would attend that night.

Thank God I joined, she told herself as she entered the Mill yard, otherwise my life would be totally devoid of excitement: at least I'm assured of a bloody good row if nothing else.

She thoroughly enjoyed the cut and thrust of debate and rarely missed the opportunity to voice her opinions. However, just lately she felt somewhat constrained, the male members sidelining the issues she raised in favour of constantly discussing substitution and dilution.

We're stuck in a rut, she told herself as she trod precariously over the icy cobbles towards the weaving shed. We asked for lavatories and hot water and got them; now we need to make further demands instead of sitting back on our laurels.

Inside the shed, wearing a thick woollen cardigan over her overall to combat the chilly draughts, Lacey watched the shuttles roving her looms.

Every now and then she rubbed her cold hands together to keep her fingers nimble, and as the cloth beams thickened she pondered on how to improve the working day? The obvious answer was better pay, but the Unions had been wrangling over that for years. Besides, she thought, it's too big an issue to resolve quickly. Our next demand should be one that's easily met to keep the pot boiling.

She glanced over at the large wall clock, its huge hands indicating half an hour and more until breakfast time at eight. Her tummy rumbled noisily as she thought of the drip sandwiches and scalding mug of tea waiting for her.

Jonas had installed a huge hot water urn, and

as she mulled over that small but vital triumph Lacey knew exactly the issue she would raise at tonight's Union meeting. Her eyes bright with excitement she turned to her left, ready to share the idea with Joan.

Joan, her distended belly obstructing her movements, was reaching into her loom, her face creasing with pain as she bent forward to catch a loose end. As she came upright, a gush of wetness trickled down her thighs.

Panicked, Joan stopped her looms.

Lacey saw her distress.

'Me waters have broken,' Joan mouthed above the din.

Lacey dashed to find Lizzie Isherwood, then Clem Arkwright, the new overlooker. 'Joan's baby's on t'way,' she mouthed, 'I'm taking her home.'

'Right you be, lass. Get back when you can.' A welcome change from Sydney Sugden, Clem treated all the women in the shed with respect and dignity.

'I'll go an' all,' Lizzie said. 'I'll see 'em to t'door an' be straight back.'

Joan in the middle, the three women slipped and skidded along the icy pavements to the house in Scar End. Hettie Micklethwaite opened the door, her sour face expressing no concern for her daughter-in-law when she learned why they had come.

'They sleep in t'back bedroom.' Hettie pointed to the narrow flight of stairs leading up from the lobby. 'Do you want me to boil t'kettle?'

'Fetch Ivy Vickerman,' cried Lacey, hoisting

197

Joan on to the first step of the stairs. 'An' tell her to get a shift on.'

Hettie sniffed. 'I'll go as quick as I can. It's bad underfoot, you know.'

She glanced scathingly at Joan's back. 'I'm not fit to be running about after her.' She unhooked her coat from behind the door, plodding out to fetch the midwife.

'How far on is she?' Ivy panted, as she entered the bedroom.

'I'm not sure.' Having only attended the birthing of lambs at Netherfold, Lacey had no idea how urgent Joan's case might be. She only knew her best friend and cousin was in distress and needed professional help.

A swift examination and Ivy turned to Lacey. 'She's fully dilated, it'll be a quick 'un, will this.'

Downstairs, Hettie Micklethwaite sulked in a chair by the fire, complaining when Lacey entered the room to fetch the kettle.

'I'm not well,' Hettie moaned, 'I can't do wi' all this carry on, yon lass of our Stanley's has no consideration for my nerves; a proper torture she's been ever since she set foot under me roof. Has me running day an' night, so she does.'

Knowing this to be to be a downright lie, Lacey ignored her. She knew Joan's willing nature wouldn't allow her to impose on the older woman, and from what Joan had told her it was she who did all the housework and cooking in the house in Scar End. Lacey hurried back up the stairs.

★ ★ ★

James Stanley Micklethwaite squalled his way into the world an hour and forty-five minutes after his mother had stopped her looms. Flushed and bonny, Joan cradled her son to her breast, none the worse for her experience.

'If he'd a bin a racehorse he'd have won The Derby would that one,' Ivy remarked, as she handed Lacey the pile of damp newspapers containing the afterbirth. 'Put them on t'fire lass, an' make a cup o' tea.'

Lacey went back downstairs. Hettie was slumped in the chair, eyes closed. Thinking to waken her and tell her she had a grandson, Lacey decided to let her sleep; she'd find out soon enough.

Joan comfortable, the teapot empty, Ivy prepared to depart. 'I'll come back this evening after Stanley gets home. He'll be fair proud you've given him a son. So will Hettie, although nowt much pleases her.' Cackling, Ivy picked up her bag. 'I'd a thought she'd a' been up to see him by now.'

'She was sleeping when I went down to make that pot of tea,' said Lacey, following Ivy down the stairs and seeing her out.

Hettie was exactly as Lacey had last seen her, save for her eyes and mouth: they hung open grotesquely.

'Ivy,' Lacey yelled after the departing midwife, 'come back. Quick!'

★ ★ ★

Stanley stood in the bedroom, a bemused expression on his face. 'I don't know whether to laugh

199

or cry,' he mumbled, his love for his wife and son radiating from his eyes, his features otherwise gloomy. 'Bad an' all as she could be, she was me Mam.' He shuffled towards the door. 'I'll go an' get the undertaker.'

'I'm ever so sorry, Stanley love,' sobbed Joan, inwardly chiding herself for some of the tears were tears of relief. Now they had the house and their new son to themselves. As she cradled her son she comforted herself in the knowledge that, even though she loathed the woman, she had never been deliberately unkind to her.

The undertakers came and went, and leaving Joan and Stanley mooning over the child in the crib, Lacey let herself out of the house in Scar End.

She trudged home feeling older and wiser. In the space of an hour she'd witnessed birth and death. It left her with the sense of how precious life was: live every moment, for you never know when the last one will be.

19

Lacey recognised the childish handwriting on the flimsy blue paper propped against the milk jug on the table the minute she arrived home from work.

Edith, her eyes moistening, nodded towards it then said, 'Read it out, Lacey. Let's all share it again.'

Pte James Barraclough, 2/4th Battalion,
Duke of Wellington's West Riding Regiment

Lacey read, her heart almost bursting with pride.

Dear All,
We're billeted in Newcastle doing our training and in January we'll move to Salisbury Plain. I like being a soldier and the sergeant says I'll make a good one because I look after my kit properly. The food is not as good as Mam's but marching and rifle practice are better than working in the Mill. Tell Mam I miss her and tell our Matt to look after the farm. Tell Dad I'm sorry for what I did and that one day I'll make him proud of me. I don't know when I'm going to France but I'm sure it will be soon.
Love Jimmy.

Lacey handed the letter to Edith and she took hold of it as one might a precious object, gazing

201

through blurred eyes at the childish scrawl. Lacey looked over at Joshua. He sat, head bowed, his hand resting on his brow to hide his tears.

'So far away,' Edith said, setting aside the letter, 'an' before we know it he'll be even further; God, don't let them send our Jimmy to France.'

Joshua reached across the table and laid his hand on Edith's. 'It might not come to that, lass,' he said gruffly. 'They said it 'ud be over by Christmas, so it can't last much longer.' Lacey heard the unspoken desire for it to be just so in Joshua's tone. She patted his arm.

Trying to sound hearty, Joshua said, 'You'd best send the lad a parcel right away while we still know where he is. Pack only t'best stuff an' don't forget liquorice allsorts an' sherbet pennies. He loves them.' Joshua trudged outside to find solace with his sheep, Matt following, but not before he had slipped a shilling into Lacey's hand to buy Jimmy treats.

Lacey ate her tea, the letter bringing home the reality of Jimmy's situation. She tried to imagine him in uniform, doing his duty, learning how to fire a rifle, learning how to kill. She tried not to think of him serving in France, up to his knees in mud or cowering in a trench, shot and shell raining down. He was her little brother and, fearing for his survival, she hoped that day would never come.

Strangely enough, although she missed Nathan dreadfully she did not fear for him in the same way. Compared to Jimmy he was so much wiser and far more capable of taking care of himself

— and he was an officer. His knowledge of warfare was bound to protect him in battle. Clinging to this, Lacey yearned for Nathan and Jimmy's homecoming.

Deprived of Nathan's company, and Joan busy with baby James, Lacey was often left to her own devices. One Saturday she ventured as far as Leeds, to a Women's Rally at which Isabella Ormston Ford was the chief speaker. Lacey was thrilled to see and hear this woman for whom she had such great admiration yet was surprised by her ordinariness. The kindly red face of the middle-aged woman wearing a turban hat squashed down on her head was not what Lacey had imagined. Yet if her appearance lacked style her eloquence was pure fire. She spoke with such conviction and knowledge it left Lacey awed and inspired. On the journey back to Garsthwaite, Lacey was bursting with fresh ideas to further the workers' cause.

★ ★ ★

'Brearley said no to a canteen,' Harry Clegg told Lacey, three days after the meeting at which she had raised the request. His expression sour, he leaned against Lacey's loom awaiting her response.

Sorely disappointed, Lacey watched the shuttle fly back and forth and marshalled her thoughts. Pick on pick, the cloth she was weaving lengthened by the minute, the thickening cloth beam lapped in khaki serge.

'See that, Harry,' she said, pointing to the beam, 'since Brearley's won that Ministry of Defence contract we've woven nowt else. Jonas'll not meet

203

his deadline if we stop working double shifts. So . . . ' Lacey clicked her fingers, 'no canteen, no overtime! We're holding all the cards, Harry; let's play 'em while we've got a full hand.'

★ ★ ★

'Is this canteen one of your ideas, by any chance?' Jonas asked, on the second day his workforce had refused to work double shifts. He had summoned Lacey to his office, and from behind his desk he now faced her, belligerently.

Lacey smiled innocently. 'No, Mr Brearley, sir: I think credit for that must go to Mr Crowther. Bank Bottom Mill has had a canteen for more than five years.'

Jonas was well acquainted with John Crowther, owner of the largest mill in the valley, and he knew that Lacey's smart reply was her way of having fun at his expense. 'By, but you're a brazen young woman,' he said.

'Aye, but not brazen enough to want to eat me breakfast an' me dinner in cold, wet conditions,' Lacey retorted, before softening her features and adding, 'all we're asking for is a bit of comfort like they have at Bank Bottom.'

Jonas pursed his lips then asked, 'How far do you intend to push me, Lacey?'

'You'll have to wait an' see, sir.'

'I'll not be taken advantage of.' growled Jonas, dismissing her with a wave of his hand.

Lacey understood this last remark was a reference to her friendship with Nathan, but she was undeterred. As far as she was concerned her work with the Union was totally separate from her love life.

At dinnertime the next day, Harry Clegg called an impromptu meeting of the workers in the weaving shed. 'As you all know, our request for a canteen has been refused. In answer to that, The Union recommends all members continue to refuse to work double shifts until the matter is resolved.'

There was a collective groan from non-members and members alike, followed by a flurry of complaints.

'We'll lose out on us wages just when we have a chance to earn a bit o' decent brass.'

'If Brearley misses his deadline he'll lose the bloody contract an' we'll be back on short-time afore you know it.'

Lacey sprang to redress the situation. 'Sometimes we have to lose a bit to gain a lot. This war won't last forever an' we'll not always have overtime, but fight now for a canteen an' you'll have it for the rest of your working days. Remember, small victories lead to bigger ones.'

'She's right,' said Harry Clegg. 'His looms standing idle an' the chance of meeting his deadline slipping away, Jonas Brearley'll have to think again.'

'Aye! For once we've got the upper hand,' shouted a voice from deep within the shed. 'Let's make t'most on it.'

A roar of approval made Lacey's heart beat all the faster.

★ ★ ★

Up at Fenay Hall Jonas paced the library, a glass of whisky in his hand.

Felicity let him rant, then losing patience, intervened.

'Oh Papa, for goodness sake, sit down and stop being so melodramatic. Look at it from the workers' point of view. You sit in a splendid dining room to eat your meals; have a little compassion. I presume you're making profit on this order for khaki; what would it cost to provide them with a sheltered space in which to eat? Not much, I'll be bound.'

Jonas slumped into a leather wing chair at one side of the ornately tiled fireplace. Felicity sat facing him, her animated expression reminding him of Lacey: another damned woman with too many opinions.

'If I don't meet the deadline, I'll lose the blasted contract,' he reiterated. 'Not only won't they have a canteen, they'll have no work.' He ran his fingers through his sparse, greying hair.

'And if they have no work, you'll have no income,' said Felicity, crossing the Chinese rug to perch on his lap. 'Really Papa, you're very short-sighted when it comes to dealing with people. You know from your own experience that if the hirer is kind to his labourer, he gets good service in return.'

She slipped her arm round his shoulders. 'How many times have we heard the stories of how you learned best from those who treated you kindly and that you had little respect for those who delighted in making difficulties because you were the boss's son.'

Jonas was not appeased. 'It's that blasted woman,' he said, 'I never had this bother before she joined the Union.'

Felicity smiled mischievously at this reference to Lacey. 'She's only doing what she thinks is right. Times are changing, Papa. Women are no longer willing to be dominated by men. They know they have just as much to offer in all walks of life, and this war is proving that. Powerful, influential women have always played their part in bringing about change: Lacey's just one of them.'

★ ★ ★

'How much longer do you reckon we'll have to hold out?'

'It makes me feel sick when I think of all t'extra money I'm losin' by not workin' overtime.'

'We're so far behind wi' this khaki order it'll not be finished in time for t'deadline; then there'll be no more orders.'

'Brearley's not goin' to give in, no matter what. We might as well do overtime, make decent wages while we can an' bugger the canteen.'

'Aye, what we never had, we'll never miss.'

Lacey looked into the angry faces of the women gathered in the Mill yard. In her heart she sympathised with them, understanding their complaints, but in her head she resolved not to relent.

It was midday on Saturday, the time the women usually clocked off for the weekend, but inside the weaving shed there was plenty of work waiting to be done: overtime for everyone and the promise of fatter wage packets.

Lacey gazed at the careworn faces, mouths clamped, eyes alert as they awaited her response. A cold fury swept through her veins. 'Give me a few minutes, lasses, I'll not be long.'

She strode away from them, across the Mill yard to Jonas' office. She knew he was still on the premises as his car was waiting in the yard. For the past two weeks Harry Clegg and the Union men had had frequent meetings with Jonas to no avail. If they could not persuade him to provide a canteen, perhaps she could. Throwing caution to the wind she rapped on the office door and stepped inside, uninvited.

Jonas was clearing his desk, placing ledgers on shelves. When he saw who had invaded his sanctuary his face darkened. 'What the devil do you mean by this?'

'You know why I'm here, Mr Brearley. We're at loggerheads, neither of us getting what we want. We need to redress the matter before it gets any worse. Harry Clegg's failed to make an impression on you, so maybe I can.'

Jonas' eyes widened. With an impatient wave of his hand he indicated for Lacey to sit in the chair facing the desk. Thumping down into the one behind it Jonas lolled back, his hands resting on his paunch, a sardonic expression on his face. 'Well . . . ' he growled.

Then, to his amazement, he heard Lacey reiterate the same argument Felicity had used earlier in the week. 'Have you been colluding with my daughter?'

Lacey shook her head, puzzled. 'No, sir, I haven't spoken with Miss Felicity about this.'

Jonas harrumphed. Could it be that both these sharp young women were right and he was wrong? He fingered his pursed lips. What was it Lacey had said about Crowther's Mill at Bank Bottom? John Crowther's philanthropy was admired throughout the Colne Valley, thought Jonas; maybe he should bear that in mind.

Troubled by the long silence, Lacey perched uneasily on the edge of the chair. Was he about to dismiss her? If so, she would go down fighting.

'It'll benefit both sides if we came to an immediate agreement, sir,' she said firmly, 'we get our canteen and you meet your deadline. The lasses will make up for time lost because they'll know they've achieved something that improves their working days for years to come. That way everybody wins.

I'll leave you to think about it, sir.'

Lacey returned to the yard. 'I've stated our case again and I've left Mr Brearley thinking about it,' she said to the waiting women, 'and while he is we have to stick to our guns so, sorry lasses, but there'll be no overtime worked today.'

The women gave a collective groan and turned towards the gate but before any of them reached it Harry Clegg dashed into the yard wearing a broad grin. 'Brearley just sent for me,' he blurted out to Lacey, and to the women he shouted, 'Hold up! Hold up! Them what's workin' overtime get back in that shed an' get them bloody looms hammerin'. Them what's coming in tomorrow can work split shifts; we'll do that all next week. We'll keep them looms clatterin' day an night to make up for lost time.'

209

'Have we got us canteen, Harry?' chorused a dozen voices.

'Course you bloody have,' he yelled back.

Lacey's heart felt as though it would burst as she watched the smiling, chattering women return to their looms, the throb and thrum music to her ears. To achieve justice and respect in the workplace you had to state your concerns clearly, take advantage of the situation to shape the matter of those concerns and be resolute. She had done just that, and would do it again, she told herself as she watched the khaki serge grow.

★ ★ ★

Lacey was still in fighting mode long after a canteen was furbished in a disused shed at the bottom of the Mill yard.

'We're still no nearer to getting equal pay than we were months ago,' she grumbled to Joan, as they walked back to Joan's house from a Union meeting.

'Aye, all we do is talk an' it gets us nowhere 'cos the men don't listen.'

'The men aren't interested in equal pay for women, Joanie. That's why we'll have to fight for it on us own. Trouble is, no two mills pay their women the same rate. While ever Jarmains, Brooksbank's and Hebblethwaites are undercutting wages by a shilling and more, Jonas won't raise ours. Then, because each mill has its own little Union we have no real bargaining power like we'd have if we all stuck together.'

Joan was beginning to wish she hadn't started this topic of conversation because once Lacey got fired up there was no stopping her.

'You see, Joanie,' Lacey continued as they turned into Scar End, 'if all the women got together to agree on common demands and threatened to strike if they didn't get 'em, the mill owners would have to listen. What we've got to insist on is unity throughout the industry.'

Lacey's fervour being such, Joan was relieved when they reached her front door. Stanley sat by the fire reading the newspaper. He grinned as Joan and Lacey stepped inside. 'Well, did you give 'em hell tonight.' Stanley viewed Joan's Union membership as something of a joke.

'Aye, we got your wages raised by five bob a week an' ours by ten.'

Lacey's sarcastic reply had Stanley laughing out loud.

'In that case I can go to me bed a happy man.' He bid them good night.

In the scullery Joan mashed a pot of tea and Lacey sat by the fire in the parlour, gazing enviously round the neat little room.

The terrace house in Scar End having only two rooms downstairs and two above, and an outside lavatory in the backyard, was by no means grand yet it was warm and welcoming. Lacey took the mug of tea Joan held out to her. 'You don't realise how lucky you are, Joan. You've a comfortable home, a beautiful son and a husband to cuddle up to in bed, whereas I'm hanging in mid-air. I don't know if I'll ever get married or have children. Nathan says we will but he's not here to do anything about it; I don't even know if I'll ever see him again.' Wracked with frustration and misery,

211

she burst into tears.

Joan, unnerved by Lacey's despair, slopped tea into the hearth as she leapt to comfort her; Lacey was usually so brave. 'Don't take on so,' she pleaded, 'Nathan'll be back before you know it. You'll be married afore the year's out; I'd put money on it.'

20

The war in Europe raged on, the belief that it would be over by Christmas now something of a joke without humour, the inhabitants of Garsthwaite inured to the absence of young men on the streets and in the mills. Worse still were the frequent obituaries in *The Huddersfield Examiner* announcing that yet another son, husband, father, uncle or nephew would not be returning to the bosom of his family. As more and more men enlisted, women became predominant in the workplace.

Lacey encouraged the women of the Weavers' Association to knit comforts for the soldiers in the trenches. They brought in wool and needles, knitting furiously in their breakfast and dinner breaks. The women not in the Union soon joined the knitting sessions, and it became something of a competition between spinners and weavers as to who could produce the most items in a week. But although Lacey was actively working to rally the women in the other mills in the valley to support the call for improved wages, she couldn't help feeling as if her personal life was on hold.

★ ★ ★

First Lieutenant Nathan Brearley arrived back in Garsthwaite on a balmy Saturday afternoon in late autumn. After briefly acquainting his parents with his return, he went in search of Lacey.

213

Lacey was hunched over her sewing machine by the window in her bedroom, preparing to sew the final seam on a dress she was making for one of Felicity's friends. Whenever she was engaged creatively it provided solace, particularly when it involved working with luxurious, expensive fabrics such as the moiré silk under the machine's needle.

Just before she applied pressure to the treadle, she happened to glance out of the window and saw him. A line of stitching zig-zagged crazily across the silk moiré as she leapt to her feet and dashed downstairs, running headlong through the kitchen and out into the yard. She met him at the gate.

Kisses exchanged, Lacey led him into the kitchen. 'We're getting married,' he said, his tone brooking no opposition. 'I stopped off in Huddersfield on the way here and made arrangements. I'll have the licence the day after tomorrow.'

'Married? Now! While you're on leave?' Her face registered both joy and confusion.

Nathan grinned. 'Yes. I'm home for ten days embarkation leave. They're sending me to France.'

France: Lacey's joy plummeted. Whilst he had been stationed in England she had felt that he was safe; but France — she'd read about what happened to soldiers in France — and now she was afraid, but Nathan seemed not to notice.

'How soon can you be ready? That's if you're still up for it,' he urged.

'Give me ten minutes,' joked Lacey, her fears suppressed as she stepped into his embrace. Lost in the magic of the moment, they stayed this way

214

until the rattle of the latch on the kitchen door broke the spell. Edith came in.

Surprised then pleased, she welcomed Nathan. 'It's good to see you, lad,' she said, glancing from one excited face to the other; something was afoot. Lacey was positively glowing, and Nathan looked fit to burst. Not until Joshua and Matt joined them a short time later was Edith's curiosity satisfied.

'Married! In a few days' time.' Edith glanced at Joshua, keen to judge his reaction. He looked somewhat bewildered, but not displeased. Both of them had often discussed their doubts about the relationship. It wasn't as though Lacey was courting an ordinary lad; Nathan was the son of a wealthy mill owner. They worried over the differences in his and Lacey's social standing. Could she really fit into his world? Would he accept hers? Would he make her happy? Looking at the pair now, neither Edith nor Joshua could deny Lacey and Nathan's joy.

'Congratulations,' Joshua blustered, shaking Nathan's hand then stooping to kiss Lacey's cheek. Matt added his good wishes although he too had reservations. Nathan seemed like a grand chap but he wasn't like them; he was a toff. Matt went to the sideboard and took out three bottles of beer. Removing the stoppers, he handed one bottle to Nathan, the other to Joshua and then raised his own. 'Here's to the happy couple,' he toasted. Nathan swigged a long draught wondering if his own family would accept his decision as easily.

Jonas, Constance and Felicity were in the drawing room when Nathan and Lacey arrived at Fenay Hall. Nathan wasted no time in telling them the news. Lacey sat on the edge of her seat and held her breath, her eyes darting from one face to another. The Brearley's initial reaction imitated that of the Barracloughs', shock and bemusement.

'It's preposterous,' gasped Constance, looking askance at Nathan, 'we can't organise a wedding in a matter of days.' She dropped her gaze to hide her thoughts; if it was postponed it might never take place.

Nathan smiled sympathetically at his mother. 'Yes we can. It will be a simple affair, certainly not the sort you possibly envisaged but just as important. I can't wait any longer to make Lacey mine. I want and need her to be my wife before they send me to France.'

Constance clutched at her bosom and choked back a sob. Then she gazed long and hard at the handsome young couple standing before her, their eager faces awaiting her blessing. Her thoughts darkened. Nathan might not survive this dreadful war. Can I really destroy his happiness at a time like this? The objections I raised initially seem petty and pointless; I like the girl — she makes Nathan happy. Flustered, Constance smiled wanly and trilled,

'In that case I suppose we can.'

Jonas got to his feet, his hand outstretched. 'Let me be the first to congratulate you, lad.' His eyes twinkled wickedly as he added 'You've chosen wisely, but don't go getting any ideas she'll be easy to handle; she has a mind of her own does this one.' He stepped up to Lacey and pecked her cheek. 'Make him happy, lass.'

Lacey's face flamed. 'I will, Mr Brearley, I promise. There's nothing in the world I'd rather do.'

Felicity squealed with delight then hugged and kissed both Nathan and Lacey. 'I'll be your bridesmaid. The blue dress you made me for my party will do perfectly, there being no time to make one especially.'

Constance smiled pensively. 'I have my misgivings, but this dreadful war has changed everything.' She stepped forward and took Lacey's hand. 'It's obvious Nathan adores you and I know you return his affections; therefore I bow to the inevitable. Now, both of you, kiss me.'

Jonas rang the bell, and when the butler appeared, he ordered champagne. Amid much discussion of plans and preparations, Constance sat back and reviewed the situation. Perhaps it would come right in the end.

She could not deny that during Lacey's visits to Fenay Hall she had grown to admire the feisty, funny girl, and had been both impressed and amused by her lively chatter as she related local matters and Mill gossip, subjects Constance showed increasing interest in.

Maybe it's time for me to broaden my outlook, she told herself. Attitudes were changing and of late she had come to realise that Lacey brought a breath of fresh air into all their lives. True, the girl didn't belong to their social class — but so what? Constance would deal with those who might censure the marriage when the time came.

The next day Nathan and Lacey walked up Town-gate, coming to a halt outside one of the double fronted Georgian houses that graced this part of Garsthwaite. Nathan produced a key from his pocket. 'This will be our home, if you approve,' he said, inserting the key into the lock then indicating for Lacey to step inside.

Lacey, utterly amazed, stayed on the pavement gazing at the fine, two storey building, its oak front door surrounded by stained glass panels. She hadn't given a thought to where they might live. Had she done so, she would have assumed she would stay on at Netherfold Farm while Nathan was away. Her senses recovered she stepped into the wide hallway, her eyes goggling at the sight of the sweeping mahogany staircase and several doors leading to other rooms. Turning full circle, she surveyed her surroundings.

'It's beautiful, Nathan, but it's huge.' She giggled. 'I'll rattle around like a pea in a drum when you're not here.'

Nathan laughed. 'If I know you as well as I think I do, you'll be so busy you'll not have time to feel lonely — and you won't be on your own for much longer.' Although his words were hearty they both heard the doubt in his voice. Unwilling to dwell on the subject, Lacey dashed from room to room, Nathan laughing at her enthusiastic ideas for refurbishment.

'I own this one and the properties either side of it; Grandfather willed them to me before he died,' said Nathan, as they prepared to leave. 'I've rented them out till now. As you know, Mr Pendlebury, the Baptist minister, lives in the one to the right, and the shop has been empty for years.'

Out on the pavement Lacey paused to gaze at the properties. The one the Pendleburys lived in was almost identical to the one that would be theirs; the shop was a single storey building with a bow fronted display window.

Lacey pinched herself to make sure she wasn't dreaming and then walked away on Nathan's arm, the seed of an idea taking root.

★ ★ ★

'See, I was right after all,' exclaimed Joan, when Lacey told her the news.

Lacey acknowledged this remark with a hug. 'I'm going to ask Jonas if I can have time off to go into Huddersfield to buy some material and new underwear.'

In Jonas's office at breakfast time, Lacey made her request. Jonas chuckled. 'I can hardly refuse. Take all the time you want, lass. Mind you,' he chuckled louder, 'I'll dock your wages.' They both laughed at this.

Later that day, Lacey sat at her sewing machine, the rhythmic clacking of the treadle music to her ears as she sewed her wedding outfit. It being wartime she'd decided to forgo a traditional wedding dress and was making a soft, off-white woollen suit. Time was of the essence, and it was after midnight when she trimmed the lapels and cuffs with military braid, the swirling black loops a striking contrast to the creamy wool. She undressed and climbed into bed. One more night after this, she thought sleepily, and I'll be a married woman.

★ ★ ★

On her last night as a single girl Lacey lay in bed unable to sleep. She wanted to marry Nathan, of that she was certain, but as she tossed and turned she was plagued with the strangest notions. She couldn't imagine undressing in front of Nathan or sharing a bed with him. Would she be capable of performing properly when her turn came to do the things she'd overheard women in the weaving shed gossip about? Until now she had classed it as 'mucky talk' and giggled with the rest of the girls but in a few hours from now she'd be expected to do these things. Did it come naturally and was it as awful as some of the women described, or was it beautiful and uplifting as poets and authors suggested in the books she'd read? And perhaps it would have been more sensible to wait. If he didn't survive the conflict she'd be married and widowed within a matter of months. Maybe his death would be easier to deal with had she never experienced one day of married life. On this sad note Lacey fell into a fitful sleep.

★ ★ ★

Like many other wartime weddings, Lacey and Nathan's was a quiet affair, the Methodist Church in Garsthwaite easily accommodating the small congregation of family and friends. A pale sun shone through two arched windows behind the altar, warming the patina of dark wood, the gleaming rays softening the austerity of the building. Two large urns of russet and gold chrysanthemums stood either side of the altar, their burnished heads like heavenly fire.

At precisely eleven o clock, the church organist struck the first notes of Wagner's wedding march and Lacey, delectable in her off-white suit, walked proudly down the aisle on Joshua's arm. As matron of honour, Joan wore the suit she had worn for her own wedding and Felicity wore the blue party dress.

Nathan, handsome in his officer's dress uniform, stood alongside his best man, John Hinchcliffe, who was also his solicitor. When Lacey arrived at Nathan's side he smiled, a hint of triumph lighting his grey-blue eyes.

Lacey returned his smile, her dark eyes flashing impishly as if to say, we've done it; there's no going back now.

Vows solemnly and honestly exchanged, Lacey and Nathan turned to the congregation, their faces radiating love and happiness. Oblivious to Alice's venomous glare and Violet's sour expression, Lacey and Nathan marched out into the sunlight, well-wishers streaming after them.

John Hinchcliffe produced a Box Brownie camera, a wedding gift for Nathan and Lacey. The guests, on learning what it did, clamoured to have their photographs taken, the bride almost overlooked in the excitement.

Laughing and smiling, Lacey and Nathan posed with each other then with the guests; Lacey thrilled to know the memories of this wonderful day had been captured forever.

At Constance's insistence, the wedding reception was at Fenay Hall; a lavish buffet instead of the tea and ham sandwiches they would have eaten in the Church Hall had Lacey married anyone but Nathan. As though by pre-arrangement the Brearleys' guests kept to one side of the room, the Barracloughs and the Mill workers to the other.

At ease in their surroundings, Nathan's guests chatted convivially, accepting as their right the food and drink served to them by uniformed waitresses. Those who had come to support Lacey hung back, ill at ease when offered champagne or canapés. Not until Jonas went amongst them cheerfully urging them to enjoy themselves did they start to relax.

With Lacey on his arm, Nathan performed a whirlwind of introductions to the members of his family Lacey hadn't yet met. Nathan's attention distracted by yet another well-wisher he stepped away from Lacey, leaving her in the company of Alice and Violet Burrows.

'So, you caught him after all,' sneered Alice. 'I suppose you think you're clever, but he'll soon discover what a scheming, vulgar person you really are.' She hoisted her hefty bosom upwards with her elbow, a habit with which Lacey would become increasingly familiar. Shocked by Alice's blatant antagonism on this of all days, Lacey was momentarily lost for words.

'You stole him from me,' Violet hissed. 'He would have married me had you not come along. Can you honestly believe Nathan will be happy mixing with the likes of those people?' She waved a hand in the direction of Lacey's guests, the Mill girls now chattering and laughing raucously, enjoying the occasion.

Lacey glared. 'Don't you dare spoil today with your petty snobberies and your delusions. Nathan would never have married you. My love for Nathan and his for me goes above and beyond your narrow minded paltry views on society. There's not a person in this room that's inferior to either of you. In fact,' this time it was Lacey's turn to wave a hand in the direction of the Mill girls, 'most of them are far more worthy. Now, if you'll excuse me I'll go and join them.'

On her way across the room she was surprised to see Matt deep in conversation with Molly Dewhirst. Matt didn't usually bother with women but now as he gazed into Molly's eyes, a warm smile on his lips, he seemed thoroughly at ease. Lacey wondered what they were talking about.

Resisting the temptation to eavesdrop she flopped into a chair next to Joan.

'Phew,' she gasped, 'I'll swing for that pair of besoms before I'm done.'

Joan adjusted the baby in her lap, not asking to whom Lacey referred.

She'd seen her talking with Alice and Violet and knew all about them. 'I know how you feel. I felt like that about Stanley's mam. I know you shouldn't speak ill of the dead but we've been a lot happier since Hettie passed over.' Strangely enough, Joan looked thoroughly miserable as she said it.

However, Lacey didn't notice. 'I can well believe it. And whilst I'm not wishing either of them dead, they'd better keep out of my way or they soon will be.' Her empty threats made Joan smile, but the smile did not reach her eyes.

'Is something wrong, Joanie?'

'Nowt,' Joan replied abruptly, quickly changing the subject. 'Look at your Matt wi' Molly Dewhirst. That's a turn up for t'books. I can't ever remember him bothering with a woman afore.'

'Nor me,' Lacey agreed, 'but he appears to be taken with Molly.'

'It wa' kind of you to invite her. She needs a bit o' cheering up, what wi' her losing her husband an' having to come back to live wi' her mam. That little lad of hers is only two.'

Lacey and Joan looked over at Matt and Molly, Matt playfully entertaining Molly's son. Joan caught her bottom lip between her teeth and her eyes filled with tears. 'Her husband had only been three days in France when he wa' killed.'

'Don't upset yourself, Joanie.'

'I can't help it! I wasn't going to say owt 'cos I didn't want to spoil your day but . . . ' She took a deep breath, 'Stanley's joined up. He went down to t'Drill Hall and signed up without telling me.'

Lacey gasped. 'Whatever made him do that?'

Joan sighed so deeply it wafted baby James's hair. 'He says it's his duty. He wanted to get it over and done with 'cos he says they'll all be called up afore long. The soldier in the Drill Hall said as much.'

Lacey glanced across the room to where Stanley stood laughing at something Joshua was telling him. 'Don't worry, Joanie. Stanley'll be all right. He knows how to take care of himself.' Even to

Lacey's ears the words lacked conviction and her heart ached, not just for Joan but also for herself. Would she and Nathan have just the next few days to get to know one another as man and wife before he was taken from her, never to return?

21

It was the furthest Lacey had ever travelled: sixty odd miles to the east coast resort of Scarborough for a honeymoon lasting three days; a rather grand idea, for neither her parents nor Joan, nor any of Lacey's married friends had had the luxury of a three day holiday in a hotel by the sea. Day trips to seaside towns being the norm for the inhabitants of Garsthwaite, it was almost unheard of to stay overnight in a hotel.

They arrived at lunchtime, having travelled by train from Huddersfield to Leeds and then to Scarborough, a new experience for Lacey. Although the town still bore the scars of war inflicted by German gunboats the previous December, it did not detract from Lacey and Nathan's pleasure, however, it did make the war seem uncomfortably close to Garsthwaite.

'We tend to think the fighting only takes place in foreign places, but here it was almost on our doorstep.'

'It was a filthy, cowardly act,' said Nathan as they walked the short distance from the railway station to their hotel. 'The Germans sailed in under cover of a fog bank, firing volley after volley of shells into a defenceless little town. It's fortunate it happened in winter when there were fewer visitors — even so several people lost their lives, children included.'

'Oh look!' cried Lacey, as they walked past the

wreckage of the fine building that had been the Grand Hotel, 'I see what you mean. A place like this would have been full of people in summer — ' she paused thoughtfully.

'Fancy, coming on holiday and ending up dead at the hands of the Germans.'

'The Germans show no respect for the laws of war; men, women and children, it's all the same to them.' He slowed his pace, and taking Lacey's elbow he ushered her up the steps into a large hotel.

Impressed by the fine Victorian façade and the atrium with its marble pillars and sweeping staircase, Lacey felt slightly overwhelmed. Fidgeting nervously whilst Nathan spoke to the receptionist, she couldn't help but smile when she heard him ask for Mr and Mrs Nathan Brearley's accommodation: Mrs Nathan Brearley; she'd have to get used to that name.

Her joy was complete when she saw the beautifully appointed bedroom with its quilt laden four poster and views over the sea front.

After they had eaten a rather sparse ham salad, they walked the high, rocky promontory jutting into the North Sea to visit the castle. As they wandered through the ruins Lacey imagined the inhabitants of long ago and the events shaping their lives, awestruck by the timelessness of it all. On the cliff edge she watched the eternal ebb and flow of the tide, waves crashing on the rocks below.

'I'd have liked to have been a pirate queen,' she said, recalling a story from her childhood.

Nathan laughed. 'Ever the renegade, Lacey: not for you the lady promenading with parasol in

227

hand but a woman with fire in her soul, giving orders to her motley crew.'

'I'd have been a pirate who smuggled in goods to help poor people, those who couldn't afford to pay the tax on tea, tobaccy and brandy, and silk to make dresses. I'd have let them have it cheap so they had some of the comforts the rich folk had.'

'Now you're sounding more like Robin Hood.'

Lacey grinned at the comparison, then, her tone serious, added, 'There's a great divide between rich and poor which must be narrowed if we're to make the world a fairer place. I know there has to be leaders, men and women with greater acumen than the rest of us, but there should be no place for cruelty and deliberately imposed hardships. That's what I hate most.'

Nathan drew her close, kissing the top of her head. 'I suppose you'll still continue to fight for your beliefs now you're a married woman — one who will very shortly be left alone.' His voice expressed his misgivings; he didn't like to think of Lacey embroiled in Union activity, challenging adversaries — or alienating his father — without him there to protect her.

'You don't have to work in the Mill now we're married. My allowance will keep you.'

Lacey eased back and gazed up at him, her expression thoughtful. 'I'll not give it up immediately; not until we've addressed certain issues but . . .'

Sounding wistfully earnest, she added, 'I do have my own ambitions. I want to make something of myself, Nathan.' Before he could respond, she pulled him close, crying, 'But hey! We're on our honeymoon so no more serious talk, Mr Brearley. Let's make these three days a joy to remember.'

Shadows lengthening, they walked back to the hotel, Lacey's thoughts straying to the night ahead. She wanted to make love with Nathan; she just wasn't sure how to go about it and, more to the point, she wasn't sure Nathan did either. He'd never hinted at a close relationship with any other woman. Still, thought Lacey, as they made their way up to the bedroom after eating a hearty evening dinner in the hotel dining room, we can learn together.

And they did.

Lolling against the plump feather pillows Lacey contemplated how amazingly gratifying it had been. Having heard the women at work grumble at having to satisfy their husband's conjugal rights, she had expected to be subjected to discomfort, even terrible pain. How wrong she had been.

Nathan's gentle caresses had aroused her to such a pitch that everything that came afterwards had seemed second nature, the most natural and beautiful thing in the world. After that first night, lovemaking was as effortless as drawing breath.

Their town pallor blown away by bracing sea breezes, Lacey and Nathan returned to Garsthwaite and the house in Towngate, eager to settle down as a married couple even if it was only for a few days. On Nathan's last night at home, in the sparsely furnished bedroom, he noticed that his usually talkative wife had not spoken for some time. Concerned, he asked, 'What are you thinking about, Lacey?' Lacey sighed. 'I was thinking how much I'll miss you when you're gone.'

'Not as much as I'll miss you: you've completely changed my life. Just let's hope nothing untoward happens to me whilst I'm away.' Nathan kissed her, Lacey aware of how much she would miss his kisses, his company and their lovemaking. They climbed into bed, luxuriating in what, for the foreseeable future, was their last night together. Afterwards, they lay entwined, hearts beating in tandem, minds filled with dread.

Nathan reached up and stroked Lacey's glorious tumble of hair. 'I swear you are the most wonderful creature I ever set eyes on. I'll carry your image in my heart wherever they send me. You have brought me more joy than I thought possible, and if this should be our last night together, the memories of the time we've shared will sustain me until the day I die.'

Lacey shuddered. Pressing her fingers to his lips, the thought of losing him left her barely able to breathe, let alone speak. Finding her voice, she whispered, 'I love you more than life itself. From when we first met I knew we were meant to share the rest of our lives together and,' Lacey's words rang with utter conviction, 'we will, Nathan, we will. I'll live every day with the certainty you'll come back to me.'

Clinging to one another they fell into dreamless sleep.

★ ★ ★

Lacey wakened later than usual the following morning, Nathan's warm, hard body pressed close to hers. Moving carefully so as not to wake

230

him she rested on one elbow, gazing down into the adored face. He looked more handsome than ever, his features chiselled, his skin tanned from the long hours he'd spent out in the open air during training.

Tomorrow, Lacey thought, I'll wake and find him gone: to where and for how long only God knows. She leaned over and brushed her lips against his. Nathan stirred, a smile stretching his mouth under hers. He opened his eyes and gazed lovingly into Lacey's then, gently rolling her over onto her back he made love to her, slowly, sweetly and tenderly. They stayed like this for several minutes, drinking in every detail of each other's face and, as though to imprint them on their memories, with hands and lips they fixed the sense of touch and taste.

Before Nathan went away, he again raised the matter of Lacey not returning to work at the mill. 'No Nathan, I'm not ready to leave just yet,' she told him, 'the issue of equal pay for equal work has yet to be resolved. I want to be there when it is. Once I start something I have to see it through to the end.'

★ ★ ★

Four days after Nathan's departure Lacey practically ran all the way to Netherfold, so eager was she to shake off the emptiness of the house in Towngate. In the yard, she clapped her hands to shoo away the gaggle of geese standing sentry outside the kitchen door. The geese stood fast, riveting her with their baleful, beady eyes. Lacey

231

tried again, this time waving her arms and hallooing. Her cries brought Edith to the door.

She laughed heartily at the sight of the geese barring Lacey's entrance then dismissed them with a sharp flick of the wrist and a few well chosen words. Lifting their wings, the geese haughtily turned tail and flapped across the yard.

Now it was Lacey's turn to laugh. 'It's well they do as their mistress tells 'em; they took no notice of me.'

Edith grinned. 'As good as guard dogs, they are. There's not many 'ud get past that lot.'

'Don't I know it. I've missed having the backs of my legs nipped black an' blue since I moved to Towngate.'

Edith led the way into the kitchen, Lacey breathing in the familiar smells. She loved the house in Towngate but Netherfold still felt like home.

'How do, Lacey, luv.' Matt, on his hands and knees in the middle of the kitchen floor, smiled up at her. 'Say hello to your Auntie Lacey,' he urged the toddler kneeling beside him.

Lacey smiled down at the bonny, blonde child. 'Eeh, if I'd known David was here I'd have brought sweets.'

'No need,' Matt said, 'me Dad buys a shop full every weekend.' He lifted David to his feet. 'Let's take Auntie Lacey into t'parlour to your Mam an' Granpa Jos.' David toddled off, Matt behind him.

'I'll come in a minute,' Lacey called after them. 'I want a word with Mam.'

Alone with Edith, Lacey said, 'I think our Matt's in love. I've never seen him so happy.'

'Me neither,' said Edith, smiling fondly. 'Molly's good for him. She's a lovely lass, an' our Matt adores little David.' Edith piled home-cooked ham and tomato sandwiches on a plate. Lacey put cups on a tray whilst Edith mashed the tea then set out a homemade cake. 'It's only plain sponge,' said Edith, clucking her tongue, 'there's no dried fruit to be had these days. I'm not short of butter an' eggs but sugar an' flour are getting scarcer by the week what with all this carry on wi' t'Germans.'

Lacey thought of the solitary tea she would otherwise have eaten in Towngate. 'It's grand, Mam, an' as long as you have your own hens an' your friends with cows to keep you in butter, we'll not starve.' She filled a jug with milk and placed the sugar bowl on the tray. 'I'm glad I invited Molly to my wedding, otherwise Matt would never have met her.'

'So am I,' Edith replied, 'I shouldn't wonder but what they'll get married in a year or so. They have to wait a while 'cos it's not a year since her husband wa' killed.' Edith lowered her voice to a whisper. 'I don't think she grieved him too much. It wasn't a happy marriage from what I can make out. It seems he wa' a boozer and quick wi' his fists.'

'She'll notice a difference with our Matt then. He's as steady and softhearted as anybody I know.'

Edith nodded agreement. 'It's good to see you all settled. Even our Jimmy, bless him, seems content. His regiment's moving to the south coast in a week or two and,' her voice wobbled, 'he thinks France will be the next stop.'

An involuntary shudder made the crockery on the tray in Lacey's hands clink noisily. She placed it back on the table. 'For all I know, Nathan could be there already,' she said, 'I haven't heard from him since he went back.

Let's hope we stay lucky. Stanley hasn't come to any harm as yet, thank God, although he's in some awful place in France, up to his knees in mud and muck. Joan worries about him something shocking and I don't blame her. Maybe the war'll end soon and they'll all come home safe.' She sounded dreadfully sad.

Edith frowned. 'Are you settling in Towngate, luv? You must be awfully lonely all by yourself in that big house. You could have stayed on here.'

'I know, but I love the house; and there's so much to do. I've sewed new curtains and cushions since you last visited. They really brighten the place up,' Lacey said, her forced cheerfulness not escaping Edith's notice.

Throwing up her hands in exasperation, she said, 'Eeh, that pot o' tea'll a gone cold. I'll have to brew another.'

The pot replenished, mother and daughter went through to the parlour where Joshua, Matt, Molly and young David awaited them.

'I wa' beginning to wonder where you'd got to,' said Joshua. 'What kept you?'

Edith flicked her eyes in Lacey's direction and shook her head, the frown on her face begging Joshua not to expect an answer. She'd confide in him later.

For the next hour, in the comfort of Netherfold, Lacey was almost her old self but all too soon it

234

was time to return to Towngate.

Lacey put on her coat. 'I'd best be off.'

'Nay, you can stay a bit a longer, can't you?' Joshua, suspecting all was not well, was concerned for his only daughter. Throughout the past hour she'd done her best to appear happy but the spark had gone out of her. Where was the funny, cocky, spirited girl he loved?

Her coat buttoned, her bag in her hand, Lacey shook her head. 'Best not. I might get too comfortable.' She didn't want to worry her parents by letting them know how dreadfully lonely she was in the rambling house in Towngate.

* * *

Letting herself in to what was now her home, Lacey went into the sitting room. With Matt's help, she had painted its walls in pale pastel shades, reflecting the light from two large windows. Curtains and cushions in rich, bright fabrics enhanced the dark leather couches and chairs.

Lacey flopped into a chair, thinking that maybe she should have stayed at Netherfold whilst Nathan was away. But the more she thought about it the more she realised she had to pull herself together and do something positive, make something happen.

Later that same evening, Lacey popped round to Scar End. Since Stanley's departure she visited Joan at least three evenings a week for now she understood how lonely her cousin must be. Like thousands of women throughout the country Joan spent her days worrying over the safety of her man, and now Lacey herself was doing the same.

'Stanley says he doesn't think he can stick it much longer,' Joan said listlessly. 'His feet are rotten, what with standing in muddy water for days on end, an' there's rats in the trenches as big as cats.' Tea slopped from the cup she was holding and she cried, 'What'll I do if he doesn't come back?'

Lacey sipped her tea, no ready answer on her tongue, and the names on the latest list of men from Garsthwaite who had lost their lives flashed through her mind. Young lads she'd gone to school with, others she'd worked alongside, and some she'd walked out with for a week or two, all dead.

Young James crawled over to Lacey's feet and fiddled with the buckle on one of her shoes. Taking him on her knee she hugged his plump little body to her own, finding comfort in his trusting innocence. Would he grow up never knowing his father?

'We just have to pray they come home, Joanie. That's all we can do. We can't sit moping.'

Joan didn't look convinced.

Lacey gave a ghost of a smile. 'Actually, I have been thinking of something; something I want to do more than anything in the world, Joanie, but I'm not letting on what it is until I'm sure of me facts.' She stood and put on her coat. 'It involves you, Joanie, so keep smiling and look to the future.'

When Lacey arrived back home she didn't immediately go indoors.

Instead, she stood on the pavement staring thoughtfully at the empty shop next door. The seed planted in her heart when the Mill had been working short-time had flourished, but before it bloomed Lacey had one last battle to fight.

★ ★ ★

Sitting in the new canteen along with her workmates, Lacey finished her sandwich then banged her empty mug on the table for attention. The women ceased their chatter, their expressions curious as they waited for her to speak.

'I've been talking with the lasses who work for Jarmain's, Hebblethwaite's and Brooksbank's. I told 'em they're selling themselves short and that if they don't demand their worth they'll always be underpaid,' she said.

'Aye, that's right; Jarmain's pay a couple of bob less than Brearley's for a finished piece,' Maggie Clegg chipped in. This being common knowledge, Flo Backhouse shouted, 'Keep your gob shut and listen to Lacey.'

'Thanks, Flo,' said Lacey. 'Now, as you all know, we've been arguing the toss over equal pay for months an' we're still no nearer to getting parity with the men. So, what I suggest is, we form our own Union an' fight for it that way. Most of the lasses at the other mills are willing to join us in our struggle, an' you know what they say; the more the merrier.'

'Aye, who needs bloody men, anyway?' whooped Flo Backhouse. A loud cheer went up followed by cries of, 'What'll we do first?'

'To start with, we'll march through Garsthwaite demanding the bosses meet their obligations,' said Lacey, thoughts of Isabella Ormston Ford in mind. 'Approaching 'em through the proper channels hasn't worked. Now it's time for shock tactics. We'll shame 'em into it. They're desperate for us to work on the new Government contracts they've negotiated; they'll not want us withdrawing our labour at a time like this.'

Lizzie Isherwood's eyebrows shot up. 'Are you saying you'll go on strike?'

Lacey grinned. 'If we have to, Lizzie; the time's ripe for it. Now, do I have everybody's backing, lasses, or am I fighting on me own?'

'I'll march to hell if it gets me a few bob extra.' Lily Skinner's shout encouraged a chorus of 'So will I.'

'We could all be sacked.'

A howl of derision met the lone, timorous voice followed by 'Don't be bloody daft. They'll not sack us. They need us to meet their contracts.'

'They do indeed,' said Lacey, 'so we'll rally the women at Jarmain's, Hebblethwaite's and Brooksbank's, and arrange a marching day.

Remember, lasses, there's strength in numbers an' by God we'll show 'em we've got both strength and numbers.'

* * *

When Lacey paid her weekly visit to Fenay Hall later that week, Soames met her with, 'Mr Jonas would like a word, madam.' He ushered her into the library.

Jonas sat behind a large, leather topped desk, his face creased with consternation. Indicating for Lacey to sit at the opposite side of the desk, he glared at her. 'Is it true what I'm hearing,' he rumbled, 'that the women are thinking of withdrawing their labour an' that you're encouraging them?'

Lacey met his gaze. 'It is. You've ignored the Union's requests to discuss equal pay, so now we're taking action.'

Jonas leaned forward, his features and tone of voice imploring. 'Lacey, you're my daughter-in-law. Do you think it right to go against me like this?'

Lacey sighed and then said, 'You have to understand how the women feel. It's unfair for them to do the same work as a man and get paid far less just because they are women.'

Exasperated by her far too logical reply, Jonas ran his fingers through his sparse hair. 'Women have always been paid less, Lacey. You know that for a fact.'

'I do, but it doesn't mean it's right. The world's changing; the war's done that and we've got to move with the times. There was a time when women of your social standing were expected to be nothing more than pretty ornaments and the mothers of your children. Now, girls like Felicity are nursing, working in munitions, driving buses or joining the Land Army — proving they're capable of anything — and women in the mills produce cloth as good as any man.' Lacey's impassioned delivery leaving her breathless she paused, fully expecting a heated response from Jonas.

When Jonas made no attempt to intervene, Lacey continued. 'Women like me keep the mills, the munitions factories and a lot of other industries going; they only thrive because of us. It's high time our valuable contribution was recognised; equal pay for equal work. We — '

Jonas slapped his palms together. Lacey fell silent. 'I've heard enough, lass. Now look at it my way. It's my responsibility to keep the Mill in profit.

I do that by securing contracts that keep you in work. If I raise your wages I have to justify it elsewhere. Furthermore, I have to keep wages in line with my competitors. I can't double your hourly rate without considering every option.'

Lacey gazed at him defiantly. 'You need us just as much as we need you.

I'd appreciate it if you could make a decision before next Saturday.'

Jonas smiled wryly. 'Are you threatening me, lass?'

Lacey didn't return the smile. 'We've waited long enough; we can't wait forever.' She stood up, prepared to leave.

Jonas stayed her with a wave of his hand. 'Before you go, lass. How do you think this makes me look, my own daughter-in-law fighting for the other side?'

Lacey's eyes flashed. 'I've always been on the other side. Just because I married your son doesn't mean I've given up fighting for my beliefs. Much as I love Nathan and respect you, I won't abandon the cause.'

Jonas sighed wearily. 'I can see that, lass. You run along now; Constance and Felicity are waiting for you. Leave me to think things over.'

For the rest of that week, every evening after work Lacey and a handful of weavers from Brearley's Mill hurried to the gates of the other mills handing out leaflets explaining their actions. With Lacey's guidance, chosen representatives from each mill approached their employers, requesting a meeting to discuss their demands. These requests were denied, some vociferously. When Lacey approached Jonas he still hadn't reached a decision.

On Saturday afternoon Townend bustled with women from several mills in the valley, their children running in and out of the noisy gathering. Lacey dashed from one group to another urging them to form a procession then, positioning herself at its head she addressed the women in clear, ringing tones.

'Ladies, we all know why we're here and what we're asking for; equal pay for equal work. So, raise your voices and make yourselves heard; show the bosses we mean business.' The women cheered their approval, Lacey waving her hands to silence them. 'We're marching to show our solidarity. We'll do it peaceably, no rough stuff. Chant if you like, but no slander, no bad language. We're ladies, remember?'

A roar of laughter drowning her words, Lacey struggled to continue.

'We'll stop outside the gates of each mill to state our demands. If the owners aren't there to meet us they'll soon hear about it. Are you ready to follow me?'

Shouting and laughing, the eager women formed a straggling throng. They carried placards with the names of their mills and the words:

EQUAL PAY FOR EQUAL WORK

daubed on them. The women from Brearley's Mill held aloft a white sheet emblazoned with the words:

WOMEN ARE THE WORKERS OF TODAY.
THEY DESERVE EQUAL PAY

The procession surged forward, the women chanting and cheering.

Listening to them, Lacey wondered if they realised the effort that had been expended in bringing them together.

'I'm worn out already,' she muttered to Joan, marching beside her, 'but look how many turned out, an' listen to 'em. It makes it all worthwhile.'

22

In the week following the march, the women waited for the mill owners' response. When none came, Lacey called for the women from each mill to withdraw their labour on Saturday morning. It being a half day, the majority agreed as they weren't losing a full days' pay.

Come Saturday, resolute crowds of women gathered outside the gates of Brearley's, Jarmain's, Brooksbank's and Hebblethwaite's Mills, deaf to the managers' pleas to go inside and attend to their looms. Irate mill owners, desperate to meet their contracts, joined in the fray, the women jeering at their half hearted threats of instant dismissal: they would not, could not, afford to dispose of the majority of the workforce.

The next Saturday, the women again withdrew their labour, although many of them were losing heart as well as earnings.

'We can't go on like this, Lacey,' grumbled Sarah Broadhead from Jarmain's mill. 'T'lasses are fed up of losing their wages, an' t'bosses aren't for shifting.'

'They will when they get these on Monday morning,' said Lacey, gesturing to a clutch of envelopes. 'If they don't agree to meet and discuss our demands we'll strike every Friday as well as Saturday.'

'Eeeh, I don't think many lasses will agree to that. They can't afford it.'

243

Lacey gave a brave smile. 'They might not have to. The bosses can't make cloth without us. They'll have to do summat about it.'

★ ★ ★

In the comfortable surroundings of Garsthwaite's Assembly Rooms four sombre gentlemen sat round a table, their snifters of brandy untouched.

'We can't go on like this,' snapped Jonas Brearley, 'I'm already behind wi' my biggest contract. I've Government officials breathing down my neck for a completion date. They're threatening to penalise me if I can't come up wi' the goods.' He reached for his drink and gulped at it, almost choking when the fiery liquid hit the back of his throat.

Charles Brooksbank curled his lip distastefully. An owner with scant knowledge of the workings of his mill, he deplored Jonas's rough manner.

'Personally, I'm inclined to hold you responsible for this debacle. My informants assure me the instigator of that ridiculous protest rally and the withdrawing of labour is in your employ: not only that, she's your daughter-in-law.'

He glanced imperiously from one to the other of the assembled mill owners to judge the effect this information had on them. 'Had you the foresight to vet your workers more scrupulously you would not have employed her in the first place,' he continued, 'and you most certainly should never have allowed your son to marry her.'

Jonas's hackles rose. 'Watch what you say. I'll not have you cast aspersions on my son's choice

244

of wife; it's nowt to do wi' you.'

'It is when she threatens my livelihood,' barked Brooksbank, undeterred.

'Listen to yourself,' Jonas sneered, 'you'd think we were all bankrupt the way you talk. Haven't we all made a killing with these Government contracts? Maybe we should give the women a bit more; we're all in profit.'

'Exactly,' Brooksbank sneered, 'and I intend to keep every shilling. Have you no control over the women in your employ?'

'Nay, I'll not take blame for summat as affects us all,' Jonas blustered, slamming the flat of his hand down hard on the table. 'The women in your mills must be just as bloody minded as them in mine. Otherwise they wouldn't be standing outside your mill gates refusing to work all day Friday and Saturday morning.'

'He's right,' Amos Hebblethwaite conceded. 'We must give this matter careful thought. We need those women just as much as they need us. I've witnessed all manner of protests in the industry in my seventy-eight years, and if we don't handle this one fairly it could be to our cost.' He sat back in his chair, the better to assess the reaction of his companions.

For the next half hour they bickered and connived. Eventually Jonas sat back, absenting himself from the argument. In his mind he pictured his daughter-in-law, Lacey. By, but she was a woman to be reckoned with. He who had known the hardships of working in the mill couldn't help but admire her. His son loved her and his wife and daughter were equally fond. Lacey had made a difference in all their lives. She might only be a working class girl but her beliefs had forced Jonas to reconsider his views on humanity. Maybe now was the time to even things up a bit, make life easier for those that struggled. It wasn't as though he couldn't afford it. He leaned forward, demanding attention.

'I've decided what I'm going to do,' he said firmly. 'The rest of you can do as you please.'

The others looked at him expectantly.

'If I miss my deadlines it'll cost me more than I care to think about. Therefore I reckon it'll be worth my while to make sure I meet 'em on time.' He swigged his brandy, then lit a cigar. 'I pay my lasses four bob less than I pay the men. Now, I'm not going to give 'em equal pay but I will meet 'em halfway. Two bob extra on every piece should satisfy 'em.' He thumped the table, a smile of satisfaction lighting his florid features.

Silas Jarmain reared up. 'It's easy for you. I'll have to pay my women four shillings more to match your offer.'

Jonas smirked. 'That's because you're a cheapskate, Silas; you've always underpaid 'em.' He turned in his seat to address Amos Hebblethwaite. 'It'll cost you nobbut a shilling a head, Amos, so what do you say?'

Amos ran a gnarled hand over his furrowed brow, his aged features revealing a weariness of the debacle. 'It seems fair to me,' he growled. 'The most important factor is to get the women back working full time. We daren't risk an all out strike. We've all got too much to lose.' His gaze roved from one face to another, the zeal in his rheumy eyes threatening them to dare disagree. Heads nodded assent.

Charles Brooksbank's face turned puce. 'Ridiculous,' he spluttered, 'we're being held to ransom.'

'Aye, we are,' said Jonas, 'but, as Amos says, we'll be the losers if we don't nip this in the bud.'

Reluctantly, Brooksbank and Jarmain agreed to comply. Brandy glasses refilled and cigars lit, the gentlemen discussed business.

★ ★ ★

Two days later, in four mills in the valley, unusual scenes were witnessed.

In Hebblethwaite's Mill the women weavers raised their voices in hymns of praise before starting up their looms. The women in Brooksbank Mill performed a spontaneous dance in the mill yard, cheering and singing as they jigged. At Jarmain's Mill they called in a local preacher and gave thanks to God, whilst at Brearley's they formed a conga line, weaving in and out between the looms, Lacey leading the way. They had triumphed and now they were celebrating.

Later that night Lacey dashed off a letter to Nathan. As she scribbled she pictured him smiling and shaking his head as he read of her latest escapade.

In bed, Lacey lay flat on her back gazing up at the ceiling, a feeling of deep content suffusing her mind and body. The past three weeks hadn't been easy: but what of it? Life wasn't easy. But you could strive to improve it. That's what she felt she had done; and not just for herself but for others too.

Sleep threatening to overtake her, she recalled Henry Wordsworth Longfellow's words; words she liked and had committed to memory. 'Perseverance is a great element of success. If you only knock long enough and loud enough at the gate, you are sure to wake up somebody.'

Lacey smiled sleepily. She had knocked at the Mill gate and Jonas Brearley had woken.

23

In accordance with Nathan's wishes Lacey visited Fenay Hall at least once a week, sometimes staying for dinner. On this particular evening, as Soames showed her into the drawing room, she was disappointed to find the odious Alice and Violet already there.

'Ah, here's your little seamstress come to call with you, Constance. Are you planning a new outfit?' Alice's arch tone and the malicious gleam in her eye were not lost on Lacey.

Constance made Lacey welcome but made no attempt to disaffirm Alice's spiteful remark. Lacey was not really surprised. She still suspected her mother-in-law's opinion of her.

Lacey sat as far away as possible from Alice and Violet, half listening to their tiresome prattle and at the same time wondering if perhaps Constance hoped that Nathan might return from the war a changed man and realise the mistake he had made in marrying beneath him. Lacey shuddered at the thought, her reverie broken by Alice calling her name.

'Lacey, is it true that you went against your employer, Mr Brearley, in that recent debacle at the mills? That you organised a strike.' Lacey heard the pretence of concern for Jonas in Alice's tone and scorned it, doing so again when Alice turned to Constance, her face twisted in mock compassion. 'I heard that there were gangs of raucous

249

women at the mill gates shouting the vilest slurs against the mill owners.' Then, addressing Lacey, she simpered, 'Were you one of them, my dear?'

'I was,' said Lacey, her gaze steely and her tone harsh, 'we were demanding our rightful dues and what's more we got them, so we must have been in the right all along.'

Alice slid her eyes in Constance's direction, eager to judge her opinion of Lacey's outburst. Constance, her cheeks flushed, clapped her hands together loudly. 'Lacey! Alice! I must admit I don't approve of women disporting themselves in such a vulgar fashion but neither do I approve of mill talk in my drawing room; so let that be an end to it.'

So much for a mother-in-law's support for her son's wife, thought Lacey, Soames's timely announcement that dinner was ready preventing her from giving Alice a piece of her mind.

Over dinner, Alice's attempts to resurrect talk about the strike were ignored by Jonas and quashed by Constance's withering glare. One could almost be forgiven for thinking my dear mother-in-law secretly approves of me, thought Lacey, as Alice wilted under yet another harsh reprimand from Constance. Still, considering all the snide remarks about my lack of breeding or my Union involvement that she's fired off in the past, I wonder how long it will be before her true colours show through.

★ ★ ★

250

The next morning Lacey took the opportunity to have a long lie in before performing her usual Sunday ritual. Later in the day, after church, she would eat her midday meal with the Barracloughs then spend an hour or two with Joan at Scar End.

Midway between sleeping and waking, snuggled under the eiderdown in the bed that always seemed half empty, Lacey was suddenly disturbed by a furious hammering on her front door. Throwing on a robe, she ran barefoot to open it. Joan's younger sister, Maggie, fell inside. 'Lacey! Lacey! Come quick! Our Joan got one o' them letters. Stanley's been killed.'

Lacey's blood ran cold as her sluggish mind struggled to register the awful news. She clasped hold of the crying girl, close enough to feel the thud of Maggie's heart; her own sinking to the very depths of her being.

Stanley! Dead! Would this soon be Nathan's fate? Gently disengaging the hysterical Maggie, Lacey steeled herself for what lay ahead.

Dressed any old how, and with her feet feeling as though they were made of lead, Lacey and Maggie hurried to Scar End. What would she do when she got there? How did you comfort a woman who had lost the man she loved? Would this terrible war snatch away all the brave young men before it ended?

Joan sat as though turned to stone, dry eyed and silent. 'She's in shock,' whispered her mother, 'hasn't said a word since she read that letter.' May whirled round, yelling at the top of her voice. 'An' you can stop that yowling, our Maggie. It's our

251

Joan as lost her husband, not you.' Maggie shuffled into the kitchen.

Lacey knelt to chafe Joan's lifeless hands, as though her own might imbue some inner strength. 'Joanie, it's me, Lacey. I'm here for you, luv. I'll always be here for you. I'm sorry about Stanley but you have to be brave for young James's sake.'

As though on cue, James let out a piercing wail. May lifted him from his pram. 'He's too young to understand an' she's in no fit state to mind him. I'll take him for a walk. It might soothe him.' Placing the howling child back in the pram, May trundled off.

In the silence that followed May's departure Lacey cradled Joan in her arms, rocking her as a mother would a frightened child and whispering what she knew were totally useless words of comfort. Maggie mashed a pot of strong tea, Lacey almost forcing Joan to take hold of the hot sweet drink.

Suddenly the impasse exploded. Joan flung the cup across the room, a torrent of tears gushing down her cheeks as she screamed, 'Stanley's dead. They've killed my Stanley an' left our James wi'out his Dad.'

Lacey caught Joan's flailing hands in her own. 'I know, luv, I know, but we're here for you. We'll help you get through it. Stanley loved you and little James. He'd want you to be strong for him.'

For the rest of the day they sat cloaked in misery, searching for something, anything, to ease Joan's anguish. Eventually she fell into a fitful sleep. Lacey fed and comforted James until he too slept. The little house eerily quiet, Lacey gazed forlornly at her cousin's ravaged face and then turned to address May Chadwick.

'I'll sleep here tonight. Ask your Maggie to nip up to Netherfold and let 'em know what's happened.'

May shook her head. 'No lass, you get off home. I'll stay with her. Our Joanie'll understand why you've had to go.'

'I'm not going anywhere,' Lacey replied firmly. 'You can stay an' all; she'll need all of us in the next few days.'

* * *

Several weeks later, weeks in which Lacey thought of little else other than Joan's grief and Nathan's safety, Constance and Felicity called at the house in Towngate. In answer to their knock, Lacey eased her foot off the treadle, the machine whirring to a stop as she went to open the door. Constance and Felicity stepped inside, the latter chirping, 'We thought you might like company.'

'Go through into my sewing room,' Lacey said, 'it's the only room that's warm. I don't light a fire in the sitting room when I'm on my own.'

Felicity and Constance did as they were bid, Constance wearing a smile of genuine concern when she saw the pile of sewing awaiting Lacey's attention. 'You mustn't overwork yourself, Lacey. Had I known you were so busy I wouldn't have suggested you make my new dress so soon after the other one.' She sat down in a chair by the hearth.

Lacey smiled warmly at her mother-in-law.

253

'Don't worry about me; I never get tired of sewing.' Removing the partially finished dress from the machine she held it up. 'What do you think?'

'It's wonderful, my dear. You are clever.'

'I just hope I'm clever enough to get the collar and cuffs right. This white pique's the devil to work with.'

'Oh, I'm sure you'll manage. I have every faith in you,' Constance assured her.

Lacey excused herself and went into the kitchen to make tea, smiling wryly at Constance's last remark. Faith indeed: you couldn't bear the sight of me a few months ago, thought Lacey, and lifted the kettle.

In the sewing room, Felicity flicked through the pages of *Weldon's Journal* and Constance let her gaze rove from the pile of sewing to the pretty cushions and curtains decorating the room. This house was Nathan's home now, a warm and welcoming haven created with love for when he returned; Lacey had made it so. Constance's thoughts strayed to when she first met Lacey; how she had despised her. But look what she had achieved since then: whenever Nathan was with her he was at his happiest; the ladies of Garsthwaite were thankful for her sewing skills, and the women in the mills praised her to the hilt for improved facilities and fairer earnings — all this achieved not just for herself but for the happiness of others.

'You're very quiet, Mama,' said Felicity, concerned by Constance's lengthy silence.

Constance gave a half smile. 'I was giving thought to a serious matter.'

Before Felicity could enquire what that might be, Lacey arrived with the tea. They sat at the fire, Constance gossiping about her work with the Ladies Charity Fund, and Lacey telling them about Joan and how she was coping since Stanley's death.

'It must be dreadful,' Constance murmured.

'It is, and for dozens of women like her,' Lacey said, going on to describe the hardships many mill women suffered. 'They rear families in overcrowded, dilapidated houses, nurse aging parents and farm out their babies to whosoever will care for them whilst they toil in the mill.'

To Lacey's surprise, Constance listened avidly to tales involving a way of life she had once denied existed. Lacey found it hard to equate the empathy Constance so obviously felt for these women with the snobbish opinions she had held in the past.

As they sipped tea by the fire, Felicity now taking part in the conversation, Lacey was surprised when Constance said, 'I would like to help. Surely I could use my position to make life easier for them.'

Lacey nodded enthusiastically, suggesting Constance persuade the Ladies Charity Fund, of which she was chairman, to do some good in their own town rather than for missions in far flung places.

Who'd have thought we'd ever sit chatting like this, Lacey asked herself as she drained the dregs from her cup and set it down before rising to take a letter from the mantelpiece. 'It's from Nathan; it arrived this morning. You can read it if you like.

255

Mind you, I'll be embarrassed if you read the mushy stuff at the end.'

Constance's face lit up at the mention of her son and Felicity rolled her eyes as she took the letter from Lacey's hand. 'We promise not to read the last page.'

Lacey responded with a grin which softened into a fond smile threatening tears as she said, 'I try to picture him out there in the trenches: First Lieutenant Nathan Brearley of the Duke of Wellington's Regiment leading his men into battle. It sounds grand but I'd prefer plain Nathan Brearley at the Mill, and have him here every day.'

Constance clamped her lips and closed her eyes for a moment. When she opened them, she gazed directly into Lacey's. 'When you write, let him know that you and I are friends, because we are, Lacey. I'm sorry I misjudged you. I'm a foolish woman sometimes.'

Moved by the heartfelt apology, Lacey gave Constance a hug, at the same time thinking, I never imagined doing this, not in a month of Sundays.

Letting Constance go, she said, 'For Nathan to know that will cheer him up no end. He loves us both, just as much as we love him. We have a responsibility to make him happy.'

Constance's eyes filled with tears. 'We do, Lacey.'

That same night, Lacey wrote a letter to Nathan telling him of Constance's apology.

Six weeks later, in yet another letter, she was able to describe how, in his absence, she and Constance were getting on splendidly.

'We are learning together,' she wrote. 'Your mother has unintentionally taught me so much;

a more refined way of speaking, table etiquette and gracious manners — all useful attributes for the businesswoman I intend to be. For my part, I'm introducing your mother to aspects of life in Garsthwaite she never knew existed, and underneath that snobbish exterior beats the heart of a very kind woman.'

Two weeks later she received his reply. Along with his usual endearments he congratulated her for 'working her magic' on Constance and on her success with the equal pay issue. In conclusion, he wrote, 'still my Lacey, fighting battles for the underdog. Rather similar to what I am doing over here, although not as muddy.'

When Lacey read Nathan's reply she loved him all the more for sparing her the gruesome details of how it truly was in the trenches. It was so like him to bear it bravely and cheerfully for her sake. Yet she knew of the horrors he faced night and day, the papers were full of it; ghastly defeats, the trenches rife with disease, food shortages and the lack of basic equipment were reported daily. Although Lacey hated the articles she could not ignore them. All she could do was pray for Nathan's safety and his speedy return. Therefore she was overjoyed when she received yet another letter from him:

God willing, I hope to be with you sometime before the end of the month (September 1915). Can't say why (classified info.) or when exactly. In the meantime, pray God preserves me and returns me safe to England's shore.

Puzzled and elated, Lacey waited, sadly unable to share the joy with Joan; it would be insensitive to crow over Nathan's imminent return knowing Stanley was never coming home. With each passing day, Lacey hugged the wonderful news deep inside.

24

Of necessity, Joan had returned to the weaving shed a week after Stanley's death leaving young James, as usual, in her mother's care. Day by day her grief appeared to lessen, but the bright, bubbly girl she had once been was replaced by a quiet, introspective and often distracted woman.

With Joan's situation in mind, Lacey decided that the time was right to put her own plans for the future into action instead of just dreaming about them.

She was hanging up her coat when she heard the sound of an engine outside and above it a familiar voice saying, 'Pick me up at this address at four on Friday.'

Lacey wrenched open the door, and, as the military vehicle roared away she fell into Nathan's arms.

'You seem pleased to see me,' he chuckled, pulling her into the house to kiss her.

'Oh Nathan, you don't know how much. I wasn't expecting you so soon.'

Lacey gazed into Nathan's grey-blue eyes, his reflection mirrored in the green depths of hers and conveying the same deep love and yearning.

Over a hurriedly prepared meal, Nathan told Lacey he could only stay for two days. 'Three days in London on military business then a quick dash up here before I'm collected and taken back to France.' Disappointed at the brevity of his leave,

Lacey determined to make every second memorable.

She watched as Nathan ravenously ate the pie she had made earlier, shocked to see how gaunt and weary he looked. Deep shadows ringed his eyes and lines etched his mouth and cheeks. In her excitement at his arrival, she had failed to notice the change in him.

They finished their meal and went to Fenay Hall, Nathan's parents and sister elated to see him, and Lacey dismayed to find Alice and Violet there.

Nathan's family clamoured for his attention and Lacey, accepting it was their right to do so stood back, secure in the knowledge that he would be hers alone once they returned home.

Unfortunately, this left her as prey to Alice and Violet. 'I gather you're living in the house in Towngate,' Alice remarked archly. 'In the event of Nathan's untimely death it will fetch a tidy sum; but then I suppose that's part of your plan. Did you fool him into believing you were with child? Is that why he married you?'

'How dare you suggest such things,' Lacey said, stung by the wicked insinuation. She kept her voice deliberately low to prevent being overheard; the last thing she wanted was for this spiteful bitch to ruin Nathan's homecoming.

'By rights it would have been my house had you not lured Nathan from me with your filthy ways,' Violet said peevishly. 'Mama says a woman who sells her body is nothing but a common whore.'

'Indeed she is,' Alice said, 'and now we have one in the family.'

Lacey clenched her teeth, biting back the words 'stick your head up your arse and go to hell, you old cow,' and saying instead, 'Your bitterness demeans you.'

'Not as much as it will you,' hissed Alice. 'One of these days I'll make you pay for ruining my daughter's future. I'll ruin yours. I haven't done with you by a long chalk.'

Lacey pushed Alice aside, feeling an urgent need to distance herself from this malevolent woman. Whereas Alice's jealous spite had previously merely frustrated, it now alarmed her.

* * *

Later that night, her fears allayed by Nathan's passionate love-making, Lacey felt invincible, and Alice's sinister threats merely nonsense spewed from an embittered woman's mouth. Yet, when she woke they came back to haunt her.

After visiting the Barracloughs, Lacey and Nathan walked up Cuckoo Hill, rejoicing in each other's company and sharing the details of their separate lives. Only when they were out on the moor, did Nathan talk about his time in France.

'It's the strain of waiting to go into action that's worse,' he said. 'It shreds your nerves, and afterwards, when we count our losses we're left wondering what it was we achieved. In whatever place we're based we can only measure what *we* have done — we never know the whole story.' He shook his head, exasperated. 'It's all so confusing, and the muck and mess of our squalid living conditions do nothing to raise morale. It's the young boys I feel for most.'

Lacey stroked his cheek. 'Anyone would think you were an old man the way you talk.'

'I feel like it out there. I'm not yet twenty-five but compared to lads of seventeen I do at least feel I've experienced some of life's wonders; marrying you being one of them. Those boys have never had the opportunity to make a career or follow their dreams; some have never had a girl and, sadly, some never will.' His face creased with anxiety at this depressing observation. 'But enough talk of war, let's talk about you.'

Lacey described the march and the campaign for equal pay, eventually lightening the mood by relating amusing incidents at the Mill, Nathan comforted as he listened to the familiar occurrences.

'I still go to the Union meetings and I sometimes help your mother with her charity work. She visits needy families, delivering clothes and useful household items she's been gathering furiously for weeks.'

'Good Lord! I can't imagine Mother doing that? There was a time when she wouldn't even walk the streets where they live.' Nathan chuckled wryly.

'Now she's hell bent on doing good deeds,' Lacey giggled.

Nathan laughed out loud. 'No doubt with plenty of encouragement from you.'

Stopping to rest on a rocky outcrop in the vast expanse of heather and bracken they watched a buzzard circle high above their heads before swooping for its prey. Lacey recalled Alice's threats.

'Why is Alice so infuriated by our marriage?'

Nathan looked puzzled. 'What has she been saying?'

Lacey told him everything.

'The vile creature!' Nathan expostulated, 'I'll put her straight when next I see her. For years now, she's foisted her bucktoothed, dim witted daughter on me, and Violet stupidly complies. I know that sounds unkind but both Father and I know what their game is. Alice's husband gambled his fortune, leaving her virtually penniless when he died. It's not me they want, it's my money; or should I say the money I'll inherit when Pa's no longer with us.'

'So it's greed that makes her so vicious,' Lacey said. 'I thought maybe you had been promised to Violet.'

'I never looked twice at Violet; as for marrying her ... ' Nathan's laughter rolled across the moorland. 'Pay no heed to Alice's idle threats, the woman's barmy.' He pulled Lacey to her feet. 'Now, let me take you home and show you exactly why I married you, Mrs Brearley.'

★ ★ ★

Shortly before Nathan's transport was due to arrive he took Lacey in his arms, saying, 'If anything happens to me, Lacey, all this is yours. John Hinchcliffe has the details and he'll advise you if needs be.' The mention of the solicitor made it sound ominous.

When the military jeep pulled up outside the door, Nathan held Lacey close and stared into her

263

face, as if memorising every detail. Lacey held his gaze, seeing in his eyes a love so deep she felt as though she was drowning.

Her parting kiss imbued all the passion she could muster. 'I love you, Nathan Brearley. I always will. Come back soon.'

The jeep drove off. A gang of children, unused to seeing army vehicles in Garsthwaite, chased after it, their arms raised to hold imaginary rifles, their voices imitating the sound of gunfire. Their childish actions jarring her nerves, Lacey watched the jeep disappear from view.

25

'By, but this weather's fit to freeze you to death.' Joan pulled the thick shawl draped over her head and shoulders all the tighter.

Lacey glanced up at the leaden sky. 'Aye, we didn't have much snow before Christmas but it's made up for it since.'

Their steps precarious on the icy footpath, they were making the early morning journey to the Mill, two women of similar nature but with different agendas; one trying her utmost to simply earn a living, the other unwavering in her determination to improve both their lives.

'Here, link me; we don't want you falling in your condition.'

Lacey slipped her arm through Joan's. Three months into her pregnancy she was taking great care, the baby she was carrying a manifestation of her love for Nathan and his for her. This child was Nathan's son or daughter, God's precious gift. She only hoped its father would live to see it and be there to watch it grow, unlike Stanley, whose son James would never know him.

Since Stanley's death, Joan was coping as well as could be expected.

Even so, thought Lacey, as they entered the Mill yard, she'll never again be as happy as she used to be; but then, what woman could be once she'd lost the man she loved?

'I hope there's a letter from Nathan when I get

home,' said Lacey, then immediately felt guilty —
Stanley would never write to Joan again — but
she needed to talk about him if only to allay her
fears. Letters affirming Nathan was alive and well
renewed Lacey's faith in God.

'I know how you feel,' said Joan. 'Whenever I
got one from Stanley it always made me feel close
to him.' She bit down on her bottom lip at the
memory.

'I don't even know if Nathan's received my letter telling him he's going to be a father. I wonder
if he'll be as shocked as I was when I first found
out.'

Joan gave a laugh. 'I don't know why you were
shocked; it's not as though you weren't doing owt
to cause it. The last time he was home on leave
you spent most of it in bed, or so you told me.'
This time it was Lacey's turn to laugh.

★   ★   ★

Shadows lengthened, the thrash and beat of
looms racing their way to the end of the working day. Out of the corner of her eye, Lacey saw
Joan darting from one of her looms to the other.
She didn't see Joan's feet skidding on the greasy
floor, but she heard her screams rising above the
noise of the machinery as she pitched forward
into a thrashing loom. Its mechanism impeded,
the loom automatically stopped, but not before it
had entangled Joan's turban and a bloodied mop
of blonde hair into warps and wefts.

Lacey knocked out her own looms and dashed
across weaver's alley, yelling at the top of her

voice for assistance. Like a broken rag doll Joan sprawled against the loom, unconscious. A dark patch, devoid of hair and skin, oozed blood from the horrendous wound to her scalp.

A deathly hush fell over the weaving shed as one by one the women stilled their looms. Fear of suffering the same fate gripping them all, they watched as panic-stricken managers sent for help. Lacey sat on the greasy floor, Joan's head resting in in her lap and blood seeping through her overall, forming a puddle between her thighs. Someone produced a length of clean white cotton cloth and as Lacey gently used it to staunch the flow of blood she willed her cousin to live and the ambulance to hurry up.

⋆ ⋆ ⋆

Joan lingered at death's door, drifting in and out of consciousness, the shock to her system more serious than the damage to her scalp. Whenever she woke she suffered terrifying flashbacks, her hands clawing feverishly at her bandaged head as she screamed and thrashed about in her hospital bed.

More often than not, Lacey was at her bedside and when she wasn't there she was relieving May, who was caring for James. She wasted no time in bringing Joan's serious injuries to the attention of Jonas and the Union, refusing to accept that they were caused by Joan's own negligence rather than an overburdened workload and a greasy floor.

Gradually, as Joan's scalp wounds began to heal, her spirits were strengthened by Lacey's devotion. She held her when she sobbed for the loss of

267

her glorious blonde curls and made her laugh by drawing pictures of the ridiculous hats she might make to cover Joan's disfigurement. She paid the rent on Joan's house and cared for James as though he was her own, all these small kindnesses giving Joan the will to get better. And throughout it all, Lacey continued to fight for Joan's right to compensation.

★ ★ ★

'I'm so glad Joan's wounds are healing nicely,' said Felicity, as Lacey brought in the jug of cocoa they would share before the car came to take Felicity back to Fenay Hall. They had just returned from visiting Joan in the Royal Infirmary in Huddersfield, Lacey thankful for Jonas placing his car and chauffeur at their disposal and grateful to May and Joan's sister, Elsie, for babysitting.

'The surface wounds might be healing but it's the hurt inside that worries me,' said Lacey, handing a mug to Felicity then sitting down with her own.

They talked about Joan for some time until Felicity changed the topic of conversation by gesticulating at the pile of garments on Lacey's sewing table. 'What's all this?' she asked.

'Everyone wants their clothes altering these days, and I want to get these out of the way before the baby comes. Ivy Vickerman tells me you can never be sure when a first baby might arrive,' said Lacey.

Felicity grinned. 'Fancy, Nathan a father. I'm sure it will be a boy, a son to carry on the Brearley name. Jonas will be delighted if it is.'

'And the day *you* present him with a grandchild he'll be absolutely cock-a-hoop.'

Felicity frowned. 'Isn't that a bit premature. I've yet to find a husband.'

She gazed dismally into her empty cocoa cup.

Lacey set down her own mug and gazed thoughtfully at Felicity. 'I've never asked but I've often wondered why a lovely young woman like you has no man in her life.'

Felicity gazed back at Lacey, her expression wary. Then, as though measuring the depth of their friendship she heaved a sigh and, carefully weighing her words she asked, 'Can you keep a secret?'

Lacey widened her eyes. 'You know I can.'

Felicity smiled gratefully. 'You know I was in Switzerland at about the time you and Nathan first met?' Lacey nodded, her curiosity agog. 'Well,' Felicity continued, 'I met someone and fell in love.' She paused, fingers twisting in consternation. 'I'm still in love but it's a hopeless cause, and that being the case I don't suppose I'll ever marry.'

Felicity looked so miserable, Lacey's heart ached for her. 'Why is it hopeless? Does he not love you?'

Felicity pressed her lips into a sad little smile. 'He says he does and I believe him, but he can't marry me. He's already married.'

Lacey, who had always considered her sister-in-law to be a carefree young woman, was astounded to learn that Felicity harboured an impossible secret love. Words failing her, Lacey took Felicity's hands in hers and held them tight. Felicity smiled wanly and shrugged. 'I don't think I could

269

ever love anyone else therefore I'll be an old spinster aunt to this little one,' she said, releasing her hands to pat Lacey's bump.

'Tell me about him,' Lacey begged, thinking it would comfort Felicity if she talked about her mysterious married man. 'What's his name?'

'Stefan; he's a doctor. He married his childhood sweetheart when they were both very young. Her uncle paid for Stefan to go to medical school so he's obligated in more ways than one.' Felicity's shoulders drooped as she related the sorry tale. 'Apparently Maria was a sickly child and now she's an ailing woman. I've met her. She's bitter and vindictive, self-obsessed. The marriage satisfies neither of them.'

'Do they have children?' Lacey asked, her thoughts struggling to come to terms with Felicity's confidences.

Felicity heaved another great sigh. 'Goodness, no! I wouldn't have pursued the relationship had there been, but Stefan is so unhappy and I love him so much I saw no harm in bringing a little joy into his life. Eventually I had to walk away, the futility of it all too hard to bear. But I can't forget him or he me. My love life is conducted on scraps of paper winging their way to and from Switzerland.' She essayed a smile. 'Mama and Pa think I correspond with an old friend from my finishing school, and I let them believe that.'

'I'm sad for you,' Lacey said, genuinely affected by Felicity's unhappiness. 'I won't say cheer up, you'll meet somebody else, because that's foolish, but I'll be here for you whenever you want to share your thoughts and feelings.'

270

Lacey stood in the smoke filled room to the rear of The Black Bull, the Union meeting about to start. Requesting permission to speak, she asked, 'What progress has been made on Joan Micklethwaite's compensation claim?'

'None as yet,' Harry Clegg casually replied. 'Brearley says it wa' Joan's own carelessness as caused the accident, an' her injuries aren't such as she can't return to work.'

Seething inwardly at Harry's dispassionate reply, Lacey cried, 'Joan Micklethwaite nearly lost her life. She's terrified of going back to the Mill. That accident will haunt her for the rest of her days. She needs compensating for loss of earnings.'

That Joan's injuries had occurred at a time when the Unions throughout the industry were fighting for compensation for injured workers and sick pay for those unable to work because they were suffering from an industrially related disease, made it all the more pertinent. However, the mill owners were reluctant to comply with Union demands. Some mills had their own health schemes, but Brearley's had none.

'You bloody women are never satisfied,' grumbled an elderly, disgruntled weaver. 'You got your extra two bob for your pieces, now you're asking for money for them what's too bloody idle to turn in for a shift. You make trouble for everybody. Afore you know it bosses'll be docking our wages to cover t'costs of a health scheme.'

'Aye, yer right there,' a bull of a fellow agreed,

271

his bald pate glistening under the light of the gas mantle above his head.

Lacey gave him a withering glare. 'You might not object to being bald as a coot but Joan Micklethwaite does.' Several members tittered. Ignoring them, Lacey continued. 'It was nature stripped you of your hair; Joan lost hers in an accident that shouldn't have happened. And when accidents or ill health prevent any one of us from working we should be compensated.'

Lacey left The Black Bull thoroughly disheartened.

The next morning, Lacey arrived at the Mill earlier than usual. Jonas was in his office. 'Can I have a word?' Lacey asked, stepping into the small, cluttered room. Jonas looked up, surprised. 'Aye lass, what is it?'

'It's about Joan Micklethwaite. I promised myself never to abuse my position as your daughter-in-law by discussing work issues outside the Mill and I've kept that promise. I left it to the Union to raise Joan's case but it appears you turned them down.'

The friendly face that had greeted Lacey was now that of an astute employer, but Lacey remained steadfast, ignoring the hooter's blast calling her to start work.

'Right now, Joan needs money to pay rent and put food on the table. She daren't go back to the weaving. She'll never get over the shock of losing her hair, or the terrible pain she suffered. I thought you might compensate her until she finds alternative employment.'

Jonas's expression softened. 'Lacey, lass, it's

272

not that I don't feel sorry for your cousin but she caused that accident by her own carelessness. If I compensate her I'll be bankrupt in six months. That lot out there will be tripping over baskets, banging their heads on beams an' getting up to all sorts to make me pay up. I daren't do it for fear they'll take advantage.'

'Yet you know it's wrong,' said Lacey, exasperated. 'Joan didn't injure herself on purpose. An accident is exactly that, only the circumstances are to blame. You say Joan was injured because of her own carelessness, but that's not true. Minding two looms means we're watching out for twelve thousand ends — '

'I do know the technicalities, lass,' Jonas said dryly. 'I own the Mill.'

'Well, in that case you'll know that the floor in that shed is thick with grease,' Lacey fired back, 'that's why Joan fell. We've complained about the floor umpteen times but nowt's been done about it.'

Jonas stared implacably.

Softening her tone, Lacey employed a different approach. 'I understand your fears but it will be up to you to use your judgement when a claim is made. If it was a deliberate act of self-harm then I agree you shouldn't have to pay, but Joan's was an accident.'

'Not in my opinion; her mind wasn't on the job, so I've been told. Now you might be my daughter-in-law and the mother of my first grandchild but I'll not have you interfering in Mill business. I know what's best for this place.'

'I'm sure you do, as far as profits are concerned.

273

You're not a bad employer, Father Brearley, in fact you're better than most but don't let profit outweigh humanity. One of these days you'll have to pay compensation, the Unions will eventually force all mill owners to do that. Don't wait to be forced; do it out of the goodness of your heart.' Lacey turned on her heel and walked out.

Back inside the weaving shed, Lacey walked up and down the alleys speaking to each worker in turn. Heads nodded affirmatively, eyes bright with defiance. Lacey went back to her looms, Isabella Ormston Ford's words running through her head: persistence must prevail.

Throughout the shed, bit by bit the thrashing faded, the noise diminishing to an eerie calm, heddles and shuttles immobile, the looms at rest, the women as motionless as their machines.

'Come on, lasses, what are you playin' at?' Clem Arkwright, tolerant as usual, hurried between the alleys gently coercing the silent women.

Arthur Allbright, a man with a decidedly acerbic temperament, was less forbearing. 'Get to bloody work the lot o' you before I send for Mester Brearley,' he roared, dashing like a madman from one end of the shed to the other.

Lacey's voice rang out clear and resolute. 'We're not working until Joan Micklethwaite is compensated. We all know she wasn't to blame. Any one of us could slip on this floor and end up in a loom. Scalped!'

A rousing cheer rattled the rafters. Lacey scanned their expectant faces, a wide smile wreathing her own. 'Now ladies, if you'll follow me.' Lacey leading the way they marched out into the Mill yard to

274

stand silently, as Lacey had instructed.

Arthur Allbright scampered over to the offices, his expression a mixture of rage and fear. Clem Arkwright shook his head despairingly then went and stood with the women. Two minutes later Jonas blustered out of the office, his cheeks reddened, his eyes flashing. 'What's the meaning of this? Why aren't you at work?'

Lacey stepped forward. Jonas reared his head. 'Oh, I might have known you'd be involved in this. What are you up to now, lass?' His eyes strayed to her distended belly; that was his grandchild in there.

'It's with regard to Joan Micklethwaite's accident, sir. This is not an official Union strike but we women in the weaving shed feel so strongly about this injustice that we will withdraw our labour as and when we choose until we have a guarantee that genuinely innocent injured parties will be compensated for loss of earnings.'

Jonas gazed into the unswerving green eyes. By rights I should have sacked her the first time she stood up against me, he thought, at the same time attempting to quell the sneaking admiration he felt. Was he forever to be plagued by this fiery young woman who stirred up long forgotten memories each time she embarked on a mission?

Jonas looked at the women, their faces determined yet hopeful. Unexpectedly, he felt warm admiration for them. It was their sweat had helped make him the successful businessman he was now. These women, some who had toiled for him for years, were like family. He knew their joys and fears: a marriage, the birth of a child or the death of a loved one. He could count the ones who had been widowed in the past two years and now he felt like a benevolent father. He smiled and nodded understandingly. 'You've made your point. Leave me to deal with it as I think fit.'

★ ★ ★

Lacey's pregnancy had brought the Brearleys and the Barracloughs closer, Edith and Joshua occasionally visiting Constance and Jonas and they reciprocating. That Constance Brearley visited Netherfold amazed both Edith and Lacey. 'I can't believe she's the woman who was so disparaging when she first met me,' Lacey remarked after one of Constance's visits.

'She's changed beyond recognition.'

'If she's owt like as thrilled as I am, being a grandmother will change her even more,' said Edith. 'It's best bit o' news we've had in a long time.'

However, the news alienated Alice and Violet to such an extent that, one evening in Fenay Hall, they openly abused Lacey. When Constance made reference to the expected birth, to everyone's astonishment Alice asked, 'Is it Nathan's?' and to compound their incredulity Violet added, 'With Nathan away so often the baby could be any Tom, Dick or Harry's.'

The rumpus that followed these outrageous remarks resulted in Alice and Violet's instant dismissal, Jonas bellowing as they hastily departed, 'Never darken my door again. I've put up with you for years and bailed you out more times than

276

enough. Now, I'm done with you, so sling your hook.'

Alice had looked to Constance for support but receiving none she and Violet had scuttled out. Nothing had been seen or heard of them since.

Of late, Edith, Constance and Felicity were frequent visitors to the house in Towngate, lured by the prospect of becoming grandmothers and an aunt.

Today Joshua and Jonas accompanied them, withdrawing to a corner of the room to discuss the news on the war and restrictions on trade. The women talked babies.

'We must hire a nurse to attend you after the birth and a nanny for the little one,' said Constance. Lacey's jaw tightened; was Constance about to spoil their amicable relationship by overly interfering in the way she wanted to rear the child.

Mentally making a note to curb Constance's enthusiasm should it get out of control, Lacey said, 'I've already spoken to Ivy Vickerman, the midwife. I won't need a nurse or a nanny; I'll look after my own baby.'

Constance pursed her lips but refrained from arguing. However she couldn't resist adding, 'You know your own mind, Lacey.'

Lacey smiled impishly. 'I'll take that as a compliment.'

About an hour after the Barracloughs and Brearleys had departed, a rapid tattoo on the front door had Lacey opening it to yet more visitors. This time it was Joan and young James.

'Ooh, Lacey, you'll never guess what's happened.' Joan, her cheeks pink and her eyes shining, blurted out her good fortune as she helped James up the steps and into the hallway. 'A man from Brearley's office came to my door with money in an envelope.'

Lacey beamed. Jonas had let his heart rule his head. The following morning, she handed a neatly written letter of resignation to a clerk in the Mill office. Her work at the Mill was complete.

26

Lacey closed the back door of the house in Towngate behind her and crossed the yard to the door of the adjacent building. Metal rasped against metal as she turned the large iron key labelled 'shop' in the lock. The door creaked on its hinges.

Lacey stepped into a long, narrow room lit by one small window; a storeroom of sorts. Walking further into the gloom she came face to face with two elegant heads on long, slender necks above bared shoulders.

Startled, she came to an abrupt halt, giggling when she realised they were just mannequins. Another door led her into the shop. She stood breathing in the dusty smell that permeated the disused haberdashery.

In the dim light filtering through the window blinds she made out an L shaped counter, and behind it a serried row of glass fronted cabinets with neat, narrow drawers beneath them. On the wall to her right an ornate gaslight jutted from the wall and under it, on a little shelf, was a box of matches. Cautiously she turned the gas tap and lit the mantle. It puttered and plopped before bursting into light, illuminating the shop.

It was quite spacious, and the cabinets and drawers were in good repair.

Lacey trailed her fingers in the dust on the polished surface of the counter top; ideal for cutting lengths of fabric on, she thought.

Next, she went behind the counter, opening drawers to disclose socks, ties, undergarments, scarves, buttons, handkerchiefs and ribbons: a veritable treasure trove. The cabinets, their shelves mainly bare, produced an outmoded shirt and a bowler hat.

Deep in thought, Lacey walked the length of the shop and back again, her imagination working overtime. Two sewing machines in the middle of the floor; lengths of fabric and paper patterns in the cabinets; sewing requisites in the drawers; Lacey could see it all. Clapping her hands in delight, then executing a circular tour of the shop and a dizzying twirl she came to a stop in front of the door leading out into Towngate.

To the right of the door was the shop window; Lacey knew this without removing the blind. She'd seen it often enough from the outside. On the inside was a narrow, raised platform. Lacey envisioned the blind removed, the window glasses gleaming, the platform draped in a long swathe of soft, grey velvet and the two dummies from the storeroom each wearing well tailored blouses of her own creation. What a display.

Her heart drumming and her thoughts flying, she turned out the gaslight, locked the rear door and went back into the house. Over a cup of tea, she wrote out a list of the things she needed to start her business. When Edith called in the afternoon, Lacey told her what she intended to do.

Edith was surprised. 'Shop? What shop?'

Lacey laughed. 'The shop next door, of course. The haberdashery.'

Edith's brow puckered. 'Oh aye, Henry Ollerenshaw's. He didn't half give everybody in Garsthwaite

280

summat to talk about when he cleared off.'

Lacey's curiosity was aroused. 'Why, what did he do?'

Edith grimaced, her eyes lighting up at the memory. Lacey settled to listen; Edith always told a good story.

'Henry was a sanctimonious old hypocrite. He never served you but what he did a bit of Bible thumping to let you know what a decent chap he was. He ran off wi' a right flighty piece that worked behind the bar in The Bull's Head. She was all fancy hat an' no knickers. Left a wife an' three children, Henry did. That shop's bad luck.'

Lacey roared with laughter. 'Fancy hat and no knickers; oh Mam, you are funny; there's no such thing as bad luck. You make your own, and you can be sure I'll be wearing knickers when I make a success of my dressmaking business.'

★ ★ ★

Two weeks later, Lacey again walked the length of the shop, this time admiring the transformation; newly painted walls courtesy of Matt, linoleum scrubbed and polished by Edith, and grey linen curtains made by Lacey to replace the window blind. Fabrics, paper patterns, scissors, tapes, spools of thread, trims and buttons in the cabinets and drawers and in the centre of the floor two sewing machines.

'Think on now,' Lacey warned Matt and Edith as work progressed, 'not a word to anyone, most of all our Joan.'

Now, alterations complete, Lacey could barely

281

contain her joy. She patted the bump that, God willing, would soon be her son or daughter, telling it proudly, 'Your Mam's in business, love; building a dream.'

★ ★ ★

Later that week, Lacey waited by her open front door in order to beg a favour from the postman, Sam Barton. He was an old boyfriend of hers; one she hoped was still friendly enough to do what she asked.

Sam came whistling down Towngate. 'Nothing for you, Lacey,' he called out, but when she beckoned him to her door he arrived with a warm smile.

'I know it's not legal, Sam, but will you shove these through the letterboxes on your round?' Lacey held out a pile of leaflets, printed by the small printing house in Towngate.

Sam took the leaflets. Out loud, he read from the uppermost one.

LACEY BREARLEY
Seamstress. Quality work assured.
Material made up to a pattern of your choice.
Alterations undertaken. Private fittings on
request.

Lacey grinned. 'I'm starting up in business, Sam. Deliver these an' I'll mend your shirts for nowt.'

Smiling fondly, Sam shoved the leaflets in his sack. 'I always knew you'd make summat o' yourself, Lacey,' he said.

'You've done all right yourself, Sam. A post-man's a big step up from mill hand.'

Flattered, Sam replied, 'Leave it to me, Lacey. I'll get you more customers than enough. You've always been a grand lass. If I'd not married Elsie Tattershall I'd o' married you.'

Lacey chuckled. 'An' if I hadn't wed Nathan Brearley I might o' married you.'

* * *

'Is anybody home,' Lacey shouted as, later that morning, she let herself into Joan's house in Scar End. It was an unnecessary question; Joan rarely went out. Still conscious of her injuries a swift trip to the grocer's was as much as she made these days.

Joan was sitting by the fire with baby James on her knee, a headsquare hiding her damaged scalp. She turned eagerly, gladdened by Lacey's arrival.

'I wa' just thinking I haven't seen much of you lately,' Joan said.

Lacey sat down, her eyes twinkling as she smiled at Joan. 'That's because there's big changes afoot, Mrs Micklethwaite; a new start for both of us.'

Joan's face registered a gamut of expressions as Lacey told her all that had taken place in the past two weeks.

'Do you really think we can make a go of it?' Joan asked Lacey in awed tones.

'We did well enough when we were on short-time from the Mill. Let's go for it in a big way this time, shit or bust.'

Joan's laughter was heartier than any Lacey

283

had heard from her in a long time. She knew she had done the right thing. Come hell or high water she'd make a success of her business.

* * *

'Keep your fingers away from the needle, Joan. Guide the material through gently, don't pull it!' Lacey's voice rose to a squeal as Joan tugged at the fabric on the machine board.

Joan stopped treadling and threw her hands in the air. 'I'll never get the hang of it, Lacey. I'm hopeless.' She looked so crestfallen Lacey hadn't the heart to be unkind.

Lacey released the mangled piece of cloth from the presser foot, rethreaded the needle and then patiently demonstrated yet again how to sew a seam. 'Let the machine do the work, Joanie. Just hold the cloth in place, then let it glide under the needle. You can do it, I know you can.'

Joan bit down on her bottom lip and set the machine in motion, the needle bobbing in and out and the material travelling freely as she joined the two pieces together. Removing the cloth from the machine she waved it in the air. 'I did it,' she yelled triumphantly.

* * *

The business soon flourished, Lacey and Joan busy making alterations to outdated or outgrown garments; 'make do and mend' as Lacey termed it.

The war that those in power had predicted

would last three months was now in its third year, the inhabitants of every town in Britain applying a certain austerity to their apparel; the poor because they simply could not afford new clothes, and the wealthy because they felt it was their duty to exercise economy in these troubled times. Whatever the reason, Lacey welcomed her clients with open arms.

'The butcher's wife wants this bedspread making into a pair of curtains, Joanie. Can you do that while I finish Mrs Dobbs' tweed suit?' Lacey asked Joan one morning at the end of their first month in business.

Joan set to work.

The curtains made, Lacey held each one up to the light, checking each seam. 'They're perfect, Joanie, I couldn't have sewn them better myself.'

'You're a hard taskmaster, Lacey Brearley. Me fingers are worn to t'bone. Weaving was a doddle compared to this. Before long you'll be expecting me to set sleeves an' pleat skirts.' Although the words were harsh, Joan's delight at pleasing Lacey was written all over her face.

Lacey and Joan soon developed an efficient system. Whilst Lacey concentrated on the more complex alterations, or the cutting out and sewing of new outfits, Joan attended to the simpler tasks; stitching buttons or sewing straight seams. Orders came in regularly and, as the month ended, they were pleased to find their earnings equalled those they had received as weavers.

★ ★ ★

'So, you've set yourself up in business,' said Jonas, an amused smile creasing his fleshy face. He had been away and this was the first Lacey had seen of him since leaving the Mill. She returned the smile, her heart swelling at the approbation in his tone. 'How are you for funds, lass?' he asked. 'It must have a cost a bob or two to put the shop to rights.'

Lacey's smile faded as she recalled the expense. 'It took all my savings, but if business continues to thrive I'll soon be in profit.'

Constance sniffed disapprovingly. 'You're beginning to sound like Jonas. I'm pleased you no longer work in the Mill, but I am concerned you may be overstretching yourself. The baby's less than two weeks away. You should be resting in preparation for the birth.'

Lacey smiled, impishly. 'I know that ladies of quality spend much longer than nine months taking things easy, it's what they are used to, but where I come from women work right up to the birth and in most cases it does them and the baby no harm. The older women in the weaving shed still talk about the time Lizzie Isherwood went home to give birth to her third baby just before breakfast time and was back at her looms in the afternoon.'

'I remember that,' Jonas chortled, 'she's a tough 'un is Lizzie. Best Mrs Weaver I've ever employed.'

Constance waved a hand in front of her face as though to prevent herself from fainting. 'But that's appalling,' she gasped, 'and you, Jonas, shouldn't allow it.'

'I knew nowt about it till t'day after.'

286

Seeing his chagrin, Lacey said, 'Sometimes, Mother Brearley, needs must. Lizzie's husband is an invalid. She's the breadwinner.'

Constance nodded thoughtfully. Her daughter-in-law frequently made her re-evaluate her opinions, and whereas once she had considered herself entitled to her privileged life she now realised how fortunate she was. 'The poor soul,' she said feelingly, 'but even so, Lacey, I think you should take things easier.'

'Sewing isn't heavy work, and I promise I'll be careful.'

Constance somewhat appeased, and pregnant women and babies uppermost in her mind, she said, 'We have two women due to give birth this week; one in Jackroyd Lane and the other in Canal Street.'

Jonas harrumphed. 'I'll leave you to talk women's talk while I attend to some unpaid bills.' At the door he turned, looking sternly at Lacey as he delivered his parting shot. 'And you, young lady, take care o' that grandson o' mine. Do as she tells you,' he nodded in Constance's direction, 'and don't be working all hours.'

'You must know something we don't,' Lacey said to Jonas's departing back, and then to Constance, 'He seems certain it's going to be a boy.'

'So am I,' said Constance, reaching out to pat Lacey's hand. 'Now where were we? Ah, yes, Mrs Stubbs and Mrs Haigh. I've seen to it that they have sufficient clothing and bedding but . . . ' she frowned as she recalled the miserable hovels in Jackroyd Lane and Canal Street, 'what they really need is an extra pair of hands. Mrs Haigh already

287

has six children to care for while her husband is fighting in France.' She shook her head, exasperated.

'He was conscripted in the last round-up.'

Lacey sighed. 'Aye, there are too many women left to deal with too many children. This war has a lot to answer for. I don't know that I'd manage to look after six children single handed.'

'Which brings me to my next problem,' Constance said acerbically.

'Have you thought any more about hiring a nanny?'

Lacey frowned. 'I'm still considering it. Let me see how I cope without one then if I do change my mind I'll rely on your help with that matter.' To pacify Constance, Lacey said these words out loud at the same time inwardly telling herself, I'll be the one to look after my baby. Stop interfering!

'Fair enough,' said Constance, 'now, what about the christening? We need to be organised for such a special occasion.'

Lacey groaned inwardly. Here we go again; Constance taking charge, and the child's not even born.

★ ★ ★

Regardless of Constance's advice that she should take things easy Lacey continued to work although the baby was due any day. She had plenty of orders and today she was in the workshop cutting out a dress for one of her new, wealthier clients. Carefully, she guided her scissors around the paper pattern pinned to a length of dark blue silk. It was

288

a warm August day and Lacey, feeling the heat, had opened the door, a welcoming breeze accompanied by rays of bright sunshine filtering in from the street.

Thinking, this baby gets heavier by the minute, she set aside her scissors to massage her aching back. As she did so, she caught sight of a young woman and an older one peering through the open shop door; it was Alice and Violet Burrows. Lacey stared. Alice looked back at her, a sneer on her lips and her eyes glinting maliciously as they registered Lacey's advanced state of pregnancy. Then, without a word, Alice grabbed Violet's arm and chivvied her down Towngate.

Lacey hadn't given either of them a single thought in months. What were they doing in Garsthwaite? Were they on their way to Fenay Hall to beg forgiveness? She hoped not; she didn't want them back in her life.

Later that evening, when Constance and Felicity called to see Lacey, she asked if Alice and Violet had called at Fenay Hall.

'Pshaw!' spluttered Constance, 'if they had I would have shown them the door. My sympathy for Alice expired long before she made those scurrilous remarks regarding yourself and Nathan. I was glad to be rid of her and her tiresome daughter. I only tolerated them out of pity: not that they were grateful for my hospitality. Alice's vindictive nature caused more arguments than enough.' She patted Lacey's hand. 'Forget about them; I have.'

27

Lacey woke with a start. The baby jiggled inside her. Smiling contentedly, she rolled over onto her back dreamily visualising the small body cocooned in its watery haven, limbs folded, small fists clenched, eyes tight shut in a tiny puckered face.

Abruptly, reverie changed to anxiety, the movement she felt next not the usual gentle shifting and stirring but an insistent pushing. She lay perfectly still, forcing herself to breathe slowly and deeply, and with each breath the pushing feeling grew stronger. Suddenly the bed sheets under her were soaked and she cried out.

'Mam! Mam! The baby's coming.'

From the room next door, where Edith had slept for the past three nights, came a thud followed by a shout. Half in and half out of her dressing gown and with her hair in curlers, Edith was at Lacey's side in minutes. With surprising composure, she quickly assessed the situation. 'Hold on now. Keep calm. It won't come straight away. I'll get Ivy Vickerman. You just stay there.'

Lacey laughed feebly. 'I'm not likely to go anywhere the way I'm feeling.'

Edith shuffled downstairs as fast as her slippered feet allowed.

★ ★ ★

Bright autumn sunshine streamed through Lacey's bedroom window. At either side of the bed, both wearing triumphant smiles, Edith and Ivy sat clutching mugs of hot tea. In the bed, Lacey held a mug in one hand, the other gentling the baby rested in the crook of her arm. She gazed down into the tiny sleeping face.

'He's got Nathan's nose and chin,' she said.

Edith leaned forward. 'So he has. He's a beautiful little boy. My first grandchild; I'm proud of you Lacey.'

At midday Constance and Jonas arrived. 'He's the picture of Nathan,' Constance said, gazing adoringly at her first grandchild. Turning crestfallen eyes on Lacey she added, 'I wish he was here to see him.'

'So do I,' replied Lacey, adding a silent prayer that his father would see him one day.

The rest of the day was busy with visitors. First came Joan and James, Joan eager to offer guidance on baby rearing. Lacey half listened to Joan's advice on feeding, winding and nappy changing while marvelling at the resilience of the human spirit. It was good to see Joan laughing and chatting as though she hadn't a care in the world, yet in the past year she'd lost her husband, the father of her only child, and suffered a horrific, disfiguring accident.

Lacey's eyes rested on Joan's animated face and the blonde curls peeping out from beneath the brim of a neat felt cloche. The curls framing Joan's face were all that was left of her once crowning glory, the ugly hairless patch on her damaged scalp hidden under the hat.

These days Joan was rarely seen bareheaded; even in the privacy of her own home she hid her disfigurement underneath a cotton headsquare. How sad, Lacey thought, that Joan would never again be able to show off her golden cloud of hair, and how brave she was that she could joke about it and her other loss. 'At least Stanley won't have to look at my bald head,'

Joan had said, shortly after her recovery. 'He's gone to a better place, an' my hair ended up in one of Jonas Brearley's pieces.'

Lacey's next visitors were Joshua, Matt, Molly and David. On their way to the house in Towngate they had met the postman. Now, Joshua handed Edith the envelope Sam had given him and recognising the handwriting, she went into another room to read it.

Matt and Molly's love affair had flourished and they were talking of marriage. As Molly relayed her plans for the wedding, Lacey watched Matt with young David. How lucky this little boy was to be getting a father as kind and gentle as Matt, she thought, and what a revelation it would be for Molly to have a loving husband, one who didn't beat her. Judging by the smile on Matt's face he obviously considered himself the luckiest of them all.

When Lizzie Isherwood and a few girls from the Mill arrived Constance welcomed them warmly, smiling tolerantly at their coarse remarks and raucous laughter.

Like a queen surrounded by her loyal subjects, Lacey lay propped up on pillows, weary but deliriously happy. After the girls from the Mill had left, Edith asked. 'Did you get a chance to read our

Jimmy's letter?'

Lacey's smile slipped. 'Don't take it too hard, Mam. He can't be that bad if he can write, and he says the hospital is looking after him really well. He expects to be back at the Front in no time.' Edith nodded, her face still glum at the thought of her youngest child hurt, and she not there to nurse him.

'I wa' hoping they'd send him back to England so he could come home to be my best man,' Matt said.

'If he pesters his commanding officer like he used to pester me, he'll grant him leave just to see t'back of him,' Joshua suggested, wryly.

This remark set everybody chuckling. Lacey was still smiling as she drifted into a well earned sleep.

* * *

Richard Brearley thrived, and if his mother was hungry for the love of his father, her love for him did not go to waste in his absence. Waking each morning to gaze into Richard's blue-grey eyes was like waking to a smaller version of her beloved husband.

The Box Brownie camera captured countless images of Richard's progress, the photographs and lengthy written descriptions of his development winging their way to France week by week. In reply Nathan wrote of his immense pride and joy. Somehow these scraps of paper with their images and words filled Lacey with a new optimism.

★ ★ ★

'We're victims of our own success,' Lacey told Joan, some three months after starting the business. 'Just look at this lot.' She made a sweeping gesture at the rack of garments awaiting alteration and the pile of fabrics for new ones. 'There was me thinking we'd mind the boys and sew at the same time, but it isn't working.'

It was a Monday morning, the tension in the sewing room particularly fraught. Lacey stuck a final pin into the military braid she had attached to a blouse she was making for the Minister's wife, and surveyed the sorry scene. Richard lolled listlessly against the side of the pram, his eyes heavy with the tears he'd shed minutes earlier. Over in the corner James banged a wooden building block against the bars of the playpen, yelling to be set free.

'I'm sorry James's so noisy. He gets tetchy if he can't run round,' said Joan, dropping the buttons she had selected for a heavy tweed coat back into the box as she gazed helplessly at Lacey.

'It's not just James bothering me. It's the whole set up,' said Lacey, going and lifting Richard into her arms. 'We should both be spending proper time with our sons, not just pacifying 'em in between sewing.'

'Do you mean we should pack it in?' Joan gasped, her disappointment plain. 'It 'ud be a shame now we're doing so well.'

Lacey grimaced. 'We're not giving up; we're giving in. If the business is to succeed, we need help. We've got the sewing organised, Joanie. We're a

294

good team. Now we need to organise someone for these little lads. Maybe it's time for me to eat my words and take Constance up on her offer to find a nanny.'

Before Lacey had time to discuss the matter further, the bell above the shop door tinkled. A woman in her forties and a girl of about twenty entered.

'Hello, Mrs Walkingshaw, come to collect your coat, have you?' Lacey raked through the garments hanging on the rack, producing a coat she'd altered earlier.

Annie Walkingshaw slipped it on. 'By, you've made a lovely job of it,'

she said, doing up the buttons and fastening the belt. 'It was me mother's, you know, an' she were twice the size of me; I knew it wa' too good to throw away but I never thought you'd make it fit as well as this.' She admired herself in the mirror next to the rack.

'It's lovely, Mam. It looks just like new.' At the young girl's compliment her mother's smile widened.

'By the way, this is our Susan,' she said, gesturing proudly towards the girl. 'She's my eldest. She's back home 'cos the family she worked for in Huddersfield have moved to Scotland. They begged her to go with them but our Susan didn't want to go so far away from home; did you love?'

Susan nodded then said, 'Scotland didn't appeal to me, that's true, but I'll miss the children terribly.'

Lacey thought 'children'? The cogs in her brain whirred, but before she could speak Susan added confidently, 'I'll soon find another nanny's position what with my experience and Dr McKenzie's excellent reference.'

She smiled brightly, as if to allay any doubts.

Susan Walkingshaw started caring for Richard and James the day after her mother had taken receipt of her altered coat. In between bouts of unhindered sewing their mothers could now pop into Lacey's house, time spent with their respective sons a bonus in the working day.

'I was right about hiring a nanny, and Susan is an excellent choice,' Constance gloated, when she called the next day. She had just spent the last half hour in Lacey's house vetting Susan and now, in the workroom, glancing at the fob watch pinned to her jacket, she said, 'I really must be about my business; four needy families await me.' She walked out to the waiting car.

Joan paused in her work. 'I never thought she'd turn out to be such a grand mother-in-law; remember what she was like when she first met you?'

Joan pulled a face.

Smiling fondly, Lacey replied, 'I do — but she's a changed woman — changed for the better.'

A short while later, Felicity, just back from a trip to London, called at the workroom with her friend, Dylis Brooksbank. Felicity, her blonde hair piled high under a pert little bowler, looked utterly charming in the sleek grey suit Lacey had made especially for the trip. Lacey shook hands with Dylis.

When she hugged Felicity she sensed her sister-in-law's excitement, felt the tension in her lean frame. Had Felicity's meeting with Stefan brought joy or woe, she wondered?

In the weeks since Felicity had first confessed her love for him, although she contrived to maintain her usual frivolous persona, Lacey had come to realise the toll this impasse took on her. When Stefan wrote to say his involvement with the Red Cross necessitated a trip to London, Felicity had immediately gone to the capital on the pretence of visiting a friend. Certain that Dylis knew nothing of Stefan, Lacey refrained from asking the questions that burned on her tongue.

When Dylis announced the need to call on the chemist across the street, Felicity declined to accompany her. Dylis out of earshot and Joan busy treadling, Lacey hustled Felicity into what had been the storeroom and was now a fitting room.

'Well, did you see Stefan?'

Felicity's eyes took on a dreamy quality and her lips parted in a rapturous smile. 'I did, and Lacey I'm full of such hope I can barely conceal it, but . . . '

Her smile fading, she plopped down on one of the little gilt chairs Lacey had bought specially for the room.

Lacey sat on the other. 'Tell me about it,' she urged, 'I won't censure you.'

Felicity blinked away tears.

'I know this sounds dreadful and that I should not seek happiness from it, but I love him so much I cannot prevent myself from being joyful at the expense of Maria's sorrow. She is not expected to live much longer. I feel wicked seeing it as an answer to our prayers, and so does Stefan. Had

297

his work not been so vital he would not have left her for fear she died in his absence. I only hope our love is strong enough to survive the awfulness of her death.'

Overwhelmed by Felicity's confession Lacey kept silent, deep in thought.

Eventually she said, 'Felicity, you're not to blame for the state of her health or their unhappy marriage. Had you never met Stefan these things would have happened anyway. If he still wants you when Maria is dead, don't let guilt come between you.' She stood, and pulling Felicity to her feet, hugged her tightly.

'Hello, I'm back.' Dylis's voice catching them unawares they sprang apart.

'Dry your eyes and put on a smile,' Lacey ordered before walking back into the workshop, 'and I'll get on with Dylis's fitting.'

★ ★ ★

Later that evening Felicity called with Lacey again. In the comfort of Lacey's homely kitchen over a cup of tea they continued their conversation, Lacey reiterating that Felicity must not let Maria's death deny her a chance of happiness. 'If Stefan wants you, don't turn him down.

Felicity, on the verge of tears, shook her head in exasperation. 'Why is it that the only time I've ever been in love it's spoiled by deceit, subterfuge and misery? I've hidden my feelings for so long I'm twisted inside, and now, when the man I love may soon be free to love me, we'll live in the shadow of his wife's death.'

298

'You will if you choose to dwell on it,' said Lacey, her harsh tone making Felicity blink. 'Of course, Stefan will have to come to terms with Maria's death, but if the marriage is as unhappy as you say it is then he'll not grieve forever. If he looks to the future, so should you. Things happen, you have to get over them and get on with your life. Trouble is, Felicity, you'd never faced adversity until you fell in love with Stefan. Now's the time to be brave.'

Cowed by Lacey's reference to her privileged life, Felicity hung her head and stared at her clasped hands. Lacey emphasised her argument.

'Consider my cousin, Joanie Micklethwaite. Her husband, Stanley, was killed in France not long after their son was born, then she was grossly disfigured in an accident in your father's Mill. She has plenty to grieve about.'

Felicity nodded solemnly, instinctively smoothing her hair as she recalled the terrible accident.

'Joanie's problems will be with her for the rest of her life,' Lacey continued. 'She can't bring back a dead husband or replace her hair, but do you see her moping? No, you don't. That only creates more problems. She's picked herself up, and with sheer determination she's made a happy life for herself and her child.'

'I never thought of her in that light,' Felicity murmured, 'she's always remarkably cheerful.' She brought her hand to her lips as if to suppress the guilt she felt at her neglect, and her own weakness.

'That's because she's made herself that way, 'Lacey retorted. 'Now, if you take my advice, you'll do the same. Give Stefan time, and if and when he asks you to marry him, don't be influenced by all that's gone before, be courageous and move on.'

Felicity searched Lacey's face. 'Is that what you will do if anything happens to Nathan?' There was no malice in the question.

The colour leached from Lacey's cheeks. She closed her eyes for a moment and then sat up straight, thrusting back her shoulders and jutting out her chin. 'Yes, Felicity, if it comes to that I would, because we can't lie down and die even if we feel like it. Life has to go on.'

Felicity flushed. 'I'm behaving a bit like the benighted heroine in one of those cheap novels I read, aren't I?'

'It's not your fault,' Lacey said. 'When you've had a life as easy as yours it doesn't prepare you for hard knocks. Learn to deal with this one and we'll make a happy woman of you yet.'

This time she managed to make Felicity smile. 'Thanks for listening to me, and for the wise words. You're such a comfort. When Nathan chose you he not only acquired a wonderful wife, he provided his sister with a true friend.'

On that fond note Felicity said goodnight.

28

Matt married Molly one blustery October day in 1916, the pretty widow and her three year old son, David, leaving her mother's house to live at Netherfold. Delighted to have another woman about the place, Edith's warm welcome was rewarded when she discovered Molly more than capable in the handling of geese and hens.

'Apart from our Jimmy and your Nathan being away in France everything else is grand,' Edith remarked, on one of her fleeting visits to Lacey's workroom.

'Isn't it just,' Lacey replied, pushing aside the coat she was altering. 'You an' Molly get along fine, and as for us here we don't know we're born now we've got Susan.' She carried on unpicking the seams of the coat. 'Not so long ago I thought I would have to give up the dream of running my own business, but now I have the best of both worlds. This morning I even found time to go with Susan and the boys to the park. It means a lot to me, and Joanie, to be able to spend time with our sons. Joanie's away with them now delivering a suit to Mrs Brook at Ferndale House.'

'Ooh,' breathed Edith, impressed to hear Mrs Adam Brook was one of Lacey's customers.

Half an hour later Joan and Susan and the boys returned, accompanied by Molly and David.

'Look who I bumped into,' Joan said, as the little party crowded into the room.

'Hello, Molly,' said Lacey, pleased to see the sister-in-law she didn't see often enough for her liking.

Richard, his cheeks rosy, slept peacefully. The two older boys scuttled off to the corner of the room, James keen to show David his toys.

Molly smiled over at them and then at Lacey. 'They get on well, don't they?'

'I wa' just saying something similar about all of us,' said Edith, 'we all seem to be getting on well these days.'

Lacey brewed a pot of tea, musing as she filled the cups on what a wise choice Matt had made when he married Molly.

★ ★ ★

That same evening, Lacey paid an overdue visit to Fenay Hall. Soames, the butler, solemnly took her coat and scarf, his usually cheerful face dour.

Lacey wondered why and the answer was in the drawing room. Side-by-side on a couch were Alice and Violet Burrows. Shocked to see them there, Lacey's puzzled gaze met Felicity's outraged glare.

'Come sit by the fire, Lacey. You must be frozen.' Constance patted the seat next to hers. 'I do hope you haven't brought Richard out on a night like this.'

Lacey moved to the sofa by the hearth, glad of the heat from the roaring blaze in the huge Adam fireplace. If she hadn't felt cold on arrival she certainly did now, the sight of Alice and Violet chilling her to the bone. 'I left him with Susan,' she replied, ignoring both Alice and Violet as she

302

sat down.

'And how is the son and heir?' Alice's tone sugar sweet, she essayed a simpering smile.

'He's absolutely wonderful, and the image of his father,' Lacey replied, flicking a glimmer of a smile in Alice's direction and thinking, 'Suck on that one, you old bag.'

'So he is,' Constance agreed. Violet looked peeved.

After a short spell of inconsequential prattle Lacey announced her departure, Felicity accompanying her into the hallway.

'Who let them back in?' Lacey hissed, unable to control her curiosity.

Felicity shrugged and groaned. 'Mama. They came bearing Christmas gifts and begging forgiveness.'

'Beware of Greeks,' Lacey muttered.

Felicity sniggered. 'Indeed. Papa is furious. He refused to sit with them.'

She adopted a stern expression. 'But you're to blame for it.' Bemused, Lacey widened her eyes.

'It's you who encouraged Mama to be charitable, and she's now extended it to include Alice and Violet. When Papa asked why, she told him it was her Christian duty and that one could hardly turn them away at this time of year.'

Lacey groaned. 'I've obviously done too good a job on her. I'll keep my mouth shut in future; I just hope they do the same.'

★ ★ ★

The next day, Alice and Violet called at the work-room.

'Damn an' blast it,' Lacey muttered, flicking bits of thread from her black skirt then smoothing her hands over her hair. What did they want?

Forcing a smile, she said, 'Good afternoon, ladies. What can I do for you?'

'We thought we should call with you before we return to Huddersfield; survey your little empire, as one might call it,' Alice said, her tone condescending. 'We came down with Constance in the car. She's taking blankets and cough mixture to one of her needy families in Jackroyd Lane.'

Her nose wrinkled. 'Personally, I think she's taken leave of her senses. She shouldn't associate with that class of people.'

'Neither she should,' tweeted Violet. 'She could catch all manner of diseases.'

'She associates with you,' Lacey snapped. 'Are you any better than those in need? Constance does wonderful work for those who cannot help themselves. She has a good heart — but then you'd know all about that — you've taken advantage of it often enough.'

Alice's cheeks turned puce. 'We didn't call to be insulted. I was merely pointing out how unwise it is for a lady of her standing to deal with such unsavoury matters.'

'It'll do her reputation no good at all,' Violet squeaked.

Lacey shook her head. 'That's where you're wrong, Violet. Constance has never been so highly respected in Garsthwaite. The poor and needy of this community look on her as guardian angel.

304

Furthermore, she's never been happier.'

'Pshaw!' Alice pushed out her jaw. 'I imagine you inveigled her into this nonsense, just as you did with Nathan when you persuaded him to marry you.'

At the sound of a car pulling to a halt outside and the slam of its door, Alice fell silent. Constance came in. 'Alice. Violet. I'm back. Cheevers will take me home then carry you on to Huddersfield.' She turned her back on them.

'Oh, Lacey, you should see the new baby. He's a healthy, bonny little chap. His mother was delighted with the blankets, and I dosed young Sammy with cough mixture before I left.'

Alice rounded on Constance. 'Is this wise, dear cousin? We can't have you associating with the lowest of the low. What will people think?'

'They can think whatever they like,' Constance replied breezily. 'Now, shall we be on our way?'

★ ★ ★

Christmas was barely a month away, and Lacey was down on her knees inside the shop window carefully covering the length of the platform with a thick white blanket. Satisfied that it looked sufficiently like the snow that blanketed the pavement outside, she spread a bright red woollen cape in the centre and placed at either side of it the two dummies she had found in the storeroom, one wearing a blouse the colour of dark green pine needles and the other a jacket in a similar shade. In between the cape and the dummies, she randomly displayed a pair of bright red gloves, a knitted cap, also red, and two green scarves.

305

She'd made the cape, the blouses and the jacket to her own design, each garment beautifully detailed with braids and trims. The cap, gloves and scarves had been rescued from Henry Ollerenshaw's abandoned stock. It was the latter items that had given her the idea of dressing the window for Christmas: her first window display.

Eager to see the display from a customer's point of view, Lacey nipped outside. On the pavement, intent on the window, she was unaware of the uniformed man approaching until he was at her side. A whiff of cologne, the scent familiar, set her senses reeling and she hardly dared to turn her head.

'Nathan!'

Nathan nodded at the window. 'I see you are still turning sow's ears into silk purses.'

'Oh, Nathan.' Lacey threw her arms up round his neck and his encircled her. Without losing hold of her, Nathan steered Lacey to the front door of their house. Inside, he slammed the door shut and covered her mouth with his, his hands roaming her body, recalling every nuance of her shape and form. Their hearts beating in tandem, Lacey responded likewise, her hands tracing the line of his jaw and his muscular shoulders.

Lacey tossed Nathan's cap aside and pulled his head to her breast, her fingertips stroking the unfamiliar stubble on his scalp. Then she broke free, her gaze questioning as she looked up into his face.

Nathan chuckled. 'Lice,' he said, 'the curls had to go. Too good a nesting place.'

Lacey shuddered, noting for the first time his gaunt eye sockets and grey tinged cheeks, skin stretched tightly over features defined by hardship.

Nathan was changed, yet he was still beautiful.

Almost as though his joy at being with Lacey had made him forget, Nathan asked, 'Where's Richard? Where is my son?'

Lacey's face fell. 'He's with Susan but they won't be long before they're back.' Her joy returning, she cried, 'I can't wait for you to see him. He's wonderful.'

Nathan smiled enigmatically. 'Does this mean we have the house to ourselves?'

Lacey's eyes twinkled.

Grabbing her by the hand Nathan raced her upstairs to their bedroom.

★ ★ ★

'Hello. Lacey. Where are you?' Joan's voice rang in the stairwell. 'Susan's back with Richard, and Molly's here.'

In a flurry of half donned clothing Lacey appeared on the landing, Nathan at her heels. Joan stared up at them, her face breaking into a knowing smile as they descended the stairs.

'No need to ask what you two have been up to,' she smirked. 'Hello, Nathan, it's lovely to see you. Making yourself at home wa' you?'

Nathan laughed and gave Joan a brotherly hug. 'Time is of the essence,' he said, letting go to push past her to where Susan stood with the pram. 'Now where's this wonderful son of mine?'

Nathan peered into the pram. A pair of grey-blue eyes gazed solemnly up at him, so like his own it took his breath away. 'Can I hold him?' he asked, reverently.

Lacey laughed. 'Of course you can. He's yours. He's been waiting for you to hold him from the minute he was born.'

Nathan picked up his son and held him at arms length. Tears blurring his vision, he surveyed the sturdy little body as if to imprint every feature on his memory. Then he held him close, nuzzling Richard's cheeks with his lips. Richard let out a wail, squirming to be free, his eyes searching for his mother. Nathan's eyes also sought Lacey.

'It's the bristles,' she said, patting Nathan's unshaven cheek and then taking Richard from his outstretched arms. 'There, there,' she cooed to the squalling child, 'it's your daddy come home to see you.'

Molly and David and Joan and James looked on, a forlorn expression on Joan's face and James staring at the tall stranger in bemusement. Suddenly Lacey was overcome with guilt and sorrow. She was celebrating the surprise homecoming of her husband, introducing him to his son; Joan would never know such pleasures again. Thrusting Richard into Nathan's arms, Lacey folded her own about her cousin. Instinctively, Joan understood. 'It's all right, luv. I'm OK. Don't let thoughts of me an' my problems spoil your happiness.' Lacey hugged her all the tighter.

Nathan addressed Molly. 'I'm forgetting my manners. Hello, Molly, and David. Welcome to the family. And you must be Susan. I've heard a lot about you.'

Both Molly and Susan flushed with pleasure.

The front door opened and Constance walked

308

in. 'Nathan!' she cried, hurrying forward to embrace her son and grandson in hungry arms.

All thoughts of work abandoned, Cheevers was ordered to take the car and collect Jonas from the Mill. A short while later the happy party sat down to tea, Jonas and Constance barely able to take their eyes off their son holding his own son on his knee.

Jonas, quick to spot the three pips on Nathan's jacket sleeve, tapped his arm. 'I see you've made captain, lad,' he rumbled, his voice thick with emotion and pride.

Nathan grinned. 'It's well I did, otherwise I wouldn't be considered for these trips back to Blighty. We've been given seven days and I've used three of them getting here.' As the happy gathering registered the brevity of Nathan's leave their joy diminished.

For three glorious days and nights, Lacey lived as in a dream, unwilling to face the realities awaiting her. However, on Nathan's last night at home as they lay in bed, sleep evading them, the burning question buried deep in Lacey's soul finally found a voice.

'What's it like over there?'

Lacey's urgent whisper sibilant in the stillness of the room, Nathan stiffened, his breathing suspended. 'You don't want to know,' he muttered. 'Don't ask.'

Lacey propped herself up on one elbow and with her free hand stroked his brow. It was clammy with sweat. A choking sound erupted from the back of Nathan's throat. He trembled. 'I can't tell — and I never will.' He fell into a restless sleep,

Lacey gazing at the dearly loved face until eventually, she too slept.

Nathan returned to the Front, and Lacey and Joan worked late into the night to fulfil their commitments before Christmas. As she sewed, Lacey's thoughts were on Nathan's brief visit; he had seen his son, held him in his arms and fallen in love with him. That's all that mattered right now.

★ ★ ★

Lacey, like many grieving widows and anxious wives and girlfriends, found it nigh on impossible to celebrate Christmas that year in the absence of their men. Without Nathan, and Richard still too young to appreciate the meaning of Christmas, she welcomed the arrival of 1917. Now they could get back to some semblance of normality.

'T'pavements are as slippy as Hell,' Joan reported one morning in late February as she arrived for work. 'I nearly went all me length outside t'butchers.'

Lacey, cutting out another red cape, grinned at the remark. 'Don't you go falling and breaking your arm. That's the last thing we need with all the work we've got on.' She snipped at the woollen cloth, the sixth cape she had made since Christmas, the one in the window bringing in a flood of requests. The blouses too, had attracted attention, affluent women still finding the urge to dress in the latest style regardless of the war.

She glanced through the window, just in time to see an elderly gentleman topple to the ground. Lacey dashed outside and helped him to his feet, dusting snow off his overcoat before releasing her hold on him. It was the elderly solicitor whose offices adjoined Lacey's workshop. 'Good morning, Mr Hopkinson; no bones broken, I hope?'

Norman Hopkinson grimaced. 'The only damage is to my dignity. I'm getting too old for these harsh Yorkshire winters. It's one of the reasons I'm shutting up shop, Lacey. Retiring. Making the most of the time I've got left.'

'You'll be missed, Mr Hopkinson,' Lacey said, sad to hear he was leaving.

Norman shook his head. 'I hardly think so. I've outlived most of my clients, and the few I had left have all taken my advice and transferred to your friend, John Hinchcliffe. I'm too old to be involved in other people's problems. My wife and I are moving to Brighton. The bracing sea air might ensure our longevity. Will you keep an eye on the place until I find new tenants? Notify me if anything's amiss.'

'I certainly will, Mr Hopkinson.'

New tenants? Lacey scrutinised the two storey dwelling as though seeing it for the first time, the seed of an idea — coming from nowhere — suddenly germinating.

The idea took root. 'Did you say you're renting out the premises, Mr Hopkinson?'

A short while later, the transaction complete, Lacey walked jauntily back into the shop, clapping her hands for attention. 'We're moving up in the world, Joanie; or next door, to be more precise.'

A day or two later, Lacey found herself involved in another business matter. The Presbyterian Minister was vacating the house next door to Lacey's

311

own, moving to another parish. His replacement not requiring the house, and Nathan not there to make a decision, Lacey decided to refurbish the house and let it, not for the peppercorn rent the Presbyterian Chapel Committee had paid, but for its true value. Garsthwaite was changing and she must move with the times.

War work had increased the prosperity of the valley, engineering personnel had been brought into the district to deal with the increase in manufacturing. If Lacey leased the house to one of these newcomers, the revenue would more than offset the rent on her new premises.

Before the end of the month, the refurbished house was let to an engineer from Oxford, and the sewing machines and materials moved into the offices next door. Joan and James, glad to leave the little terrace house in Scar End that was full of bitter memories, were living on the upper floor above what was now the new workshop.

'I'm going to love living here,' panted Joan, as she and Lacey humped the last of Joan's possessions upstairs into the sitting room. Joan dumped a box on a table then flopped into a chair by the window. 'I can keep an eye on the goings on in Towngate from up here.' She leaned forward, crying, 'Oh look, Lacey, there goes Ivy Vickerman into Sally Bevin's across the street; the baby must be due.'

Lacey chuckled. 'The folk in Garsthwaite had better watch what they do from now on. They'll have no secrets with you spying on them.'

Joan sniffed. 'I'm not nosey; I just like to know what's going on around me.'

'Aye, you'll be better than a watchdog. It'll be lovely having you next door. I'll not feel so lonely on a night knowing you're only a couple of rooms away.' She hid her own sorrow at being a woman with no man to keep her company by admonishing, 'Now get off your backside and get this stuff put in its rightful place.'

* * *

The new premises were open for business, and the clientele no longer limited to the residents of Garsthwaite, so Lacey concentrated on designing and making garments just as she had for the Christmas display. This time, with spring in mind the window regularly sported dresses and blouses in the latest style.

'We're falling behind with the orders,' Lacey told Molly, one morning in April when Molly called in on her way back from the grocers. 'We've umpteen customers wanting stuff finished for this week and next.'

'I'll give you hand if you like,' said Molly. 'I used to work for a dressmaker in Halifax before I got married to David's dad.'

Askance, Lacey gasped. 'You sew? Why ever didn't you mention it before?'

Sweet, self-effacing Molly shrugged. 'I didn't like to. I thought you might think I was muscling in on your an' Joan's business. You've all been so kind to me since I married Matt, I didn't like to take advantage.'

'Take advantage! You'd be a godsend; what can you do?' A quick inspection proved Molly was

313

indeed a skilled seamstress.

'It 'ud be a positive waste not to use your talent,' Lacey said, as she admired Molly's handiwork, 'and Susan won't mind looking after David.

One more won't take a feather out of her.' She cast a quick glance round the workroom. 'Where is David, by the way?'

'In your house,' Molly replied. 'James saw us through the window and David pestered to go to him. Susan said she didn't mind.'

Laughing merrily, Lacey and Molly went through to the house to find Richard, James and David happily playing with a Noah's Ark and a farm set. Down on her knees, Susan was cheerfully supervising the game.

Lacey smiled warmly at the energetic young girl who never tired of entertaining her charges. 'What do you say to having one extra?' Lacey asked Susan.

'The more the merrier,' Susan replied, knowing her generous employer would reward her fairly.

* * *

With Molly installed for a few hours each week, Lacey found her workload considerably eased. So much so, that when the Brearley's large maroon Jowett rolled majestically to a halt outside the door, Lacey strolled out to greet its passenger. Constance lowered the window and, after a brief exchange, Lacey agreed to accompany her on a visit to one of her problem families.

Cheevers drove the car to the far end of Towngate and into the warren of mean streets close by the Mill. As they travelled Constance told Lacey

314

about Lily Bottomly, widowed with six children. 'Her husband was conscripted last autumn and killed at the beginning of this year. He never knew he had fathered another son.'

Cheevers brought the car to a standstill outside one of the shabby little houses in Jackroyd Lane. Constance and Lacey got out, Cheevers handing Constance the large basket stowed on the front seat.

The house was damp and cold, a pathetic fire burning in the grate. A skinny woman huddled up close to it, a puny baby at her breast. She smiled eagerly at Constance and Lacey's arrival, her parted lips exposing stumps of blackened teeth. Two pasty faced toddlers played with torn paper in the corner of the sparsely furnished room, their eyes widening in anticipation when they saw Constance.

After a few words of concerned enquiry Constance went into the small scullery, and, taking a bag of porridge and two bottles of milk from the basket she filled a large blackened saucepan. Lacey stared in amazement at her mother-in-law performing the menial task, she who never carried out such tasks in her own home. Startled into action, Lacey emptied the basket of a loaf of bread, margarine, the remains of a ham shank and a soft, squishy package.

'Make sandwiches with the ham; that poor woman has hardly strength enough to make a meal,' Constance advised in a whisper. She filled three chipped dishes with porridge then set the pan and its still plentiful contents to one side. Lacey made sandwiches, Constance instructing

315

her to put some on a plate and to wrap the rest in the greaseproof paper that had contained the ham. They carried the porridge and sandwiches through to the living room.

'Now,' said Constance, briskly efficient, 'There's more porridge in the pan and sandwiches for the older children when they return from school and enough bread and margarine for breakfast tomorrow. There's also a parcel of leftover chicken. It's cooked, ready to eat.'

'Chicken!' Lily Bottomly almost choked on her porridge. 'Eeh, I couldn't tell you when I last tasted chicken.'

The children and their mother addressed the porridge and sandwiches like a ravening horde. Lily, old before her time and wearing an air of defeat like a shroud, raised her head to smile gratefully, her eyes moist with unshed tears. 'Thanks, Mrs Brearley; we'd never manage without you.' She left the table and resumed her position by the hearth.

Good God, thought Lacey, she's barely older than I am, and look at her.

A spurt of anger seared Lacey's chest. There was something dreadfully wrong with the world that it expected a poor war widow with six hungry children to survive on next to nothing when there were others who had more than enough to eat and could still afford to buy the clothes she made.

Guilt at her own affluence enveloped her. She knelt at the hearth to bank up the fire. Still on her knees she thrust her hand into her pocket. Extracting the coins she found there, she dropped them into the woman's lap. Lily's eyes widened,

316

tears she had been holding back falling as she mumbled her thanks.

In the car, riding back up Towngate, Lacey said, 'More needs to be done for people like that. I've always known there are people who struggle to make ends meet but I've never before come across such abject poverty. It makes me ashamed.'

'That's why I do what I can for them,' Constance said briskly. 'You opened my eyes to the inequality in society, and like you, I'm shocked by their suffering. Families who once eked out a living have been plunged into despair by the loss of their men; the husband was usually the breadwinner. A war widow's pension barely covers the cost of rent and coal, and it's not just sustenance they require, it's a physical presence; someone to share the chores as they rebuild their shattered lives.'

'You've mentioned that before, but I was too involved in my own business to take much note,' Lacey said, thoughtfully. 'You say it was me who had opened your eyes to their suffering, but it's you who's opened mine.' Her tone expressing deep concern she added, 'There must be something we can do.'

Constance sighed, 'I coerce my Charity Ladies into raising funds to buy food but, try as I might, I can't persuade them to make house visits. They're afraid to step inside dwellings as insalubrious as the one we've just left. Until I succeed in disturbing their consciences sufficiently, I'll carry on alone.'

Cheevers brought the car to a halt outside Lacey's house. Lacey turned to Constance, and her tone rich with sincerity she said, 'You are

317

an amazing woman, Constance Brearley.' Lacey paused, weighing her next words. 'To think I once despised you and doubted your integrity shames me. You're twice the woman I am.'

Constance accepted the compliment with a dip of her head, then said,

'Don't denigrate yourself, my dear. You had good cause to despise me.' She chuckled softly. 'I was protecting my own and Nathan's interests, so I thought. That was before I realised how narrow was my view on the world.

I know now that privilege and respect must be earned, not merely taken as a birthright. As for being twice the woman you are, I can't accept that honour.

Where once I would have scorned your efforts I now praise them — not least for giving Jonas and I a wonderful grandson.' She patted Lacey's hand fondly. 'Never underestimate yourself, my dear.'

'I won't,' said Lacey, opening the door and stepping out to the pavement, her expression determined.

29

'There has to be something we can do,' Lacey told Joan, on her return from Jackroyd Lane. 'Women like Lily Bottomly are so bowed down with their loss they can hardly lift their heads of a morning.'

Joan sighed. 'I know how they feel — or I did,' she corrected.

'Course you do, love.' Immediately contrite, Lacey made amends, but the hopelessness of the situation still plagued her conscience.

Whenever time allowed she took food and clothing to 'Constance's families', each visit increasing her awareness of their extreme poverty; not just financial paucity but the loss of dearly loved husbands who should have been there to give them support in the ordinary, everyday events that all families experience.

To add to her worries, Nathan had yet to reply to the letters Lacey had written telling him of the newly leased premises and the refurbished house.

Well aware that letters went astray, and that Nathan was involved in far more important matters, she attempted to shrug off the sense of foreboding.

Yet it was so unlike Nathan not to write. Anxiety increasing with every waking moment, she sought to stem the inner terror gnawing at her soul by denying herself time to think.

'Still no word from Nathan then?' Edith set a mug of tea in front of Lacey, her gloomy face mirroring her daughter's. 'You shouldn't burden yourself with imaginings, Lacey. If anything bad has happened you'd have heard by now.'

Lacey managed a watery smile. 'I know, Mam, common sense tells me that, but you know me, I've always had a vivid imagination. At one time I only imagined lovely things; silly dreams like all young girls have. Now I imagine the worst. It must be a sign of old age.' They both giggled at this last remark, Lacey not yet twenty-five.

Edith sat down at the table. 'There's weeks go by without a word from our Jimmy, an' don't think I don't worry about him 'cos I do, but I promised him I wouldn't be miserable. I keep that promise by thinking positive, an' that's what you've got to do, Lacey. You haven't heard owt bad so don't go thinking it.'

Lacey grinned at her mother's good old Yorkshire common sense. She could always rely on Edith to take the hurt out of a situation, and a visit to Netherfold always lightened her heart.

'That's better,' Edith said, relieved to see a glimmer of Lacey's old spirit returning. She scooped Richard up into her arms. 'You don't want this little lad to see you moping. Children are quick to sense when something's wrong. Be happy for him.' She walked towards the door. 'Now me an' this young man are going to pick gooseberries an' you Lacey, get a bit of fresh air; put some colour in your cheeks. Go an' find your Dad an' Matt up in t'top field an' tell 'em I'll have the tea ready in half an hour.'

Leaving Edith and Richard by the gooseberry bushes, Lacey walked to the top field where

Joshua and Matt were planting turnips. Her Mam was right. There was enough horror, death and destruction in the world these days without imagining any more.

Joshua jumped down from the plough at Lacey's approach. 'It's nice to see you, lass. We don't see enough of you these days, what wi' you bein' so busy.'

'I'm skiving today. I work too hard.'

Matt hooted with derision. 'Hard work, you don't know the meaning of it,' he cried, waving the seed drill aloft. 'All you an' our Molly do is sit an' drink tea.'

Whatever he said, Lacey knew that Matt was delighted that Lacey had accepted Molly into the business; it brought the family closer together.

'How are you, Dad? Everything all right?' Lacey swung on Joshua's arm and smiled up into his sweating face.

Joshua's automatic response of, 'Aye, everything's grand' was no sooner spoken than his jowls creased pensively in consternation.

Lacey, sensing something awry asked 'What's up? Is summat bothering you?'

Joshua rubbed his stubbly chin. 'Aye, you might say so.' His gaze strayed to the fields beyond the one in which they now stood. 'I allus thought they were mine.'

Exasperated, Lacey cried, 'What are you talking about?'

'He's talking about them.' Matt indicated two fields left to grass. 'Arnold Beaumont says they're his by rights. He came t'other night an' told us he wants 'em back.'

Lacey looked mystified. 'Why ever would he say that? Grandad Barraclough farmed those fields before Arnold Beaumont wa' born.'

'We know that,' said Joshua, 'my father an' his father afore him, but Beaumont says they were on'y lent because Hardacre Farm had no use for 'em. He says they never charged rent 'cos his father an' mine were friends.

Now he wants 'em back.'

'Wi'out them fields we might as well pack it in,' Matt grumbled.

'Netherfold's small enough as it is, an' if we don't have winter fodder for t'sheep we're buggered.'

Lacey knew Arnold Beaumont, the owner of Hardacre Farm. The most prosperous farmer in Garsthwaite, he had the reputation for being a greedy, grasping employer, the lads who worked for him complaining of poor wages and ill-treatment.

'But why, after all these years, has he suddenly decided to re-claim them?'

Matt grunted. 'He says it's summat to do wi' expansion. He says t'government want bigger farms, not piddling little muck holes like Netherfold.'

'The cheeky bugger!' Lacey gazed at the disputed fields, her thoughtful expression furrowing her brow. 'Can he prove ownership? Has he summat on paper?'

Joshua scratched his head. 'He hasn't shown us owt yet, but he seems certain they're his.'

'Ask him for proof,' said Lacey, 'an' you must have something to prove you own Netherfold, some old deeds or maps that show how much land you have.'

Joshua frowned. 'Aye, we have, but God knows where. I've never been called on to prove Netherfold's mine. It's allus been taken for granted.' He looked so confused, Lacey's heart went out to him.

She patted his arm affectionately. 'Don't look so worried; we'll get it sorted. Now get cleared up here 'cos Mam'll have the tea ready.'

Later, wheeling Richard in his pushchair back into the workshop, Joan pointed to an envelope lying on Lacey's machine. For a split second her heart plummeted then soared again; the envelope was blue, not brown.

Careering the pram forward, she snatched it up, Nathan's bold print making her heart sing.

'See, I told you everything 'ud be all right,' said Joan.

In the solitude of the house, Lacey opened the envelope. Nathan congratulated her on extending the business, asked after Richard and the folks up at Netherfold and finally instructed her not to worry.

It will take a lot more than the Hun to keep me from coming home to you. As I have often reminded you, nothing can stand in the way of love like ours. My love for you and yours for me is my sword and my shield. Thus protected, my safety is ensured.

Lacey wept.

The next day, as Lacey was returning from a trip to the butcher's she met Maggie and Sarah, two old friends from the Mill. The girls were dawdling along the street, arm in arm. 'No work today, lasses?' Lacey asked by way of a greeting. She already knew that the Mill was on short-time, the lucrative contracts the mills had thrived on in the early years of the war no more; for large quantities of serge were no longer required.

Maggie scowled. 'We're on'y on two days this week.'

'If we don't go back full time in t'next week or two I don't know what I'll do,' Maggie grumbled.

Sarah added her complaints. 'Aye, it's awful being without wages but having nowt to do's nearly as bad. I'm sick o' traipsing round trying to fill a day.'

Both girls unmarried, they had plenty of time on their hands. As this thought crossed Lacey's mind, so did another. 'I've got summat you can do on your days off.'

'We can't sew,' they chimed as one.

'It's not sewing; it's summat far more worthwhile.'

Maggie and Sarah glanced quizzically at Lacey and then at one another.

Lacey pressed on. 'There are families in Garsthwaite, some as poor as crows, where the women aren't coping. Most of 'em are war widows with young children. Then there are old folks who've lost the son who provided for them. My mother-in-law, Mrs Brearley, helps as much as she can

324

but she requires assistance.'

'We've got nowt to give 'em,' Maggie inter-rupted, 'we've barely enough for us selves.'

'That's where you're wrong,' Lacey urged. 'You've got your health and strength and time on your hands. Now if you popped in and out, gave a hand with the bairns, made sure they had a fire on the go and a warm meal at dinnertime it 'ud make their lives easier. That way you'd be doing some good and earning a bit of brass at the same time. I can't pay the same rate as you get for weaving but it'll be a few bob you wouldn't have otherwise.'

Maggie and Sarah looked at one another, weighing up the situation. 'Who buys t'food to make dinners if there's nowt in t'house?' Maggie asked shrewdly.

'I arrange that,' said Lacey. 'You just collect it from me as and when you need it.'

Sarah laughed. 'You're a right one you are. You're always organisin' summat.' She nudged Maggie. 'Remember the time we marched through the town an' got two bob of a rise for every piece?'

Maggie smirked. 'I remember t'lavatories bet-ter.'

This time all three women laughed.

'Will you do it then?' Lacey smiled appealingly. 'You can ask another couple of lasses to join you if you like. Choose two who are on different shifts at the Mill. That way somebody can call every day.'

That same evening, after Lacey had told Con-stance of the new arrangements, she said, 'We need more contributions if we're to help more families.'

In no time at all, the butcher was supplying

325

scrag-ends cheap, the bakery cut-price oats and leftover bread, and the greengrocer bruised apples and wizened potatoes, Lacey and Constance having convinced them it was their Christian duty.

'We call ourselves Lacey's League,' Maggie piped when she and Sarah called to collect the supplies they delivered to the needy. 'Sarah wanted to call us Lacey's Ladies League but,' Maggie gave a hearty guffaw 'I reminded her, we're not ladies.'

'You are to me,' said Lacey, 'ladies with good hearts.' She waved them off, still chuckling at the title they had given themselves.

★ ★ ★

Thrilled to have achieved yet another goal Lacey was content for much of the time, yet there were moments when she was seized with irrational panic.

What would the future hold if Nathan didn't come home? What if their mutual love was not protection enough?

One night, Richard asleep, Lacey sat at the dining room table with her ledger, invoices and receipts spread out in front of her. She opened the ledger, scanning each page, checking the columns of credits, debits and totals; entries she meticulously recorded at the end of each working day.

Satisfied they were in order she crosschecked invoices and receipts against the entries in the ledger. Further calculations appertaining to the house she rented out to the engineer, and the outlay for Lacey's League also proving satisfactory, she pushed the ledger and the invoices aside. Finally she checked the balance in her bankbook.

Lacey was inordinately proud of her bankbook. Never having had one before, she took great pride in the balance it showed: not a king's ransom but a tidy sum proving that her sewing business was a thriving concern.

Consoled by her findings Lacey sat back and rubbed her tired eyes.

The rush of adrenaline that had accompanied the mental activity gradually wore off, replaced by a gnawing sense of foreboding. What if Nathan didn't return? Without him Lacey feared she might be too grief stricken to further her ambitions. Better to do it now whilst there was still hope, for if Nathan made the ultimate sacrifice she must provide for her future and Richard's future. She owed Nathan that much. Wearily she climbed the stairs, only to toss and turn restlessly in the half empty bed, sleep evading her until the small hours, when she at last fell into a deep, dreamless slumber.

★　★　★

The next morning, after putting the final touches to a dress for the doctor's wife, Lacey went into the house and asked Susan to dress Richard for outdoors and put him in the pushchair. Leaving Susan to carry out this problematic task — Richard didn't like being strapped in the pushchair — Lacey went back to the workroom.

'Joanie. Molly. I'm going out.' The determined twinkle in her eyes did not escape their notice. Of late they had grown used to the wistful gazes or distracted glances each day without Nathan produced. Their hearts saddened, they were quick to

327

sense the new vitality in her voice.

'You're up to summat,' said Joan, knowing Lacey well enough to detect the energy coursing through her.

'I am,' chirped Lacey, 'an' I'll tell you all about it when I get back.'

Out on the street she caught sight of a young lad in uniform riding a bicycle: the telegram boy. He pedalled swiftly towards her and her heart plunged into her boots, her knuckles whitening as she gripped the pram's handle. The boy sailed past, whistling. Lacey sagged with relief. His news, good or bad, was for someone else.

★ ★ ★

By the summer of 1917, Lacey's sewing business had undergone monumental changes. Outside, above the door, a sign in large green and gold letters announced:

Lacey's Modistes

and under that in smaller letters:

Purveyors of Ladies' Quality Fashion.

Inside, the sewing machines and cutting tables were relegated to rooms at the rear and the haberdashery had been reinstated. What had been the sewing room was now a dress shop, complete with fitting rooms and rails of garments; some bought in, others designed by Lacey. With its dark blue carpet and gold and blue striped curtains hanging at the fitting room doorways, Lacey considered her dress shop almost as grand as Brown Muffs in Bradford: and all achieved with a bank loan.

She had been pleasantly surprised at how readily the loan had been granted. A brief check on her assets and the manager of The Yorkshire Bank in Huddersfield, smiling expansively, had shaken her hand and then ushered her out of his office saying, 'Always pleased to be of assistance.'

To himself he had added, 'and should you fail to meet your commitments I can always call on Jonas Brearley to honour them.'

Had Lacey been aware of this she would have roundly, and possibly crudely, told him what he could do with his loan; she'd succeed without her father-in-law's assistance but, blissfully ignorant, she had rushed back to Garsthwaite to expand her empire.

Now, the workforce included Sarah Walker, a seamstress who had trained in Leeds, and two young trainees, Katie and Ann. Both bright, willing girls, they were the daughters of women Lacey had worked alongside in the Mill. This pleased her for, along with the work done by Lacey's League, she felt as though her good fortune was spilling over into other people's lives.

30

Head down and pencil in hand, Lacey made swift, deft strokes on a large sheet of white paper. The past nine months had been hectic and now she was taking advantage of the lull in business to create new designs for the coming seasons.

'Gentleman to see you, Mrs Brearley.'

At Katie's announcement, Lacey glanced round to see a tall, smartly dressed man hovering in the workroom doorway. She smiled in welcome and then ushered him into the dress shop, away from the noise of the machines.

'Adam Brook, at your service, madam.' He held out his hand. Lacey shook it, impressed by his elegant manner.

'What can I do for you, Mr Brook?'

'My wife suggested I should call on you to discuss a matter of business.'

A frisson of expectation surged through Lacey's veins. Outwardly she remained calm. 'Would that be Mrs Adelaine Brook of Ferndale House?'

Adam Brook smiled. 'The very one: she's delighted with the work you've done for her and suggested I approach you with a view to putting business your way, should you feel able to fulfil the requirements.'

'Lacey's Modistes are extremely competent, Mr Brook. What are the requirements?'

'I've recently inherited a ladies' mantle house in Leeds. My research shows that the demand for inexpensive, ready to wear dresses is increasing, therefore I wondered if you could make up a selection of garments to capture that corner of the market.'

Lacey's heart thudded so loudly she thought he must hear it. A contract to supply dresses on a regular basis would ensure work for her girls for months, if not years to come.

'Mr Brook, I'm flattered that you should consider us.'

'My wife assures me there's no better dressmaker in the district.'

'Please convey my thanks to Mrs Brook. Now, if you'd follow me through to the house we can discuss the details over a cup of tea.' An hour later she returned to the workroom, triumphant.

'Girls, we've just landed a contract to supply dresses to a shop in Leeds.

If we do a good job — and we will — it'll keep us in work until we're old an' grey.'

By October, Lacey's Modistes had produced such a successful winter collection that Adam Brook extended the contract for the following spring and summer. Lacey was overjoyed.

During this time, Lacey not only wrote letters to Nathan, she included tiny sketches of the garments they had produced, Nathan praising her initiative, and the main content of the letters they exchanged about Richard's progress (with accompanying photographs) and, as usual, hopes for the future and their devotion to each other. But come December there was no seasonal greeting from Nathan to mark Christmas or the New Year.

'I can't understand it,' said Lacey, barely

acknowledging the greetings cards it was increasingly fashionable to send at this time of year, 'It's not like Nathan to miss sending a Christmas letter, of all letters.'

And so, the festive season being anything but, Lacey watched and waited for the post. As the Old Year ran into the New she still waited, her fears for Nathan's safety deepening with each passing day and her temper unusually irascible.

'Katie, clear this table. I can't work until you shift all this clutter. I've Susan Hepplestone's wedding dress to cut out.'

Hurt by Lacey's sharp tone, Katie attempted to lighten the mood. 'I wouldn't want to get married in January; it's too cold. I'd like a summer wedding, the sun shining an' me wearing a white lace dress.'

'Well, just make sure you keep yourself right so's you can choose when you get married,' snapped Lacey. 'Susan Hepplestone didn't have any choice. She's four months pregnant.'

The bell above the door of the dress shop shrilled. Lacey hurried to answer it; she liked to serve her customers personally.

The sale of a jacket completed, the satisfied client left, remarking 'it's nothing short of a miracle.' It reminded Lacey of something Nathan had once said: 'The impossible I can do. Miracles take a little longer.' She'd laughed then but with no letter from Nathan for almost three months, miracles seemed thin on the ground. She gazed wistfully through the shop window.

Outside, a telegram boy was dismounting from his bicycle. For one second her heart missed a

332

beat, and in the next the boy thrust open the door.

'Letter from the War Office for Mrs Lacey Brearley.' His urgent cry practised, he fished in his leather pouch and withdrew the dreaded missive.

Having delivered the now familiar envelopes on too many occasions he was almost certain of the contents.

Somehow, Lacey managed to remain upright although her legs trembled uncontrollably. 'That's me,' she croaked, 'I'm Mrs Lacey Brearley.'

Not daring to move, she stretched out her hand. It shook so badly she had difficulty grasping the small brown envelope the boy handed her. 'Sorry to be the bearer of bad news,' he muttered before turning tail.

Lacey crushed the unopened envelope to her chest and then tottered into the workroom. Joan glanced up from the paper pattern she was pinning to a length of material. At the sight of her cousin's ashen face she tossed it aside, paper, pins and fabric flying from the table. She dashed across the room. 'What is it, Lacey? What's wrong?'

Lacey proffered the envelope, croaking, 'Open it. I can't.'

Joan paled, memories of receiving a similar envelope springing to mind.

'Katie, bring Mrs Brearley a chair, an' you, Ann, make a pot o' tea; good an' strong wi' two sugars.'

Katie placed a chair behind Lacey then hovered impotently, shaken to see her employer stripped of her usual brisk efficiency.

Lacey sat. Again, she proffered the envelope. This time Joan took it.

Molly and Sarah hurried over, Molly placing a comforting hand on Lacey's shoulder.

Joan opened the envelope and withdrew the flimsy yellow paper. Taking a deep breath, she scanned the missive, relief of a sort on her features.

'He's missing, Lacey. Not dead. It says he's missing.'

Lacey snatched the letter, forcing her eyes to focus on the small black type:

I regret to inform you that a report has been received from the War Office to the effect that No. 12934, Rank: Captain, Name: Nathan Jonas Brearley, Regiment: 1st Duke of Wellington's, was posted 'missing' on the 24th November, 1917.

The report that he is missing does not necessarily mean he has been killed, as he may be a Prisoner of War or temporarily separated from his regiment.

Official reports that men are Prisoners of War take some time to reach this country, and if he has been captured by the enemy it is probable that unofficial news will reach you first.

The letter fluttered to the floor. Katie picked it up, holding it gingerly between finger and thumb, unsure what to do with it. Lacey hid her face in her hands and sobbed.

Ann arrived with a mug of tea. 'Here, drink this,' Joan said firmly. Lacey withdrew her hands from her face and fumbled for the mug, tea slopping into her lap. She brushed at the damp patch distractedly, took a deep drink and then thrust the mug back into Joan's hand.

'It doesn't say outright that he's dead. It just says he's missing.' Lacey's voice strengthened as hope soared and she began to gabble hysterically. 'He could be anywhere. Just not with his regiment. In all that chaos men must get separated all the time. An' if he's been taken prisoner it means he's still alive.' On the verge of tears, she glanced wildly from one to another of the women and girls.

Joan nodded eagerly. 'That's right, Lacey. Somebody'll find out what's happened to him, an' when they do they'll let you know.' Again she thought of Stanley; the letter she had received more than a year ago had given her no hope.

★ ★ ★

Throughout the following weeks Lacey simply went through the motions, numb inside and blindly impervious to all but the necessary tasks. In her mind's eye she conjured pictures of Nathan staggering under the influence of mustard gas or suffering from shell shock as he tried to find his way back to his regiment; or wounded and lying in a morass of mud in No Man's Land, waiting for help that never came. At other times she imagined his broken body left to rot in a hastily dug, unmarked grave.

She stopped reading newspapers, the reports and grainy photographs only exacerbating her

335

imaginings. At other times she tried to picture him as a prisoner, alive but subjected to cruel treatment at the hands of the murderous Germans. Although she hated the thought of him being captive, this was the scenario she most hoped for.

At Fenay Hall the Brearleys too, were numb with grief. Constance bore the news with fortitude, bravely continuing with her charity work although her heart wasn't in it. Jonas spent increasingly long hours in the Mill office pondering on the absence of his son and heir. If Nathan never returned, who would run the Mill until young Richard was of an age to take command?

Felicity also grieved but whilst she, like her parents, lived in hope for Nathan's safe return she had another secret hope burning deep inside.

When Lacey and Richard went to Fenay Hall to take Sunday lunch with the family, Lacey was disappointed to find that Alice and Violet were also there. They had come to offer their commiserations, so Alice told her.

Irritated by her simpering manner, Lacey swiftly removed herself, and thinking it far more likely that they were there for a free lunch, she crossed the room to where Felicity stood gazing pensively through a window overlooking the garden.

'Stefan has written; Maria's dead,' she whispered, as soon as Lacey joined her. 'If he's allowed to leave Germany, he says he will come to Garsthwaite after a suitable period of mourning.'

Lacey squeezed Felicity's arm affectionately. 'I'm pleased for you, Felicity. At least one of us has good news.'

Felicity looked doubtful. 'I'm confused. One

part of me fears for Nathan, another is saddened yet relieved by Maria's death and the biggest part of me sings with joy to think Stefan will come for me.'

'Nathan will come back as well,' Lacey replied stoutly, 'I'd know if he were dead, I'd feel it in here.' She thumped her chest, her words sounding braver than she felt, but of late she had convinced herself he was alive, and now, partly to comfort Felicity and also to bolster her own belief she added, 'Wherever Nathan is, he's not dead.'

'I do so hope you're right. Not only for our sakes but the sake of this little chap.' Her voice shaking with emotion, Felicity lifted Richard into her arms who, in order to escape Violet's cloying, and false, affection had hurtled across the room to join them in the window recess.

'Vi'wet howibble,' said Richard, protruding his top teeth over his bottom lip in imitation of Violet. Felicity laughed out loud, Lacey remarking, 'For one so young he's an excellent judge of character.'

'Isn't he just,' said Felicity, 'I wonder what he makes of Alice?' She set Richard down, groaning, 'and to think we have to endure their company over dinner.'

At the dinner table Alice's bracelet clinked noisily as she applied her spoon to her plate. 'I've lost so much weight even my jewellery is too big for me,' she twittered.

The bracelet, a chunky collection of green stones, dangled loosely from her scraggy wrist. When it clattered against the plate a third time she removed it, setting it on the table.

Constance smiled tolerantly. 'Was it your mother's, Alice?'

'It was. One of the few remaining pieces I've managed to hang on to since we were so cruelly left in straitened circumstances.' Her eyes sought the sympathy she considered her due. Only Violet responded.

'Yes,' Violet lisped, 'poor mama has had to sell most of the pieces that by right should have come to me.'

'You'll have to find yourself a husband to buy you replacements,' Jonas growled. To hide her amusement at the barbed comment, Lacey fussed with Richard's napkin, tucking it firmly under his chin.

Violet cast her mother an embarrassed glance. Smoothly, Alice responded, 'Alas, Violet has pledged her dear, loyal heart to one who failed to appreciate her worth; isn't that so, my dear?' She laid a comforting hand on Violet's, causing her to fumble with her spoon. Soup slopped onto the table. Richard crowed with delight, Violet's chagrin palpable. 'See,' piped Alice, 'the poor darling is quite heartbroken.'

'Balderdash!' barked Jonas, tossing his napkin onto the table and pushing back his chair. 'It's you that's brokenhearted, Alice. You failed to get your sticky hands on my brass and now you're going to make that poor girl suffer for the rest of her days.' He marched to the door. 'I've heard enough of your twaddle for one day. Make sure you're gone before I come out.' To Soames he said, 'I'll take my dinner in my study.'

'As you will, sir,' said Soames, although his

338

words were drowned by Constance protesting, 'Really Jonas, is this necessary?' and Alice wailing, 'How can you be so cruel as to say — '

Jonas didn't stay to listen.

The meal over, the ladies and Richard retired to the drawing room. After an uncomfortable half hour of tedious chat, Lacey bade Richard take leave of his grandmamma and aunt. Hugs and kisses delivered, Lacey ushered Richard into the hallway. She set her handbag on the hall table then stooped to button his coat, surprised when she came upright to find Alice standing beside her.

'I gather your business is flourishing nicely. What with that and the property you're soon to inherit, you'll be a wealthy widow.'

Stung by the remark Lacey hissed, 'You bitch! I'm not about to inherit anything. Nathan isn't dead.'

Alice opened her mouth to make what would, no doubt, have been a vicious response, but before she had chance to air it, Felicity appeared. 'I'm coming with you Lacey,' she said.

Outside the house in Towngate, Lacey delved in her handbag for the door key. Withdrawing her hand, she dangled Alice's bracelet in front of Felicity's face. 'Now how did that get there?'

* * *

The police constable who presented himself at the shop in Towngate was unknown to Lacey. Even so, she smiled a welcome. 'What can we do for you, officer?'

The constable coughed self-consciously as he

looked at the respectable, pretty woman who stood calmly before him. 'Are you Mrs Lacey Brearley?' he asked.

Lacey affirming she was, he mumbled 'Sorry to trouble you madam but . . . er . . . we've been informed that some jewellery belonging to Mrs Alice Burrows has gone missing, stolen whilst she was a guest at Fenay Hall. We have . . . er . . . reason to believe you may be implicated.'

Lacey accepted the accusation calmly. 'And what jewellery would that be, constable?'

'An emerald and gold bracelet so I've been informed.' Dropping all pretence at formality he gabbled, 'She says you stole it yesterday evening.'

Lacey heaved a sigh of exasperation. 'Have you a car to take us to Fenay Hall or do we have to walk?'

The constable, taken aback by Lacey's response, muttered that he had come by bicycle. Without another word they made their way up to Fenay Hall, Soames looking bemused when Lacey arrived with a policeman in tow. Then his face fell as he imagined the worst; Master Nathan was dead.

To add to his bemusement, Lacey asked Soames to take the constable to Constance and Jonas. 'I'll wait here,' she said.

Soames ushered him into the breakfast room where Constance and Jonas lingered over coffee. Jonas leapt to his feet, his features expressing the same unwelcome thoughts as those of Soames. Constance paled and clutched at her breast. 'What is it, officer?' Jonas's croak betrayed his fears.

The constable drew himself up to full height. 'A robbery at these premises was reported early

340

this morning by a Mrs Alice Burrows, a guest of yours, or so I was told.'

Constance and Jonas sagged into their seats, the colour returning to their faces along with puzzled expressions. 'So you're not here about my son, Nathan?' Jonas gasped.

The constable looked bemused. 'No sir, a bracelet was stolen yesterday evening according to Mrs Burrows. The accused person is out in the hallway.'

Jonas barged to the door, yanked it open and saw Lacey. 'You bloody idiot,' Jonas yelled at the constable, 'this is my daughter-in-law.' The constable's face fell. Jonas charged to the foot of the stairs. 'Alice! Alice!'

He turned to Soames. 'Go get that bloody woman and bring her down here this minute.' Soames darted upstairs.

In the drawing room, Alice and a dithering Violet faced their irate hosts.

Lacey and Felicity looked on, their lips quirking. The constable looked from Lacey to Alice. 'Is this the lady who stole your bracelet?'

Alice said, 'It is. I saw her slip it into the large, black handbag she was carrying when she was here yesterday, the same one she now has with her.'

Felicity burst into peals of laughter. 'Oh, Alice, how foolish you are.

Here's your bracelet.' She dangled it enticingly. 'You left it on the table at dinner and Soames brought it to me.'

'No! Mama put it in Lacey's . . . ' Violet's hand shot to her mouth in an attempt to smother the incriminating words. Alice glared at her, then recovering a shred of composure tweeted, 'How . . . how silly of me. I thought it had been stolen.'

The constable harrumphed. 'This could be classed as wasting police time, Mrs Burrows. What with a war on, we've enough to do.'

After the constable had left an icy silence fell over the room, Alice and Violet darting anxious glances at Lacey, Felicity, Constance and Jonas and then finally at one another.

'What will you do next to bring me down, Alice?' Lacey asked calmly.

'Nothing, if she's any sense,' screeched Constance, 'I can't for the life of me understand why she acts this way.'

'Because she's a spiteful, grasping parasite with a wicked mind,' Felicity said blithely. 'She deliberately placed the bracelet in Lacey's bag. She found it there, and I kept it until such time as it was needed. You see, Alice, you're not the only crafty one.'

'By God!' roared Jonas, 'you've done it this time. The pair of you, pack your bags.' He turned to Constance. 'There's to be no more kind gestures where these two are concerned. They don't deserve any.'

Constance glared icily at Alice and Violet. 'Please leave my house this instance. I no longer regard you as relatives of mine.'

After Alice and Violet had left, Lacey apologised for any aggravation she had caused by allowing them to think the constable had called with regard to Nathan's disappearance. 'Alice can't forgive me for marrying Nathan. At first I considered her vicious threats to be nothing more than the ramblings of a thwarted woman with a warped mind. I never imagined she would try to blacken my character by having me charged with theft.'

'But we didn't let her get away with it,' piped Felicity, grinning impishly.

'We plotted to expose her, and it worked.'

Constance hurried to Lacey's side and held her close. 'Oh, my poor darling, we were all aware of Alice's careless tongue but I for one never thought she would stoop to mendacity.'

Jonas groaned. 'That's because you refused to listen to me; I've had the measure of that woman for years. This time, however, she's overplayed her hand.' He stood up and crossed the room to pat Lacey's shoulder. 'Go on home, lass,' he said kindly, 'Alice Burrows'll trouble you no more.'

31

Richard Brearley was a happy, sturdy young-
ster, the light and life of all his mother's hopes
and dreams. Too young to remember the father
he had seen only once, Richard spent his days in
the company of his mother, his nanny, his doting
aunts, uncle, cousins and grandparents, his little
world unhampered by sadness and loss. On the
other hand, although his mother appeared outwardly calm and briskly efficient, her soul was in
turmoil and her heart an aching, yearning weight
inside her chest. Only those who knew her well
saw through the façade, understanding that she
would never again be the fun loving, cheerful,
cheeky girl they had once known.

Lacey's Modistes continued to thrive, her
wealthy clients always able to locate and pay for
new materials to make their garments, and her
poorer clients often needing a worn out dress
refurbishing or coats and suits altering for a wedding or a funeral; for life and death went on apace
in Garsthwaite. So too, did romance.

On a breezy March morning in 1918 Lacey kept
her morning vigil at the open shop door, on the
look out for the postman. Behind her, the whirr of
sewing machines and muted chatter let her know
it was business as usual.

'Morning, Lacey.' Sam Barton shoved a pile of
envelopes into her hand.

'They all look like bills, luv. Sorry about that.'

Like most people in the town, he knew Nathan was reported missing. 'Better luck tomorrow, eh.'

Off he went down the street, whistling.

Lacey watched him go, thinking, I might have married Sam had I not met Nathan. How different life would now be if I had. I wouldn't be standing here worrying about where my husband was. I'd know. But she knew in her heart, no matter how much pain it caused, she'd never exchange Nathan for Sam.

She thumbed through the envelopes. Just as Sam had said; no personal letters, only bills. As she turned to go back inside she caught sight of a heavily built young man leaning against the lamp post outside the house next door. He wasn't anyone she recognised but now she came to think of it he'd been there yesterday and the day before. Fleetingly, she wondered why, the thought escaping her mind as quickly as it had come when the shop door opened and Jonas stepped inside.

It was the first time he had set foot in Lacey's establishment since its inauguration and Lacey, surprised to see him there, paled. Was the purpose of his visit to relay the news she least wished to hear? Jonas's face creased into a wide smile and her fears evaporated. 'Good morning, lass,' he boomed cheerily.

'Whatever brings you here?' she asked.

'I thought it was high time I visited your little empire; see how you run your business.'

Lacey clapped her hands to her cheeks in mock horror. 'Checking up on me, are you?'

Jonas laughed. 'Not at all, I trust you know what you're doing. I've come to collect Richard.

345

Constance and I are going to take him to Hollingworth Lake for a picnic; begging your permission
of course.'

'He's with Susan in the house,' said Lacey, 'I'll
go and get him ready. He'll be delighted; a ride in
the big car, and a picnic.'

Lacey led the way into the house. 'Ganpa.'
Richard ran to his grandfather, Jonas rewarded
by the warm welcome.

'Hello, young man, what do you say to coming
for a car ride to Hollingworth Lake? We'll have a
picnic and feed the ducks.' David and James, on
their knees playing with toy cars, stood expectantly, but Jonas had eyes only for Richard, who by
now was so excited that Lacey had trouble dressing him in his topcoat and boots.

'Stand still, you little monkey,' she laughed, as
she pulled on his cap.

Richard planted farewell kisses on Susan and
Lacey's cheeks then, hand in hand with Jonas,
walked happily out to the street. Cheevers lifted
Richard into the car beside Constance, Lacey
waving until they were out of sight, saddened that
the Brearleys had not thought to invite James or
David to join them.

To make it up to them, Lacey popped across the
street and bought ice creams, a rare treat. As she
waited to be served it suddenly occurred to her
that Constance and Jonas were preparing Richard
for the future. Before long they'll want to send
him to a private school then boarding school, she
thought, educate him as they did his father.
They don't believe Nathan will come back.

When she handed the treats to James and David

346

she thought, these boys don't have their futures mapped out for them but mine does. She couldn't decide whether to feel angry or elated. Her son was the heir to one of the most prosperous mills in the valley and not yet three years old; was it a boon or a burden?

Leaving the delighted boys with Susan, Lacey wandered out into the back yard deep in thought. Nathan loved the Mill, and knowing it would be his eventually, he had taken pleasure in planning for the future. But what if, years from now, Richard didn't want to be a manufacturer? He might choose to be an academic, an artist or an actor. What then? Would he be allowed to choose — she wanted that for him — but would Jonas?

Back inside and deep in thought, Lacey slowly surveyed her surroundings: the refurbished haberdashery, the busy workroom with its colourful clutter of fabrics and Joan, Molly and Sarah behind their machines, the steady whirr and clack mingled with Katie and Ann's lively chatter. So much to be thankful for, thought Lacey, walking through into the dress shop and nodding pleasantly at Isabel, the sales assistant. If Nathan is dead and if, years from now, Richard chooses to carve his own future then this will give him the freedom to do so.

Through the shop window she saw the young man she'd seen earlier now standing right outside the door. She eyed him curiously and then marched into the workroom.

'There's a fellow hanging about out there. He was there yesterday and this morning. I don't like the look of him.'

347

Katie and Ann giggled. Molly laughed out loud. 'That's a pity,' she said, 'Joan won't like that. He's her young man.'

Lacey stared at Joan, askance. 'Your young man?'

Joan, her cheeks pink, nodded affirmatively. 'He's Lizzie Isherwood's nephew, home from the war. He came to stay with her a while back. We're walking out.'

This time it was Lacey's turn to flush. 'I didn't know . . . Oh, Joanie. I've been that wrapped up in meself I've not taken any notice of you or anybody except Richard.' Lacey sounded as though she was about to cry. 'Why ever didn't you say summat?'

Joan looked wounded. 'You've a lot on your mind, what wi' Nathan an' the business. I didn't like to bother you.'

'I'm sorry,' said Lacey, 'an' I'm sorry I said I didn't like the look of him.' She grinned impishly. 'Ooh, you dark horse, Joanie Micklethwaite; go an' fetch him in an' introduce us.'

Alfie, wearing an embarrassed smile, stepped into the workroom. He was a tall, beefy lad with a shock of thick black curls. Lacey went to greet him.

Only when she held out her hand for him to shake did she notice that the cuff of his right jacket sleeve was pinned to the upper part. Alfie had lost an arm. Burning with shame she clasped his left hand in both her own.

'Pleased to meet you, Alfie; you be good to our Joanie. She's a very special person.'

'I know that, Mrs Brearley. She's special to me.'

Joan flushed with pleasure and pride. 'Alfie an' me are going to eat our sandwiches down by the river,' she said, 'we're taking James with us.' Joan picked up a basket and linking Alfie's good arm, she went to collect her son. 'I'll be back inside an hour, Lacey.'

'Take your time, luv. It's precious.'

Molly followed her. 'I'll take David to the park. We'll eat our lunch there.'

Lacey watched them go, a feeling of sadness creeping over her. Her son was lunching at Hollingworth Lake, and taking his first tentative steps towards the life of a gentleman and heir to a fortune. Please God, she thought, as she made her lonely way into the house and into the kitchen, don't let Constance and Jonas steal him from me.

She filled a teacake with cold, roast meat and sat down to eat it. As she chewed she mulled over the events that now affected her life and the lives of those she loved. Firstly there were her fears for Nathan, and now Richard. Then there was Joshua and Matt, still worrying over Arnold Beaumont's claim on the fields; she really must get back to John Hinchcliffe about that; and now there was Joan, married and widowed before she'd barely had a chance of happiness, in love again with a man who surely had known grief. You didn't lose an arm and not have regrets.

I've no right to monopolise sadness, Lacey thought. We all have sorrows in some shape or form. We have to learn to live with them.

Her hunger satisfied but her spirits still low, Lacey left the kitchen and strolled across the yard to the shop. As she entered by the rear door a

349

woman dashed out into the street. Damn it, Lacey thought; she'd been so distracted she'd forgotten to lock up after everyone went for lunch.

'What did she look like?' Joan asked, after Lacey had relayed the incident.

Lacey looked blank. 'I only saw her from behind: old, wearing a black coat. Apart from that I've no idea.' She paused, a frown wrinkling her brow. 'On second thoughts, there was something familiar about the shape of her. Maybe we made something for her in the past.' She shrugged dismissively.

★　★　★

'We've had a splendid day,' Constance declared when she and Jonas brought Richard home. 'He was a perfect little gentleman.'

At the use of the word 'gentleman', Lacey bristled, her thoughts returning to the reason for the Brearleys taking Richard out. Hiding her fears, she listened indulgently to Richard's garbled account of feeding ducks, eating a picnic and riding in the big, shiny motor.

'We must make a regular habit of it,' Jonas said, as he and Constance took their leave.

Later that same evening, as Lacey tucked Richard into bed, she was still somewhat disconcerted by what she thought of as Jonas's and Constance's interference in his future. They mean well, she told herself, but he's my son, not a replacement for theirs.

The thought still bothered her when she climbed into bed and fell into a fitful sleep.

Crash! In the still of night somewhere close at hand, something shattered. It sounded like a large amount of glass. Lacey leapt out of bed, running barefoot along the landing to peer through the window overlooking Towngate. It was past midnight, the street deserted, the pavements slick with rain.

Lacey placed a foot on the low windowsill to obtain a better view, craning her neck to look down on the pavement immediately in front of the haberdashery. Shards of glass glinted in the light from the nearest gas lamp.

Someone had smashed her shop window!

Back in her bedroom, Richard was still sleeping soundly. Lacey put on her slippers and hurried downstairs. In the haberdashery she felt the draught of cool night air blowing through the gaping hole in the window. A large red brick nestled amongst garments now sprinkled with broken glass and a display dummy lay drunkenly on its side.

'Bloody vandals!' Probably some drunk who'd fallen out with his wife or his mates had decided to vent his temper on her window, she thought. Or was it thieves? She crept into the dress shop and then the workroom.

Ears pricked and breathing suspended, Lacey listened to the footsteps padding nearer and nearer. She stretched her arm, her fingers trailing the wall in search of the light switch. Thanking God for the recently installed electricity, she snapped down the switch.

Joan's scream split the air. Blinking in the sudden glare, her hair on end and her nightdress hitched up to her knees, she stared at Lacey. Lacey stared back. Then they both began to giggle.

'I thought I heard summat,' Joan gasped, 'it sounded like breaking glass.'

'It was. Come and look.'

'The buggers!' cried Joan, when she saw the ruined window display.

Lacey smirked. 'I thought you were a burglar when I heard you coming across the workroom. I'd have clobbered you if I'd had something to hit you with. It's a good job we don't still have gas mantles; I'd have torn you limb from limb.'

Joan shuddered. 'Don't joke, Lacey. It's nasty work is this; I wonder who did it?'

'Probably a drunk on his way home to beat the wife.'

Joan pointed to the broken windowpane. 'We'd best get it boarded up.

We don't want cats traipsin' in an' pittling on everything.'

'It would have to bloody pour down tonight of all nights,' grumbled Lacey, as a flurry of rain spattered through the hole.

'There's a roll of oilcloth in my spare room,' Joan volunteered.

They went up to Joan's apartment. 'You living above the premises is proving handy in more ways than one, Joanie,' Lacey said, as they struggled down the stairs with the oilcloth. 'Otherwise I'd have been here all on me own. It's awful not having a man about the place.' There had been no further word of Nathan and, whilst he was never far from her thoughts, times like this cut through her armour like a knife.

'There might be a man about the place afore long. Alfie's asked me to marry him,' said Joan, resting her end of the oilcloth on a step.

Lacey let go of her end and, as the oilcloth slid towards her she grabbed at it wildly, crying 'Oh, that's wonderful, Joanie. I'm happy for you.'

'So am I,' Joan cried, yanking the oilcloth back. 'There was a time when I thought I'd be left on me own for t'rest of me life. I still think fondly of Stanley but I love Alfie, an' I need him. James loves him too, an' he needs a dad.'

Lacey tugged at the flapping oilcloth, the chink in her armour widening. She too, needed some-one to love, and Richard needed a father. She didn't begrudge Joan her happiness, but Lacey didn't want to consider giving her love to another man. No one could replace Nathan.

The garments from the window display sal-vaged and the window sealed, they mashed a pot of strong tea. When their eyes began to droop they bade one another goodnight, one woman filled with hope for the future, the other nursing a heartbreaking sadness.

* * *

Jack Eastwood, the local police sergeant, solemnly studied the window, his embarrassment tangi-ble at such a thing happening on his watch. He pushed up his helmet and wiped his brow. 'Jim Braddock's on duty tonight,' he said, 'I'll tell him to keep a look out, Lacey.'

'It'll hardly happen two nights running, Jack. It was most likely a drunk with a nasty turn of mind. Maybe I made his wife a dress he didn't like.'

Jack grinned. 'Aye, it's hardly likely you'll have any more bother.'

But Jack was wrong.

One week later, Lacey woke to find the dress shop window daubed with black paint. 'Who's doing this?' she ranted, out on the pavement with her dismayed employees. Only when they stepped back inside and surveyed the damage from a different angle did Lacey interpret the random slashes. Although the paint had dribbled, she was able to make out the letters W H O R E.

'I know who's behind this,' she said.

★ ★ ★

Later that day she told Jonas of her suspicions.

'Press charges,' he said.

'I won't for a number of reasons: I don't have any proof and I don't want the good name of my business or yours dragged through the courts. If Alice is charged, her connection with you will be made public; think what that will to do to Constance. She'll be mortified. Her feelings are more important than a brick through a window or daubs of paint.'

Touched by Lacey's consideration for his wife's feelings, Jonas squeezed her hand affectionately, saying, 'But you can't go on —'

Lacey didn't let him finish. 'I know Alice's pranks are annoying, but that's all they are; stupid pranks. They're hardly likely to ruin me.'

354

32

'Well, what did John Hinchcliffe have to say about the fields?' Lacey asked Joshua, as soon as she entered the kitchen at Netherfold.

Joshua's leathery face creased in consternation. 'He didn't say owt much, except them old maps are drawn so badly it's hard to say who owns what.'

Matt took up the strain. 'He says we could pay one o' them fellows what measures the land, but even that might not prove owt. They didn't keep accurate records in Grandad Barraclough's day.' Matt covered his face with his hands. His eyes, still visible above blackened fingernails, begged Lacey for a solution.

Lacey didn't have one, but she wasn't giving up the fight. 'Let's talk things out. Arnold Beaumont says he owns the fields and that his dad let your dad farm them rent free because Hardacre Farm had no use for 'em.'

Joshua nodded. 'Aye, that's what he says.'

Sneering disbelief crossed Lacey's face. 'I think Arnold Beaumont's trying it on. I can't believe he'd not charge rent for summat he owned. He doesn't have a reputation for being generous.'

'You can say that again,' Edith cried. 'Do you remember t'winter afore last you asked for a loan o' some fodder. You told him you'd pay him back next season. He wouldn't let you have as much as a blade o' grass, the miserable sod.'

'Aye, I remember that,' Joshua said wearily, 'but

355

when I asked him why he hadn't asked me for any rent in over twenty years he said he wa' being kind.'

'Kind be buggered,' Matt snarled. 'He hasn't a kindly bone in his body.'

Lacey chipped in. 'Does he have documents to prove he owns the land?'

Again Matt answered despondently. 'He showed John Hinchcliffe a map of Hardacre. It showed our fields marked off as though they were his, but John says that map could have been drawn up yesterday for all we know.

He says we need title deeds if we're to prove owt.'

Lacey left after tea, her heart aching for her family. If Netherfold was no longer a viable farm how would Matt earn his living? She could support them sufficiently to prevent them from starving, but that wasn't the answer.

Her Dad and Matt loved the land, and if the baby Molly was carrying turned out to be a boy, Matt would want to pass the farm on to him. There had always been Barracloughs at Netherfold for as long as anyone in the district could remember.

* * *

Lacey was restocking the haberdashery with new spools of thread when the heavily set man in a shabby pinstriped suit shuffled in. He looked like a travelling salesman down on his luck. Although her supplier was a reputable merchant in Leeds, her kind heart wouldn't let her send this chap off without making a purchase.

356

'Good morning, sir; what might I do for you?'
The man cleared his throat nervously and handed Lacey a card. As she read the words:

FREDERICK LYNCH

Lawyer and Private Investigator

she couldn't help thinking he wasn't a very prosperous lawyer by the looks of him.

'Are you Mrs Lacey Brearley, widow of the late Nathan Brearley?' he asked, his accent letting her know he was Irish.

Widow? Lacey took an instant dislike to him. She drew herself up to her full height. 'I am Lacey Brearley. I'm not a widow. My husband has yet to be declared dead.' Then, not wanting young Katie, who was standing behind the counter awaiting customers, to be party to this exchange, Lacey reluctantly said, 'You'd better come this way.'

Lynch smiled ingratiatingly. Lacey led him out of the shop and into the hallway of her house. At close quarters a sickly sweet smell emanated from his person. Lacey recognised it as whisky. 'What is it you want, Mr Lynch?'

she asked, her voice sharp as she eyed him suspiciously; for a professional man he was decidedly ill at ease.

Lynch's left eye twitched. 'My client, Mrs Alice Burrows, seeks recompense for a wedding dress you were to make for her daughter but failed to produce.' His delivery sounded as though he had rehearsed it several times.

Lacey gave an exasperated groan. 'Mr Lynch,

neither Mrs Burrows nor her daughter have ever been, or ever will be, clients of mine; there are no circumstances requiring compensation.' Her final words biting the air, Lynch squirmed uncomfortably.

'My client has a receipt proving the transaction. It bears your signature and shows quite clearly that Mrs Burrows paid in full for the said garment.' He fumbled in his shabby briefcase then, giving Lacey an oily grin, he handed her a scrap of paper. Lacey gasped when she saw it was indeed a receipt from Lacey's Modistes. She was further shocked to note the handwriting on it was very similar to her own. The wording however was not. 'Paid in full' would have read 'Received with thanks' had she written it.

'I didn't write this,' she said, her voice shaking with frustration, 'I never made any garments for Mrs Burrows.'

'Certainly not to her satisfaction,' Lynch sneered. 'In due course my client will produce this receipt as evidence in a court of law.'

Too late, Lacey regretted ignoring Jonas's advice. Her patience worn thin she threw the offending receipt at Lynch, shouting, 'Take your rubbish and your lies and get out.' She pointed to the door.

A sheen of sweat moistened Lynch's brow and upper lip. He stuffed the receipt in his pocket. 'My client is not prepared to accept an out of court settlement. She fully intends to bring the full weight of the law down on your shoulders.' His voice cracked under the strain. If Lynch had thought to frighten Lacey with the threat of appearing before a court, he had completely misjudged her.

Lacey laughed bitterly. 'I didn't offer a settlement. Now listen to me, Mr Lynch. Your client is a deluded, resentful hag, only concerned with seeking revenge. I won't delay you by explaining her actions other than to say Mrs Burrows has a personal vendetta against me. This is not the first time she has sought to blacken my character.'

Lynch's confusion apparent, he blustered, 'My client intends to take this case to court.'

Exasperated beyond bearing, Lacey heaved a huge sigh. 'Mr Lynch, pardon me for saying this but you're not much of a lawyer, are you? That's if you really are one. I have my doubts.' Lynch flushed at the insult. 'Now,'

said Lacey, 'I suggest that in future, you do your homework before throwing scurrilous allegations in people's faces. I can't explain how Mrs Burrows came by that receipt but I do know it has no validity. If you wish to pursue the matter I suggest you contact my solicitor, John Hinchcliffe.

You'll find his offices at the top of Towngate.' Lacey walked to the door and opened it. 'I'll bid you good day.'

Lynch shuffled off. Lacey picked up the telephone. Recently installed, like the electricity, it was proving to be a valuable facility in times of stress.

'John? Lacey here; I've just had a visit from a strange character by the name of Frederick Lynch. He says he's a lawyer acting on behalf of a supposed client of mine.'

'Fred Lynch.' John sounded both startled and amused. 'Is that old fraudster still practising? I

359

thought he'd been disbarred years ago. Was he sober?'

Lacey chuckled. 'I can't vouch for that. He reeked of whisky. He's been hired to prove I took money from a client without producing the goods.

She's filled his head full of nonsense and downright lies.'

John's laughter crackled down the line. 'And poor old Fred believed her.'

'It appears so. I've sent him up to you. He should be with you shortly, if he's taken my advice. Set him straight, will you? I'm tired of this woman's barmy games.' Lacey gave John a brief account of Alice's other spiteful tricks.

There was silence on the line. When John spoke his tone was sombre. 'She may be barmy but these are dangerous allegations, Lacey. If you're hauled through the courts it will be unpleasant,' then in a lighter tone, he added, 'although if she's relying on Fred Lynch to present her case, it won't hold water. Leave it with me.'

Lacey thanked him and was about to replace the receiver when she remembered Joshua's problem. 'John, before you go, any further progress on Dad's land?'

A sigh through the receiver whistled in her ear. 'Like I told your Dad, Lacey, without title deeds it will be hard to prove. Don't despair though. I'm still on the case.'

Problems, problems, problems, thought Lacey, setting the telephone to rest. Was this to be the pattern of her days for years to come? She went through into the sitting room and gazed at Nathan's photograph on the mantelpiece.

'Oh, Nathan, where are you when I need you,' she said out loud. His smiling image gazed directly back at her. Suddenly the light in the room brightened and flickered across the photograph. Lacey jumped. Had Nathan nodded his head affirmatively, because that's what it looked like. She clasped the photograph in both hands, staring hard at it. The image was lifeless, fixed a time long ago. The light dimmed, and although Lacey's common sense decreed that the movement she had seen was caused merely by changing rays of sunlight shining through the window, she took it as an omen. He was thinking about her, giving his support no matter how far apart they were.

* * *

'Has anyone seen my little black notebook; the one I jot ideas in?' Lacey opened first one drawer, then another, in the cutting table. 'I haven't used it for ages but I usually leave it in here.'

Molly looked up from her machine. 'The last time I saw it was in the cupboard where you keep the new receipt books.'

Receipt? Although it was several days since Lynch's visit the word still held unpleasant connotations and Lacey flinched. Molly carried on sewing.

Later, in John Hinchcliffe's office, Lacey explained what she thought had happened. The woman who had dashed from the shop that day Lacey had forgotten to lock up must have been Alice. 'I'm sure now that it was her. She must have stolen the receipts and my notebook. They copied

361

my style of writing from it but the wording on the receipt was all wrong.' Demonstrating with a used receipt book, she pointed out the differences.

'What's more,' John said, 'the receipts are numbered. The stolen book's numbers will not correlate with the ones you are currently using. Your duplicate receipts will show a history of use in strict order and the correct wording.' He went on to discuss how he thought the case should be handled, Lacey leaving his office with a much lighter step.

No longer overly concerned by Alice's threat, Lacey concentrated instead on forthcoming pleasures: Joan's wedding to Alfie and the birth of Matt and Molly's baby.

Once again, Lacey designed a wedding dress for Joan. 'Eeh, Lacey, I can allus rely on you to make me look a picture on me wedding day,' Joan commented, when she tried on the dress for its final fitting.

'Aye, well, don't be expecting a third. I draw the line at two.'

Joan smiled dreamily. 'Who'd a thought I'd be married twice, me as never thought I'd find anybody. I can't believe how lucky I am. Everything seems to be going my way, what with Alfie getting his . . .' Joan looked puzzled. 'What do you call it, Lacey?'

'His prosthesis.'

'Aye, that's it, a propereesith.'

Lacey laughed. 'If I were you I'd stick to calling it his false arm.'

'It's ever so clever,' Joan said. 'It has this clip like thing at the end where his fingers should be. It fastens onto his elbow an' he can open an' shut it just by squeezing the muscles in his upper arm. He's got really good at picking things up. He wa' thrilled when the army sent for him to go to the hospital to be fitted with it.'

'I'm sure he was.' Lacey shuddered. 'I'd hate to lose one of my arms. I'd not be able to sew.'

'Alfie says he wa' lucky because there isn't enough of 'em to go round.

When he wa' in hospital in France just after it happened, he says there wa' dozens of lads wi' no arms an' legs.'

'And God love each an' every one of 'em,' Lacey said fervently. 'This war has a lot to answer for.'

Joan's face clouded. 'Eeh, I'm sorry, Lacey. Here's me babbling on 'cos I'm so happy an' you still haven't had any news of Nathan. I'm a thoughtless, selfish pig, so I am.'

'Don't upset yourself, Joanie. We can't go round being miserable all the time. God knows I miss Nathan every minute of the day. In fact I'd give my eye teeth just to have him home, but don't let his not being here spoil your happiness.' Lacey paused, a wistful expression on her face. 'I don't think he's dead, Joanie. If he was I'd know in here,' Lacey thumped her hand over her heart.

'Alfie thinks he's in a prison camp,' Joan said, her tone firmly indicating she hoped this was true.

'I hope to God Alfie's right. Now what's this about Alfie's new job?'

'He starts the week after the wedding. It's in Tommy Jackson's hardware store. He'll be weighing out nails an' screws an' serving behind the counter. He says he can do that wi' no bother now he's got his you know what.'

They celebrated Joan and Alfie's wedding with as much aplomb as wartime allowed, the ceremony prompting Lacey to dwell on memories of her own wedding day. Not even four years ago, it seemed a lifetime away.

* * *

'Gentleman to see you, Mrs Brearley; he's waiting in the haberdashery,' said Ann, colouring as she added, 'I think he's had a drop too much to drink.'

'In that case I'll go an' get rid of him,' said Lacey, setting her scissors aside.

Frederick Lynch was even more slovenly than when she last saw him.

Lacey's spirits sank. She thought she'd seen the last of him.

'What is it this time, Mr Lynch? More ridiculous allegations?'

Lynch cleared his throat and peered at her through bleary eyes. 'My client, Mrs Alice — '

'Yes, I know all about that,' Lacey snapped. 'Get on with it.'

'She's instructed me to take the case to court.'

Lacey flew at him, shouting in his face. 'Get out before I call the constable. I refuse to be harassed by a drunk on my own premises.'

'Only carrying out my client's orders,' Lynch slurred.

Lacey watched him stagger up the street and then made another call to John Hinchcliffe.

Later that day, in need of comfort, Lacey and Richard paid a visit to Netherfold. After an hour in Edith's company, Lacey's frayed nerves were soothed sufficiently for her to turn her mind to more mundane matters.

'I'm popping upstairs to the attic. There's an old fox fur in Grandma Barraclough's trunk I might use to trim a suit or two in my winter collection.'

'Your winter what?' Edith sounded bemused.

'My winter collection; the new outfits I'll make at the back end of the year. That's what the magazines call the stuff fashion houses make each season, collections.'

'It sounds awfully grand. You've come a long way, our Lacey. Folk from miles around talk about your sewing. I'm fair proud of you.'

Lacey mounted the stairs to the attic, glowing from the compliment. A musty smell rose from the trunk as she rummaged for the fox fur. The trunk's contents disturbed, Lacey could now see a pile of tattered papers, brown with age and tied up with a ribbon. Her curiosity aroused, she untied the ribbon, scanning the papers one by one.

Receipts for hoes, ploughshares, livestock and oats made dull reading, and she was just about to bundle them back into the trunk when a pair of little beady eyes and a whiskery snout peered over its edge. Lacey leapt to her feet.

It was hard to say who was most startled — Lacey or the mouse — one unsuccessfully attempting to hold onto a sheaf of papers, the other springing to the floor and scuttling to safety. Catching her breath and inwardly cursing her nerves Lacey gathered up the papers.

Edgar Beaumont. The name on the document jumped out at her. She read on, whooping with delight as she hurtled downstairs, fox fur forgotten.

'Look what I've found!' Lacey cavorted round the kitchen table waving the flimsy sheet of paper, brown with age and curled at the edges.

Edith, kneeling at the hearth with Richard, turned so quickly she demolished his tower of building blocks. Richard roared his disapproval. 'What is it?' Edith cried, scrabbling to her feet. Just then Joshua and Matt came in from the yard.

'Hey up, our Lacey. What's to do?' Joshua exclaimed, seeing his daughter jigging round the kitchen waving a piece of paper.

Lacey shoved the document under Joshua's nose. 'Read it, Dad, read what it says.' She turned to Matt. 'I found it in Grandma Barraclough's trunk.'

Joshua screwed up his eyes and read the faded print, his lips wobbling as a great gust of air escaped his lungs. 'By bloody hell! I knew all along them fields wa' ours. Me Dad 'ud o' told me if it had been otherwise.'

Matt craned his neck to peer over Joshua's shoulder. 'What does it say?'

'It says on the first day of July eighteen seventy-nine, Edgar Beaumont sold ten acres of land to Jacob Barraclough for two hundred an' forty-nine pounds, seven shillings an' sixpence.'

Joshua handed the receipt to Matt. Matt scanned it, his face lighting up as he read. In awed tones he said, 'It wa' witnessed by Norman Hopkinson, so it must be legal.'

He pointed out the signature of the now retired solicitor.

Lacey flung her arms round Joshua and hugged him tight. 'See Dad, everything's going to be all right, so stop worrying.' She laughed merrily. 'It'll be one in the eye for Arnold Beaumont when you produce this. It's proof without a doubt.'

They celebrated with mugs of tea and a lardy cake Edith had baked that morning. Joshua scratched his chin thoughtfully. 'I thought it were just women's clutter in that trunk. If I'd done owt about it I'd o' saved meself an awful lot o' damned worry this past while back.'

'Mebbe you should look through the rest of the papers, Dad; you might own half of Garsthwaite,' chirped Lacey. 'In the meantime you've got mice in the attic.'

★ ★ ★

Three evenings later, Lacey was again at Nether-fold, this time in the company of Ivy Vickerman, the midwife. In the bedroom, in the final hours of labour, Molly sweated and intermittently dozed. The clock on the mantelpiece showed half past eleven.

'She'll have it afore midnight,' Ivy said sagely, 'second babies always come quicker than first ones.'

For the umpteenth time that evening Matt stopped pacing the landing and peered round the edge of the door. Ivy tutted, her eyebrows raised in mock indignation. 'They're all the same, first time fathers. They think 'cos it only takes 'em two minutes to put the baby there in the first place, it'll take t'same length o' time for it to come out nine months later.'

Matt mumbled an apology. Lacey laughed. 'Don't fret, Matt. Ivy knows what she's doing. She's delivered half the population of Garsthwaite.'

'I couldn't bear it if owt happened to either of 'em,' muttered Matt.

'It won't,' Lacey replied confidently.

She was right. As the clock struck midnight Matt's son squalled his way into the world: another generation for the Barraclough family.

★ ★ ★

The following morning John Hinchcliffe called on Lacey. 'I've got the contract for the new tenancy on the property next door for you to sign,' he said, the engineer from Oxford having been replaced by a family from London.

Dozey from lack of sleep, Lacey invited him into the kitchen where she was preparing breakfast. 'Bear with me, John. I was up half the night.

Molly had a boy. Our Matt's like a dog wi' two tails.'

John conveyed congratulations and accepted a cup of tea. Lacey told him about the bill of sale she'd found in Grandma Barraclough's trunk.

'Well done,' he replied, 'that will stand as proof in court if Arnold Beaumont still persists in claiming the fields. I'll go and see him tomorrow.'

Lacey lifted Richard into his high chair then set a bowl of porridge in front of him. 'By the way, any more word of our friend, Mr Lynch?' she asked, refilling John's cup.

John shook his head. 'Not to date; maybe Mrs Burrows has come to her senses. Lynch has yet to file the case in court; I checked. If he does it will be unpleasant for you, to say the least.' He drained his cup and prepared to leave. 'Try not to worry, Lacey,' he said fondly, his respect and admiration for this woman having grown considerably since she married his friend, Nathan. 'Whatever she throws our way, I'll make sure we win.'

After John had left, Lacey sat sipping tea and nibbling a bacon sandwich. Richard contentedly crumbled crusts into the remains of his porridge, Lacey too distracted to stop him. Deep in thought she weighed up her present situation.

Mentally she ticked off the positives: Richard: bright and bonny. Business: thriving. Joshua's problem: more or less solved. Matt and Molly: son safely delivered. Joan: new husband, healthy son. Lacey's League: providing sustenance and comfort to the needy. Everything as it should be, except for my own problems: No word from Nathan or the War Office to let me know whether he's alive or dead, and Alice's threats still hanging over me like a storm cloud. I seem to have a knack for making things right for other people, but I have no control over the problems in my own life. Feeling cheated, she cleared the cups and plates into the sink.

'But I've got you, my little love, and that makes everything worthwhile,' she said cheerily, lifting Richard and transferring him to the draining board. 'Sit there now while Mammy wipes you down. You've made a right mullock of yourself.'

369

★ ★ ★

Days dragged by, Lacey in a perpetual state of waiting; waiting for news of Nathan's whereabouts, and Alice's court case. And whilst she waited, she worked.

All day, bright April sunshine had streamed through the open doors of the workroom. Now, with the afternoon drawing to a close, the shop shut and the seamstresses oiling their machines, Lacey lolled in the doorway looking out into the yard.

Close by the door, Molly's Joseph slept in his pram and across the yard Richard, James and David played pig-in-the-middle.

'When the sign over the door was painted it should have had Lacey's Modistes and Nursery written on it, 'cos ever since we started up we've never been without a baby in the place,' said Lacey.

'It's Joan's turn to provide the next one,' Molly quipped, 'I've done my bit for the time being.'

'I'll be pleased to oblige,' chirped Joan.

Lacey loved the camaraderie of the workroom. We're blessed, she thought. It's a luxury to earn your living with your children close by throughout the day. Not like the weaving shed where women were forced to farm out their younger offspring from early morning until late evening.

Richard toddled towards her, his sturdy little legs pumping as he chased the ball, and his grey-blue eyes, when they met Lacey's, so like Nathan's.

My son's no longer a baby, she thought, he's a grown boy. He can run, jump and kick a ball.

370

He can feed himself and even hold a simple conversation. He's learning to form opinions, telling me his likes and dislikes, the latter in no uncertain terms on some occasions. He learns or does something new almost every day, and as he grows into a proper little person his father isn't here to witness any of it.

She shook her head in despair. All over the country there were children like Richard, children who didn't know their fathers, and fathers who didn't know their children. The war had deprived thousands of men the pleasure of seeing their children grow. When it was over they'd come home, strangers to their own sons and daughters. And the fathers who didn't return would be forever strangers, no more than a photograph on a shelf, remembered, or forgotten, by only the older family members.

Although she often showed Richard photographs of Nathan and had taught him to call the tall, handsome man, Daddy, she knew it had no tangible meaning. He had no memories of the feel of Nathan's strong arms, the sound of his voice or the soft touch of his lips.

Joan broke Lacey's reverie. 'Me an' Molly are off up to my place. Come up when you're ready.'

Lacey lingered in the doorway lost in thought then, hearing footsteps, turned to greet Alfie, just returned from work.

'Hello, Alfie; how's the new job?' Lacey liked Alfie. He was kind and sensible, and he made Joan and David happy.

Alfie grinned. 'Not bad, Lacey; I'm managing rightly.' He waved his prosthesis. 'You'd be surprised what I can do wi' this.' He flexed the muscle in his upper arm, the false hand opening and closing with ease.

'I bet I would,' Lacey observed saucily, 'and it'll come in useful for keeping our Joanie in line; a few sharp nips with that and she'll soon do as she's told.'

'Oh, I don't think it'll come to that. She's grand is your Joan. I couldn't believe it when she said she'd take me on, what wi' me being only half a man.' He flicked the prosthesis again.

'You're a man an' a half, Alfie,' said Lacey, her tone brimming with admiration. 'You've come through the war, seeing and doing things too horrible to imagine, but you haven't let it beat you. You might have left a bit of you behind in France but now you're going forward, and I wish you every success.'

'Thanks, Lacey.' Alfie glanced down at his false arm. 'I wa' shattered when it happened. I couldn't imagine how I'd live without it, but when I wa' at Roehampton getting it fitted I saw lads wi' both arms an' legs missing. I realise how lucky I am.'

'Lucky and brave, Alfie; it takes a lot of courage to overcome something like that.'

'I don't consider meself brave, I wa' scared out o' me wits half the time, but I fought alongside men who had the courage of lions. There wa' one lad in our regiment went out into No Man's Land twice to bring his wounded mates back; third time he wasn't so lucky.'

Alfie's eyes darkened at the bitter memory. 'This war's done some terrible things to thousands of us. I saw chaps blinded, gassed and shell shocked; an' they were the lucky ones. Them as weren't were blown to bits.'

Lacey sighed heavily. 'When will it all end, Alfie?'

Alfie smiled. 'Well now, if you can believe what you read in't papers we've got Gerry on the run. T'allies are pushing 'em back rightly. Up on t'Ypres Salient an' the Hindenburg Line we've had some cracking victories. T'Germans are said to be running out o' food an' firepower. If we keep it up we'll beat 'em in no time.'

Lacey was impressed. 'You're very knowledgeable, Alfie.'

'Aye, well, once you've been involved an' know what them lads out there are going through, you tend to take an interest. I'd still be there but for this.' He flicked the prosthesis.

'I don't read the papers; it's too depressing. But tell me this; do you know anything about soldiers who were taken prisoner?'

'Aye, there wa' whole units of 'em rounded up in some places. Some of our lot were captured. It wa' a right bloody shambles. We never saw 'em again. One o' t'officers said they'd be taken to a camp in Germany. They don't kill 'em. There's rules an' regulations for taking prisoners.'

A surge of hope flared in Lacey's chest; if Nathan had been captured he could still be alive. Lacey's eyes begged Alfie for reassurance. 'Your husband hasn't been declared dead,' he said. 'He could well be sitting out the war in a camp in Germany. Never give up hope, Lacey.'

Joan and Molly clattered downstairs from the apartment above, Molly clutching an armful of

373

baby clothes Joan had passed down. 'I'll be off then, Matt'll be wondering where I've got to,' she said, and amid a chorus of goodbyes she stepped out into the street.

'An' I was wondering where you'd got to,' cried Joan, squeezing Alfie affectionately and pecking his cheek.

'Me an' Lacey wa' just talking,' Alfie explained.

'We were,' Lacey agreed, patting Alfie's good arm. 'And I really appreciated our conversation, Alfie. Thanks very much.'

Alfie went off upstairs. Lacey watched him go then addressed her cousin. 'He's a lovely man, Joanie.'

'Isn't he just. I can't believe how lucky I am to have found him.' She adjusted the pretty scarf covering her damaged scalp. 'What wi' my bald head I thought no man 'ud ever look at me again. But it doesn't bother Alfie. I suppose we're two of a kind. We've both got summat missing.'

'There's nowt missing about you two. You're as whole as anybody I know, and I love the pair of you. Now get off upstairs and make his tea.'

Alfie's personal courage, and his belief in the recent successes of the British troops filled Lacey with hope. Furthermore, if Alfie believed Nathan was a prisoner of war then so would she.

Later that evening, as Lacey and Richard played merrily, the telephone rang. It was John Hinch-cliffe. 'Is it convenient for me to come and see you within the next hour? It's with regard to Alice Burrows. I'd rather talk face to face than tell you over the phone.'

The happy feeling Alfie had inspired suddenly dissipated. As Richard's tower of brightly coloured

374

blocks tumbled into disarray, Lacey wondered if Alice was about to shatter her hopes in the same way.

Richard was tucked up in bed by the time John arrived, Lacey waiting fretfully for what he had to say. She led him into the sitting room, his warm smile and cheerful greeting raising her spirits. 'Tea?' she offered.

'I'd love a cup. It's been something of a day, I can tell you.'

In the kitchen brewing a pot of tea and setting cups on a tray, Lacey mulled over John's attitude. He didn't sound like the bearer of bad news; perhaps she was worrying unnecessarily, or maybe he was delaying the blow he was about to deliver. Her hands shook as she lifted the tray, the cups rattling in their saucers.

'Thanks.' John took the tea Lacey handed him and settling back in the armchair, drank deeply. Lacey sat in the chair opposite him, her mouth dry, her tea untouched.

'I needed that,' John said, setting down his cup and wiping his lips. 'Now! Down to business. Alice Burrows is hell bent on punishing you. The case has been filed.'

'Does this mean a court case?'

John nodded solemnly. 'It does. The woman hasn't a hope of winning, but it will mean you have to defend yourself in court. Any hopes you had of keeping the Brearleys and your business out of it will go up in smoke. We can't prevent it from going public.'

Lacey's eyes glittered angrily. 'In that case, prepare a counter claim; charge her with theft, libel and an attempt to defraud. Do whatever it takes to prove that that woman is a menace to society.'

After further discussion of how he would handle the case, Lacey saw John out and for the rest of the evening she seethed with rage. By bedtime her anger had turned to determination; she would not let this bloody woman ruin her.

★ ★ ★

'I'm taking Alice Burrows to court,' Lacey told Joan the next day.

'An' so you should,' said Joan fervently, 'she's evil.' With Lacey so downcast, Joan hugged her comfortingly.

A shadow blocked the sunlight in the open shop doorway and they drew apart. Sam Barton lolled against the doorframe. 'I think I've got summat you've been waiting for,' he said, smiling fondly at Lacey and holding out a letter. 'I hope I'm not mistaken.'

Lacey reached for it with trembling fingers. She knew that Sam, like any regular postman, recognised the identity of the senders by the handwriting or postmarks on the envelopes he regularly delivered. Her fingers grasped the envelope. She didn't dare lower her gaze. Her eyes on Sam, they begged him not to have made an error of judgment. Sam stared back, then nodded encouragingly.

Lacey lowered her gaze.

33

'Tell us again what he says,' Joan urged.

Lacey didn't need to refer to the letter, its contents were already printed on her heart and in her mind. 'He was captured in a battle on the Ypres Salient and taken to a prison camp somewhere in Germany; I don't know which one, the name's been crossed out. There were other men from his regiment with him. They weren't allowed to contact anyone.'

'That's downright cruel, keeping a man's family in the dark, letting 'em think he's dead when all the time he's alive,' Joan protested.

Lacey shrugged sadly. 'It's war, Joanie. War is cruel.'

'If they weren't allowed to write to anybody, how did Mr Brearley manage to get that letter to you, Mrs Brearley? Has he escaped?' Katie's eyes grew large as her imagination ran riot.

Lacey's lips quirked and she shook her head, almost sorry to dispel Katie's vision of a heroic Nathan duping the German guards and then making a hazardous journey through enemy countryside to freedom.

'No, Katie; he's still a prisoner. They were moved to another camp, one the Red Cross has access to. Then they were registered as prisoners of war and allowed to write home. Thank God for the Red Cross. Nathan says they supplied them with food parcels and soap.' She chuckled. 'He says he hasn't had a proper wash in months.' She stood up, crackling with energy. 'He says I can send him parcels. He's asked for cigarettes, chocolate and socks. Once I've recovered my senses I'm going to pack the best parcel you've ever clapped eyes on.'

Later that day, the joyful news having been relayed to Constance and Jonas, Lacey sat with Richard on her knee and a photograph of Nathan in her hand. Although the little boy was too young to understand the import of what Lacey told him, she repeated the miraculous tale yet again. 'Your Daddy's alive and well, and if God is good he'll come home to us once this war is over.'

Richard pointed at Nathan's image. 'Daddy come home,' he lisped.

'Yes,' Lacey replied with conviction, an inner voice asking, but when? How long before I see him again?

★ ★ ★

Lacey stepped out of the post office, her third parcel to Nathan about to start its journey to Hesse in Germany. In reply to Nathan's second letter she had included toothpaste, lice powder, gravy browning and more soap, each item bought and packed with loving care in the hope that these simple comforts would reach him and make life more bearable.

'Oh, Lacey, I'm glad I bumped into you. We've another case of flu in Jackroyd Lane.' Maggie, the team leader of Lacey's League wore a worried expression as she delivered the news.

The League, now a respected body of women,

378

had gone from strength to strength, now with six full time employees caring for the needy. Lacey and Constance's motto being 'share what you have with the have-nots' they still covered much of the cost, but just recently Lacey had persuaded the local Council, businessmen and churches to contribute to the League's wage bill.

Persuading them had not been an easy task. As usual, Lacey's persistence and Constance's influence triumphed, the worthy members of Garsthwaite society taking pride in the knowledge that its poorest inhabitants did not suffer unduly. In fact, the Garsthwaite Echo and the Huddersfield Examiner had both written articles praising their 'magnanimous humanity.'

Concerned by Maggie's news, Lacey asked, 'How many cases to date?'

'Four; an' that young woman who gave birth last week has it really badly. T'doctor says she'll not see tomorrow.'

'Is there anyone to care for the child?'

'Aye; her sister's already minding it.' Maggie shook her head, frustrated.

Lacey sighed. 'If that poor lass goes, it'll bring the death toll in Garsthwaite to eleven. That young lad who works for the butcher died almost immediately he caught it, and according to the newspaper there's hundreds of people dying from it all over the country.'

'They're callin' it Spanish Flu,' Maggie said, her lip curling distastefully. 'We might a known it 'ud be foreigners that started it. It's bad enough them bloody Germans killin' our lads in France without the bloody Spaniards sending us their

379

rotten flu.'

Lacey suppressed a smile at Maggie's distorted vitriol; but the flu epidemic was no laughing matter. Most of those who had fallen prey to the deadly virus appeared to be aged between twenty and forty. Usually the very young or the very old succumbed whenever a plague of illness struck, but not this time. Was this a punishment intended for her generation? First, so many young men killed in the war, then people of both sexes dying from Spanish flu.

Maggie hurried off, Lacey promising to meet with her later, at the same time reminding herself that after she had visited the sick woman's house she'd take a bath before going anywhere near Richard. She mustn't bring illness into the house; not now she and Richard had everything to live for; Nathan was alive.

★ ★ ★

The flu epidemic continued to take its toll, but whilst there was great sadness in the homes of the victims, by the end of October 1918 the inhabitants of Garsthwaite were agog with anticipation.

'The Germans are definitely in retreat,' announced Jonas, flourishing the newspaper Soames had brought to the evening dinner table. 'According to this report Ludendorff has resigned and the American President is refusing to negotiate for an amnesty until his demands are met. It looks as though the war's almost won.'

Constance reached across the table to clasp Lacey's hand, Lacey returning the pressure as they smiled at one another through eyes blurred with tears. 'It won't be long now until Nathan's home,' said Constance, her voice thick with relief.

In the days that followed, Garsthwaite buzzed with talk of victory over the Germans. People smiled more often and stopped to chat, their faces mirroring the hope they all felt for the future. It finally came on a cold, bright day in November, at the eleventh hour on the eleventh day. War was over, peace declared.

★ ★ ★

Everything was changed, yet in reality nothing changed. Lacey's Modistes worked throughout the winter months sewing heavy coats and suits in tweed and flannel, some trimmed with fur for those who could afford such luxury. The new shop with its ready to wear garments did a roaring trade in the month before Christmas, the wealthier customers casting aside the parsimony war had induced and celebrating freedom from German oppression by splurging on new outfits. Those with little to spare always found something to suit their purse.

'Spread the happiness,' Lacey said to Joan, after selling, very cheaply, two dresses of her own design to a mother and daughter, both hard working but under paid women from the weaving shed.

'You're too soft by halves, Lacey Brearley,' Joan chided, 'but you do make people happy.

'I'm a bit like Robin Hood,' Lacey said, the words Nathan had spoken on their honeymoon in Scarborough springing to mind. 'I charge them that have it full price, and set it against the few bob I knock off for them who deserve a treat. It's swings an' roundabouts, Joanie.'

34

Although a thick layer of snow blanketed the fields and an icy wind had blown across the moor for the past few days, Joshua Barraclough sat in a chair by the fire, his expression one of utter contentment. Arnold Beaumont had relinquished his claim; the fields were Joshua's.

Edith set the table for tea; plates of home-cured ham accompanied by a thick mustard sauce, pickled eggs and boiled potatoes, and a rich, dark boiled fruit cake for afters.

'That looks tasty,' said Lacey, lifting Richard up on to a chair piled with cushions so that he could reach the table.

Edith flushed with pleasure. 'Aye, we've never gone short o' much, what with having us own eggs an' a pig or two; although I can't say I'll ever get used to this margarine, it's not a patch on butter.' Disdainfully, she scraped the pale yellow substance onto slices of bread. The family sat down and tucked into the spread, talking nineteen to the dozen as they ate.

'How are you feeling now you've got over the morning sickness, Molly?' Lacey asked the sister-in-law she had grown to love and admire.

Molly, nursing Joseph on her knee, smiled at Lacey's concern. 'I'm gradely. I have a feeling this one might be a girl. It feels different to when I wa' carrying David and Joseph.'

'I hope it is,' said Matt, his features alight with

love and pride. 'We've got two lads already; we're due a little princess.'

David looked quizzically at his stepfather. 'If the new baby's going to be a princess, does that mean I'm a prince?'

Matt, who loved David as his own, laughed. 'Aye, you're a prince among men, an' so's our Joseph. I'm fair proud knowing I've got two lads to help me run Netherfold when I get too old to do it meself.'

'Just like I am wi' you, Matt; you've helped me keep this place going. I couldn't a done it wi'out you.' Not used to showing his emotions, Joshua's cheeks reddened and he cleared his throat noisily.

Although Joshua had spoken from the heart, no barbed insinuation intended, Lacey immediately thought of Jimmy who, much to his father's regret, had chosen to work in the Mill rather than on the smallholding. 'What time does our Jimmy arrive on Tuesday?' she asked.

'His train gets into Huddersfield at three. We're all going to meet him; your Dad an' all.' Edith's face softened, her excitement at welcoming home her youngest son palpable.

'If I get me work finished afore noon,' growled Joshua.

Edith shot him a warm smile. She had been desolate when Joshua disowned Jimmy after his scandalous involvement in the Mill robbery. His refusal to visit Jimmy in prison had torn Edith apart. The rift had been partially healed when Jimmy was found to be nothing more than misguided, and his enlistment to fight for king and country had done much to restore Joshua's pride in his younger son. Now, Jimmy soon to be welcomed back into the bosom of the family, Edith could give him the homecoming he deserved.

'I'll come too,' Lacey said, 'make it a real family welcome: Barracloughs united.'

'Have you heard from Nathan, lass?' Joshua's eyes conveying sympathy, he smiled tenderly at his much loved daughter.

Lacey, knowing how much he understood her pain, smiled back. 'Not since the letter telling me he was being moved to another camp, ready for repatriation. He says it could be weeks before he finally arrives back in England. I've waited so long; a bit longer won't hurt.'

Edith's eyes filled with tears. 'Just to know both our boys are coming back makes me feel more than blessed.'

'Me an' all,' Lacey said, quelling a frisson of fear. Nathan was still far away. Please God, don't let there be a last minute catastrophe. She had, much to her horror, read a newspaper article reporting that the Germans had shot some Prisoners of War rather than set them free when the Armistice had been declared. She lifted Richard from the chair next to hers and sat him on her knee, hiding her face in his neck to stem her tears.

Sensing Lacey's anxiety, Molly changed the subject. 'I hope you've got your best bib an' tucker pressed for tomorrow when you go to Felicity's wedding. We can't have you letting Lacey's Modistes down.'

Lacey grimaced. 'It's a society wedding; I'll have to look me best.'

'You will,' Edith said archly. 'You've done well

for yourself, our Lacey. You're that respected in Garsthwaite I wouldn't be surprised if you got an invitation to Buckingham Palace.'

Lacey laughed at Edith's boast. 'Jonas Brearley's mansion will do me.' She smiled mischievously. 'Remember how it was when me and Nathan first got together; Ma Brearley couldn't stand the sight of me and Jonas wasn't too keen either. I bet when he first employed me in his weaving shed he never imagined I'd end up as his daughter-in-law.'

* * *

Yet again, Lacey stood in the drawing room at Fenay Hall but, unlike her first visit to the mansion five years ago when Nathan invited her to the Mill managers' party, she felt completely at ease. Today nobody would belittle her; she had earned their respect. Mind you, she thought, taking a sip of champagne, it was damned hard work in the beginning but it's all been worth it.

She watched with pride as Felicity and Stefan circled the drawing room greeting their wedding guests. He looks like a learned prince with his gold rimmed spectacles and bushy beard, and she looks like an ice queen, thought Lacey, her eyes on the shimmering moiré silk dress she had made.

Stefan had arrived in England shortly before Christmas, Felicity dashing to meet him in London. 'You should tell your parents about him,' Lacey had advised when Felicity told her of his arrival. 'If you want to be truly happy, you can't go on meeting him in secret.'

Felicity had taken Lacey's advice, and to her

amazement Constance and Jonas had issued a somewhat hesitant invitation for her to bring Stefan to the Hall.

'If only to assess his suitability,' Constance told Lacey on the day Felicity left for London. 'She's inclined to be headstrong and not the best judge of character, yet, knowing Felicity, our opinion will count for nothing.'

'She's not the flighty young girl we all thought we knew,' responded Lacey, 'she's loved this man for more than three years. Circumstances being what they were, she hid her feelings but she never lost faith in him. Their love wouldn't have stood the strain had it not been true. As it is, it's as strong as ever. I'm sure you'll approve of him.'

They did. Charmed by the quiet, serious young doctor who made their daughter deliriously happy, Constance and Jonas had acquiesced to Felicity's request to marry as soon as possible. What better way to start the New Year 1919 than a wedding. Now here Lacey was, clasping a glass of champagne and enjoying the occasion, saddened by Nathan's absence but delighted for Felicity.

It's nothing short of marvellous how things have worked out, she mused, as she surveyed the happy scene. Felicity has her Stefan, I'll soon have my Nathan back where he belongs and here I am surrounded by family and friends, completely at home in a house where once I was ostracized and scorned for being working class.

She gazed around the spacious drawing room, admiring the elegant, velvet covered chairs and sofas and the fine pieces of furniture, their rich patina gleaming under the light cast by two huge crystal chandeliers in the ornate ceiling.

I helped pay for some of this, she thought; every pick my loom made, every loose end I caught, every bobbin I changed, every piece I wove bought a tiny bit of this splendour. There was a time when I couldn't have imagined such grandeur; now I'm part of it.

'She looks beautiful, doesn't she?' Jonas, bursting with pride, gestured with his glass to where Felicity stood posing for a photograph with some of her guests.

'She does, Jonas,' Lacey agreed wholeheartedly, 'Felicity is beautiful inside and out. It was a privilege to make her wedding dress.'

'Aye, and you made a damned good job of it; you've come on rightly since the day you bullied me into giving the lasses at the mill decent closets.' He laughed at the memory. Lacey laughed too.

'Thanks for the compliment, and the closets.'

Jonas laughed again. 'You don't alter do you, lass? You say exactly what you're thinking. That's what I like about you.'

'There's no point in burying yourself in thoughts,' Lacey replied. 'If you think something needs doing then it usually does. I've only ever tried to do what I thought might improve my own and other people's lives.'

'And you've done that, lass. You're a proper businesswoman these days.

I'm sure Nathan's as proud of you as I am. You kept your independence; not once did you come crying for a handout, as some do.' He grimaced, Lacey knowing he referred to Alice. 'You deserve all the credit you get. You've come a long way.' Jonas patted Lacey's shoulder fondly then moved off to greet a fellow mill owner.

There it was again, that phrase. I have come a long way, Lacey thought, and if I can continue the rest of the journey with Nathan by my side I'll be the happiest woman in the world.

★ ★ ★

On a Tuesday afternoon in January 1919, at exactly three thirty, the Leeds to Liverpool train chuffed into Huddersfield station, wheezing and clanking as it drew to a halt. Doors flew open, the Barracloughs craning their necks, each wanting to be the first to catch sight of Jimmy.

'There he is!' Joshua's roar startled Richard enough for him to look fearful. He, who had never seen his Uncle Jimmy, scanned the faces of men crowding the platform, many of them dressed in drab brown greatcoats.

Joshua, Matt and Edith surged forwards, behind them Lacey, Molly and their children, the young ones watching in amazement as their parents and grandparents hugged and kissed a stocky little man wearing a huge overcoat and a lopsided cap. Eventually they released him, all except Edith who clung to Jimmy as though she would never let go.

Jimmy glanced from one family member to another, a huge grin on his face. 'By, but I wasn't expecting a full turn out.' He fixed his eyes on Joshua. 'It's good to see you, Dad.'

Joshua clapped Jimmy heartily on the shoulder. 'It's good to see you, lad. Good to have you back.'

His voice wobbled, tears springing to his eyes. To stem them he jested, 'Now your mother can get summat done instead o' sitting moping.'

'An' this must be Molly.' Jimmy gave Molly a cheeky wink. 'What did you do to get this miserable brother o' mine to t'altar. I thought he'd always be an old bachelor farmer.'

Molly blushed. Matt came to her rescue. 'She didn't have to force me. I fell for her t'minute I saw her.'

'An' now you're the father of two lads an' one on the way. Congratulations, pal.'

Matt pumped Jimmy's hand yet again, eyeing him up and down. 'You've filled out since we last saw you. What happened to the skinny kid what joined up?'

Jimmy grinned. 'I left him in France. He wa' a useless, stupid bugger, so I dumped him.'

★ ★ ★

The kitchen at Netherfold hummed with happiness as they all crowded in for Jimmy's homecoming, Jimmy delighted when Joan, Alfie and young James joined them. 'You lucky bugger,' he said when introduced to Alfie. 'She left me high an' dry when she married Stanley, now she's gone an' done it again.' Knowing Jimmy was joking everyone, including Alfie, laughed.

'Take your coat off, lad, make yourself at home,' cried Edith, undoing the brass buttons on Jimmy's coat. Jimmy flapped at her hands playfully, saying, 'She still thinks I'm a bairn.'

'What are you still wearing an army greatcoat

390

for?' Lacey asked as she hung Jimmy's coat behind the door.

'Eh, don't sneer. I paid for that. They gave me fifty-two shillings and sixpence in place of a demob suit an' told me if I wanted to keep the greatcoat I had to pay a pound for it.'

'They charged you for a coat you've been wearing for the past four years fighting for king an' country,' squealed Edith, her eyes popping. 'Well I never.'

'If I return it I can get me money back, but I don't think I'll bother. I've grown fond of it.' Jimmy's face softened, memories of his days at The Front suddenly surging back. 'You'd be surprised at the things we used to treasure over there. That old coat's kept me warm an' dry many a night.'

'I know what you mean,' Alfie said softly, 'I brought mine back wi' me. I only wish I'd brought this.' He tapped the table with the prosthesis.

Jimmy gazed at Alfie, his eyes full of sympathy. 'Aye,' he said heavily, 'there were lads in my regiment ended up t'same way, the poor buggers. But hey, you're here an' alive an' wed to our Joanie. How lucky does that make you?'

'The luckiest man alive,' Alfie said, his voice thick with emotion.

Edith set about preparing a spread fit for a king, Molly and Joan assisting. Lacey sent the boys to play in the parlour, telling them to be good for this was a special occasion. 'Your Uncle Jimmy's a hero,' she said, 'and you've got to behave when there's a hero in the house.'

'By bloody hell,' Jimmy exclaimed, coming in behind her, 'I never thought I'd hear you saying that about me. You always thought I wa' a daft little bugger.'

Lacey ruffled his hair, 'Not any more. You've fought a war and made Dad proud. You've grown into a grand man, Jimmy. I always knew you would. Though you're still careless with your tongue. Mind your language in front of these youngsters.'

Jimmy saluted. 'Sorry, Lacey. Over there we did plenty of cursing, but then we'd plenty to curse about.'

Lacey ushered him out of the boys' earshot. 'It must have been terrible; was it truly as bad as the newspapers made out?'

'Worse. You couldn't describe some of the stuff I've seen an' done. An' don't ask me now 'cos I don't want to remember . . . not today. Mind you, there are some things I'll never forget; good mates that were blown to bloody smithereens an' others who were gassed an' went crazy.'

Jimmy's face creased painfully and he shook his head to dispel the ghastly memories. 'But hey, I wa' one o' t'lucky ones. Here I am. An' don't you go getting all mopey, 'cos like me your Nathan will be home any day. They're repatriating 'em as fast as they can. A whole lot o' them fellows I travelled up from London wi' had been POW's. They're all coming home; wait an' see.'

* * *

Wait and see, Jimmy had said. Lacey did, but it wasn't easy. Every day she waited for the letter that would herald Nathan's arrival. Would he have changed so completely she'd have to get to know him all over again? Jimmy had changed. There was a serious side to him now.

'It's a bit like the parable of the Prodigal Son,' Matt groaned to Lacey, when he called to collect Molly from work. 'If me mother serves up another dinner like the ones she's dished up ever since he came home, we'll all be as fat as Fred Porter's pigs. Mind you, our Jimmy's certainly earnin' his keep; an' I never thought you'd hear me say that.'

Jimmy had decided to stay at Netherfold, his intention being to expand Edith's chicken and turkey business. 'We'll increase t'number o' birds,' Jimmy told Edith, 'an' now I can drive, we can be poultry merchants. I've already organised gettin' a lorry from a mate in me old regiment, an' I'll have them new rearing pens and chicken houses built before t'end o' t'month.'

When Lacey heard of Jimmy's plans she said, 'By, he certainly has changed.'

Two weeks after his homecoming, his family discovered exactly how much.

★ ★ ★

'Did you see this in t'paper?' cried Matt, bursting into the kitchen at Netherfold waving a copy of the Garsthwaite Chronicle. He'd gone into the town earlier that day to deliver mutton to the butcher.

Edith and Lacey looked up from the paper patterns they were examining for Edith's new dress. 'What is it?' they chorused.

'It's our Jimmy. He's a bloody hero. Just listen to this.' At that precise moment Joshua lumbered in from the yard. Matt waved the paper at him.

'Dad, listen to this.' Matt held the paper up and began to read, his voice ringing with pride.

A HERO IN OUR MIDST

Matt paused. 'That's the headline. Now hear the rest of it.' He paused again to clear his throat:

It has recently come to our attention that we have a hero in our midst: none other than James Barraclough, son of Joshua and Edith Barraclough of Netherfold Farm. Whilst serving in France with the 3rd Battalion Durham Light Infantry, Lance Corporal James Barraclough risked his life to save that of three of his comrades. Under heavy fire, Lance Corporal Barraclough single-handedly destroyed a German gun emplacement which was threatening his own and the lives of his fellow soldiers. On a separate occasion he rescued an injured comrade, again under a hail of enemy fire, the unlucky soldier having been left for dead after the Hun invaded their trench. For these acts of gallantry James Barraclough has been awarded the Military Medal. We are extremely proud and honoured to learn that a son of Garsthwaite distinguished himself so bravely on the battlefield.'

In the silence that followed, each member of Jimmy's family digested the glowing report and then reflected on the feckless young lad he had once been. Edith shook her head, bewildered: how

394

was it 'her bairn', as she still thought of him, had had the courage to perform such heroic deeds? Lacey felt her heart swell with pride for the lad who had once endangered himself to protect her honour, and Matt silently acknowledged that his useless little brother wasn't so useless after all. Joshua recalled the times he had badgered the boy for his dislike of farming. Now, he wiped tears from his eyes, and choking on his words said, 'He never mentioned nowt about that.'

'He didn't even mention it when I asked him what it was like in France,' said Lacey, lifting Richard up on her knee and hugging him tight as she marvelled at her brother's bravery.

Matt set the paper on the table so that they could read the article for themselves. 'Our Jimmy, a hero,' he said, his tone filled with awe. 'He kept that one quiet.'

'He never wa' boastful,' said Edith, her face pink with pride, her tone loving, 'but I never thought he wa' brave enough to do summat like that.'

Lacey chuckled. 'He'd do it without even thinking of the consequences. That's our Jimmy all over.'

'What's our Jimmy all over? What have I done wrong now?' Jimmy ambled into the kitchen, just in time to hear Lacey's last remark.

'It's what you did right, lad, that we're talking about.' Joshua stood and stuck out his hand for Jimmy to shake. 'I've never been prouder in all me life.'

Ignoring Joshua's outstretched hand, Jimmy asked, 'What are you on about?'

'This. In t'paper.' Matt shoved the Chronicle at

Jimmy. 'Why din't you tell us you wa' a hero?'

Jimmy skimmed the article, a gamut of expressions flitting across his face. Finally, he grinned. 'I'm no bloody hero. I just did what I could. It's what you do out there. You looked out for one another. They'd a done t'same for me.' He tossed the paper onto the table, his eyes darkening as memories flooded back, a poignant smile curving his lips.

The smile stretched into a wide grin. 'When t'commanding officer told me they were givin' me a medal, I thought he were kidding. Then a bit after, they had a ceremony and pinned it on me uniform.'

'Where is it now?' cried Lacey.

'Upstairs wi' me other stuff.'

Matt gave Jimmy a gentle shove. 'Go an' get it, you daft ha'porth; let's see it.'

Jimmy returned with a small leather box in his hand. 'I wasn't only one as got one,' he said self-effacingly, and handed the medal to Edith. 'Here Mam, you have it. You deserve it for puttin' up wi' me when I wa' a young 'un.'

Edith clasped the medal to her lips, then passed it to Joshua who handed it to Lacey who gave it to Matt, each of them marvelling at the silver disc suspended from a bar threaded with a red, white and blue ribbon.

Tears streamed down Edith's cheeks. 'Eeh, lad, you'll never know how proud I am; words fail me.'

'That'll be a first then,' said Jimmy, his cheeky remark making everyone laugh, and easing the solemnity of the moment. He picked up the paper and scanned the report again. 'Last time me name wa' in t' *Chronicle* nobody wa' happy,' he said, recalling the report of the mill robbery.

'That's all in the past, luv,' Edith said, 'forgiven an' forgotten like this rotten war should be. From now on we'll not look back. We'll look forward to a better future . . . for all of us.' She smiled fondly at Lacey. 'You an' all, luv; it'll not be long now before Nathan's home.'

Lacey walked back to Towngate feeling happier than she had for some time. Her elation stayed with her throughout the evening and she went to bed feeling contented for the first time in ages.

* * *

It was past midnight, Towngate devoid of all human activity save for that of two women, a young one who dithered nervously as she scuttled in the shadows behind an older woman whose steps were determined and whose eyes glinted with demonic zeal.

At the entrance to the alleyway leading to the rear of Lacey's Modistes the older woman signalled a halt. She glanced left, then right and, sure of being unobserved, dodged into the dark passage, dragging the younger woman in behind her.

'Mama, this is madness!' The young woman's quivering whisper betrayed extreme consternation.

Alice clamped a hand to Violet's mouth. 'Shut up, you little fool,' she hissed, 'Nathan's coming home and if he is to be ours you must do as I say. Now stop your whimpering and keep an eye out for anyone approaching. It's not likely at this hour, but should I be disturbed you must alert me at once.'

Wild eyed, Violet struggled to free herself. 'Mama, I beg you, please don't do this. I promise to find another man to marry; one just as wealthy as Nathan.'

'I want none other than Nathan Brearley for you,' snarled Alice, tightening her grip. 'Once this night is over, you will have what should have rightly been yours in the first place. I'm doing it for you. Don't I always put your needs before my own?' She scurried down the passage. Violet, paralysed, listened to Alice's fading footsteps.

The small pane of glass broke easily, the sound muffled by the wad of cloth Alice placed against it before striking a sharp blow with a hammer. She stowed the hammer in her capacious cloak pocket; it clinked against the smal'l bottle already there. The cloth wrapped round her hand, Alice cautiously reached for the key Lacey had left in the lock.

At the top of the staircase Alice paused, unsure where Lacey slept. Judging it to be in the room overlooking the street she took the bottle from her pocket and sprinkled its contents on the cloth still in her hand.

Lacey smelt the sweet, cloying odour before she felt the fingers clawing at her neck. Instinctively, she rolled away. Something damp slapped against the bare flesh above the neck of her nightdress. Dizzied by the fumes, she struggled to free herself from the iron grip on her shoulder. With one tremendous surge she threw herself out of the far side of the bed, wincing as a clump of her hair stayed in the frantic, restraining hand.

On her feet, Lacey woozily faced her assailant. Alice glared back, her eyes wild and her breathing laboured. For several seconds they stared at one another, each waiting for the other to make the first move. The chloroform's vapour dissipating, Lacey's head cleared, her mind sharpening. She fixed her eyes on the door. Deliberately.

Down in the passage Violet trembled at the sound of heavy footsteps tromping along Towngate. Incapable of suppressing the urge, she stepped out into the street, almost colliding with Constable Jack Eastwood, patrolling his patch on night duty.

Up in the bedroom, Alice anticipated Lacey's next move. She darted to the door, utterly confounded when Lacey scrambled across the bed and dashed to the window. Throwing it wide open, Lacey yelled at the top of her lungs.

* * *

After that, it was all a blur.

Lacey tottered downstairs to find Alice struggling with Jack Eastwood, Alice screeching maniacally as she tried to break his grip and attack Lacey again. Violet cowered in the corner by the door, sobbing and blabbering apologies. Joan and Alfie, alerted by the racket, burst in from next door, Alfie's urgent telephone call bringing two burly policemen and the Black Maria. As Jack and his two colleagues led Alice and Violet out, Alice's eyes met Lacey's. 'Whore,' she shrieked.

Lacey thought she would never forget Alice's

crazed glare.

Joan made a pot of tea, and for hers and Alfie's benefit, Lacey shakily went over the terrifying events from the moment she realised Alice was in her bedroom to Jack Eastwood's intervention and Joan and Alfie's arrival. 'The evil bitch,' Joan exclaimed, 'she needs locking up.'

They talked into the small hours, Alfie eventually leaving with Richard in his arms. 'I'll put him in with James for the rest of the night,' he said to Lacey and to Joan he said, 'You stay and keep an eye on her.'

Lacey had thought she would never sleep again. Now, she awoke to find herself in the parlour, slumped in the same chair she had fallen into shortly after the Black Maria had taken Alice and Violet away. It was daylight, shafts of bright sun were lancing through the gaps in the curtains. Her body ached and inside her head she could still hear the shrilling police whistle, the thudding feet and the shrieks and yells that had followed her own screams.

It was like waking from a nightmare.

Her fingers strayed to the wheals on her neck put there by Alice's clawing hand. They were real enough, and although she had earlier rinsed her face she could still smell the cloying sweetness of chloroform that clung to the neck of her nightdress.

In the opposite chair, Joan stirred. 'You're awake then?' she said.

Lacey yawned and sat upright. 'I need a bath,' she said, but when she stood her legs buckled under her. Joan leapt up and caught her. Taking strength from her cousin's warm embrace Lacey said. 'Thank God that's over and done with. Wasn't Jack Eastwood absolutely wonderful? He probably saved my life.'

'Aye, so you keep saying. You told him that a dozen times last night.'

★ ★ ★

About an hour later, Lacey walked wearily to Fenay Hall. She had to let them know what had happened before anyone else did. A dank fog hung over the mansion, drops of moisture dripping from the bare branches of the trees onto Lacey's head as she trudged up the drive. It seemed to Lacey like the perfect setting for what she was about to tell her in-laws.

Soames answered the door, surprised to see Lacey at such an early hour. 'They're just sitting down to breakfast,' he said.

This will spoil their appetites, Lacey thought, as she entered the breakfast room. Two anxious faces met hers as she sat down — had she come with bad news about Nathan? On learning she had not, anxiety changed to anger as she told them what Alice had done.

'That appalling bloody woman,' growled Jonas, 'I hope they lock her up and throw away the key.' He rang for Soames, asking him to summon Felicity and John Hinchcliffe. 'Felicity needs to hear this from us,' he said, 'and we need John to set the wheels of the law in motion.'

John arrived almost immediately and Felicity a short while after, her curiosity at being summoned at such an early hour having sent her into

401

a complete tizz. 'Is it Nathan?' she asked, her eyes wide with fear. Assured that it wasn't, she listened and was shocked to the core as Lacey repeated the gory details yet again. 'I always thought she was a barmy old bat,' she said, 'but I never for a moment thought she'd commit murder.'

Constance fanned her face in an attempt to dispel the nausea that had plagued her from the moment she first heard the news. 'I can't believe it,' she moaned, 'that a member of my family would stoop to such a vile crime.'

Jonas harrumphed. 'Alice is deranged. I've been saying so for years. Now do you believe me?'

Lacey patted Constance's arm. 'Don't feel guilty, Mother Brearley. You're not to blame for Alice's madness,' she declared stoutly. 'It was just lucky for me Jack Eastwood came along when he did.' She let out a deep sigh. 'God knows what might have happened if he hadn't. I'd have probably ended up strangling the old bitch.' She essayed a shaky laugh, the events of the previous night still raw. Felicity laughed out loud at the idea and said, 'If I'd been there I'd have helped you.'

'It's no laughing matter, Felicity,' Constance said disapprovingly.

'Indeed it isn't,' John Hinchcliffe said, 'but it's over now, Lacey. There'll be no more trouble from Mrs Burrows.' He smiled encouragingly into Lacey's wan face. 'She'll most likely be incarcerated in the asylum at Storthes Hall and held there until her mental state is fully assessed. Then she'll stand trial. So, there you have it.'

'Poor Alice.' Lacey's concern was genuine.

'Poor Violet,' echoed Felicity, 'she'll feel responsible for this for the rest of her life. It was bad enough her mother using her to snare a rich husband, but now she's doomed to spinsterhood; any decent man will run a mile once he hears of Alice's exploits.'

'Perhaps we should extend the hand of friendship to poor Violet,' said Constance, hesitantly, 'she'll need some support after all this.'

Jonas gave her a warning glare. 'It's over and done with. Leave it at that.'

At her own insistence, Lacey walked back to the house in Towngate alone wondering why she didn't feel more elated.

35

They say hope springs eternal; and so it does.

A chill March wind was blustering its way along Towngate as Lacey ushered one of her most prestigious clients out of the dress shop to the car waiting at the kerb. Idly, she watched it drive off, and was fishing for the keys in her pocket to lock up for lunch when a scruffy young lad hurtled across the street, coming to a breathless standstill in front of her.

'Are you Mrs Lacey Brearley?' he gasped. Lacey confirming she was, the lad gabbled, 'you've to go to Cuckoo Hill at two o'clock. You've to meet him there.'

Lacey stared. 'Meet who?'

'The fellow what told me to tell you to meet him at Cuckoo Hill at two o'clock. He said you'd give me a couple o' bob if I delivered the message.'

'Did he now?' Lacey's mind whirled. Why Cuckoo Hill? And who would presume she'd pay for the privilege of meeting him there? A flame of hope sparked inside her only to be quenched instantly by doubt.

'Where did you meet this man, an' what did he look like?' Lacey's anxiety was such that the lad jumped back.

'In Townend. He wa' tall an' thin an' he must have a bad leg, 'cos he wa' limpin'.'

Exasperated, Lacey begged, 'I mean his face. What did he look like?'

The lad shrugged. 'I don't really know. He had this big, long coat on wi' t'collar turned up. I din't get a good look at him. Are you goin' to give me a couple o' bob or what?' he asked impatiently.

Lacey crossed to the cashbox and withdrew a florin. 'I hope this isn't some sort of trick on your part, 'cos if it is I'll set the bobby on you.'

'Honest missis, it's true. I'd not make summat like that up.' Clutching the money, he turned tail and ran.

'No, I don't imagine you would,' Lacey said to the shop door.

She hurried through to the workroom, and taking Joan to one side whispered the details of the strange incident. 'It must be Nathan. Who else could it be?' Joan insisted. 'Who else knows Cuckoo Hill is your special place?'

Bemused, Lacey shook her head. 'But why wouldn't he come straight here? Why make a mystery of it? It's not the sort of thing Nathan would do.'

Joan looked thoughtful. 'Maybe you're right. It could be a trick.' Her eyes reflecting a mixture of fear and excitement she said, 'Perhaps it's somebody who wants to get you up there on your own so they can demand money. Maybe they're plannin' to kidnap you till we pay up.'

Lacey laughed outright. 'Joan Micklethwaite, I mean Haigh,' she exclaimed, correcting herself to give Joan her married title, 'you are the most ridiculous fantasist I've ever come across. You read too many tuppenny novels. Kidnap indeed!'

'Well then, if you don't believe that you must believe it's Nathan. So what are you waiting for?

405

Go an' meet him.'

Lacey dashed through to the house. 'Susan, dress Richard in a warm coat and leggings; we're going out.'

Wearing a warm, dark blue coat with a fur collar and a little fur hat, Lacey took the pushchair from under the stairs and wheeled it to the door. 'Come on, darling; climb in. We have someone to meet.'

Richard jutted out his bottom lip and shook his head. He strongly objected to this mode of transport, but Lacey knew his legs would tire long before they reached Cuckoo Hill. She wondered if she should leave him with Susan, but somehow it didn't seem right. Nathan would want to see his son.

Then why didn't he come straight home, she asked herself for the umpteenth time, strapping a recalcitrant Richard into the pushchair.

Lacey ignored his pleas and hurried to find Joan. 'If I'm not back in an hour send out a search party.' Joan grinned.

Lacey collected the now squawking Richard and, the wind whipping at her heels, she hurried along Towngate pushing the chair with one hand and holding on to her hat with the other. Why did it have to be so blustery today of all days?

The pushchair wheels skimming the pavement, Richard soon forgot to protest, the speed at which he was travelling making him laugh. On the edge of the town, away from the narrow streets that channelled the gusting wind, there was a sudden lull. Lacey slowed her pace and began the ascent to Cuckoo Hill. Unbidden, Joan's ridiculous scenario planted itself in Lacey's mind.

What if it was a ploy to harm her? All at once the memory of Alice's attack surged back. For one fleeting moment Lacey recalled the slimy Frederick Lynch and wondered if he was waiting for her at the top of the hill. She shook her head impatiently. You daft ha'porth, she told herself, you're as bad as Joan.

★ ★ ★

Sheltered in the lee of the cairn on Cuckoo Hill, Nathan Brearley gazed across the moor, watching the hypnotic sway of drifting heather. It looked like a vast ocean rippling towards the horizon, the rocky escarpments of millstone grit little islands washed by a verdant tide. He tugged the collar of his greatcoat up round his ears as he limped to the other side of the cairn, his eyes smarting in the bracing wind.

Nathan had chosen this place and this time because it was here, at two o'clock one summer's day, that his most beautiful memories had taken root. In the long, dark, fearful night hours in the trenches and then in a hard, narrow bunk in a prison camp hut he had often traced the course of his life, his reminiscences taking the same route each night, the starting point of his journey Cuckoo Hill. It was here Lacey had stolen his heart. This is where it will begin again, Nathan told himself stepping forward to watch Lacey's approach.

At the bend near the top of the hill Lacey paused, her heart beating more with trepidation than the exertion of the climb. Richard, wearied

407

by the excitement of his speedy journey and the fresh air, had fallen asleep.

Lacey rounded the bend.

'Nathan! Nathan!' Her cry floated on the wind like that of a bird winging its way over the moor. She quickened her pace but Nathan made no attempt to run to meet her.

He stood with his back to the wind, his body rigid, no movement at all save for his overly long hair, blown against his cheeks by the stiff breeze. Lacey's eager footsteps faltered, something in his stance making her afraid to rush and hold him as she had intended. Her next steps tentative, she stumbled to a halt, gazing at him across the distance. No more than six feet separated them, but to Lacey it felt like a hundred miles and a hundred years. The joy at seeing him evaporated, an icy dread replacing it.

'Nathan?' She heard the fear in her voice as she struggled to understand what was happening. On the way to Cuckoo Hill, she had imagined him running to meet her then taking her in his arms, kissing her and she kissing him back. 'Nathan,' she cried.

Nathan stayed where he was, his gaze riveted on Lacey and the child in the pushchair, his eyes absorbing every detail and his lips moving soundlessly. Lacey returned his gaze, looking deeply into the grey-blue eyes that were so like Richard's. But whereas Richard's eyes shone with happiness and mischief, Nathan's reflected torment and the fear of rejection.

'Oh, my love,' breathed Lacey, 'my poor, poor love.' Steps uncertain, she crossed the chasm and placed her arms around him crying, 'You're home now; home and safe.' The tremors coursing through Nathan's body threatening to unbalance them, she tightened her grip.

'Lacey. Lacey.' The words sounded as though they were stuck in his throat.

Releasing her hold, Lacey stepped back to gaze into Nathan's face. His eyes had lost some of the fear and uncertainty she had seen earlier, but his gaunt features were etched with unspeakable suffering.

Nathan returned her gaze, his lips trembling as though he was afraid to speak. Without a word he stepped away from her and limped over to the pushchair. Only then did Lacey notice he leaned heavily on a slim cane.

Nathan stooped and gazed into Richard's sleeping face. 'My son, my son,' he sobbed. His eyes brimming with tears he turned his face to Lacey, and in a voice shaking with wonderment, he said, 'He's beautiful, and so big. The photographs you sent don't do him justice.' With his forefinger he gently stroked Richard's cheek.

Richard frowned and slept on.

Then, his steps unsteady, Nathan wheeled the pushchair behind the cairn, into the lee of the wind. Lacey followed. 'Why did you send the strange message with the young lad,' she asked softly. 'Why did you not come straight home?'

'Because I thought the cairn on Cuckoo Hill would bring me the same luck as it did when first we met.'

Lacey stared at him.

Nathan's eyes begged understanding. 'I want

us to start all over again in the same place where it began. I have to be sure you can love me again. I'm not the same man you fell in love with and married, Lacey.' He turned away, gazing into the distance, Lacey suspecting he did not see miles of beautiful Yorkshire moorland but some other scene; a place straight from hell.

She turned him gently back to face her. 'It's over, love. Put it behind you, and,' she gave a little laugh, 'whatever do you mean, love you again? I've never stopped loving you. I never will. You're my Nathan, just as you've always been.' Her voice rang with conviction.

Nathan shook his head. 'Look at me, Lacey. I'll never be the same.' He tapped his left leg with the cane. 'This will never function again as it should and . . . ' his eyes clouded, his face twisting in unconcealed rage, 'then there's this.' Pulling aside the collar of his greatcoat he pushed back his hair.

His left ear was missing, and in its place an ugly red knot of flesh. Below it, an attenuation of livid scars spread under his chin and down his neck. 'Shrapnel,' he said.

Lacey stood on tiptoes, her lips tracing the scars before coming to rest on his mouth, the sense of taste and touch rekindling a love they had both thought was lost forever. In between kisses, Lacey whispered, 'I didn't marry you for your looks, Nathan Brearley. I married you because I fell in love with your beautiful mind.'

Nathan averted his head. 'I'm sorry, Lacey. You'll have to say that again. I'm deaf in that ear.'

Lacey giggled and gently cupping his face in both hands she repeated the words in his good ear, adding, 'An' don't think you can use that as an excuse to ignore what I say in future.'

Nathan visibly sagged, the fear of rejection that knotted every muscle in his body dissipating. His laughter woke Richard, Lacey releasing him from the pushchair and into Nathan's arms. 'This is your Daddy, come home to love us again.'

Richard gazed solemnly into Nathan's haggard face. 'He doesn't know who I am,' said Nathan, looking as though his heart would break.

Suddenly, as though a light had been switched on in a dark chamber, Richard threw back his head, a huge smile curving his rosy lips. Pointing a stubby finger at Nathan's face, he crowed, 'Daddy! Daddy! My Daddy.'

Nathan held Richard closer, Lacey embracing them both as she cried tears of relief on Cuckoo Hill. Here they had fallen in love and together they had overcome his mother's harsh objection to their marriage. Then, torn apart by the war, they had struggled for survival each in their own way, their love for one another giving them strength to carry on. No matter the hardships, they had won through.

Lacey released her hold and stepped back, smiling. 'I think maybe we should attach our own plaque to this cairn. It will say 'Here, on Cuckoo Hill, love was born; and love conquers all adversity.'

Acknowledgements

First and foremost I thank my agent, Judith Murdoch, who took a chance on an absolute beginner; her sound advice and encouragement got me this far. Thanks, Judith, for keeping the faith. I am also extremely grateful to the team at HoZ/ Aria for their friendly guidance, particularly my fantastic editors, Sarah Ritherdon and Rose Fox, proof-reader Sue Lamprell and team member Vicky Joss; what a difference a sharp eye and a broad vocabulary makes to any story.

My love and sincere thanks to my son, Charles, and his wife, Martina, whose IT skills rescued me on numerous occasions, and to Paul and Anne-marie Downey, June Shields and Elizabeth Rice for reading and patiently listening to me as I waffled on. Thanks to Andrew Downey and my brother, John Manion, for keeping me right with their local knowledge of the Colne Valley, and to Matthew and Jack Downey for keeping the gardens under control and my grandson Harry for simply making me happy.

This story and all the main characters, places and events are entirely fictitious.